'Mir offers us a fascinating glimpse into ... ...ayed in fiction.'

Guardian, best crime and thrillers

'With *The Khan*, Saima Mir delivers a once-in-a-generation crime thriller and in Jia Khan has created a female South-Asian protagonist who is fierce, passionate and absolutely compelling. This is not simply black-and-white on the page. It's blood. It's emotion. It's tears, anger, betrayal and revenge. An outstanding debut which deserves to be read widely.'

A.A. Dhand, author of *Streets of Darkness*

'This impressive debut reveals a world in which monsters exist "in the guise of friends and behind smiling faces". It is a considerable achievement.'

The Times, best crime fiction

'Compelling and gritty.'

Cosmopolitan

'A tremendous debut (Jia Khan is a fascinating, multi-layered protagonist). Timely, authentic, immersive and powerful. Hints of *The Godfather*. SUPERB.'

Will Dean, author of the Tuva Moodyson mysteries

'Bold, addictive and brilliant.'

Stylist, best fiction 2021

'The book operates on various levels: crime family saga, character study and an exploration of clan-run organised crime. A sterling debut.'

Vaseem Khan, author of
The Unexpected Inheritance of Inspector Chopra

'It's a joy to read a book set in Northern England that does not veer into cliché. It's so good on motherhood, morality and gender.'

Nell Frizzell, author of *The Panic Years*

'A brilliant debut from an exciting new voice for our times. A thrilling book with a thrilling hero in Jia. Brava.'

Imran Mahmood, author of *You Don't Know Me*

'A Bradford take on *The Godfather*.'

Mail on Sunday, best new fiction

'An eye-opening look at a world that rarely makes it into fiction.'

Evening Standard

'It's an amazing piece of work.'

Lesley McEvoy, author of *The Murder Mile*

'Blown away by the intricacy of such a clever, complex plot and the sense of unease.'

Huma Qureshi, author of *How we Met*

'*The Godfather* retold as a feminist tale with the romantic notions of wise guys obliterated... A truly outstanding debut novel.'

NB magazine

'A unique and compelling read.'

The Skinny

'Saima Mir reinvents the gangster genre with dark lyrical prose that explores trauma, being an outsider, white privilege and revenge.'

L V Hay, author of *The Other Twin*

'Superb.'

Khurrum Rahman, author of the Jay Qasim series

THE

KHAN

SAIMA MIR

POINT
BLANK

A Point Blank Book

First published in Great Britain, Australia and the Republic of Ireland
by Point Blank, an imprint of Oneworld Publications, 2021
This mass market paperback edition published 2022
Reprinted 2022

ISBN 978-0-86154-089-1
ISBN 978-1-78607-910-7 (ebook)

Typeset in Geethik Technologies
Printed and bound in Great Britain by Clays Ltd, Elcograf S.p.A.

This book is a work of fiction. Names, characters, businesses,
organisations, places, and events are either the product of the author's
imagination or are used fictitiously. Any resemblance to actual
persons, living or dead, events, or locales is entirely coincidental.

Oneworld Publications
10 Bloomsbury Street
London WC1B 3SR
England

MIX
Paper from
responsible sources
FSC® C018072

To Ami and Abu, thank you for putting my happiness above the gossip.

However dirty and coarse his hand he will stretch it to a king for a hand-shake. However meagre his meal he will invite an emperor to share it.

The Pathan, Ghani Khan

PROLOGUE

The frayed fabric of the black niqaab scratched at her nose and she raised her hand to adjust it, bringing it taut over her lips. She hurried on. The setting sun worried her. She would be late for work.

Broken syringes and greying condoms lay spent, caught between the pavement and the road, trying to disappear into the sewers beneath. Engine oil mixed with rain pooled around them and spread into the gutter.

Ahead of her a new Bentley waited, its engine purring gently. Further up and across the road a bruised, blonde working girl leaned into a sheenless VW Golf. Hidden behind grubby old textile mills, this forgotten strip of land equalised rich and poor. They all came here. From near and far. To have their cars looked at and their bodies serviced.

The young Muslim woman's eyes, watchful, hollow and kohl-rimmed, moved from lamp post to lamp post and then to street corner. For one brief moment her resolve weakened and she considered turning around and heading home, but then she remembered the Final Demand letter her mother had handed her as she'd been leaving and something tightened in her stomach.

Sakina, her name was, and as she pulled her arms tight around herself, hoping their warmth would melt some of the hardness that had set in, she reminded herself of its meaning: serenity. '*Bas thorai saal hor nai putar*,' her mother had told her, her tone as gentle as her coarse Punjabi would allow. 'Once your brother finishes university he will take care of everything.' But only Sakina knew what those few years were costing. She was paying with more than money for the university fees, rent, bills and bread her family needed. Her father's death had come suddenly and he hadn't had time to make provision for his wife and children. He had been a good man and she missed him with an all-encompassing heaviness in her heart. He had always been proud of Sakina and she wondered what he would have thought of her now.

But there was little time to stop and contemplate such things today. Quickening her pace, she stepped over the shadow of a short, stocky man who was leaning against a blackened wall. He sucked on a cigarette, pulling smoke into his fat fist as he spoke to the driver of the Bentley. Sakina walked past him. He paused as if recognising her and then offered his 'salaam'. She nodded in acknowledgement and crossed the road.

The red heels of her shoes clicked hard; they weren't made for cobbles. The blonde prostitute was also struggling to balance on the stones. Brushing back her hair, the hooker rubbed her hand suggestively up her thigh, her small skirt leaving little to the imagination. She leaned into the driver's window of the car, the skirt rising further up her thighs, revealing the marks left by previous clients.

Sakina stole a glance at the punter in the Golf as she passed, measuring him up, taking in his cropped black hair, pock-marked cheeks and the blue-green tattoo on the side of his head. There was something menacing about him, something that made her take the black satin of her niqaab and pull it tighter over her painted lips. He turned and looked back at her, his empty eyes burning right through her, as if he could see what she looked like under her purdah. She hurried on.

Realising she was about to lose another customer, the prostitute swore loudly at Sakina. 'That's right, why don't you just fuck off? Bloody ISIS lover.'

Her words backfired and her potential client looked at her in disgust. 'Ladies shoun't talk like that,' he said, peeling her fingers off his car and drawing up the window.

She stood her ground, refusing to leave. 'Aw, darlin', don't be laike that. For some dirty Paki?'

But the driver had made up his mind and he turned the key in the ignition, the car edging forward slowly and hugging the curve of the kerb. When he reached the 620 bus shelter where Sakina was waiting, he switched off the headlights and rolled down the window, the engine still letting its readiness be known. The sun had now buried itself deep into the ground; the only light came from the street lamp next to Sakina, spotlighting her in its orange glow. She tried to look past the man, focusing on something, anything, in the distance. His smile remained fixed. She turned away, but not before catching a glimpse of the purple bank notes he was holding. She turned back, watched as he counted the cash slowly and deliberately. She looked at his face again, making a mental note and itemising his features as she'd been taught to do by the other girls. She eventually stood up, walked to the car and climbed in. The punter leaned across the leather seat and respectfully helped her adjust her seatbelt, breathing her in as he did so.

'You brown girls are hard work,' he told her, 'but your smell alone is worth it.'

Sakina pulled down her niqaab and smiled. She lifted the folds of her black burqa to cross her legs, revealing thin, red leather stilettos and dark olive skin. The man grinned. He loved this city.

CHAPTER 1

His forehead touched the worn patch of his mat as he prayed. Deep in supplication, Akbar Khan whispered the Arabic phrases he'd been taught as a child, invoking blessings on the Prophet, praising Allah and calling on His infinite mercy. The old man moved back to the sitting position, his knees now folded under him, and adjusted the tan-coloured woollen hat covering his black hair. He wore it as a sign of respect and honour to his people. It reminded him of how far he had come; its presence kept them in his prayers. The day he had taken it from the rebel soldier was still fresh in his mind, even though more than half a century had passed since he came across the body as he played in the street.

A single thought flickered through his mind and stole him from his prayers. He scratched his clipped beard and made a note to ask his wife to pick up a box of Bigen from the Pakistani grocery shop nearby. The dusty streets and winding walkways of his homeland may have been decades behind him, but the grey-and-orange packaging of hair dye, like the hat, was another reminder of his birthplace, and one of the few constants in his life. The hair dye, the hat, a beaten brown leather suitcase that used to rest above an old cupboard in his father's house, and odd memories: these were all that remained of those times. He had heard that suicide bombers had destroyed much of his home town. He had heard that the women cried blood and the children played with Kalashnikovs, and though his Pukhtun blood meant it was not in his nature to take much to heart, he wept for Peshawar.

He slid his hands from his knees to the faded pink of the prayer mat once again and sank into the sajdah. Prostrating before his God, he gave thanks for the cotton kameez of his youth, the only one he'd owned then, and for the row upon row of suits and shalwars and chadors and chappals that were housed in the wardrobe in his home here in England. His wardrobe was larger now than the house he'd been born in, the house where he had watched his parents die.

Akbar Khan knew well the harsh realities of life, realities that had branded him and defined his path. He knew that standing alone in the wilderness of despair, shunned by God, men often found themselves contemplating dangerous things. When children writhed in hunger, their mothers suppressing their screams, when debt collectors knocked on doors, when elderly parents with eyes full of dead dreams turned to you for hope when you yourself had none, you had to find a way to keep standing. Carrying the burden of family, their hopes bearing down, men turned to cigarettes and beedi, and all methods of intoxication, to escape the reality of poverty and despair...even when that intoxicant dried up their veins and ate up their souls. And it was through this deep understanding of man's struggle that Akbar Khan had found himself supplying substances of all criminal classifications. And as he stood before the God of Abraham and Moses, of Jesus and of Muhammad, Akbar Khan felt his heart to be unblemished, because he knew he was providing for his people and fulfilling their needs.

That battered old suitcase on the shelf above his starched, crisp shirts belonged to another Akbar and another Khan. One that he had long since buried to serve his people.

He turned his head to the right and then to the left – '*Asalaam-o-alaikum wa rahmatullah*' – praying for prosperity and peace in the world. The world he inhabited believed the Khan would never bow before another man. It was a necessary belief. Akbar Khan understood this well. He knew that people would be prepared to ignore the flaws of their masters if they believed their icons were born to serve a higher purpose. Because people were weak and truth was only for the brave.

He reached over to roll the prayer mat up and then stopped, running his fingers over its faded patches. The rug needed replacing, worn away at the place where his forehead touched it in prostration and frayed where his feet rested when he stood; it served as a reminder of all the nights he had spent in prayer. Especially after having someone killed. And there had been many such nights. Akbar Khan's business interests led and fed the city and most of its people. They would not survive without him. Those who called his dealings 'illicit', his associates 'criminal' and his methods 'illegal', what did they know about hunger? What did they know about survival? About seeing the life leave your sister, tiny in your arms, as you weep and beg the doctor to save her but he coldly turns away because you cannot pay his fees?

He picked up the prayer beads from the table beside him and as he did so he noticed his hands were those of an old man. They had not aged as well as his face. The skin covering his long, slim fingers was almost translucent; a tiny brown liver spot nestled between his thumb and forefinger. The world had pointed fingers at him his entire life, and it had judged him harshly. He knew he had made mistakes and would one day have to answer for them. His own daughter had cursed him, demanded that life extract payment for her loss. How could he expect the rest of the world not to? He wondered how much more he owed on the debt, and how much of his blood others had demanded. He sighed deeply as he considered all this and more. His decisions had been reasoned and measured and coloured by knowledge not held by those who sat in judgement. Prayer bead to prayer bead he read the Ayat-ul-Kursi. The verse had served him well and allowed him to reach old age. He was acutely aware of the ripeness of this time. He knew that it would be over soon, and he would not need to carry the demands of the world alone for much longer. There came a point in every life when another was needed to lean on, someone stronger, younger, one who was ready. Akbar Khan had arrived at that point, and now he waited for the other to join him.

The room was almost in darkness now. The house was silent, the only sounds coming from the storm outside. A loud crash startled him and he turned to see the branches of the heavy apple tree that reached up to the house thrashing against the bedroom window. It had grown fast and become unruly in the last twenty years. The gardener had advised it be chopped down before its roots destroyed the foundation of the house but Akbar Khan had resisted. The sound of its branches tapping on his window helped him sleep, as did the pies his wife made from its fruit every summer, a delicious taste he'd acquired in the early days of his arrival in this country. But now the time had come to heed the gardener's advice; the tree would be cut down after the wedding. Akbar Khan watched as its boughs bent low, so heavy with fruit that some touched the ground. They bowed lower than all the branches of all the other trees in the garden without damage to themselves, just as the Khan, laden with power and knowing just how to wield it, prostrated himself before his Maker.

He prayed aloud; the sound of his voice brought with it clarity of thought. 'I have made mistakes, my Allah. I have made them knowingly, willingly, and in the cloak of darkness, but you know why I have done the things I have... The world does not need to witness the birth of another Akbar Khan. Do not let my sacrifice go to waste, my Lord,' he said.

He brought the beads to his eyes before kissing them and putting them aside. He folded up the prayer mat and moved to the bed. His wife slept soundly, the kind of sleep that is brought on by warm milk, turmeric and blessed ignorance. Her children would be together tomorrow and the preparations for their arrival, the desire to fulfil their every whim, had exhausted her.

How many years had it been since all the children had been under this roof? Akbar Khan could not remember... Fifteen, perhaps?

Sixteen? Sixteen years since his daughter Jia had made a necklace of arms around him and discussed her plans? She had called him her 'Baba jaan'. But the 'jaan', the life, was leaving his old bones and he needed to make peace with his strongest-willed child. There were things to discuss and things to reveal. Time had taken too much; it could not be allowed to take any more. Tomorrow, he would start anew. Tomorrow, all his children would be together, all but one.

CHAPTER 2

In the end it wasn't the drug cartels, the prostitution rings or the money laundering that made Jia Khan leave her father's home. It wasn't the various fraud cases, it wasn't the police raids, and it wasn't even the fact that her father was head of the city's biggest organised crime ring, the Jirga. It was simply a matter of a broken heart.

The sound of the podcast helped numb her mind to the day she'd had. Defending guilty men left her devoid of feeling and in need of the kind of understanding that comes from family. But this wasn't something she was ready to admit to herself, or to anyone else. She needed no one. This independence had been hard won and she bore the scars of battle.

Solace in the arms of a man or at the bottom of an expensive bottle of wine – the traditions of the successful circles she frequented – were not for her. She needed the ordinariness of life to restore order. Dressed in black lounge clothes, a cashmere blanket waiting for her on the couch and the vegan take-out on speed dial, she let the normality of the evening seep in. The dulcet tones of Reza Aslan came on, as *Metaphysical Milkshake* asked its listeners, 'Why are we so lonely?' The room was warm; the soft scent of Jo Malone filled the air. Candles were dripping on to the windowsill, rivers of wax pooling from one to the other and setting to form islands. Their light was the only kind she could tolerate at the start of a migraine.

Her friend's Pakistani grandmother who'd visited had asked, '*Yahan kya bijli bahut jaatee hai?*' They'd laughed at the suggestion that electrical companies might cut the power to London homes. It was a regular occurrence in Karachi, Lahore and Peshawar, done to avoid placing an excessive load on the generating plant, but here among the tenants of Jia's Knightsbridge apartment building, it would have caused uproar.

A mobile phone began to hum persistently somewhere in another room. Jia left the comfort of her couch in search of it. It was rare for her to receive calls this late.

She stepped across the scattered clothes in her bedroom and moved towards the bed. She had undressed quickly, not caring where things landed. The maid would pick them up and hang them and send them to the dry cleaners in the morning. Cheeks to the carpet, the red soles of her work shoes chastised her. A skirt lay in a heap next to the kingsize bed, along with a soft silk blouse. Its mate, the Savile Row jacket, was neatly placed on top of the covers; beside it sat a pebble-coloured Birkin handbag. It was vibrating. It was fair to say that Jia Khan was a gently vain woman.

The phone stopped ringing as soon as she found it. 'Baba jaan' flashed up on the missed call log. She was about to put it down when it rang again. He knew she was avoiding him. 'Jia Khan never whines,' she'd overheard him saying to her mother once, 'she protests in silence.' He was goading her to hit 'decline', and so she did. A minute later the phone buzzed, signalling he'd left a voicemail.

Akbar Khan's message was as concise as his relationship with his daughter: 'The car will be with you at 6.00 P.M. I am sending my personal driver, Michael. Do not be late, and don't make him wait.' The sound of his voice made her bristle, almost pushing her back to teenage strop and pout. She was tempted to call him back and tell him she wasn't coming. But far too many years had passed for her to act that way. And besides, she'd made a promise to her little sister Maria.

'Don't fall down that rabbit hole of rage when Baba jaan calls.'

'I don't do that. Do I do that?'

'I won't get married if you don't come. I will send the baraat away.' And although Jia knew Maria's threat was empty, she had agreed. After fifteen years away, she was going back to Pukhtun House. Now was as a good a time as any to face old foes, even ones that were family.

She put the phone down on the bedside table and returned to the warm sofa. She tried to get back to the podcast she'd been listening to but found herself unable to concentrate. Her mind kept wandering back to the call; something about it wasn't right. Her father's voice, normally strong and decisive, had sounded worn. She had never known Akbar Khan to waver. It was one of his countless strengths; it was how he controlled a room. As she picked over his words and pauses, someone walked over her grave and she shivered. She remembered something he'd said to her a long time ago: 'Heaven, hell, present, past and future are all dimensions that operate in the same space. What you experience depends on how you see the world.' She wondered which of the dimensions he was caught up in today and what he was planning for her.

CHAPTER 3

Though Jia Khan had not visited her parents in fifteen years, the wedding wouldn't be her first time back in the city where she was raised. A court case had taken her there less than a year ago. It had felt strange to be back and not stay at her parents' place, but she hadn't been ready for a family reunion then, so she'd stayed in a hotel across from the Crown Court, venturing into neighbouring streets only to grab some lunch and return. She'd eaten dinner in the hotel and spent her evenings in her room, poring over case files. It had been a relief, therefore, when the trial came to a close, and not just because it meant she could return to London, but because the case had been an unsettling one.

Jia remembered that last day in court well. Windscreens were iced over, chins buried deep in scarves, any escaping breath turning to mist, as she crossed the courtyard from the hotel to the Crown Court. Buttoned up, her boots warm and her leather gloves protecting her from the bitter wind, she'd felt calm and controlled, ready to demand justice for her client.

The court dates had been issued earlier than expected, as her client had predicted. 'My cousin will make some calls,' he'd said. But Jia hadn't taken him seriously. She'd heard clients drop the names of people they said would get them off or out of their predicament too many times to believe it. She'd learnt to recognise it as a last-ditch attempt at bravado, one that rarely proved true.

But in this case it did, so it was lucky that Jia had been ready – although those who knew her well understood that luck had little to do with it. A seasoned barrister, Jia Khan prepared for her cases earlier than most. 'Be twice as good as men and four times as good as white men.' This had been the mantra of her mentor. She'd picked it up early on in her career and it had served her well. Shortcuts and fast tracks came with the culture she had inherited. Meticulous, methodical planning came gift-wrapped from the country she was born and educated in.

Pulling strings in law courts was not unheard of. Lawyers, barristers, legal attachés and judges were no strangers to nepotism, but for it to be this blatant had surprised even Jia Khan, and not much surprised her these days.

She saw her client climbing out of a supercar as she approached the building. She guessed that his cousin and benefactor, and the man responsible for arranging the early court date, was sitting in the driver's seat, behind the blacked-out windows of the car. She'd met him briefly at a meeting. Her client tipped his head at her before heading to the back of the courthouse for a cigarette.

Jia took the stone steps to the front entrance. The security guard greeted her warmly, stepping up to lift her case on to the X-ray machine. She'd been here two weeks, during which time she had made it her business to get to know everyone who worked in the court. Learning about the people who oiled the machinery of the judicial system was part of her process.

'How's your wife today, John?' she asked the guard.

He attempted a smile but quit, knowing that his tired eyes betrayed him. 'The weekend was hard,' he said.

Jia took a clean handkerchief from her bag. 'You call me when you're ready to take this to court,' she said, handing it to him.

The guard wiped his eyes, reining in his emotions. Kindnesses were hard to come by in court, and he made a mental note of Jia Khan's.

'It's your last day, then?' he said. 'Good luck.'

Jia thanked him, though she didn't need the luck. She knew she had this. What the guard couldn't know, however, was that she had no desire to win this case, not since Jimmy Khan had come to see her.

'Why are you representing this guy, Sis?' he had asked, his voice filled with emotion.

Khan was a title, a name given to rulers from China to Afghanistan and on through to Turkey; it belonged to the Tatars and the Mongols. It represented honour and valour, leadership. This Khan shared her surname but was not related to her by blood, so when he referred to her as 'sister' it was as a sign of respect. It had stopped her, that word 'sis'. It was a term she had left behind in her past. This white world she inhabited felt no place for the ties and honour that came with simply calling someone 'sister'. She had softened at its sound. Maybe it was because this was the first time her past had crossed her present; maybe it was because someone had traversed the north–south divide to ask for her help; or maybe it was simply a question of timing. Whatever it was, it triggered the domino effect that would change Jia Khan's life and eventually take her home and into the arms of the Jirga.

Jimmy had taken his phone from his pocket and held it out to her, insisting she flick through his photographs. Images of his daughter filled the screen, a wide-smiling little girl, her first day at school, bike rides, Halloween costumes, pretty cakes with candles, laughing with her daddy, arms around her mummy, on and on, image after image until smiles turned to blank expressions, and blank expressions became a tiny child in a hospital bed, surrounded by machines. 'That's what he did. That's what he does,' Jimmy had said, and Jia had taken his hands in hers to stop them trembling.

The world no longer shocked her. She'd represented violent repeat offenders, rapists, and men and women who had committed heinous crimes. There were some who would say, being the daughter of

Akbar Khan, she had even lived in the company of one. She knew monsters existed in the guise of friends and behind smiling faces.

But the photographs triggered something in her. Maybe it was because the little girl reminded her of her own sister, Maria. Or maybe it was because she knew that this kind of thing would never have happened ten years ago, that her father would have prevented it.

'It's bad, Sis. These bhain-chods have been tryin'a cause trouble. But…t'be honest, it's been comin' for a while. The Jirga han't been listenin' t'us younger folks, y'know? Times have changed an' some kids have got degrees and shit. Our people, they never hurt children or women. Akbar Khan would never allow it. He would skin us alive before we even considered it, but these Eastern Europeans have no honour. Our children mean nothing to them, and our women are fair game, Sis. They have no izzat.' His words had taken her by surprise; they were sharp and burning, like acid, and seeped into her skin. She had little to do with her father's business, and hardly any knowledge of what it had become. According to Jimmy Khan, the edifice that was her father's castle was crumbling, and with it, it seemed, was the protection it had afforded people who looked like her.

'I was high when I got the call,' Jimmy had said, the words reluctant to leave his lips, his shame evident. 'I'm not high any more. I'm never high now.' He'd shifted, his voice navigating emotion like a new driver, his accent thickening with every bend. 'I'm here because of your dad. Out of respect for what he's done for me and my family. My wife…she took our daugh'er to her homeland to see 'er family. We needed money. An' the kuttee listened to some shit her cousin said.' The disbelief was still written large on his face.

His daughter had been admitted to hospital with severe abdominal pain. Doctors found half a kilo of cocaine in her stomach. 'I wanted to fucking kill my wife, but your dad and Idris convinced me to go to the police. Fat lot of good that did – arrested some stooge of Nowak's on bullshit charges. But then I heard you were representing him and I had to come and see you.'

Andrzej Nowak, the man she'd supposed was at the wheel of the supercar. When Jia had met him that one time with her client, most of his questions had been posed with the assurance of a public schoolboy. At times he had turned to his cousin, appearing to reassure him in their mother tongue. He'd been charming, dapper, young – his silver hair, like his money, was inherited. Jia remembered being struck by how soft his hands were, and how tapered his fingers. He was not used to getting his hands dirty.

'Jimmy, I wish you'd come to me sooner,' she'd told him. 'You know I'd do anything to help you. But you should know that Andrzej Nowak is not my client.'

'Nah, but his fall guy is.'

Jia hadn't been able to argue with that: she was representing one of Nowak's henchmen. She had thought something was off about the case and seeing Jimmy had confirmed it. She'd been a barrister for almost two decades. Some people were obviously guilty, some obviously innocent, and then there were those who fell into the grey, people like her own family. She had initially read law to arm herself, to be better equipped than those who tried to use it against her and those she loved. But once she'd turned her back on her father, she came to believe in the justice system. She'd liked that the lines were clean and clear. If you stepped over them you deserved punishment, but only if it could be proved you'd done so. The law, unlike men, was dependable. It was easy to navigate; you always knew where you stood with it.

Jimmy had begged her to do something. He knew her client was a pawn and that the actual man responsible for what happened to his daughter was paying for his defence. When he'd heard that Akbar Khan's daughter was representing the guy, he had come to her in the hope of a better, cleaner kind of justice.

But Jia Khan was not ready to deliver.

***

Andrzej Nowak sat in the gallery, watching as the barrister looked through her notes, placing them face down after finishing each argument. He noted her every movement, every flicker of emotion. She was striking, not as tall as they'd said, but steeled, like the exterior of an armoured vehicle. He watched her hands, her lips, her long, olive-skinned neck, and wondered what it would take to break it. He parked the thought. It interested him. Very little did nowadays. Boredom had set in. He leaned forward to listen as she questioned the officer responsible for the operation that had brought in his man.

'Just a few questions, Officer Swan,' said Jia.

This was the first time the officer had given evidence since returning from maternity leave. Her baby was teething, and she hadn't had much sleep. Adjusting to work again was proving harder than she had anticipated. The laddish culture of the drugs division was well known across the force. She didn't want to give them any excuse to judge her.

Jia smiled gently at the woman. 'Can I get you some water?' she asked. The police officer nodded. The sign of solidarity from the only other woman on this side of the court allowed her to exhale.

Jia looked up from her place at the defence desk and ran through some general questions about the investigation, putting the officer at ease. Then she seemed a little straighter, her eyes clearer: 'Were you sleeping with the defendant's wife, Officer Swan?' she said.

The police officer looked confused, as if she'd been reading from a script and lost her place. She'd prepped for procedural questions. She was unprepared for this line of questioning. She stared at Jia Khan, her groggy head wondering what had just happened.

'How do you know the defendant's wife, Officer Swan?' Jia pressed.

The officer stammered over her words, before managing to cobble a sentence together. 'We met at a mother and baby class,' she said.

'And how soon after you met did things become sexual between you?'

'They didn't.'

Jia took off her glasses and picked up a sheet of paper: '*I miss you so much, and can't wait for us to be together again,*' she read out. '*David doesn't understand me the way you do. I love you so much.*' She put the paper down and her glasses back on. 'I'm afraid the evidence speaks to the contrary,' she said.

The witness looked from Jia Khan to a woman sitting at the back of the gallery, her eyes lowered.

'We're just friends. That's all,' said the policewoman, her media training kicking in.

The freelance court reporter scribbled furiously in the press gallery. Salacious copy was lapped up by newsrooms. '*Married mother-of-two police officer in lesbian love tryst with defendant's wife,*' he wrote.

Text messages were a dangerous thing, especially between women. The absence of nuance, coupled with emotional vulnerability and the tendency to overshare could be twisted. Jia knew this.

The defendant's wife had come to Jia with the allegations of impropriety on the part of the officer a few weeks ago. Jia didn't know if they were true or not; she didn't know if their meeting at the mother and baby class had been genuine or contrived. All she knew was that it was her job to defend her client to the best of her ability, and to this end she needed to plant a seed of doubt in the mind of the jury. All it took was sullying the reputation of an officer. She would get over it.

The jury listened intently. Nowak watched each one carefully, leaning in again as Jia Khan put forward her closing arguments. He knew each one of them from the photographs his men had taken after the first day of the trial. He was not troubled by defeat and he cared little for the defendant, despite him being family. Family, in his experience, was only ever a burden. He would ordinarily have left by now, but Jia Khan interested him. 'Who is she?' he'd asked his men after the first time they'd met.

'She is the daughter of the man who runs our rival operations: Akbar Khan,' he was told.

'So that is what it is,' he had said, more to himself than to his men. He had recognised something in her; he had seen himself.

The closing arguments done, they waited for the decision. The clock ticked slowly on to lunchtime and recess. When Jia left the courthouse, Nowak followed. She crossed the street and headed towards the parade of restaurants on the other side, walking past shops bathed in orange light and filled with pretty pastries and cakes. She chose the nondescript café at the corner of the terrace of shops, and took a seat in a booth at the back, ignoring the menu and ordering from memory. She removed the multiple layers she was wearing to protect her against the elements. She was scrolling through her emails, when he interrupted:

'Could I join you?' he said.

She looked up to see Andrzej Nowak standing beside her booth. The fragrance of bitter almond, lavender and tobacco wafted towards her, and she registered his Penhaligon cologne, the same as the one worn by her most disliked tutor at university. Images of Jimmy Khan's little girl flashed before her like an Instagram story.

'Thank you, but no,' she said.

He didn't move, but continued to stand and stare, as if the very act of looking would bore into her brain and change her mind. She felt his eyes on her, willing her the way owners will their pets when establishing a hierarchy. The silence remained thick, neither of them needing to fill it or knowing what to do. Jia picked up her fork as her lunch arrived, hoping Nowak would understand the signal and leave. But he didn't. He stayed there, his gaze never straying from her face. She began to feel porous, as if he could see straight through her. She pushed her salad slowly around her plate.

Eventually, he spoke. 'What happened to you?' he said. Despite his slim frame, he was blocking the light, and his presence felt more and more oppressive. 'What happened to make you this way?'

She looked up, hoping to catch the eye of a waiter, but the café was busy and all the staff dealing with customers.

'I hope you don't mind, I'd like to continue with my lunch,' she said.

'You are not afraid. Most people are afraid of me. Unless they are stupid. And you are not stupid.'

He was right: she was not afraid. There is not much that frightens a woman who has had to fight to live life on her own terms, but experience had taught her when to save her energy and when to pick her battles. The waiter caught her eye, and she gestured for the bill. He came over with the card machine. She continued to ignore Nowak, paying quickly and asking for her lunch to be packed up. The waiter returned moments later with a cardboard box, which Jia thanked him for. She left Nowak alone in that café pondering what had just happened. It was rare for him to be refused, and rarer for him to fail at lighting a fuse. He was not to know that Jia Khan had had years of practice at not rising to the slights of men. She had cultivated the skill of calm. Years of chaos, watching defendants talk themselves into trouble and out of acquittal, meant the skill of diplomacy was second nature to her. She had learnt to let the silence breathe.

When the verdict came in a few hours later, it was in the defendant's favour. The evidence had been insufficient. Nowak looked around for Jia, but her colleague informed him that she had left the courthouse earlier to attend to another matter.

She had in fact gone back to her hotel to pack. She was desperate to get away from this city; it held far too many memories. Little did she know that a year later, she would be back for good.

CHAPTER 4

Akbar Khan had raised his eldest daughter like a son, shunning his wife's advice and ignoring the town talk. She was, after all, both the daughter of a great Pukhtun and a daughter of Great Britain. 'My child will live on her own terms,' he had told his wife plainly, repeating it like a daily affirmation, embedding it in his daughter's bones.

His wife had not agreed easily. 'But she is a girl, Akbar jaan, what will people say?' Sanam Khan's protests fell on deaf ears. Her husband had made up his mind and when Akbar Khan made up his mind only Allah and His angels could change it.

'We are Muslims,' he said. 'Our women were given equality over fourteen centuries ago, yet you want to hold her back? The enemy of women is woman herself.'

Sanam Khan was no fool; she was well acquainted with the world and its ways. 'You are the Khan of our people,' she said, 'but I'm her mother. And as a woman I know that what you are teaching her will make our people turn against her. She will be shunned for having an opinion and looked down upon for speaking her mind. And what if she goes astray and brings dishonour upon herself?'

Akbar Khan tried hard to allay her concerns. 'My blood will not allow her to lose her path. Dignity and honour course through our veins and hers. Have more faith in me and in your child, and in yourself. In any case, every great leader is shunned before they are admired.' And when he realised that the fear in her eyes was for her child and not for their family honour, his voice softened. 'My love, my jaanaan, trust me.' She shook her head, and he whispered terms of endearment, tracing his finger across her forehead and gently moving wisps of hair from over her eyes and tucking them behind her ear. Through the warm tears of a wife and mother, she relented, as she always did.

'My daughter will marry a very important man,' Akbar Khan had announced to the midwife the first time the baby was bundled up and handed to him. The hours, days, years passed more swiftly than he'd have liked, but he continued to whisper his many plans into his daughter's small ears, first the right and then the left.

At just ten months old, Jia Khan waddled around the office, her father discussing business with various men of ill repute. Brushing aside her curly fringe, she would cup her father's wide, dark face in her chubby hand and try to kiss him, as he unflinchingly made decisions about work and the fates of men. No one dared question the presence of the child or why she was allowed in the quarters of men while they discussed business affairs. She was the daughter of their leader. She was their honour.

And so, some would say, it was inevitable that things turned out the way they did. 'Men of Pakistan's North-West Frontier know better than to question their Khan. Yet you raise your voice to me?' her father had said the day she left, the day her heart was broken into pieces so small that not even the angels could put them back together.

'It's a good job I'm not a man,' she told him. 'You're a liar and a murderer. You killed Zan, you destroyed my hope, my marriage, and you have the audacity to tell me that you did all this out of love?' The last words had, in fact, been more a statement of fact than a question; she had no need of his excuses any more. And with her broken heart, she had smashed his in the way only a daughter can: 'I hate you.'

The years had passed quickly, blurring together. She hadn't managed to escape the voice in her head – *his* voice – and even now, for better or worse, it echoed through the many recesses of her mind. She'd been running away from him so fast she hadn't noticed how far she'd come. It was only as she packed her bags, ready for the journey home, that Jia realised how much she had changed.

Akbar and Sanam had raised their daughter to be the wife of a respectable man. But respectable families don't choose to marry their sons off to the daughters of drug smugglers and money launderers. Her father found this out the hard way, when Jia wept salty tears on to his shirt the first time her heart was broken. 'It's not you. But your father...' the boy had said, his words like ground-up glass. And that day Jia learnt a lesson she would never forget: she would have no control over her honour – her father had seen to that. And although she didn't believe the things he had said about her father, that young man had laid the first row of bricks in the wall that was to stand between Jia and Akbar Khan.

Ironic, then, that it was Akbar Khan's pain that had known no bounds when his daughter wept. He had believed his wealth and power would allow his daughter to find an honourable match. He, who made men bow to his will, had forgotten that the heart is held between Allah's thumb and forefinger, and it is He who turns it at His will. In the world of arranged marriage, the daughters of criminals married criminals and the daughters of noblemen married nobility. Money was not their concern, bloodline and izzat were. 'I fix the world's problems but what can I do for her?' Akbar Khan said to his wife. 'I never thought this would happen to our children. They talk of honour, but is this what honourable boys do? Make a young girl cry?' He did not know that, huddled on the other side of the door, Jia Khan was listening to every word.

After this, Akbar Khan had taken matters into his own hands and paid a visit to the matchmaker, because a young Pakistani girl is nothing without a husband.

'There isn't a boy good enough for your daughter on my list, Khan sahib,' the old lady said. 'I'm afraid I don't know anyone who would match her.' The china teacup rattled in her ageing hands as she handed it to him. 'Sugar?' she asked.

Akbar Khan shook his head. 'We have been good to you,' he said. He held the dainty cup and saucer awkwardly, ill at ease, and the matchmaker was relieved when he placed it on the table before him.

'You have,' she said. 'You have. And I say this with respect, it is a new zamana we live in, sahib.' She was getting old. Gout had taken hold of her foot and her knees were riddled with arthritis, making her gait more of a waddle than a walk. But none of this stopped her working. She was greeted with respect, fed hot samosas, called constantly and pandered to by her people. Girls' mothers brought her gifts, while boys' mothers brought her gossip. She was acquainted with every Pukhtun family in England, Scotland and Wales, and was privy to their intimate affairs, and so she knew none would consent to a union with the daughter of Akbar Khan. Families who had worked hard to hide their histories and bury their bloodstained pasts didn't want to build alliances with a family so freshly connected to crime.

Now in her eighties, she had seen too many good women age and wither away in the hope of a good match, sacrificed at the altar of honour, faith and family name. It was a crime to ask a woman to give up her dreams of being a mother and a wife. It was a sin to expect a woman to safeguard her chastity her entire life because a man of appropriate upbringing or station could not be found within the system. She knew her ideas would disrupt an age-old system and rain a mighty backlash down upon her, but her children were married and her husband was long dead, and so the courage to speak the truth was not hard to muster. Sitting directly opposite Akbar Khan, she put down her cup and rested her hands on the table. 'Jia is a good girl. She can be trusted to make her own decisions. Let her find her own husband.'

Her words broke the dam, and rage spread across Akbar Khan's face. She had anticipated this and was ready for him. 'Now, now,' she said, taking his hand in hers to restrain more than comfort. 'Spit out the anger and think again. Izzat, honour, both these fade and are nothing in the eyes of Allah. What lasts is love, and you know this better than most.'

Akbar Khan nodded. Heart heavy and mind muddied, he learnt that day the hardest lesson of fatherhood: even the Khan cannot save his favourite child from the trials God chooses to heap upon her. He knew the world of his heritage well, a world where a woman was considered 'left on the shelf' when she turned twenty-five. A world where boys' mothers visited house upon house, sipping chai and eating sweetmeats and fried savouries as they viewed potential brides as though they were buying cattle. It was a hobby, a time-pass. They forgot that they too had daughters; they gossiped about girls and spread half-truths about families, and the cycle continued from one generation to the next.

The daughter of the Khan had struggle upon struggle heaped upon her. Like water dripping on a rock, it slowly wore away at her, revealing someone new beneath.

And so it was that, with time, Jia Khan developed a thicker skin. She built a wall around herself and tried to do the same for Maria, planting her feet firmly between the world and her sister. Maria could not be allowed to feel the pain she had felt. 'Let me raise my children my way,' her mother had shouted at a nineteen-year-old Jia. 'Why do you think it is your place to always play lawyer for everyone else in my house?'

'Because if you'd had faith in me instead of worrying about the rest of the world and what it has to say, I wouldn't be cleaning up the mess my life has become,' Jia had said. Head down and gloves up, she stood her ground. Her actions meant the world in which her younger siblings grew up was less restrictive than the one she had experienced. Having learnt his lesson with Jia, Akbar Khan had allowed his wife to raise Maria in ways she saw fit without interfering, and Sanam, seeing the hurt heaped upon her older children by others, had softened her approach.

One day Jia walked away from that life without looking back. But years later, memories of the wagging tongues and pointing fingers could still make her smart a little.

There had been a time when her wardrobe, like her manners, had been neatly divided into two sections, one half for polite white life and the other for Pakistani society. The two parts of her life ran in parallel like the lines of latitude on a map, the space between widened by language and custom. The number of occasions she'd heard old aunties gossip about some poor girl or other, before turning to Jia and reminding her that 'nice girls speak quietly, nice girls are patient, nice girls don't answer back'. So-called 'nice girls' were demure and non-confrontational, their opinions of no threat to the status quo. But England was full of not-so-nice girls, because white society demanded each person speak up to be heard.

After the matchmaker's failed attempts, Jia had tired of the balancing act of being a Brit Pak girl. There came a day when her heart felt heavy as she looked into the long mirror beside her after finishing her Isha prayers. The soft drape of the chador across her hair and shoulders made her feel safe and she'd pulled it tighter. Then, remembering her father's words – 'I fix the world's problems but what can I do for her?' – she'd pulled the shawl from her head, leaving her brown hair exposed.

From then on the two parts of her wardrobe, and the east and west of her, became as one: she'd wear kurta and jeans, shalwar and buttoned-down shirt; she'd laugh loudly when the urge took her, ask impatiently for what she felt was her right. She showed the nice Pakistani girl the door.

And so it was a very different Jia who stood in front of the mirror, taking off her make-up, the eve of her first trip home in fifteen years. She wondered how she had managed to keep away from her mother for so long. As a child she had loved her family wholly and greedily, but the loss of Zan left the air thin, making it hard for her to breathe, and the people she had loved most become the people she could bear least.

The divide that now separated them had opened up unexpectedly; no one could have predicted its coming. But she knew life to be dangerous that way, bringing one's worst fears forward and setting alternate plans in motion. But as the Quran stated, and as she herself had learnt, with hardship comes ease. And so here she was, less than twenty-four hours away from the car journey that would take her back to the arms of the family who had wiped her tears, nursed her through childhood fevers, promised to love her without condition, and then made it impossible for her to stay when she needed them most.

CHAPTER 5

Elyas Ahmad was packing when his son called to him. He put down the shirt he'd been folding and went to the boy. He was sitting up in bed, exhausted and unable to focus. The squint he'd had in infancy returned whenever he had a migraine. 'I'm so tired, Dad,' he said. Elyas felt that familiar pang of helplessness that comes with finding yourself unable to solve your child's problems. The gruelling schedule of babyhood was nothing compared with this.

He sat down beside the boy. 'You shouldn't be reading,' he said, taking the book from his son's lap and glancing at it before placing it on the bedside table. '*The Dark Web?* No wonder you have a headache.' He gently pressed his fingertips over the boy's forehead, the way he used to do for Jia all those years ago. The tiny, almost invisible dimple on his son's chin wasn't all he shared with his mother. He also had her eyes, and her drive. But stubborn and prone to overstimulation, Ahad had inherited his mother's worst qualities as well as her best. 'I'm bored and I'm sick of being sick,' he said.

'I know. Hopefully the change of air will put an end to the headaches,' said Elyas, and then he watched as Ahad's face turned suddenly pale. He grabbed a bucket, bringing it swiftly to his son's mouth. The boy threw up violently, then tired and clammy, clutching his head, he leaned back on to the pillows, the exhaustion leaving him grey.

Elyas's concern was evident across his face; he'd never been able to hide his feelings when it came to his son. 'That settles it, I'm not leaving you like this,' he said.

'I'll be fine. And I'll catch you up the day after. I'm an adult now, I can do this.' But his words did little to allay Elyas's worry. Both of them were booked on the 11.10A.M. from King's Cross out of London tomorrow, as Elyas was due to start his new job in the next few days. But Ahad came first. He always came first. He was also the reason Elyas had accepted the position.

'Son, you're only fifteen. You don't want to be in any hurry to take on the responsibility of adulthood, trust me,' Elyas said. He pulled the duvet up, tucking Ahad in, and then leaned in to kiss his head. Illness was the only time the boy allowed his father to look after him – it had a way of pushing people back to infancy. His father's touch soothed him and the pain ebbed a little. So too did some of Elyas's concerns. The migraines didn't worry him so much as what might be underlying them. Elyas wondered what demons were yet to appear. He wished Jia could see how much of her was in their son. He knew she'd be proud of the man Ahad was becoming, despite the problems he'd been having at school and with the police. But she had made no effort to see him and, as yet, Elyas had no way to explain her absence.

He wiped the boy's forehead and helped him to take a sip of water. Sometimes he worried he was trying too hard, but guilt and parenting seemed to go hand in hand, and he reminded himself that some things were beyond his control. He was doing the best he could.

Ahad finally asleep, he slipped quietly out of his bedroom, breathing a sigh of relief in the hallway. He paused to look at the row of pictures and awards that hung on the walls. The British Press Association's 'Foreign Reporter of the Year' for five consecutive years, 'Journalist of the Year' for the Foreign Press Association, one of *Time* magazine's 'Most Influential People'. He was privileged. He had worked in television and film, doing the things he loved. And the offers were still there, but after the events of this week, he was looking forward to the simplicity of print.

'You want to close the production company because of some trainee camerawoman?' His business partner had been livid, refusing to accept what he was hearing. 'You've known me for twenty years. You've known her for twenty days. Come on.'

'I do know you. And I know that this partnership is over,' Elyas had said. He remained steady, trying to maintain some dignity in front of the man he'd once regarded as a friend, the man he had started his company with, who'd handled the business side so that Elyas could make the films he wanted. They'd won awards and accolades together, broken stories and changed lives. But accusations were being made and it was clear that his partner had crossed a line, one he could not come back from. 'When I return, I want you gone,' said Elyas.

'You've lost your mind. If we fold now, we'll never work in the industry again. No one will commission us.'

Elyas leaned forward. 'You took advantage of a defenceless woman,' he said. 'You got off on a technicality.' He paused, waiting for some response. Waiting for his partner to fill the silence. 'I've spoken to her. I've seen the police report. You belong in jail.'

His partner's face showed no remorse. 'She was asking for it,' he said. 'She wanted to climb the ladder, and I helped her.'

Elyas stood up and walked towards the door. He needed to leave the room; if he didn't he was worried he would punch him. He wanted to pummel him until he was bloody and broken, but he wouldn't. That's not the kind of man he was. The once-friend's inability to keep it in his pants, his inability to take no for an answer, had landed them here, in a place where the thing he had toiled over, poured blood, sweat and tears into, was about to die. This was business. But it was also personal. That was Elyas's line: if it wasn't personal, it wasn't worth doing.

The young woman had come to him in confidence, frightened that speaking up would spell the end of her career. But Elyas had spent enough years as a journalist to know the truth from a lie. She'd broken down when he'd said he believed her.

'She's a fucking liar,' his partner said to him as he was about to leave. 'You and your fucking feminist rhetoric. You always were a pussy.'

'Daniel, you've mistaken my kindness for weakness again,' Elyas replied, taking a breath and turning round. 'I've already spoken to our lawyers and instructed them to begin the process of dissolving the company.' His voice was as calm as still waters. 'Or I can buy you out. It's your choice.'

It was decided: the company would fold. It was a blow that Elyas would accept willingly. His life was built on knowing when to duck and when to take the hit. He would start over. His reputation was intact, and that was all he needed. He tucked ten pairs of identical black socks into his suitcase before closing the zip. Single fatherhood had made a practical man out of him. That eternal problem of the disappearing sock was not one he had time to deal with.

He was about to spend six months at the paper where he had started out as a trainee. It was a world away from documentaries, but the memories of his first proper job in news were so strong that he was unable to turn down the offer to guest edit the paper. Returning as the boss was something his younger self could never have imagined. In a city where white media dominated, a brown editor was an interesting proposition, even if the paper was failing.

It was more than twenty years on from his first day, but he remembered well the smell of freshly inked news-sheets, the hard-won camaraderie of old school hacks. The sound of news editors pouring curse words over grammar and the whine of highly strung sub-editors still filled his dreams.

It had been a tough place to be but a great place to be. In a city of brown ghettos, it was a white enclave, but that made the victories, when they came, even sweeter. He'd not found anything to match those highs or those lows, except Ahad's mother.

Losing her had driven him to the edges of war-torn Afghanistan and the fringes of Pakistan. He'd fought hard to make sense of his loss and understand the ways of her family. His Urdu, Punjabi and Pashto had come in handy and he had found himself spoken of with respect among locals and journalists alike.

The awards had come and so had the women, but they meant little to a man who was hiding from life. Elyas Ahmad had the kind of face that betrayed him, a face that held no secrets. Some said it was because his heart was pure, and he liked that idea, but others saw it as a weakness: a man unable to control his feelings was a liability. His eyes invited admiring glances and whispered wants, his olive skin kept time at bay. But success and admiration did little to fill the loneliness left by his wife's departure.

The guest editorship at the paper in West Yorkshire was a well-timed excuse to spend time with his son. Taking Ahad out of London would give them an opportunity to reconnect, away from the place they had come to call home, away from his friends and from the trouble that seemed to seek him out there.

They lived in a terraced house on a south-west London street lined with cherry trees. It was a quiet neighbourhood, full of 'French Grey' doors and *Guardian* readers. The kind of place that was home to people *Time Out* referred to as 'intelligentsia'. As idyllic as it seemed, this middle-class existence wasn't without its problems, and the absence of brown people had troubled Elyas.

At the back of his mind, flowed a steady stream of concerns. Some were the sort that all parents have about their children, things like falling in with the wrong crowd, dabbling in illicit substances – and Ahad had given him reason to be worried. But there were other, more niche concerns, to do with raising a brown son, and one who was Muslim. He worried about Ahad's self-esteem and how he saw himself. He hoped that being around youngsters of similar racial background would help him make sense of his place in the world.

In a couple of months Ahad would be starting sixth form at one of the best colleges in Yorkshire. Ahad was bright – bright enough to have been bumped up a school year at the age of thirteen – one of those kids who gave the impression he avoided learning all year but always came out with excellent grades. Elyas had never been that kind of student. Elyas had had to work hard for everything in life.

The early years of raising a child alone had been particularly challenging, but once Ahad started school Elyas discovered that, under the surface of the world of paid work, there was a network of fellow parents, people who raised you up on tired days, picked your child up when meetings overran and offered understanding words when you felt yourself failing at every step. He could hardly believe his son was now a teenager: in a few years Ahad would swap their home for university digs. That time would fly fast on the wings of A levels and campus visits, application forms and interviews. The empty nest was approaching.

The spectre of reflection hovered close by, and Elyas knew it would result in the raising of the dead. He was acutely aware of the baggage he had stuffed away. He hadn't made peace with ghosts of the past and he hadn't sorted and sifted through old memories to categorise and make sense of them. No, he had compartmentalised his life, he had held on to his son, and together they had survived.

But this last year, Ahad's migraines had become more and more frequent, as had his questions. The consultant had said that stress was a possible trigger and suggested it was exam pressure, but deep down, Elyas knew the truth. He'd been running from it long enough. And when the exams were over and the migraines persisted, that confirmed it. Ahad needed to see Jia and place his unanswered questions before her.

Elyas sat down, overwhelmed by the reality of the journey he was about to take his son on. Much had happened since he was last in the hills and valleys of Yorkshire. The boy who once greeted him in the mirror was now a man with flecks of grey scattered through his black hair. That boy had wanted to see the world and make it his. This man wanted to unsee it. The monsters he now knew lived inside people, those who shunned their ordinary lives to run amok, making those around them question everything they held dear – he wanted to purge them from his mind and start over.

He picked up the handwritten letter that had arrived a few weeks ago. The flourish of real ink on Conqueror paper, a rare sight in today's digital world, was his father-in-law's penmanship, unmistakeable and impeccable. The man had not learnt to read until his twenties, and pride had driven him to overcome and surpass the challenge.

It came with a wedding invitation, and was brief.

Elyas jaan,
You must come and see me.
Bring my grandson. It is time.
Regards,
Akbar Khan

Elyas stared at his father-in-law's succinct words. As he turned the paper over in his hand, he wondered if the timing of the letter was a coincidence. Akbar Khan knew of Ahad's troubled mind and the migraines that came as a result. Since leaving his grandson in Elyas's care, he had corresponded regularly with Elyas. Was he responsible for the job offer that was taking them back to the city where it all began? He had always been well connected, of course. Elyas wondered how far those connections now extended. Was it paranoia to suspect a link between the timing of the job and the letter, or was it journalistic instinct? Hard news had made him cynical. It had taught him that even the most democratic of countries, and the whitest of white establishments, called on the criminal fraternity occasionally. And vice versa.

The knot in his stomach tightened as he thought of Jia. He knew it wasn't the wisest decision to accept his father-in-law's invitation, he knew nothing good would come of it, but he had never been able to resist temptation when it came to her. He was curious. What was she like now? What kind of woman had she become? Did she ever think of him?

Then he put these thoughts aside and considered the other, more likely option: the two events were unconnected and the timing was merely coincidental. He had landed the job on merit. And Akbar Khan had finally decided it was time to meet his grandson. And maybe he was right. Maybe it was time to sew up old wounds.

CHAPTER 6

Benyamin Khan watched from his car as the woman in the burqa left with the punter. He had been raised in the family business and understood its workings better than most, but the mind of these men was lost on him. He got that the punters had sexual proclivities they could not satisfy elsewhere, but not that someone might be willing to sell their sister, girlfriend or even mother to meet the needs of those people. And while he'd been raised in a world of grey areas, there were still lines of morality whose blurring made his stomach churn, and he knew his revulsion made him better than these men.

'A Pukhtun's woman is his honour,' his father had told him. 'Her seating place is in the heart. If you want to succeed in life, remember this: hear and heed your sisters and your mother, and in time your own wife. It is their birthright to speak, and it is your duty to listen. Women are like prisoners in our hands because they are physically weaker than men, but we must not abuse that power. A society that dishonours its women dishonours itself. Remember that; that is how He will judge us,' he had said, pointing to the sky.

'Then why do we take money from these men and their women, Baba?'

'Man is neither good nor bad, Benyamin Khan. It is the deeds that are thus divided. And money is money, my son; it is not honourable or dishonourable, it is just necessary. That said, the world confers honour on the man who holds it. These men will whore their women without regard whether we allow them or not. By taking them under our wing we regulate things, make sure of the girls' safety. In a way, it is an act of charity on our part.' Benyamin had nodded at his father's words, taking them as others might take Quranic scripture.

Despite his youth, he understood the workings of the family business and that times of austerity meant turning one's hand to all kinds of work. Men needed to eat, and women had families to feed.

And in the Khan house that meant hundreds of families. Especially this week, since there was a wedding. One that Benyamin was responsible for overseeing.

He pulled his cuff back and glanced at his watch. He wore the price of a house on his wrist, thanks to his sister Jia. She had sent it to him on his twenty-first birthday. The vintage Patek Philippe went unnoticed among the gold Rolex watches his friends wore. His older sister had always been one for subtlety, looking dowdy among what some described as 'the Chavistanis'. She hated the way people dressed themselves in their money. The watch told him he was late the way any other watch would have done, but this one did it while reminding him of his sister, her rebellion and her unconditional love for him.

Ordinarily, tardiness wouldn't have bothered him, but today was different. Maria would not forgive him if anything went wrong tomorrow and he knew he'd never hear the end of it. He still couldn't believe his young sister was about to become someone's wife. She was so disorganised and frazzled in her thoughts, it astounded him that she was about to build a life apart from her family. He would miss her more than he could say. The accident had brought them closer, as had Jia's departure. It had been so sudden that Benyamin had been lost in the haze of it.

She was coming back, Jia, his older sister, his protector, his adviser, the one who had abandoned him. Her presence in the Khan household had made it a warm place, whether it was by her singing of Hindi songs into an old brush, smuggling pizzas into his room at midnight, telling him ghost stories on the steps or doing hilarious impressions of their father's friends. She had been his partner in crime, his cool big sister and his best friend. Losing her had been a lot for a ten-year-old to bear, and he had never forgiven her.

Not a day went by when he didn't wish things were different, that the accident hadn't happened, that his brother Zan was still alive and that Jia understood their father. But wishing didn't bring change and it never would. Life was about doing not dreaming.

The untested bravado of a twenty-five-year-old meant it was rare for Benyamin to be afraid, but there was something about this weekend that made him nervous. He was the son of Akbar Khan, and as such he believed that fear should fear him, not the other way around. But this would be the first time the Khan family were together in over a decade. He hoped that the past would stay buried and not raise its bloody head.

He turned his mind back to the job at hand and to the pimp renting this 'bitch pitch', who was leaning against a wall and carefully counting out a wad of cash. It was unusual for the son of Akbar Khan to do the 'milk run', but he wanted to make sure that everything was ticking over smoothly. His father would have enough to deal with over the next few days.

'Business is good, bro,' said Khalid, when Benyamin asked him. 'Since your dad's been running things all our girls are clean. Tested an' that. We keep a *close* eye on 'em, y'know. And kasmai these gorai, bro, they do like a bit of exotica.' The pimp was in good spirits as he flicked away his cigarette butt and passed the money to Benyamin through the car window. 'Going for a shisha after work and then watching the big fight. Our boy Amir Khan is up. You wanna join us an' that?'

Benyamin took the cash and shook Khalid's hand. 'I'm afraid I'm busy. You understand?' He nodded his head once, the way his father did when he was implying trust. Business of this kind was built on trust and on distance. It was one of the many things he'd learnt over the last few years. Akbar had wanted Benyamin, his youngest child, to experience the family business from the bottom up, to see it from every angle, in order to prepare him for what was to come. There was no room for fear and little forgiveness left in the bank of Khan. Not any more. There had been once, back when Akbar had planned to hand his empire over to his eldest son, Zan. But things hadn't worked out as he'd hoped. He had outlived his son, and the daughter he'd primed for the business had proved herself obstinate.

And so the apprenticeship had fallen to Benyamin Khan. His being out on the streets was risky – the child of the Khan was rarely put in a place of high visibility. But he was being closely watched over by Bazigh Khan, Akbar's younger brother and the most loyal of all the Khan's men. He would keep him safe and out of trouble.

Benyamin was only to collect from certain streets but the responsibility gave him a sense of pride. Unknown to him, Bazigh Khan had gone ahead and swept the area of anyone who might seek to implicate the Khan's son in illegal activities.

Having inherited his family's good looks, Benyamin was not easily missed. A chubby, waddling Pukhtun baby, his cheeks had been heavy with puppy fat, probably to protect the chiselled cheekbones and large eyes that emerged in adulthood. As with all Akbar's children, people would often ask him about his origins. Greece was the most popular guess. Benyamin was young enough to still enjoy the game. He felt it set him apart from the average Asian kid. If there was one thing he didn't want to be, it was like everyone else.

As Benyamin put the cash away, the pimp said to him, grinning, 'I hear there's gonna be a meeting soon, the Jirga getting together. Must be serious.'

Benyamin nodded, but added nothing more. It was time for him to leave. Khalid the pimp had forgotten that the code of the Jirga required silence as much as loyalty. One did not speak casually on the streets about the Khan and his 'Jury'. Benyamin left saddened and burdened. A way would have to be found to reinforce the old lesson and make sure Khalid never made that mistake again.

CHAPTER 7

The Rolls-Royce purred through the broad streets of Knightsbridge and Belgravia, its navigation system telling the driver that he was almost at his destination. He was on schedule, despite the Friday rush-hour traffic.

Michael had only driven a few hundred miles, but the climate and pace of this city was a world apart from where his journey had begun. Though he felt out of place, the car he drove was not. Bentley, Ferrari, Mercedes-Maybach...few knew that the streets of his home town were also paved with prestige vehicles. Whether parked up in Frizinghall Square or cruising through Mayfair's New Bond St, the cars on the roads were the same. The social demographic that sat behind the wheel, however, was not.

In his city, cars were the favoured symbol of how far you had travelled in life – the milometer clocked resilience. They spoke of high achievement, a PhD from the School of Hard Knocks. Like the diamond in an engagement ring, an elite car signified the spending of care, attention and copious amounts of money. It showed one's rank in society: a white Audi for foot soldiers, a black Bentley for the kingpin, a Rolls for his family.

Michael knew the cash that was flashed to purchase these beautiful machines came fast and easy to the boys moving up the ladder of the Khan's organisation to become men of means.

As he drove through London in the Rolls-Royce Phantom, he felt the city's magnificent stucco buildings embrace it, recognising it as one of their own. But the broad, sprawling Yorkshire stone edifices to which it actually belonged stood squarely detached from everything around them, whereas the slim homes of Mayfair gentry stood shoulder to shoulder, stretching upwards, and downwards. No room for anyone or anything new. Michael wondered if cars, like people, looked down on each other, Skodas and Peugeots put in their place as they tried to climb the social ladder. 'But then...new money is better than no money,' he said to himself as he turned the corner into White Horse Street. He'd reached his destination. He parked up and made his way to the address he'd been given.

He waited uncomfortably at the concierge desk of 100 Piccadilly, looking down at his shoes. He quietly raised his right foot and rubbed it behind his left trouser leg in an attempt to shine away the signs he didn't belong here.

'Ms Khan left this for you, sir,' the concierge said, handing him a note and a parking stub.

'What is this place?' he asked the concierge, showing her the note.

'It's a warehouse, sir. Not far from here.'

He thanked the woman and climbed back into the car. He was entering the new postcode in the satellite navigation system, when the phone rang. It was Akbar Khan.

'I'm on my way, Khan Baba,' he said. 'She got held up at work. I will call you as soon as I have collected her... Yes, Baba. Salaam.' He never knew how much detail to give the Khan. He didn't want to say anything to upset his employer, especially in this case, since he was collecting his daughter.

The concierge had been right: the location was not far. A young man in a high-vis vest waited at the entrance to the street named on the parking stub. Michael showed him the paper and he waved him on and down towards what looked to be a vacant plot. As he got closer, he counted ten cars parked up, each one worth more than his house. He felt ill at ease as he left the car park. Even if he achieved his dreams of becoming a surgeon, he was unlikely to live the kind of life on show here.

The attendant was waiting for him and recognised the look. 'Obscene, in't it?' he said. 'There's people visiting food banks and these guys get to live like this.' They walked on through a tunnel of wet cobblestones the colour of copper when it rusts, towards the light and roar of a crowd. The passageway opened out into a courtyard. A sign on one of the walls dated them as Victorian.

'What is this place?' said Michael.

'A private venue – for those in the know,' the attendant replied, tapping his nose.

'This must be some party.'

'That ain't exactly what I'd call it,' said the young man, as he led him towards a door into the warehouse.

The smell of sweat and the taste of iron hit Michael hard as the metal door swung open. A crowd was gathered around a huge cage that stretched around ten feet high; inside it, two bloodied men were pummelling each other. 'Ms Khan is at the front, on the right,' said the attendant, pointing.

A solitary woman stood in a sea of angry men, their adrenaline-fuelled fists punching the air, their faces contorted as they roared, and hers no less so, possibly more. Her dark hair fell across her face, her voice was strong, echoing as she shouted to the fighters, telling them to punch harder, move faster. Michael felt the crowd around her blur out, and when she came into focus, she was primal, her pull so strong that he couldn't stop looking at her.

'How did you know I was here for her?' he asked the attendant.

'None of your beeswax how I know. She's been coming here for years. She's paying for my little brother's posh school. Proper bright, he is. Anyway, I can't stand here yapping. My shift's nearly over – bit like this match,' he said, as one of the fighters slumped to the floor.

When a few minutes later the bell sounded and the winner was announced, Michael took advantage of the interval to make his way through the gentrified cage-fight enthusiasts towards Jia Khan. 'Did you find the place easily?' she asked. He nodded. 'Follow me,' she said.

He did as she instructed, walking a couple of steps behind as she navigated the crowded space. She was swift, moving faster than the women he knew. She stopped next to a stocky woman in a loud shirt and a black hat.

'Jaani, I'm leaving now, so we need to talk about my winnings,' said Jia. The woman waved her quiet, frowning. She was sweating to the point of melting; the synthetic shirt was a bad decision. 'You're the only person I let get away with that kind of rudeness,' said Jia, and the woman smiled, her rouged lips wide over her yellow teeth.

'It's already done, my darling, take a look at your app. You know I always do you first,' she said, winking.

Michael watched as Jia checked her phone, before thanking the stocky woman.

She led him back to the car park, where the parking attendant was waiting with a small suitcase and an overcoat. He handed Jia the coat and she slipped it on before getting into the car.

'We'll give you a lift, Ali. I need to say hello to your mother.' she said. 'Come on, get in.'

She gave Michael directions as they drove. Half an hour later, they reached an old council estate. The kind haunted by the smell of fried bacon and the sound of dogs barking, and where Union Jacks hung out of windows. It looked uninviting to people like them, and as Michael pulled up, he worried for their safety and that of the car.

'Wait here, I'll only be a few minutes,' Jia told Michael. His phone rang just as she began walking with Ali to his front door. It was Akbar Khan.

'Yes, Khan Baba, she is with me. We have made a slight detour.' Michael watched as Jia waited outside a ground-floor flat, while the parking attendant disappeared inside. He returned a moment later with a tired-looking woman in a crinkled dupatta. She looked grateful to see Jia. A young boy hovered behind her. Ali said something that made the woman take her mobile from her cardigan pocket. She pressed it against Jia's phone before hugging her tightly, gratitude spreading across her face. From the car, Michael could see Jia's discomfort, her arms hanging limply as she tolerated the show of emotion. 'I don't know, Baba, I think it is a family your daughter helps.'

Jia was subdued when she returned to the car. They sat in silence all the way to her apartment building, where Jia needed to pick up her bags.

Michael waited in the hallway as she unlocked the door to her apartment. It was the first time he'd really looked at her. She'd tied her brown hair up in the car. Her eyes were like rum-soaked almonds, her skin golden and soft. She took off her shoes and stepped barefoot on to the parquet floor of the entrance hall. A crystal chandelier hung in the centre of the room, and stairs curved up one side.

'Why don't you wait in there,' she said, pointing to an open door. 'I'll be down shortly.'

He did as she asked, and found himself in a large hexagonal library. Four of the walls were covered in shelves stretching from floor to ceiling. Books by writers as diverse as Chimamanda Ngozi Adichie, Chuck Palahniuk, Manto, Byron, Bukowski and Ghalib reached up to the ornate mouldings of the ceiling. A moleskin chesterfield stood to one side of the room. A glass wall adjacent to it looked out over a courtyard garden. Photographs, mainly in sepia and black and white, but the occasional colour image too, hung on the opposite wall.

Michael felt suddenly small, a rare occurrence for a man who stood six foot two. He had retained the lankiness that teenage boys have when their arms outgrow the rest of their body, and found himself awkward as he tried to sit in one of the armchairs. He stood up again and waited.

He wanted Jia Khan to be impressed by him. He didn't know why. Maybe it was because she was so different to him. Privileged and self-assured, she knew her place in the world and how to move through it. He was a mixed-race medical student in his early twenties, and still trying to figure out what that meant.

The Khan's daughter was infamous among his father's people, spoken about in hushed tones; the rumours about her were many. She was the only person known to have challenged, confronted and abandoned the Khan and lived to tell the tale.

He was lost in thought when she walked in. 'Do you like it?' she asked, startling him. He pulled his eyes into focus, took off his glasses, wiped them on his shirt and put them back on to study the image he'd absentmindedly been staring at. It was a copy of *Life* magazine, framed, mounted and hanging on the wall. The photograph on the cover – one he'd seen hanging in chai shops across Pakistan – was of an old man with aquiline features wearing a peaked hat of the kind worn by the people of Kabul. The sight of the qaraqul resting on Muhammad Ali Jinnah's head always left him queasy. What kind of people used aborted sheep foetuses to make headwear?

'It's from 1948,' said Jia. 'That particular one took quite a lot of effort to track down.'

Michael was surprised. His Pakistani heritage had not served him well and he'd dropped all ties to it, other than his father. It was one less moth-eaten coat in his cupboard. This woman was not like him. She hung her heritage on her wall for everyone to see and judge and question. He didn't know anyone second-generation who did that.

'My sister thinks I'm overcompensating for my "polite white lifestyle".' She tilted her head slightly as she spoke, and he could see traces of her father in her face. He noticed that she'd changed into a sari blouse and petticoat under the shawl she'd wrapped herself in. She turned back to the picture. 'Who knows, maybe I am. A little.' She smiled. 'I don't mix with Pakistanis or Pathans much. Not unless

I'm defending them in court. You'd be surprised how much one can miss those ways... Shall we go?'

She handed him her case. He nodded.

'So, what did the good people of our city tell you about me?' she asked as he placed the bag in the car. He didn't answer, instead holding the door behind the driver's seat open as his father had taught him to do for women of 'good' families. Jia ignored the protocol and climbed into the passenger seat.

'I'm not sitting in silence in the back of the car for three hours,' she said. 'This isn't Pakistan.' In that moment Michael knew that he liked Jia Khan, but that it mattered little to her either way.

CHAPTER 8

The boy searched the pockets of his red jacket for his car keys as he stood at the front door. He noticed his mother watching him from the kitchen. She was enveloped in the smell of masala, in her hand a powdered rolling pin. The boy stepped into the street to escape the scent.

He wasn't really a 'boy' and when the newspapers would caption his photograph they would describe him as a 'youth'. It was a legal technicality that mattered little to his mother.

'No more chapattis, Mum. I'm in training,' he said, waving her away as she followed him to the door. Her constant need to cook, showing her love through complex carbs, cakes and jalebis, annoyed him and hampered progression towards his muscle-building target. She stepped forward to kiss him but he brushed her off. 'Acha, acha,' he said, softening as he saw the look on her face. 'Don't wait up watching those Hum dramas.'

She stood by the door whispering prayers as the headlights of his red Ferrari flashed and the boot clicked open. She knew of no other way to keep him safe.

Taking a package from the back of the car, he placed it inside his jacket and pulled the zip up high before looking around. A group of kids were staring at him, one with his mouth wide open. They'd been kicking a football back and forth down the alley that hugged the side of the terraced houses. The flashing lights of the car had interrupted their game.

'What you looking at?' he shouted. The shortest of the group gave him the finger, before turning and tearing down the alley, his friends following fast behind. They all wanted to be like the man in the red Ferrari.

He climbed into his car, the sound of loud music exploding through the quiet street. The neighbours were relieved when his car disappeared down the road.

Twenty-three years old, Atif spent daylight hours at the gym trying to make up in muscle what he lacked in height. The evenings were spent making money.

He pulled into another terraced street, where his friend Aslam was waiting on a bench in the low sunlight, playing with his phone.

Atif greeted him warmly and told him to get in. 'Bro, it's been time, man!'

Aslam was a student at Manchester. His parents had encouraged him to move away in the hope that he'd leave his old friends behind. 'Yeah, just, you know, been studying and that.'

'Right. Right. Good for you, bro. Good for you. Me, I didn't like it. Uni wasn't for me. Dropped out.'

'What were you studying?'

'Politics and law. Then Abba got sick, I came back to help Mum an' that... You know how it is, family.' He stopped under the weight of the conversation, and pulled at his jacket. 'It's all good, though. See this?' he said. 'Ralph Lauren. Cost me a few hundred quid. There's no way I could afford this if I was a student. Or even if I was working in an office. I make plenty Gs selling this shit. It's the milk round that pays for my mum and sisters,' he said, and winked at Aslam as he pushed the package further down into his jacket. Real men didn't talk about their feelings in this town; they drove fast and flashed their cash.

He took a left into a narrow one-way road off Stourley Street. There were cars parked on either side, the drivers still in their seats. Aslam was about to mention this when his friend stopped the car. He watched Atif reach out of the window, his fist becoming a

49

handshake as it met the hand of the driver parked alongside him. When he brought his fist back into the car, he was holding a twenty-pound note. He flicked his fingers making a clicking sound.

'And that's how it's done,' he said. 'Help a bro out?' He handed a small package to Aslam and gestured to let him know he was to do the same on the passenger side. Aslam tore open the brown paper of the package and tiny sealed plastic wallets fell all over him. 'Easy. Easy,' Atif said firmly.

Gathering himself and his goods, Aslam attempted to copy his friend's fist to handshake move. It wasn't as easy as it looked but the customer handed him a few carefully folded banknotes and seemed relieved to have his stash. They continued, driving and exchanging, until there was only one car left on the street.

As they approached the last car, Aslam realised he'd been holding his breath. He moved back into his seat, his sweat-soaked shirt clinging to his back.

The next customer was dressed in a vest, shalwar and prayer hat. 'You're delivering early,' he said. 'I'm supposed to be at mosque praying Maghrib righ' about now.'

'Sorry, bro. It's Akbar Khan's daughter's wedding. The Jirga wants to shut up shop early for the weekend. They don't want'a bring no bad luck or owt,' said Atif. A look of respect fell across the buyer's face. He nodded in understanding and pulled away.

Aslam had heard stories surrounding Akbar Khan. He wanted to separate the myth from the reality. 'How long the Jirga been running things?' he said to Atif.

'For time. They're like the law lords of this city. You know how the twelve of'em Supreme Court judges run Great Britain, keep everything, you know, running tight. In the same way the Jirga runs this city.'

'But what exactly does Akbar Khan do?'

'He owns this town, bro. He and the Jirga make sure the councillors do their jobs, the hookers do theirs and tossers like that dick back there don't start gettin' up in our faces and start another riot...'

Atif's voice trailed off. Distracted, he slowed the Ferrari down to a crawl. Aslam caught sight of a group of pretty girls in the wing mirror. His friend rolled down the window, staring at the girls but addressing Aslam: 'The Jirga and Akbar Khan run this city.'

Backcombed hair, bright red lips and teetering on heels, the girls had looked older from a distance. They were barely eighteen.

Atif carried on speaking as he reached out of the window: 'They got their own rules, their own ways, not all people can function in a democracy, see. Tell me, Aslam, why would we groom white girls when we've got high-quality arse like this on our doorstep?' He grabbed the rounded bottom of the girl closest to his car.

The girl calmly turned and looked at him as if he'd asked her for the time or directions or notes to a lecture…and then she spat on his car.

'What's a matter?' said Atif.

'Fuck off,' was the girl's response. Her friends tried to pull her away, giggling as they walked. She refused to go with them, standing her ground and staring at the Ferrari.

'Where you working? Will you go out with me?' said Atif. He nodded at the girl in a 'you know you want to' kind of way.

The girl narrowed her heavily made-up eyes; green contact lenses gave them a snake-like quality. 'I wouldn't go out with you if you were Amir Khan. Anyway, whose car you robbed?' she said.

Atif broke into a grin. 'It's mine. You wanna ride?'

Shouts echoed across the street and they looked to see what was happening. On the other side of the road, two bouncers outside a bar nightclub were arguing with a couple of well-dressed Asian men. One of the well-dressed men pushed the bouncer: 'You fuckin' racist. I'm gonna see you very soon with me shooters.'

The bouncer turned to his colleague. 'Check out 50 Cent over here.'

Hearing the response, the younger man's shouts grew louder and more vicious, but his friend dragged him off.

'I like his style,' said Atif. 'You gotta love it. Home of two riots. And we ain't afraid to start a third. I'll do it just to get you in my car, girl.'

The girl looked at the car and then at him and then at his car again, but said nothing.

'Alhamdolilah! God made me Asian, baby, I got skin like Caramac, you know you want to lick it!' Fireworks began exploding across the sky. 'See, it's a sign from Allah. Subhanatallah!' Atif wasn't going to let her go without a fight. 'My last girlfriend said I look like Zayn Malik,' he added, nodding his head and acting the man. 'Or was it Dynamo?' He winked.

The girl's narrowed eyes widened and then crinkled with laughter. She pointed to the small drum that one of the girls was carrying. The instrument was played at parties in the run-up to Pakistani weddings. 'We're singin' and playing the dholki at Akbar Khan's house later. Pick me up at the Beauty Spot, I'm getting my hair done first,' she said, before teetering along the road and climbing into the car where her friends were waiting.

'What time?' he called after her.

'You figure it out.'

The men watched as they drove off.

'This must be one expensive wedding,' Aslam said as a second batch of fireworks exploded.

'Them's not for the weddin'. That's the next delivery. Don't you know nothin'? When the big drugs haul comes in, the fireworks go off. Come on, let's go to Pasha's. I need me some shisha.'

The bouncers watched the red Ferrari leave. One of the men was slightly taller than the other. He shook his head as the car left and then continued with his conversation: 'Yeah, it's her birthday. She's been going on about wanting some fairy castle.' He pulled out his phone and showed his colleague a photograph of his five-year-old daughter. 'They say it changes your life but you don't believe them.

And then one day your little girl wraps her hand around your finger and nothing's the same.' He smiled as he put his phone back into his pocket.

A silver Subaru turned the corner next to the nightclub. It circled back and a man in a suit leaned out of the passenger side. The shorter of the two bouncers clocked who he was just as the spray of bullets began. Revellers collapsed on top of him, their legs taking the hit. By the time he was able to stand, all he could see was blood. And his friend's body in a heap on the pavement.

CHAPTER 9

A lone security man watched from his tower and bowed as Benyamin
Khan did a last sweep around the grounds of the private residence,
under the gaze of countless security cameras, to check everything
was ready. Grandiose and imposing, the Victorian mansion was
exactly the kind of place befitting the city's kingpin, and the perfect
setting for a wedding.

Built by a wealthy textile merchant, it had fallen into disrepair
when Akbar Khan bought it. It was part of the city's heritage, but
to Benyamin it was just home. The extensive gardens bloomed all
year long thanks to their two gardeners. They kept the varying
green hues of the lush landscape visible from every window. From
its hilltop, the house watched over the two aspects of the city, the
white and the Asian, a divide not visible in the landscape but etched
on the minds of the people who lived there. Pukhtun House was
the one place where the two met as equals to discuss matters of
importance.

The inside of the house was suitably dignified, thanks to Sanam
Khan. She had spent years collecting artefacts and antiquities, and
restoring pieces of furniture to their former glory. She had once
belonged to generational wealth and looked down on the gaudiness
of new money. This house was a labour of love. The family finances
had dwindled when her grandmother was a young woman, but she
had tried to keep the legacy alive by training her grandchildren in
the art of the gentry – familiarity with the knot counts of Persian

rugs, how to tell if a fabric is silk or synthetic, the choosing of chai, discernment in the quality of china, the purchasing of pure spices – all skills that had proved useless until now. According to the genteel ways in which Sanam Khan was raised, weddings were the one time ostentation was allowed, and Benyamin was pleased to see the how well the preparations had gone. It had taken an army of men to drape every tree on the estate in lights but not one of these workmen was visible now.

The wedding guests began to arrive in all their splendour, their black, blue, grey and white cars lining the driveway of the sprawling family house, each one more expensive than the next. Hidden away from prying eyes, they were able to enjoy Akbar Khan's keen hospitality. The grounds swelled with powerful people, some of whom did not want to be seen, others who had a price on their head: they needed assurances that their safety was guaranteed. Discreetly placed cameras covered every part of Pukhtun House. Connected to a hi-tech security system, they allowed guests to maintain a sense of privacy and safety. The army of loyal men who were known to watch over the Khan and his home continued their surveillance from a distance. All that was needed was one simple signal and the house would be surrounded and in full lockdown. But few people other than Akbar Khan and his family were ever seen in the grounds of Pukhtun House. The Khan's justice was known to be swift and his men skilled in its delivery. This and their undying loyalty struck fear into the hearts of anyone who would attempt anything. Though no one was visible, everyone was being watched.

A marquee covered the entire north side of the garden; no expense had been spared. Ladies in swirls of bright silks filled one half of the tent like sweet fruit coulis, as they admired and envied each other's jewels. The younger generation dressed more simply, opting for pearls in place of their mothers' gaudy gold necklaces, the children of immigrants tempering the vibrancy of their heritage with shades of their new homeland. At the other side of the marquee their fathers, husbands and brothers knocked back whisky in sharp suits, shalwar kameez and silk Nehru coats, laughing raucously as they patted each other on the back and shook hands over stories of love, war and business.

At the end of the garden, a young man waited on the bridal stage. Tapping the mic he gently drew the crowd's attention. He grinned and winked at the older ladies, who feigned offence, as the younger women stole glances, hoping to catch his handsome eye. Confidently, slowly, he began humming a well-known Pukhtun love song. The hum turned to words, the men began to clap, the women sway, and he had control of the crowd. He sang of the beauty of Pukhtun women and of the strength of their men, and of the love of their homeland. His words took effect and a loud cheer went up from the men, and the women clutched their hands over their mouths, muffling their laughter. One particularly stout man dressed in cream shalwar kameez and a heavily embroidered waistcoat started miming to the song. He took his wife by the hand, his other arm in the air, and began copying the ways of folk dancers. The crowd clapped loudly and whoops of delight travelled across the gardens and into the house, where Benyamin was. He was holding the basket of motichoor ladoo, each one as big as a fist. The yellow sweetmeat balls had been sent as a mark of respect from a friend of Akbar Khan and were to be given out to the guests at the end of the night.

Benyamin entered the kitchen. The counters were filled with fresh meat, coriander, bulbs of garlic, onions and other produce, the hobs with large pots of bubbling curry. The fragrance of rice and kewra water filled the room. A burly man wearing a blood-stained apron was chopping mutton with a cleaver, the knife cutting through shoulder after shoulder with ease.

'Why are you cutting the meat, Lala? We have people to do this.'

'I know, beta. I came in to oversee things but they were making a mess of it! And I want it all to be perfect for your sister. And will it be you next?' Bazigh Khan raised a jesting eyebrow at his favourite nephew, who brushed him off affectionately; he was used to the question.

Bazigh Khan was a stout man with a red beard, and his business was butchery. Those who knew him understood that he was a man to frighten Iblis and his army of fallen angels. He was a man of myth. There were those who would swear blind that he was responsible for all chaos in the world, saying that when God ordered the angels to bow before Adam, it was Bazigh Khan who whispered in the ear of Iblis. Growing fat and arrogant on the butcher's friendship, the devil raised a rebellion that took on the Lord of heaven and earth Himself.

In the real world, Bazigh Khan owned the country's largest supplier of halal meat, and his produce was eaten in all the best restaurants, halal and haram alike. Today, he had personally taken it upon himself to prepare the roasting lamb, the baby chickens and the keema for chappal kebabs. This was his gift to his niece. After all, she had been raised in his arms and was his heart and honour.

'You're looking a little skinny, Benyamin jaan. Eat! Make us proud, like a real Pukhtun!' he told his nephew.

'Yeah yeah… Look, I've brought poison for all you REAL Pukhtun diabetics. It's part of my plan to kill you all and take over the family business.'

'It will take more than a little sugar to kill that old man!' called a familiar-looking man stirring the curry pot on the stove. The wedding was awash with family; Benyamin wasn't even sure how some of them were related to each other – they were 'cousins' and that was all he needed to know. 'Have you not heard? Even the plague runs and hides from Bazigh Khan!'

And Bazigh Khan laughed wholeheartedly at his cousin's words. The men's lungs filled with air, their bellies with food. It was a good day to be alive. It had been too long since this house had heard such laughter.

'Put the mithai in the dining room,' Bazigh Khan said to his nephew. 'It will start to smell of karahi if you leave it here.'

Benyamin took the basket into the dining room. He looked around for a place to leave it, but boxes of Maria's wedding trousseau lined the walls. He was about to exit when he felt someone's eyes on him. A woman with a familiar face, one much thinner than he remembered, was standing by the window. He flinched at the sight of her. She'd caught him off guard.

'What are you doing here?' he said. His voice was soaked in annoyance, the kind one saves for family. It surprised her.

'Benny?' she said. She'd been slow to recognise him.

But he knew her instantly. She didn't look that much older, and although something about her manner said she wasn't the girl who had fled this house years ago, he knew her. And in that moment, it felt as if not a thread of time had elapsed since they'd last met. Seeing her, the responsibility briefly slipped from his shoulders, falling to the floor along with the years that had passed, as he felt himself becoming her little brother again. He wanted to embrace her, but his pride stood like a glass wall between them. He stepped back. 'Have you seen Baba?' he said.

She shook her head. 'You've lost weight. You look like a man.'

Benyamin straightened up.

'I am a man,' he said. He had enough attention from both sexes to know he was no longer the overweight kid he used to be. His baby fat had been replaced by muscle; his chest was wide and his eyes proud, but something in them told Jia that that pride was not whole. Her little brother had grown up and his aura was hard and cold, tinged with self-preservation. But in spite of all that, to Jia he was still the same little boy who wanted to eat ice-cream sandwiches and kebab-topped bagels every day, the one wiping dripping ketchup from the side of his mouth.

'Don't say anything stupid to Mama,' he said. 'She's old now, she can't handle your stuff any more.'

'Benny, I'm here for the wedding. Maria asked me.'

'You know how you get. Just leave it alone, OK?' He was picking a fight with her the way one picks a scab. He didn't really want it to bleed, he just wanted to know what was under it. She didn't reply, and it pissed him off even more. 'Just do what you want and leave. You do anyway.'

She reached out to touch him but he turned away, and reflected in his eyes, for the first time, she saw what she had done. The walls that she had built to protect herself had left those more vulnerable than her on the outside. In taking care of herself she had forgotten those for whom she was responsible. Benyamin was holding on to his anger; it had started to define him. She had done that to him and it hurt her a little to know he was right. Unable to stay in her presence, he walked out of the French windows and into the garden.

The guests were feasting; the air was scented with tender lamb, hot roasting coals and warm naan, and rang with the sound of rhythmic clapping and singing. The smells and noise drifted in through the open doors as Jia watched her brother walk across the lawn towards their father. The old man was laughing and dancing with her mother; she was pushing him playfully away and he was bringing her back into his arms. Benyamin joined them, his father enveloping him in a hearty embrace. It was rare to see Akbar smile. It was rarer still to see him laugh so heartily. As Jia watched the garden full of merriment, her heart filled with memories of Zan Khan. She moved back into the shadows, waiting for the longing to pass.

CHAPTER 10

Akbar Khan quickly descended the staircase of his home. His wife had been fussing over his attire and he had kept the men waiting longer than he deemed acceptable. Twelve of them, all immaculately dressed, were sitting patiently in the study.

The room spanned the length of the house, its large bay windows, covered with heavy velvet curtains, faced each other at opposite ends. The Khan's antique desk sat in front of one of these windows, a leather captain's chair behind it. Across from it was a tall, carved wooden jhoola, the kind of cradle swing found in the homes of feudal families of Pakistan and the royalty of pre-partition India. Matching chairs lined the sides of the room, each one intricately carved from rosewood with a small table beside it. Each one filled except for one.

The talk was small, of the weather and Eid and Hajj, and ended with Akbar Khan's arrival. Each man stepped forward to shake his hand and they embraced thrice, as was the custom, multiplying between them the greeting of peace.

Akbar Khan surveyed his men. They were his brothers in arms. Although their work was not an appropriate subject at other weddings, it was welcome at Pukhtun House. Akbar Khan knew his men were here today as much for connection as for celebration. They needed to hear him speak, the way congregants need their preacher on Fridays.

He thought carefully before he addressed them. 'One mouth but two ears,' his mother used to say, and he had taken it to heart.

'Our role on this earth, my brothers, is to serve God and to assist His people,' he said. 'We understand that this is the dunya and not the jannah. This world is meant as a trial. It is harsh on the believers, and its pain will not cease until we are in the ground. As holders of this knowledge it is imperative that we ease that pain in whatever way we can. Even if the world judges us harshly. Remember this, that you and I are believers, and the world itself is a prison for the believer.'

The call for prayer interrupted him, coming from a speaker in the corner of the room. He stopped immediately. 'Come, let us offer Isha together,' he said, and stood aside to let his men make their way to the wet room.

They lined up before the twelve taps, the water sweet and clear, washing away their differences as it poured over them from their face to their feet, taking with it their sins. Ritually cleansed, they entered the room where the imam was waiting.

Ibrahim Khattak knew prayer to be a seminal part of these men's lives. His father had spent his life in service to the mosque that Akbar Khan had built forty years ago. Since his death it had fallen to Ibrahim to tend to the Khan's needs, helping him navigate the knottier laws of Allah, laws that could otherwise have kept the Khan up at night. Ibrahim was steeped in the old ways and well versed in the new, as were all the men who gathered there that day. They knew what was expected of them and Akbar Khan was well acquainted with their needs. Linked by blood, marriage and business, their families had been bound together for centuries. These powerful men pledged unwavering allegiance to the Khan; they were his Jirga; they were his right arm and his left.

As the imam began to speak the Arabic words of salah, silence fell. Shoulder to shoulder they stood before the God of Muhammad, who was also the God of Moses and Jesus and Krishna and Confucius. They knelt before him as men have done for fourteen centuries, their foreheads pressed deep into the prayer mat, whispering the words of repentance and supplication and praise, hoping for wisdom and wealth. The fardh offered, some stood for the sunnah, the optional prayers. Others remained seated, turning their attentions to their private tasbeeh.

Afterwards, as their wives offered envelopes of banknotes to the bride's mother outside, the men returned to the study and promised their property, lives and honour to their God and then to Akbar Khan. Each man brought gifts, some brought requests; all brought respect.

One of these men was Sher Khan, Akbar Khan's brother-in-law. He had waited twelve months for this day, and considered it auspicious to find himself seated next to his Khan. So when his protector asked him to pray for his daughter's happiness he found the knot in his tongue loosened.

'Inshallah and ameen, Khan sahib,' he said. 'I will surely pray for Maria. And I ask the same of you for my sons. They are good boys. They made only one mistake and trouble has followed them since.'

Akbar Khan's eyes were downcast as though deep in thought. In truth, they were hiding his disappointment. He believed man's role in the world was to evolve spiritually and emotionally, but Sher Khan's family shunned self-improvement. Rough and abrupt, he'd not made the best impression on Akbar Khan when his sister had expressed her intention to marry him. Today was yet another reminder of Sher Khan's ineptness.

Unaware of the Khan's feelings, however, he continued to press his case, his voice betraying his ego. 'I believed we were equal when we came to this country,' he said. 'I worked hard every day. I looked after my wife. I sent my children to school... I wanted them to live a good life, a happy life. Did we want to see this rioting? No! I was a law-abiding man. The boys' mother, she listened to the police, we trusted them... She told the police where they were. She thought they would help us. But they took our sons and locked them away for twelve years, and since then they are like marked men, in and out of prison whenever they happen to be in the wrong place at the wrong time. The gorai,' he said, spitting out the word for 'pale skin' as though it had a bad taste, 'they burned our houses and abused our women but nothing was done to them. They get community service. What is this community service? Tell me. They have no idea about community, about honour, about friendship!'

On this, Akbar Khan agreed with him: the treatment of their men by the British law courts had not been just, and had only served to feed people's anger. That Akbar Khan had the means to manipulate both the people and the police force meant that he could bring about the demise of the city if he wished, but he knew that doing so would serve no purpose. There were no winners in war except for dealers of arms and carpetbaggers. He had not become Khan by opening the gates of hell; he had become Khan by keeping the devil at bay. He measured and held his own tongue, while cutting the tongues of others out.

He looked at his brother-in-law, the pain he felt for his people evident on his face. 'Treat a man like an animal and that is what he becomes,' he said. 'The justice system does not see us as human. I understand what you are saying, my brother, but I am not happy that you have raised this matter with me now, at my daughter's wedding. Could it not have waited?'

Sher Khan fell to apologising. 'Khan Baba. I have five daughters myself. If I could have waited I would have, but my sons... They will be released from jail tomorrow and I have been trying to find the most respectful way of making my request. I want them to be with me. I am an old man and my life is almost done. I wish to ask, to request most humbly, that my sons take my place on the Jirga.'

A murmur ran through the men. Akbar Khan held up his hand and silence fell once again. 'The law of this country saves a man after he has done wrong,' he said. 'Our customs stop him from doing that wrong. Are our customs as good as their laws? Some would say not, we would say yes. But your boys have tasted of their laws, and now they want to live by ours. I do not know if they will be able to administer justice when they carry the desire for vengeance, but... this is how our life is. It is up and down. As for taking your place in the Jirga, you are not the first to ask this, and you will not be the last... Come enjoy the wedding. Today, eat and spend time with your wife and daughters. You and I will speak more about this tomorrow night, inshallah.'

Hearing these words, Sher Khan began calling down blessings upon Akbar Khan and his family. He moved forward to embrace him but Bazigh Khan stepped in, quickly ushering him and the other men out of the room. When he returned he found Akbar Khan standing by the window, watching the guests, his face pensive.

'There is that one final matter of business, Lala,' he said.

Akbar Khan turned to face his brother. 'The chief of police wants me to help him with something?' he said. 'It was so much easier when they were the enemy.' He shook his head slowly at the changing times and blurring boundaries. 'This matter, what is it?' he asked.

Bazigh Khan relayed the news of the nightclub shooting to his brother, who listened silently, his face dark, his brow furled. 'If the young are not initiated into the tribe, what else will they do but burn the village down?' Akbar Khan said. 'Still, we do not need another race war. Our people do not know fear. They will destroy everything that we have spent years building. Tell him, the policeman, to come to the house tomorrow... Let us listen to what he has to say, and hope he listens to us before our boys find a way to get heard.' Bazigh Khan nodded at his brother's wisdom, understanding the implied and the unsaid.

Theirs was the camaraderie of soldiers and of family, of shared secrets and of blood. As brothers, they had stood apart from other men and back to back with each other. The things they had done and the things they had seen were never spoken of, but, like white-hot irons on flesh, they had left their mark.

Akbar Khan turned back to the window and watched his family enjoying the evening. Standing in the middle of the garden was Maria, as radiant and blushing as a bride should be. And there, too, was Jia, so much like him, and so unlike her sister – one golden and the other pale, one gentle and the other sharp. 'I see both my daughters are here today,' Akbar Khan said to his brother. He regarded them from afar as the sisters hugged one another.

'You look beautiful,' Jia said.

'I'm in good company, aren't I?' laughed Maria, and Jia noted the ease with which her little sister opened herself up to life, her soft brown curls falling around her face, her shoulders loose, her touch light. Maybe this is what she herself would have become if things had been different.

Maria taught at a primary school nearby. That's where she had met the man she was marrying today. Loved and beloved, Maria changed lives in ways that Jia once hoped she would too. Out of everyone in the family, Maria alone had managed to maintain some kind of relationship with Jia despite the circumstances. It was what sisters did with ease. It was what brothers let slip. It was what made men and women need each other.

Jia adjusted her sister's jewellery. The string of pearls that ran along her centre parting had twisted, turning the gold pendant that hung from it over. 'Benyamin is angry with me,' she said.

'He's angry with everyone. Except his girlfriend, Mina,' said Maria. Several questions sprang to mind but Jia put them aside. She made a mental note to talk to Maria about it after the wedding.

'You really do look lovely,' she said, admiring her sister's outfit. 'I'm glad you made me come.' A rogue silk thread was coming away from the pinks and the plums of the brocade of Maria's wedding dress. It occurred to Jia that family was a little like jamavar: countless delicate threads woven together to make an intricate and somehow robust fabric, but one that frayed quickly if not looked after. She looked around for a pair of scissors, but finding none, she leaned forward and broke the thread with her teeth the way she had seen seamstresses do in Zainab Market.

'Ben can be an idiot,' said Maria.

'I think it might be my fault,' answered Jia, her voice distant.

Maria waved at her groom. He was watching her from the other side of the garden. He looked in need of rescuing. 'He can't quite handle the outfit,' said Maria.

'Are you sure you want to marry this man?' asked Jia.

Maria laughed again, and it filled Jia with a lightness, like hope.

'I should go help him before Baba sees. By the way, you know Elyas is here?'

The lightness evaporated instantly. Jia nodded. She knew he was here. She just didn't know if she was ready to see him.

She watched her little sister traverse the space, feeling both pride and envy at her youth. She handled the silk gharara with the same ease as she handled everything else in life. Sanam Khan had succeeded in protecting at least one of her daughters.

Back in his study, her father was thinking the same thing as he watched them.

'You seem troubled, Brother?' Bazigh Khan said.

'A little. I want you to take these papers. There is a letter in it addressed to you. Open it tomorrow before you come to see me, and then burn it.' Akbar Khan placed his right hand on his brother's shoulder, as if to stress the importance of what he was about to say. 'I know it is a strange request, but everything will become clear. Tomorrow evening, we'll talk like we used to before things changed, yes?' His voice was weary. Bazigh Khan had not heard him speak this way since Jia left. 'I trust you above all others. And I know that you trust me. I know that you will stand by the family no matter what,' he said. He locked eyes with his brother, unwilling to look away until understanding passed over Bazigh Khan's face. The matter was too important to be avoided, yet too delicate to be ridden over roughshod with empty words. 'No matter what happens,' he said.

Bazigh Khan nodded. 'Yes, Brother,' he said. 'You have my word.'

CHAPTER 11

He scanned the other guests with a mix of nerves and excitement. The thought of seeing her had kept him up all night. He wondered if this was what a mid-life crisis felt like. He wondered why he was here. He wondered if this was a mistake.

Across from him, surrounded by his closest friends and his children, Akbar Khan danced with his wife. The man who'd damaged Elyas's life was still happily continuing his. The last time he had been in this place, words had been said and tragedy had followed. The last time he'd seen Akbar Khan was when he had left Ahad in Elyas's care.

Watching the crowd encircle his father-in-law, clapping and singing and making merry, he felt time fold back on itself. It brought with it pieces of his past…the scent of his new bride's skin, the henna on her hands, the light as it poured in through the blinds the morning after their wedding night, and the sound of her singing in the bathroom. He was hit by an ocean of longing for old times, followed by a wave of hatred for the man who had taken it from him. Akbar Khan hadn't aged a day and watching him now, acting as if his life had lost none of its vigour, anger began to rise inside Elyas. He wanted to march over and wrap his hands around the old man's neck and squeeze and squeeze until the life ran out of him.

'Drink, sir?' a voice said, snapping Elyas out of his thoughts. He knew now he should not have come. He turned to leave, but stopped. A woman was waving at him from the other side of the marquee.

She began walking towards him, pulling the edge of her pink sari tight around her shoulders, the lace of her blouse delicately framing her slender neck, and he felt that old pull in his stomach return. He watched as she effortlessly crossed the crowded marquee and the years of missed opportunities and unsaid words. She stopped before him, and he realised he was holding his breath. He realised, again, that this was a mistake. He realised he hadn't really got over her.

'Elyas,' she said. 'I wasn't sure you'd come.'

'Jia Khan,' he said, and then nothing. They stood in awkward silence, watching as others who hadn't met since the last family event embraced, laughed and posed for photographs. The oft-imagined overcooked words saved up for meeting one's past love fell away as Elyas shifted uncomfortably from one foot to the other, his new shoes cutting into him. He was grateful when she finally broke the silence. 'You've started wearing glasses,' she said.

The ordinariness of the conversation managed both to annoy him and put him at ease. 'I'm getting old,' he said, as he touched the bridge of the solid black spectacles, pushing them into place.

'They suit you. You look clever.'

Where the hell were you? Why am I here? And what the fuck is going on? – all words he wanted to say, but didn't. Experience had taught him the consequences of rash actions, and he understood better than most the power of words. Maybe being tongue-tied in front of an old flame was where small talk originated, he thought wryly.

'You didn't think I looked clever before?' he batted back.

'You look good. And you still haven't learnt to take a compliment.'

'No, you're right, I haven't. You would know that if you'd answered any of my letters.'

His words surprised her, and as she fell silent he noticed all the ways in which she'd changed. Her eyes, once shy and unsure, now pooled with self-assurance. Her words were measured, and despite what had transpired between them, her smile was warm and forthcoming. She ignored his dig. 'I catch you on-screen occasionally,' she said, and now it was his turn to be surprised. Their parting had been so sudden and her reaction so severe that he had assumed she had cut him out of all existence, like taking scissors to old photographs. That she hadn't, pissed him off.

'Where are you staying?' she said.

'The cottage.'

'You still have that?'

'Never got around to selling. Not much changes here, does it? Same place, same city, same people, same bed… Everything's the same… Well, almost everything…' Nothing was the same. Not since she'd left. They were skirting around an elephant and he wanted to name it and shame her, along with all the other pent-up accusations, but the words wouldn't come. He searched her face for something, anything, *anything* that would betray her feelings. And then he saw it, that look in her eyes, the way she gently reached up and touched her neck, her fingers spread wide, and he knew that she too was caught up in the folding back of time.

She changed the subject quickly, and he accepted that small talk was all there was for now. From trivial things, to work – his and hers – to politics, science, old friends; they spoke, and all the while he stole snatches of her, each blink of the eye a mental snapshot, greedily stashing them in his mind for days when things were dark and his memory unforgiving. The bright young thing he'd fallen in love with all those years ago had become a woman. And while he saw that she was now cleverer and more accomplished, he felt sadness for the innocence they had both lost. Standing before her he understood exactly why no one had yet managed to replace her in his affections. She was simply the most extraordinary person he had ever met. His greatest misfortune was that he had met her too young.

Their conversation had reached a natural pause when Bazigh Khan walked by, carrying a plate of precariously balanced meats, his hair the colour of the flames on which the barbecue was to be cooked.

'Would you like some?' asked Elyas.

'Actually, don't say anything but…I'm vegan,' said Jia, letting Elyas in on her secret.

'Bloody hell! Is there anything you can eat here? They've carved up an entire abattoir!' said Elyas. His eyes met hers and they laughed as they used to, years ago.

'I had this moment where I suddenly became aware that I was eating flesh. Obviously, I can't tell my father. He'd bring me chicken and say, "This is not meat!"' Their laughter airbrushed the edges of the past, and everything softened, the way the borders of old friends melt into each other.

'Is he a relative?' asked Elyas, pointing at Bazigh Khan. 'He looks too hard a man to henna his hair.'

Jia laughed again. 'He is. You don't remember him?' Elyas shook his head. 'I don't think you would like him,' she whispered, leaning forward.

'Why? Who is he?'

'I never told you the story about my uncle?'

'No, tell me now.'

'Are you sure?' she said. 'Sometimes you ask for the truth when you don't really want it.'

Elyas raised his eyebrows, and mouthed: 'Me?'

'OK, listen up…' she said.

Elyas nodded, moving closer in anticipation, his eyes down ready for the story that was about to unfold. But she didn't speak, and when he looked up at her face, he could tell she was lost deep in thought. He followed her gaze and realised she was staring at three men who were making their way towards them across the marquee, their strong strides swallowing up the ground beneath them.

CHAPTER 12

Elyas held out his hand to each of them in turn.

'You remember my cousins?' said Jia. 'Brothers Idris and Nadeem, and Malik.' The men were immaculately dressed, their suits perfectly cut and stitched to accommodate their broad shoulders. They had the kind of golden skin tone that comes with money and Mediterranean holidays. One of them had a Turkish beard, of the type favoured by jihadis and hipsters. *Nowadays who can tell the difference?* thought Elyas, feeling a little shabby in his off-the-peg attire.

'So, what's the deal with you two? Aren't you divorced?' one of them asked.

'They're still direct,' Elyas said to Jia.

She smiled at her cousins in that way women do when men step out of line. 'Elyas was just asking about Bazigh Khan,' she said to the eldest of the three, Idris.

'Stories made up to scare children,' said Malik. He was the youngest of the men, and the one with the beard.

'If you're looking for a news story, you won't find it here,' said Idris, his tone cold. He was the kind of man who favoured silence over small talk. Although his jawline was square, his cheeks rounded when he smiled, which wasn't often. His eyes had the potential to tear strips off men. Elyas remembered Jia referring to him as a 'hellhound'. Seeing him now, he understood why. 'If I'm ever in trouble, call Idris,' Jia had said. 'He'll drag me back from hell if he has to.' It had been a strange conversation, as were most conversations that featured his wife's family.

Nadeem put a hand on his brother's shoulder. 'Steady on, Idris. It's just a question.'

Elyas liked Nadeem. Of all Jia's cousins he was the one he had warmed to most. He was an actor, a rare one, of the kind that made a lucrative living from his talent.

'I'll tell you about Bazigh Khan,' Nadeem went on. 'It happened a long time ago,' he began, 'when Bazigh Khan and Akbar Khan decided to go into business together. Pathans like snuff.' He splayed his hand and tensed it to show Elyas the groove that appears on the back, near where the thumb meets the wrist. He raised it to his nose and inhaled. 'But you couldn't buy it here and so, seeing a gap in the market, the two men, they started selling it. Soon, they were doing well, really well, and that's when things changed –' Nadeem stopped abruptly, as if choking on the words. Jia gently laid her hand on his arm as if to steady him.

'Then what happened?' Elyas said softly.

'Then what happened,' said Jia, 'is that the gang who controlled the estate where they lived came to see Bazigh Khan.' As she spoke, her demeanour changed and her tone lowered, and something in her voice made him wish he hadn't asked about Bazigh Khan. 'Mica, the man who ran all the drugs in town, offered him a deal: Bazigh and my baba smuggle heroin into the country from the borders of Pakistan and in exchange their families get to live. Bazigh Khan refused.' And then, suddenly, it was as if her voice drained of all emotion and she was reading from a book she'd read too many times. 'So the men went to Bazigh Khan's house. By the time he arrived home all that was left were the three tiny bodies of his children, and the remains of his wife, Liza. My father said his howls were heard across the valleys and hills that night. I still remember the fire engines and the faces of the two little boys, one three and one five, who survived. They were huddled in a corner together, their faces grubby with smoke. My father and his brother went to the police. Bazigh Khan begged them for help. They said the officer in charge whispered "Paki" to his colleague and told them to go home. It was the last time either man would ask anyone for anything again, and then they turned to the old ways for justice. The police had no trouble figuring out the fires in the white parts of town were arson. The men who had threatened Bazigh Khan died. Their families died. Their wives died. And their parents died. The places where the men had worked were destroyed. The places where the men drank were destroyed. The fires raged for three days.'

Elyas wondered if her detachment was due to countless retellings of the story, so that the events had lost their power over her, or whether the pain was still so fresh that she could not allow herself to feel it. Either way, as she spoke, Elyas was reminded of the boy soldiers he'd met in Afghanistan, the ones who knew no other life than death and despair.

'Are you saying he killed all those people?' he asked slowly.

'I'm simply stating the facts. And the facts are that, for the three days the fires raged, Bazigh Khan was at my father's house mourning the loss of his family, as is prescribed under Islamic law. The police suspected him, they even arrested him, but eleven men stepped forward to say he had not left the house in days.'

'And his children? What happened to them?' Elyas asked.

Jia pointed at Idris and Nadeem. Elyas looked from the brothers to their father. Bazigh Khan was across the garden, greeting some guests. He thought of his own son and what he would do to anyone who dared to hurt him. He thought of what Jia's leaving had done to him. And he wondered what damage lay within Bazigh Khan and his sons. He couldn't even begin to fathom.

In the distance, Bazigh Khan was shaking hands with the men of the Jirga. No one knew exactly how many police officers had tried and failed to bring them to justice, how many lives they had taken to achieve their ends or what it was that drove them. They embraced and laughed raucously, like any other group of greying old uncles at a wedding, making merry and over-indulging.

CHAPTER 13

Jia watched Benyamin from afar. Even from a distance she could tell he was flirting with the young girl in the emerald green. She wondered what Zan would have made of their little brother. Things had been so very different when she and Zan were young.

Zan Khan had been fiercely loyal, with his mother's charm and his father's intelligence, but he had been a lot less carefree than Benyamin was. The absence of her eldest sibling was a constant knot in her stomach. She wished he was here, to pick over food and family gossip with, and to help her make peace with her father, because she couldn't bring herself to do it. But Zan wasn't here, and he never would be. Akbar Khan had seen to that. Time unrolled and wrapped like a ribbon around her and she could almost feel his presence; there he was taking his mother by the arm, laughing, making her smile in that way only he could. He was eighteen again, captain of the debate team, playing cricket at county level and getting straight As. She remembered how he'd argued with his school when they'd asked a student to remove her hijab. He'd won, and his name appeared in all the national press, making him a celebrity for a while. Girls her age worshipped popstars, but Jia worshipped Zan; in her eyes, he was matchless and fearless. But Zan was not quite fearless enough to tell his father about his own plans. Maybe if he had, things would have been different. She was deep in thought when Benyamin walked by. Caught up in the past, she instinctively reached out to stop him.

But he answered her abruptly. 'What do you want, Sis?' He was annoyed, and his gaze kept drifting towards the girl in the emerald green. 'I've got things to do.' This wasn't the right time to talk. The right time had been aeons ago. She let him go.

'I just wanted to make sure you'd be here for the rukhsati.'

'I'll be here,' he said. 'Some of us have always been here.' He walked away, his words stinging gently, like antiseptic on a cut. Is this what healing felt like?

Jia turned and walked towards the house, making her way up the stairs to her parents' bedroom. She remembered how she and her siblings would hide in here when extended family overstayed their welcome. She stopped by her mother's dressing table: a picture of the Khan children stood beside the perfumes and powders. She ran her fingers over their faces. Zan would never have spoken to her like that.

He was full of practicalities, but he knew about the power of kindness. He had been a budding astrophysicist, drawing constellations and carrying out calculations on scraps of paper, on napkins, notebooks – and then on walls, after his sister asked him to. Tall, tanned and sociable, to Jia's pale and introverted, everything came easy to Zan, including grades and girls. Nothing came easy to Jia. Except, of course, her father's love.

Jia opened her mother's armoire and took out the old photograph albums. She flicked through them slowly. Pictures of holidays, and Eid, Christmas and birthdays. They had travelled so much, mainly to Pakistan and the US. Zan had loved it. He had planned to take a gap year and see Eastern Europe and West Africa and then South Asia. He wanted to see the world before settling down to discover places even more distant, through telescopes and mathematical calculations. But as the time to tell Akbar Khan grew closer, he found he wasn't as courageous as his little sister.

She had looked down her nose at him and through her rose-tinted glasses. 'You have to tell him that you hate law, and that medicine is boring!' she said. Their father wanted what all South Asians wanted back then, for their children to be doctors and lawyers, not stargazers. Dreams did not pay bills. Dreams were for people with white privilege.

Zan had laughed at her naivety and followed his father's wishes, which was to win a place at Oxford. 'A lawyer,' his father said. 'A lawyer from Oxford!' and Zan finally felt he'd made Akbar Khan a little proud.

Zan was golden in more than just skin tone. Distanced from their parents by a cultural divide and with that tight sibling bond common to children of immigrants, Jia would listen to her brother the way the believers listen to a scholar. Zan was the font of all knowledge and the team leader. He helped make GCSE selections, advised on homework and fought for his siblings and cousins to take part in extra-curricular activities. As with most first-generation immigrants, the value of these things were lost on their parents. Maths, English and science were surely all that a child needed to succeed in life. Thanks to Akbar's money and Zan's tenacity, the Khan children basked in an innocence that was afforded to people of means. Life was good. At least for a while.

Then everything changed. Looking through the pictures now, Jia could almost map the changes, the point at which her brother lost his shine, when his face started to become gaunt, his eyes sunken.

It was incremental. For Zan, it started with simple questions, then pushing, followed by bullying, which turned to out-and-out intimidation. Soon, there was no doubting the fact that Zan was being targeted by the very people who were supposed to protect him.

The first time it happened he was driving home with his school friends. They'd been to play football at the recreation ground. Zan had just got his licence and his father had bought him a car to celebrate. There were other drivers on the road travelling much faster than the new silver Golf GTI. 'You drive like an old man!' Zan's friends laughed.

'I don't want to break the law,' he told them.

There was no reason to stop him. But they did. The flashing blue lights behind him told him to pull over. He waited on the side of the road. He'd not had dealings with the police, but he knew enough to stay polite and to answer any questions. He watched a policeman get out of the car and walk over to the Golf. Something about the way the officer walked betrayed his arrogance. Watching him from the rear-view mirror, Zan could see that he was grinning. Discomfort began to seep into him.

'Well, aren't you a good-looking one, eh?' the policeman said, leaning into the driver's side. A second officer had got out of the police car and was waiting just a few feet away.

Zan's response came stammered: 'Er...is everything OK, officer? We were just going home from football practice.'

'The tread is worn on your back tyres,' the policeman said.

'That's not possible, it's a brand-new car!' said Zan.

'Are you saying I'm making it up?' The officer's voice was sharper.

'No. No. I'm just... I...'

'You know you need a driving licence to drive in this country?' the officer said, waiting for him to take the bait.

But Zan knew better than to answer. Tight-lipped, he waited, acidity rising in his throat. He handed the policeman his licence. The officer looked at it with disinterest. 'Come and look at the back tyre,' he said. 'You've been racing hard, haven't you? The tread is gone. You can't drive like that in this country, y'know.' The blood rushed to Zan's face. He climbed out of the car and walked to the back.

'Over there,' the officer said. He made him spread his arms and legs up against a cold, hard wall. The officer leaned in, his breath on Zan's neck filled with a sickly nicotine gum smell, mixed with stale beer and stolen cigarette puffs. The policeman moved closer, patting him down, moving his hand deliberately up the boy's leg and bringing it to rest on his thigh, his heavy belly pressing against his back. Zan felt the sickness rise from his throat to his mouth. It would never leave him.

'You look a bit like my ex,' he said. 'He was Asian too.' The officer grinned, revealing a gap where one of his top left teeth should have been. He whispered again, his mouth close to Zan's ears. 'Give great blow jobs, you Pakistani boys. Especially in handcuffs.'

Zan froze at the officer's words. He knew his friends would be watching from the back seat of the car but this brought little relief. The smell, the words, the touch of the man, seared themselves on to him. For days afterwards the reek of the officer's body odour and cheap antiperspirant would linger around him. He was crippled by hot, relentless shame. He prayed for the moment to end, for the officer to step away, his insides twisting and somersaulting. Then suddenly he threw up. The policeman sprang back in disgust, his shiny black shoes covered in vomit.

'Urgh! Who's going to fucking clean these?' he shouted at Zan, who was gasping for air. 'I should get you to do it! Right now, you fucking –'

The second officer appeared, and said something to his colleague. The first policeman's tone changed. 'I'm going to let you off this time, little boy. But you won't be so lucky if I catch you again.'

Zan climbed into his car. He sat there shaking as his friends' questions came at him hard and fast. He didn't know how he managed to drive home, and when he got there, he didn't tell anyone what had happened. He closed the door, climbed into bed and waited for sleep. If he didn't tell anyone, then it hadn't happened.

But a few days later, he was stopped again. This time the officer's partner took the lead. Polite and apologetic, he was quick to let Zan go. 'Sorry, mate, just doing my job, you understand?' he said, handing back his driving licence. The fat officer with the body odour and wandering hands watched, his eyes sharp, his shoes clean and firmly planted on the pavement. His partner's apology restored Zan's faith and he breathed a sigh of relief. It was always best to do the right thing, he reminded himself, especially in a country where everyone's rights were safeguarded. Maybe the last time hadn't been as bad as he remembered. Maybe his brain had played tricks on him. He went home happy and relieved. His mother, who had been worried about her son's sullenness, put his behaviour down to his teenage years.

But then it happened a third time, the fat policeman leaning over him again, his breath still stale and alcoholic, his hands travelling further, deepening the scars of shame. Zan could not bring himself to tell his family. He tried to talk to a teacher at school. But it turned out that his wife was a police officer, and he took it as an affront. He told Zan he was overreacting.

Zan, like many others, still believed the justice system was essentially fair; he thought his family and wider community would blame him for what had happened. He blamed himself. He was the Khan's son, but wasn't man enough to sort out his own problems. He told himself this was all a mistake, a blip, and it would all go away. But it wasn't. It wasn't a blip and it didn't go away.

Things went from bad to worse and on from there. Zan found he couldn't leave the house without being stopped and searched by the police. He lost weight, dark circles appeared around his eyes, and he became withdrawn, preferring to stay in his room. On days when he did leave, his face was set hard and questions were met with snapped answers and sharp words. It ended only when Jia Khan demanded to know why her father hadn't stepped in to find out what was going on with Zan.

Akbar knocked on his son's door, Jia a few steps behind. 'Not you, beta,' he said, telling her to wait outside. Akbar Khan came out an hour later, his face dark, his eyes burning with rage.

'What happened, Baba?' Jia asked.

'Nothing for you to concern yourself with,' he told her. 'Your baba will fix everything. I will make it right. Get some chai for your brother.'

He'd kissed her and gone to his study to make a phone call. And he had fixed it, in a way. The stop and searches ended after that.

Then the CID arrived, bringing with them the two officers who had terrorised Zan. Seeing them walk in through the front door of his home without permission stripped the boy's soul.

Those memories of the night they came to take her father and brother hadn't faded at all. Twenty years on and Jia found that the old monsters hadn't died, they had simply found new places to hide. The images ran like an 8mm film before her eyes, beginning with the door catching on the rug as Maria pushed it open, unable to speak, the words refusing to leave her mouth. 'Some men are here… to arrest Baba!' she'd cried.

Jia had rubbed her eyes, trying to clean them of sleep, and reached for her glasses. Her sister's frightened face came into focus, signalling the severity of the situation. Jia remembered getting out of bed. It was cold that night, and she had pulled on a hoodie, zipping it high and hiding her hands in the sleeves.

'It'll be OK,' she had said, guiding Maria down the stairs, her arm around her shoulders reassuringly. But her gut told her it wouldn't.

From the staircase, through the open doors, Jia could see five men rummaging through their cupboards and belongings. There were three of them in her father's office, and two went past them up into Zan's bedroom. She followed them. Her brother was sitting on the edge of his bed, his head down. He looked small and scared.

The policemen finished their search and gathered in the hallway. Akbar Khan gently removed his wife's hands from his arm when the officer in charge told him he needed to go with them. Zan, who had been staring down at his feet, looked up on hearing his name. For the first time in his life, Akbar Khan put his arm around Zan. 'It is OK, beta. Just tell them the truth, my son,' he said. Jia remembered Benyamin clinging to his mother's leg as the door to Pukhtun House sucked shut behind them, like the closing of a vault.

CHAPTER 14

With the wedding party in full swing, Benyamin decided it was time. He looked around for his girlfriend, Mina. She was waiting patiently by the house. Catching his eye, she turned and began walking to the gate. Something about the way her sari clung to her hips, her waist pinched like a sixties Bollywood heroine, made Benyamin grin. He was one lucky guy, and he couldn't believe she'd agreed to what they were about to do.

His mind flashed to Jia. She always thought she knew best. Well, she didn't have a fucking clue. He quickened his stride, flicking her from his mind, and slipped his hand into Mina's, leading her towards his car. Of course he needed to be there for the rukhsati; he didn't need reminding. He checked his watch. They would be back in time to give the bride away.

Finding his car blocked in by the other guests', he shouted to the valet, who threw him a set of keys and pointed to a yellow Ferrari. The doors clicked open and the couple slipped in, the car purring into action. He put his foot to the gas and gunned down the driveway, seamlessly disappearing out of the gates.

Once outside the grounds of Pukhtun House, Mina unbuckled her sandals and began unwrapping her sari. From the corner of her eye she could see Benyamin stealing glances, young lust flooding through him. She played up to the attention. He reached over to rub his hand up her thigh, and she pushed him away. 'Keep your eyes on the road!' she said. He laughed loudly, the adrenaline coursing through his veins and making him hard. Before he could try anything else, Mina had pulled on a black dress and was slipping her heels back on.

Twenty minutes later, they pulled up outside an exclusive boutique hotel, The Mansion. Owned by Arab money, sitting in acres of rich green fields, the place promised privacy and discretion to its select clientele. Benyamin parked up outside the reception and Mina climbed out. 'See you in a bit. Good luck,' he said and drove towards the car park.

Once in the hotel, Mina made her way to the bar and ordered a vodka and lemonade. The bartender, who had been waiting for her, handed her the lemonade minus the alcohol. She took the glass without argument – she knew he'd been paid to keep an eye on her – but she really could've used a drink right now. Her mind turned over the delicious idea and then put it aside. Since she'd started seeing Benyamin, falling off the wagon had become impossible.

She scanned the bar and saw Juliet waiting for her, every curve and bump of her friend's body visible in the red dress that wrapped around her like a badly applied bandage, flashing slithers of bare skin. Juliet had always liked attention, irrespective of whom it came from. And it was usually the wrong kind.

Mina followed her to a deep alcove where two men were sitting on a sumptuous velvet chesterfield. They were deep in discussion. As they approached, Mina noticed that the first was distinguished and tall, and the other was doubled up in pain. Their conversation was over, and the tall man wiped his hand on a white napkin before offering it to Mina. 'And you are…?'

'Mina,' she replied, averting her eyes from the bloodstains on the white cloth.

'Andrzej Nowak, at your service,' the man said, this time bowing as he spoke.

He reminded Mina of a stained-glass window saint, the kind she'd seen at the church Benyamin took her to last Christmas. His face was long and slim, his eyes piercing blue. But she'd heard enough about him to know that Andrzej Nowak was no angel. He liked his women, and he liked them like his liquor: cold, old and hardened. This was evident from the ladies at the other end of his table who were enjoying his hospitality and champagne as if at the last-chance saloon. For most of them, it probably was.

Nowak signalled to a passing waiter, who came running, almost tripping over a table as he did so. Service was fast at The Mansion, but the Pole was renowned for his generosity, making staff work harder to win his business. Rumour had it he had paid off one waiter's student loans and had given his BMW to another. The staff fought over his business and he encouraged the competition. Courtesy had been missing from Nowak's childhood and had become very important to him as an adult.

Tonight, the hotel's newest waiter had won Nowak's custom and he was eager to impress. The hotel's policy of discretion was well known. The staff took their work very seriously, and for those with aspirations The Mansion was the place to be. Fulfil the needs of the right client and you could find yourself living a much wealthier lifestyle. To keep the drink flowing and the customers socially lubricated, the waiters had developed their own system of signals. It was faster than the tech devices favoured by chain restaurants and didn't leave a trace, something that was important to The Mansion's clientele.

Nowak's waiter took his order and signalled the bartender, who was ready and waiting. He, in turn, crushed a small white pill into the bottom of a tall glass, poured coffee liqueur over it, then vodka, and gave it a good shake in a silver cocktail shaker before serving it in a glass over crushed ice. He placed the drink on the tray, and poured out two more, then handed them to the waiter, who safely delivered them to the table. Nowak knocked them back fast. He was celebrating the safe arrival of his shipment, which was currently sitting in the boot of a new Ferrari. Nice touch from the suppliers, he thought. It would be fun to christen the car. He leaned in towards Juliet. They'd met last week at the races and he had been showering her with expensive gifts. He believed this gave him the right to partake of her today. He ran a finger under one of the scarlet strips of her dress, just beneath her cleavage.

'You know, my Ferrari is waiting outside,' he said. 'You...you would look beautiful behind the wheel.' He moved forward to kiss her but she backed away. Offended by her rejection, he turned his attention to another woman to his left. Juliet placed her hand on his thigh. He watched as her slender fingers moved slowly upwards. Her eyes widened and she parted her glossy pink lips, moving them closer to his. She waited for him to meet her mouth and when he didn't she pulled him in, one hand behind his head, the other deftly reaching for the keys in his pocket and secreting them in Mina's open purse.

Mina picked up her clutch bag. Reality had suddenly hit her and her stomach turned. 'I don't feel too good,' she said to Juliet. 'I think I'm going to be sick.'

Seeing her pallor, Nowak stood to attention. 'Take her to the ladies room, please,' he said to Juliet. 'This is a five-thousand-pound jacket. I don't want her vomit on it. She couldn't afford the cleaning bill.'

Juliet put her arm around her friend and ushered her towards the cloakroom, Mina tripping on a stool and bumping into the bartender as she did so. He held out his hand to steady her, and in one well-timed move she passed the keys to him. The bartender walked steadily over to an open window and, making sure no one was looking, threw the keys down to where Benyamin was waiting.

The Khan's son picked up the keys and headed towards a red Ferrari. He'd had time to size up the situation and knew that the car was parked awkwardly for a swift getaway. He wiped his brow and started the engine. The key turned like butter, encouraging him, and he backed out of the space slowly at first, slamming his foot down in reverse the moment he knew he'd be clear of the cars on either side. The engine responded with a roar, but the tyres skidded wildly on the gravel, forcing Benyamin to swerve and brake sharply. The car stalled. He started her up again, glancing round to see three men hurrying towards the car park, alerted by the noise. By the time he'd manoeuvred the car out of the tight spot, the exit was blocked. The men shouted loudly, signalling frantically at each other to *move, move, move,* and within seconds Benyamin was surrounded. A heavy man with a broad head and no neck stood in front of the bonnet; two equally ugly heavies stood on either side of the car. Behind was the solid brick wall he'd just managed to avoid hitting.

Benyamin grasped the gearstick in his sweaty palm, and revved the engine in warning, but no-neck stood firm, and suddenly there was Nowak beside him, and more men at his back pulling out weapons. Pistol in his palm, Nowak stared intently, his cold gaze locked on to the Khan's son. Benyamin slowly raised his hands. The game was up.

CHAPTER 15

Jia walked across the garden towards the house. The last of the wedding guests had left. The night had fallen silent. She wondered where Benyamin was; he hadn't returned in time to give Maria away and their father had had to do the ceremony alone. She assumed he was off somewhere with the girl in the green sari.

She climbed the steps to Pukhtun House, moving one foot along the gentle dip in the centre of the first golden slab. The Khans had spent years climbing, walking and running up these five steps, from childhood through to adulthood, swinging coats and bags and ditching them all at the front door as they left the cold and entered the warmth of home.

She had sat on these very steps for what felt like hours after the police had taken Zan and her father away. This was where Sanam Khan had cried salty tears, clutching her son's jacket against her cheek, unable to speak. It was where Jia had greeted Bazigh Khan later that night. His arrival had been swift and she had crumpled at the sight of him. He smelt like her father, his aftershave and his starched shirts. His arms and fragrance enveloped her, and the dam that been holding back her tears broke.

He rebuked her gently. 'Child, you are to face stronger trials than this,' he said. 'You are a daughter of the Khan. Struggle is our life.' She had never seen him so gentle as when he wiped her tears. 'You are the niece of Bazigh Khan, yes?' he said. 'And have you not heard the mothers tell their children about me? And you know that Bazigh

Khan is beyond the laws of the land and more powerful than all the jinn and bhoot of it put together?' With these words he'd succeeded in making her smile. Then he turned away, his face darkening. 'Ya Allah! I will burn the city down if I have to, but I will bring my brother and yours home.'

Several hours later he made good on his promise, or half of it at least. Akbar Khan came home the next morning; Zan Khan did not. The prayers continued, the janamaaz spread in one long row, the family side by side, pressing their foreheads to the ground asking for Zan's return.

The tears and prayer ended only when the boy walked through the doors of Pukhtun House later that afternoon. The women rushed forward to embrace him but his arms dropped, hanging limply by his side. Unresponsive, he waited for them to stop. Dark circles around his eyes told them he hadn't slept. They tried to fuss over him, but he was tired, he needed a shower, he wanted the sweetness of home.

He waited quietly in the kitchen as his sister poured tea into two mugs. It had been steeping all day, its flavour deepening with each passing minute, the colour from the leaves darkening the milk. Jia added spoonfuls of sugar, hoping it hadn't tipped over into bitterness.

Eyes lowered and face dark, Zan was not the boy who had left the house the night before. Akbar Khan embraced him, his arms bear-like, leading him away from the women and into the study.

Jia followed but Akbar Khan stopped her, his body between her and the doorway. Something in his voice told her not to argue. She sat down on the floor outside, waiting patiently until Zan emerged. She looked at him expectantly, but he said nothing and walked to his room.

It was early morning when he knocked on Jia's door.

'There is no justice for people like us,' he said quietly, his head in his hands. His weakened smile made Jia's heart ache. She felt so helpless. Sitting on the floor of her room, as he had done many times before, he counted the painted stars. 'Still two hundred and eighty-two,' he whispered. 'Some things do not change. Take one down when I die?' he said.

'Must we be so melodramatic?' she said, equally irritated and frightened. She wanted to lighten things but couldn't, and they found themselves sitting in silence. Zan's gaze remained on the floor as he tried to process the past few days of his life. The silence was only broken when the family manservant came in, clumsily carrying a tray of more milky chai and parathas. He placed it on the floor in front of Jia and left. Jia marvelled at her mother's abilities; she was aware of every waking soul in the house and knew exactly what they needed.

'Tea?' she said, and Zan nodded. He took the cup, and their eyes met for the first time since his homecoming. It gave her the courage to ask the thing most on her mind. 'What happened at the police station?' she said.

'More than you want to know…' His voice was measured, but his tone was low, as if the act of merely speaking the words would awaken a nightmare again.

'Tell me…please?' she said. 'I'm worried about you.'

'You don't need to be. I'm fine. I really am.'

'It's his fault, isn't it?' Jia said. 'It's to do with the things they say at school about Baba, isn't it?' Her words hung in the air like the speech bubbles in a comic book. They had never discussed their father's line of work. They had heard people say things, but had left them on the other side of the door when they came home from school, falling instead into homework and TV. Some things were too immense to be processed by children. The mind had a way of compartmentalising and filing them away in order to survive. Now, though, one of them had fallen victim to Akbar Khan's business dealings and there was no way to avoid what was being said in the wider world, and what, on some level, they already knew. Their father was all the things people said he was – Jia knew it and Zan knew it. Nevertheless, she waited for him to speak the words. But he didn't. His silence was deafening.

Jia's love for her father was as encompassing as the ocean, but her brother was the cloudless sky above her. Zan was a spiritual soul who seemed out of place in the Khan's life. There was no doubt that their father loved him, but this didn't stop him from trying to toughen him up. Zan never complained, and Jia was always ready to defend him. But now Akbar Khan had hurt him in ways that she could not have envisaged.

'Our father is a good man,' Zan said slowly. 'He's not what you think he is.' Something in his voice wavered, and it was all Jia needed for rage to take root. Like spitting masala in an earthenware pot, this rage would grow with time until it bubbled out of control and consumed her.

'They arrested you because of him!'

Impassive, dispassionate, Zan sat cross-legged, his back against the wall. 'He's my father. I'm his eldest son,' he said. 'He trusts me. I know that now. It's time you realised that too.' Despite all that happened, Zan had managed to wipe his father's slate clean. His forgiveness was lost on Jia.

'I'm going to kill him,' she said matter-of-factly.

'A lot happened, a lot of things you don't know about.' And he began slowly to unravel his story, of recently opened bank accounts, of their father's business interests, of the business Akbar Khan had set up in Zan's name for tax purposes, without Zan's knowledge, of the money laundering the police suspected him of being involved in, and of much darker, graver things. 'That was why they took me in for questioning,' he said. 'They wanted me to help them put Baba behind bars. They showed me photographs, so…many… photographs. Pictures of people they said were missing under mysterious circumstances, of wives and children of men dead as a result of vendettas, drugs and being in the wrong place at the wrong time. Some of the pictures were brutal, others were just sad. They said Dad was responsible. They thought I would turn against him.'

The images were etched into his mind. He saw them every time he closed his eyes. He thought about what the officers had said, how they had stared at him from across the desk as though looking down the barrel of a gun. 'They talked to me like I was shit on the street, Jia. I was born here. I've been to better schools than they have. I speak better English. But they didn't see any of that. All they saw was what they wanted to see, a dirty Paki with a criminal for a father.'

'They can't talk to you like that! They should be reported!'

'They can, Jia. Don't you get it? We are nothing but who they say we are. They don't hear us. They only hear their own privilege. They've been getting away with it for years. Look at the riots. Segregation, poverty, deprivation, no jobs, no future. Those guys had no chance, still have no chance. Add to it trying to navigate a white world with brown sensibilities and Muslim pressure – it was a melting pot for disaster. Is it any wonder the kids kicked off? And when they did, Asian kids got years more than the white kids did for the same crimes. You and I, we just ignore these things because we think we're better, because we go to a good school and wear expensive clothes and live in a nice house. But to white people we're all just filthy Pakis who wear bling and live in cramped terraced houses. They've been tormenting me for days before this. They tried to make me afraid. They…touched me.' He stopped, watching her for some reaction. She swallowed hard, not wanting to understand. 'They had power and I did not,' he said. 'Well, soon I will have power. And I will take theirs from them.'

The rage that had been simmering in the pit of Jia's stomach dissipated. For the first time in her life she was afraid, really afraid for her brother and for her family. She placed the piece of paratha she had been about to put in her mouth back on the plate and pushed it away.

'Don't say that word again,' she said.

'What word?'

'Paki. Don't say it again.'

'But I am one and so are you. And in the minds of some people, that's all we'll ever be.' Zan spoke slowly, his hands perfectly still, staring into his chai. He told his younger sister everything he knew about the family business, and the fog around him began to clear. 'I listened to the things they said about Baba,' he said. 'I didn't speak. I just listened.'

The police had accused the teenager of knowing more than he claimed. They had pushed him gently, insulted him, and then they had turned nasty. 'We're going to have fun fucking with you on the stand,' they had said. 'You're going away for a very long time.' The lead interviewing officer had fed on the fear in Zan's eyes, his chest becoming broader. He'd leaned back in his chair. 'And you know what happens to pretty brown boys in prison, don't you?'

Zan's eyes were still red with the residue of the pictures he'd seen in the interrogation room. When they finished telling him he was scum, they asked him to turn traitor, to sign documents that gave them access to his father's accounts. 'It's not like you've got a choice, is it? We are your lord and master.' And it was then that something snapped, something tiny and inconsequential, something not worthy of note to anyone else but to Zan. Every man has a limit. If pushed hard enough he will either make a leap, fulfil his potential and become the thing he is meant to be, or else stumble to his knees and crawl. If the heat is high and the pressure pronounced, the result can be kundan, the purest kind of gold. As the officers poured scorn and stress on Zan in the hope of breaking him, they unknowingly flipped the switch that would make him the next Khan. Hunched and crumpled in the hard plastic seat, he began to straighten up, and leaned back in his chair. 'Yes, alright, I'll do it.' he said. The men smiled. They pushed over the necessary paperwork and handed him a pen. He took both and then met their gaze.

'I'll sign. But first you need to bring me the man who burned my aunt and my cousins alive. Then bring in the policeman who assaulted me. Then go and get every racist who stops someone like me and my father getting on in life, from moving on to the next level, from taking what is due to us, from getting a place at a good university, from finding a job that's slightly better than cleaning your shit, from setting our minds free from the sense of inferiority you'd have us believe in. Then, and only then, will I give you all the information you need.'

The switch threw the men. They'd been cocky and they'd been arrogant, and in playing games, they had run out of time. The budding law student knew his rights and he knew how long he could be held without charge. He had played them, and now they had no choice but to release him.

Back home, sitting with Jia, Zan had clarity. He knew what he had to do. 'I'm not going to take the place at Oxford,' he told her. 'I've spoken to Baba already. I know he wanted to keep us away from his line of work and I respect him for it and love him even more now I know what that means, but I need to stay and help with the family business.'

'What? No! We should get as far away from here as possible! Why don't you understand that?' Jia said.

'You still don't get it, do you? I've tried to get Baba's approval my whole life. Now, at last, I understand the world he lives in. He wanted to make me tougher, strong enough to deal with life, but he also wanted to distance us from his work, to live like respectable white people. He expected too much too quickly.

'He wanted us to be spotless and know nothing about where our family money comes from, and what he has to do to earn it, so that no one can use it against us. But his plan didn't work. We can't have the lives he wants us as a family to have while the business exists as it does. Someone has to act as a buffer or the past will bleed into all our lives. I need to be that buffer, so that you and Maria and Ben can get out.

'Do you remember the goat herder's daughter, Jia, the one who Mama put through school?'

'The one who killed herself?'

Zan nodded. 'You know why?'

Jia shook her head.

'Not really. I remember Mama blaming herself.'

'She was really bright. Graduated top of her class, but after she finished her MA, she no longer fitted anywhere. She knew there was a better life out there than the slums – she had seen it. But the people in that world didn't accept her, they didn't want her to marry their sons, live in their houses, be their equal. In the end, the fight broke her. Change has to be slow, has to be incremental, otherwise people don't accept it. We have to do it together. I have to help Baba evolve the business, clean it up now, so that by the time you are ready to leave, the past is buried. The business holds our family together. If we dismantle it too fast, it will collapse and we can't live like ordinary people yet. We need the money to clear the way.

'You can still stay out of all of this, Jia – keep your head down and your hands clean. I will stay to make sure that happens. And I will stay so that the rest of you don't have to. It's OK – I want this, don't you see? I finally feel like Akbar Khan's eldest son, and I am a Pukhtun: my place is with my family. Baba knows his world, and I know this one. Together, we can find a way forward.'

Jia wanted to make him see that sacrificing himself was no answer, that their father loved him and he did not need to prove himself to him, but she could tell that he was gone; he was too far down the rabbit hole to come back.

The money, the education, the status, it had all failed to protect him. His dreams, his intelligence, his manners all amounted to nothing. White privilege had pushed him one finger at a time to the edge of the cliff and he had jumped. And as he fell, Zan promised himself that the day would come when his people would have justice. He would make sure of it. This would never happen to him or his family again.

CHAPTER 16

Two years later Jia took Zan's place. She left home for Oxford University and quickly fell for its prestige and privilege. Privilege divided people into them and us, and was celebrated among the spires of Oxford.

Handing in essay after essay left little time for anything other than work, and it made the forgetting easier. Falling asleep before her head hit the pillow, or at her desk, there was little time to think of the troubles of family and home. Words like *debate, discussion, opinion, argument* – all considered unbefitting of a young woman in the culture of her parents – were encouraged here. Slowly, she began to revel in them. Her father's pride in her achievements and her mother's concern for her virtue were fed to her in equal measure. She took both on board; they kept each other in check.

Zan, who had remained true to his plans, enrolled at a university closer to home and continued living with his parents. The police had dropped their investigation, citing a lack of evidence. His evenings were now spent locked in his father's study, learning the family business. Life seemed to return to normal, but the constant fear of a knock at the door stayed with them, as if a part of them had remained in suspended animation and could reanimate at any time.

When, four years later, Jia Khan came home and announced she had married, her mother, standing in the kitchen up to her elbows in flour, took the news with grace. Sanam Khan had been preparing for a storm, but in the end what had come was drizzle. Her daughter had brought home a young man. It would have been shameful in generations gone by, but it had come to be expected of Jia Khan.

Sanam Khan was reassured to see her daughter scarlet with shame, having dragged her chador from her bosom to her head. 'A woman's chador is her honour,' was something she'd said often to her daughters, a way of reminding them of what was expected of them. She had predicted this day years earlier. 'A woman knows her children, Akbar Khan,' she had said as she packed Jia's belongings for university. 'And that daughter of yours will be the end of us!' But she had been young once, and she knew the fears a young girl harbours before her parents. So when she saw Jia's shame, she took her hand gently and asked to be taken to her son-in-law.

Elyas waited quietly in the living room, trying to look suitably respectful. His face glowed golden and Sanam Khan was pleased at what she saw. At least the girl had had the good sense to pick a Pukhtun and one who had grown up with her own brother. 'Women have been known to give their hearts to one-legged donkeys,' she said to her daughter. 'But you have chosen well. Your heart and head are one.' With warmth and speed she ushered the couple into the dining room.

'It's a lovely room,' said Elyas, looking around, trying to hide his nerves. White flowers filled the place. Even years later the smell of jasmine would make him feel sick.

'Yes, it is,' she said. 'My husband had the furnishings brought over from his home city in Pakistan. He loves to bring bits of Peshawar back with him. You must have such things in your house?'

'Our furniture is more Ikea, I'm afraid,' he said. 'My grandfather came to England to study at the Bar when he was young and never went back. He said he liked the weather here too much, but I suspect it was my grandmother, and the whisky...' Elyas stopped, thinking he shouldn't have mentioned his grandfather's liking of the haram. But Sanam Khan knew there were worse things than a family that drank.

Elyas and Zan had been friends since primary school, but apart from a smile at the school gates Sanam Khan knew little about his parents. 'Both my parents were born in England,' Elyas said. 'I'm really sorry, Mrs Khan, I don't know anything about the protocols of our culture. I'm sorry.' He was babbling and he knew it. He should have brought his parents with him, but everything had happened so quickly that he hadn't had time. And he doubted they would have fared any better.

Elyas had been in love with Jia for as long as he could remember. She was his friend's little sister, goofy and geeky and funny. Buried under books and her head filled with song lyrics, she was oblivious to him. It was only when he confessed his love one Valentine's Day by giving her a bottle of perfume that she realised.

'I can't accept that,' she'd said, pushing her chunky brown glasses back with her forefinger. He noticed how grubby the lenses were. She was fifteen at the time, dressed in blue jeans and an oversized jumper she'd borrowed from her father's wardrobe. She buried her nose in its neckline – it smelt of stale tobacco and her father's aftershave – and she shook her head. 'I definitely can't take it.' Black-and-red wrapping paper lay strewn around her as she sat cross-legged under the large pine tree in the garden. 'My mother won't like it,' she said matter-of-factly.

'OK,' was all he'd managed to say, his face reddening. He'd spent months saving up to buy the perfume, and she'd rejected it in seconds. He got up to leave. 'You really shouldn't sit out here when it's so cold,' he said, and then left. He took the gift home and handed it to his mother, who wiped his tears and listened to his heartbreak and told him there was plenty of time for girls after studying and travelling. She nudged him towards other things, and after that Elyas stopped visiting Pukhtun House.

They'd run into each other by chance, years later. It was at a pro-Palestine demo in London. She was dressed in skinny black jeans and a fur-lined parka, placard in hand. He recognised her instantly. He'd just finished his journalism qualification and was looking for a story; she was an idealistic student. He spent the day following her, with her consent, to document the events. She had lost none of her fire and she still held tight the strings that tugged at his heart. When he found himself sharing the same train home with her, he convinced himself fate was contriving to show him his future.

She also thought fate had brought them together, but for very different reasons. The arrest, and university life, had made Zan distant. She missed him and she missed her old self. On the rare occasions they were in a room together, he was silent, his eyes full of thoughts to which she was not party. Seeing Elyas walk through the crowds towards her on that rainy November afternoon, was like finding some part of what she had lost.

The train journey home placed them in a sea of nostalgia. Like the foam that sits on the ocean, it lapped her up. Elyas was easy company. He entertained her with stories of Zan and their escapades, things she'd not known. She laughed at his tales of their ineptness and their failed attempts to 'get girls'. He walked the length of the train and brought her back sandwiches and biscuits from the buffet bar. He surprised her with his memory of her favourite crisps, and he made her laugh in a way she realised she hadn't for a long time. And as she listened to him talk she noticed all the ways in which he was like her brother. And all the ways he wasn't. Zan before the arrest. Zan now. Zan happy and sad, good and bad.

Over the coming weeks they saw more and more of each other. Jia's questions about her brother were incessant but Elyas stayed patient, waiting, hoping that she would see him, really see him. And then one day she did.

She found herself thinking about Elyas more and more. She could still smell him after they'd spent the day together, like cinnamon cookies and Hugo Boss. He reminded her of home, which raised an ache within her. He was a warm glass of milk in a world full of cheap wine: innocent, easy and good for her.

The world looked broadly the same to them both, only differing in its minutiae. But youth has always argued over the trivial. Philosophical and political, literary or culinary, they debated with a certainty blind to all alternatives, a certainty drawn from the bottomless pit of passion that is only found at the start of life. They were young and time had yet to set its limits, disappointment yet to curb their passions. Brick by brick, crack by crack, the dam that Jia had painstakingly built around her heart broke. The passion of ideologies spilled over into love of another kind, the kind that is hard to stop. They talked. They fought. They laughed. They kissed. She pushed him away. But he would not be dissuaded.

'We live in a world that holds romantic love up as the ideal, over everything else. *Romeo and Juliet, Heer Ranjha* and *Laila Majnu* – our culture is steeped in this notion that love is a drug that makes us blind to our differences.'

'I get the feeling you're trying to tell me something, Jia.'

'I don't know, I'm trying to figure us out. I never expected to be with someone like you.'

'What do you mean, "like me"?'

'I've lived like the Virgin Mary, I expected only ever to be with one guy, the guy my parents introduced me to, and yet here I am. You've lived a totally different life, been out with lots of women, had so many more options – and yet here you are.'

'I'm confused. Does that bother you? Because it doesn't bother me or change how I feel. What are you saying?'

'I have no idea!' she said. The truth was she didn't know what it was about her that made him want her. She was difficult, her family was hard work, and things were complicated, so why on earth would someone like Elyas choose her? It didn't make sense.

'You don't think love has anything to do with it?' he said. 'Human beings are not logical creatures. We're emotional.'

'Yes, exactly. And how do you trust those feelings? We've had such different upbringings and there's nothing wrong with that, but wouldn't you rather be with someone who gets all of you?'

'Maybe, but that's asking the impossible, and love doesn't work like that. I like that you challenge my ideas.'

Jia saw things in black and white; there was no room for grey. She was clear and consistent and hard work, but he loved that about her. She was the most interesting woman he knew, and while they had a similar outlook on life, her experiences meant that she came at things with a unique perspective that intrigued him.

'It's sad,' he said, 'that you feel that love is a compromise, or shaped by thought processes rather than passion and instinct. Me, I believe in crack-cocaine love, addictive and maddening. It does happen to people, you know. Maybe it'll happen to you. One day.'

'Yes, well, it shouldn't.'

'You're crazy,' he said. 'But I love you.' He leaned in to kiss her. She placed her hand between his lips and hers and pushed him away.

'Don't be stupid,' she said.

'It makes no sense to you, I know. But I love you. Do we have to go through this every time I want to kiss you?'

He was a junkie and she was his addiction. 'There is nothing I can do about it,' he told her over and over again. His words wore down her defences and slowly she succumbed. She loved him but was afraid to admit it, choosing instead to put up obstacles and hide behind practicalities.

When, eventually, the question of telling her family about their relationship came up, Jia knew, sure as one and one equals two, that Elyas Ahmad loved her. Even so, he sensed her reluctance.

'So what's the problem?' he'd asked.

'You know the problem. You can't be my boyfriend. I can have a husband and a friend but not a boyfriend. It's just not done. How would I face my mother? And what would I tell my father? I can't lie to them.' They had been arguing for hours and she couldn't get Elyas to understand her predicament.

'We don't need permission to live our lives! Why do you still care what your father thinks? Are you afraid of him?'

'This is not about my father. I may love you and I may have crossed some lines by being in a relationship with you, but I am still a Muslim woman.'

'And this is why you still refuse to stay the night? No one will know, Jia, so no one will care.'

'I'll know and God will know. It doesn't matter about anyone else.' Jia knew that this made little sense to the world in which they lived but she had expected Elyas to understand. He didn't.

Elyas had no ties to his beliefs. He was raised Muslim but most of that fell by the wayside when he discovered girls. But he'd never met anyone like Jia before. Her black-and-white life left him seeing red. 'You're a maulvi in a mini-skirt!' he told her. 'You seem like the kind of girl who will, but really you're the kind of girl who won't, wouldn't and doesn't. How can someone so open-minded about the world be so closed-minded about sex?' She didn't reply, but he kept trying in the hope that she would thaw.

Admitting that she loved him had been an excruciating process. Before him, work and family had consumed her, and her thoughts had never wandered to anything else. Love affairs and lust were for the weak-willed. Life was to be planned and those plans implemented for the attainment of long-term goals beyond any childish infatuation. The men she knew were complicated, secretive creatures. Admitting that she had defied logic and fallen for one of their kind wasn't easy.

Elyas was honest and handsome, good-natured yet strong-willed, and he loved her, but he was a divergence from her plans and a reminder that she too was at the mercy of chemical reactions, just like the rest of the human race. Her falling for him had surprised her. She'd pushed him, turned him this way and that, and tested him constantly. He had not come up wanting.

'There's nothing sordid about any of this,' he went on. 'How can there be? You've not even let me come near you! And yet still I'm here!'

'Go, then. I won't stop you.'

'I don't want to go. I want to be with you! You drive me crazy sometimes!' Exhausted, Elyas collapsed on to the sofa. He'd tried so hard to make her understand but nothing seemed to convince her. How could he make her see that he was all in? Hook, line and sinker, the works, done for, and all the other clichés reserved for a man who has lost his heart and found his head. He had no choice but to see it through.

'I get it,' he said. 'I understand your sensibilities. I love you for them not in spite of them. And I'm not like him. I'm not like Akbar Khan. I'm a straight-down-the-line, honest-to-goodness guy. I've never even had a speeding ticket. And I can promise you this... I will never ever hurt you, on purpose, or otherwise. What else can I possibly do to make you understand? Marry you?' He stopped.

That was it. He had been ignoring the obvious and not listening to her. He'd seen her as an indie chick, a debating diva, a girl like any other, but in among it all she was still a young Muslim woman and the way to get a young Muslim woman to stay was to make her your wife.

After all the times she had turned him down, her change of mind took him by surprise. His hormones racing, he wasted little time. The nikaah was conducted that evening. The imam was an old school friend, and Zan was 'wali' for his sister, standing in as her guardian until Elyas met Akbar Khan, which happened the very next morning...

The silence was rich, brimming with the unsaid. Sanam Khan had pulled her kameez straight over and over again, as if removing the creases would somehow iron out the problems that lay ahead. Her mind raced from obstacle to obstacle, aware that women and their honour had caused great wars among the Khans. Elyas knew her concerns. His grandfather's stories had not been pretty, and he knew that Jia's reluctance was in part due to them. Tight-lipped, her mother beside her, her husband adjacent on the soft cream cushions of the carved wooden sofa, Jia sat, waiting for her father to arrive.

The silence was broken by a clatter of plates from the kitchen. Sanam Khan took her daughter's hand. 'It will be OK,' she said. And for the first time Elyas noted how similar mother and daughter were. Tall and slim, Sanam Khan was an elegant woman. When she laughed, her eyes were more hazel than green, and when she stopped they darkened to emerald. This they did with the arrival of Akbar Khan. Everyone got to their feet. He looked from his daughter to the young man.

'Who is this?' he asked. The room remained silent, tempered only by the sounds of activity coming from the kitchen. It ended with the arrival of the manservant, who came in balancing plates of buttered naan in one hand and fried eggs in the other. The old man's vision was poor. He didn't see Akbar Khan standing in the doorway, and as he sidestepped to avoid him, he lost his balance, almost losing one of the plates. Sanam Khan moved swiftly forward and rescued it.

'Chilli Chacha, how many times have I told you to use the trolley?' she said. The old servant nodded in short, sharp bursts before scuttling off back to the kitchen. 'Here, sit here,' Sanam Khan said to her husband, directing him towards the table and beckoning Jia and Elyas over.

Legs crossed, his eyes low, Akbar Khan waited as everyone sat down. The room was pregnant with tension, the waiting unbearable. Sanam Khan finally spoke. 'This is our guest, Elyas,' she said.

Akbar Khan looked up at his daughter. 'Jia jaan, you know our ways well enough to know that women in our family do not have male friends, and you have brought one to the dinner table?' he said.

He waited for her reply but none was forthcoming. He softened his tone a little. 'Bacha, speak to your father.'

Elyas, who had been poised for a fight and a barrage of abuse, was taken aback. The Pukhtun ways were legend in his home. His grandfather had been hard on his children, saying it was the custom of the 'old country' and the best way to instil discipline in one's offspring. That Akbar Khan would be anything else had not occurred to him.

Jia reached over and touched her father's cheek. 'Baba jaan...' she said. And Elyas saw a tender expression fall across his face. He listened to his daughter quietly, his head bowed throughout her explanations. He seemed like a good man, a just man, and Elyas wondered if there was any truth to the stories about Akbar Khan. When he finally raised his head, he looked down the table at his son-in-law, and Elyas was reminded of the oversized eyes of a maindak, but of course he could not be as harmless as a bullfrog. Jia finished speaking and Akbar Khan called Elyas towards him. 'Bacha, come here.' He patted the empty place to his left. Elyas did as he was asked.

He both feared and revered Akbar Khan. So when asked for his father's name, Elyas answered in more detail than was necessary. His knowledge was sketchy and he found the names difficult to pronounce, but Akbar Khan seemed impressed with his effort. He smiled and patted him on the back. 'Good, good. I am pleased my daughter has chosen to marry into such an honourable family. Even if the manner has been a little less than honourable. We must correct that oversight and organise an official wedding. I know you have already had your nikaah, but in my house that is not enough. I am a forward-thinking man but many in my family are not. I do not want them to point fingers at my daughter and her honour, you understand?' Elyas nodded. 'Then write down your parents' name and address on here and leave the rest to me,' Akbar Khan said. The scribbled details were taken gratefully by Akbar Khan and slipped into his shirt pocket.

'He's probably going to have me beaten up,' Elyas had said half-jokingly to Jia on the way over, 'and then thrown out of the house.' Akbar Khan had done neither. Instead he had only smiled.

After the meal, Akbar Khan said he had much to attend to, and stood to take his leave, his son-in-law following suit. Akbar Khan placed his hand on Elyas's head. '*Kor di wadan!*' he said as he kissed him.

For a second, fear filled his new son-in-law's eyes, but Sanam Khan smiled, and Jia whispered in his ear, 'It means "a blessing upon your house!"' And he relaxed.

Akbar Khan pulled out a roll of purple banknotes from his kameez pocket and called Chilli Chacha towards him. 'Buy some mithai and send the rest of this to your family,' he said. 'Tell them my daughter has found a Khan worthy of her!' Jia kissed her father without reservation and he responded with laughter, turning to hug his new son-in-law once more.

No one even noticed the small slip of paper that made its way into the manservant's hand and from him to Bazigh Khan.

CHAPTER 17

That unnoticed slip of paper destroyed the house that Jia built. It took two years, but at the end of it, her father-in-law was implicated in a complicated tax fraud.

A company once registered by him became one in a long line of businesses used to commit carousel fraud. Signatures had been forged, invoices drawn up for products that never existed, and VAT falsely claimed from HMRC. She had no proof of his involvement, but Jia blamed Akbar Khan. 'Are you listening to me?' she screamed.

He ignored her, and carried on writing on his notepad, his gaze unflinching. She could feel the pressure building up inside her, his disinterest like screws tightening her sinews. From the corner of the room, Elyas watched. He knew his father to be meticulously law-abiding, a man who had never even had a parking ticket. He had fallen under Akbar Khan's spell and revealed personal information. Information that had taken him to the verge of a jail term.

Akbar Khan put down his pen. What his daughter did not know was that Elyas's father had come to him for help. The man was in financial trouble, mortgage repayments long overdue. He had no stomach for business and his start-up company had swallowed up his income and more. Akbar Khan had agreed to help, but reluctantly. He'd considered this the best of a bad deal, and now his daughter blamed him.

'These honourable men you worry about so much...I know things about them that you do not,' he said. He turned to Zan, who was standing beside him and gestured for a glass of water. It was bitterly cold outside, and inside the central heating was drying out the air, leaving skin chapped and mouths dry.

Zan placed his hand on his father's shoulder, to show his allegiance as much as to protect his sister. But Akbar Khan wasn't annoyed with his daughter. He was proud of the rage that ran through her. It was a sign of her loyalty to those under her care, but she hadn't yet learnt to win. 'My child, life is ugly,' he said. 'The only people who survive it are those who make themselves its equal.'

'My father-in-law trusted you and now he is ruined.'

'Well then, he was a fool,' said Akbar Khan, his words so matter-of-fact, his manner so calm, that they snatched the fight from Jia's mouth. Violence was her only option. She lunged at him, her face contorted in anger and heartbreak, and found herself being held back by Zan. He had stepped in between her and his father. Her arms were flailing; she had lost control of herself.

The investigation, the court case, the jury's deliberation, all of it had chipped away at her. She had held it together until now. She couldn't do it any more. The shame of what her father had done, the embarrassment before her in-laws, their silence on the matter, had made it all worse. If they had blamed her, she could have fought them and argued for her father, but they hadn't; they had simply looked broken. And now here she was, her shame leaving her ravenous for blood.

Taking her by the shoulders, Zan forced her out into the hallway. 'Calm down,' he said. Stoicism was rare in Pukhtuns, but Zan had mastered it. Controlled, disciplined and intelligent, his mix of British sensibility and Pukhtun courage had brought him respect in his father's eyes. He had become the kind of son a Khan could be proud of. His sister, however, did not share the sentiment.

'I hate him,' she said. She spat the words like hot fat. 'For what he has done to us and for what he has done to you.'

'I know,' he said. The immediacy of his response disarmed her.

She sat down on the floor and cried. The adrenaline that had been coursing through her had dissipated now, and she was exhausted. She wondered what was to become of them. Her head hurt at the thought of Zan in her father's world. He had embarked on a path of pain, and there was nothing she could do to change that. She cried salty tears, for him and for herself. They dripped down her face and into the crevice of her mouth, their taste reminding her of the grazed knees and minor scrapes that had ended with childhood. There was shame and embarrassment today, but no one was going to prison. She realised that though her anger was justified, it was wasted, and that there were bigger battles to come. So she opened her eyes, wiped her face and got to her feet.

She was considering her next move, when her husband's voice cut through the silence. It made its way through the thick walls and closed doors of the study and left her cold. He was shouting at her father, his words clear and hurtful, like sharp objects being ground into her wounds.

Zan watched her flinch. 'Not nice, is it,' he said, 'when someone attacks your family?' Jia remained silent, her confusion evident on her face. 'Your father-in-law should have known better. No one forced him to sign the papers, and the courts have found him not guilty, but you have given Elyas permission to shout at Baba. It's not our father's fault that your husband's father did what he did.'

He said the words slowly, deliberately, and was ready for retaliation, but she dropped her head into her hands, and by the time she looked up, black lines of mascara and kohl were smudged across her cheeks.

'I watched an old man standing in the dock and fighting for his life, day after day, knowing that I was partly responsible for putting him there. While we sit safely in our houses, that is what Baba does to people. He doesn't care who it is or what happens to them. He just keeps on going. It's business to him, just business. He destroys lives, livelihoods, and all for what? For money. He's kept it from us, this business of his, but this time I saw it, every last drop of pain. I watched it being wrung out of an innocent man. All because his son had chosen to marry me, and because I am Akbar Khan's daughter.'

Her father, her hero, the hypocrite, and so was she. She couldn't forgive him and it was tearing her apart. 'He's done all these things, all these awful things and more, and yet I still love him? What can I do?'

'Why do you need to do anything?' Zan replied. 'Why do you care so much what people think?' His arrest and the years that followed had changed him from the inside out. 'Making peace with the differences between our birthplace and our parents' is hard. Making peace with their choices is even harder.' Jia looked up at her brother: his face was unblemished, his eyes were tired. Standing in their father's house they would both have given anything to turn back the clock and be children again. But there was no way back. Life had shown them its disfigured face. 'Jia, we're not like white society. They look after their own and that's what Baba does. The day you see the world for what it really is, you'll realise the lines drawn between right and wrong are not black and white, and they are not drawn for or by people like us. That day, you will see our father for what he really is, and you won't be able to forgive yourself.' There was nothing more to say. Jia knew that words could not change who they were and what had happened. They stood in silence, looking at each other, each one helpless in their own way.

A sudden crash interrupted the quiet, then Akbar Khan's voice, angrier than either had ever heard it before. 'Get out of my house,' he said. Suddenly Elyas was standing in the hallway, his face red with rage, and Jia knew he would never speak to her father again. He moved at speed, making his way out of the house, letting the solid oak door smash against the frame as he left.

Jia followed him into the driveway, hoping to stop him, bring him back, to calm the situation, but she found herself standing alone in the darkness. A gale was blowing; its bitterly cold fingers wrapped itself around her face and permeated her bones. The wind swept through the branches of the trees that lined the long driveway, bending and twisting them to its will, their boughs refusing to give up control. The night made them menacing, like the monsters of childhood nightmares. She heard a loud crack above her head and she dodged as a chunk of the apple tree fell to the ground. Through the sound of the raging storm came the angry revving of an engine and headlights appeared. It was Elyas. She ran to him, climbing into the car, hoping to make him change his mind, but he was reversing before she could even close the passenger door. From the other side of the darkness came Zan, rain pouring down his face, dripping off his jaw, shaking his head at Jia, mouthing the words: 'Don't go. Please.' He could see he was failing. He had to bring them back. If they left now, things would never be the same again. He moved swiftly towards the driver's door but Elyas was faster. He put the car into gear and hit the accelerator, tearing down the driveway.

Jia turned to see her brother climbing into a BMW, the speed they were travelling and the rain making him almost invisible at once. At the end of the driveway, Elyas jammed on his brakes, stopping inches away from the wrought-iron gates. The impact threw Jia back in her seat. 'Slow down,' she said. 'You'll get us both killed.' She was angry at her father, at Elyas, at Zan, and at herself. The blood pulsed through her temples making it hard for her to think.

'I'm sorry,' he whispered. She softened, letting go of her pride and taking his hand in hers. They sat in silence, watching as the iron gates swung slowly open. Maybe when they got home, they could talk things through properly and figure out a way through this mess. She pulled down the visor in front of her, wiping her face clean of tears, rain and make-up. As she looked in the mirror, Zan's car came into view. The rain was easing and she could see his face looking back at her.

Elyas turned into the main road and Jia lost sight of her brother. In that moment, she realised that no man, no matter how beloved, would ever take the place of her family. She reached down into her handbag and took out her phone, dialling his number.

Lying in her old bed years later, her face washed clean of the make-up she'd worn for Maria's wedding earlier that day, Jia could still feel the cold sting of that stormy night against her cheeks. The smell of the wet gravel and the sound of it crunching as the car tyres spun out of control was still fresh in her mind. And then the flash of silver from the opposite side of the road, the shrieking of brakes on the rain-soaked tarmac, followed by glass smashing and the sharp screech of metal cutting through itself: it would never fade from her memory. The smell of burning rubber would never leave her.

The crash had been loud; it must have echoed for miles. Zan's car turning into the road, the boy racer coming the other way, jumping to the wrong side of the road to overtake a driver who was navigating the precarious driving conditions.

She remembered running and losing her shoes somewhere along the way. She reached the site of the crash before Elyas had even made it out of his car. She saw the BMW Zan had been driving in front of her. It had crumpled like a tin can, the Subaru sandwiched through its centre. Frantically, she'd searched for her brother, screaming his name until her throat was ripped to shreds. The driver of the Subaru was dead; the air bag had failed to open, his crushed head resting against the steering wheel. In the passenger seat, his girlfriend was pressed against the side of the car, whimpering for help, but Jia was not there for her, she was there for Zan. And then she saw him, lying lifeless on the other side of the road.

Through the heavy rain and darkness, Elyas watched Jia cradling Zan in her arms, her face up to the heavens, twisted in agony.

Family trickled out of the gates of Pukhtun House. Stumbling over each other, they washed on to the street.

Sanam Khan was the first to see them, a hand reaching out for her son as she stood in the road, her youngest child clinging to her in fear. She clutched her last-born to her chest and screamed out for her firstborn, the anguish in her voice reaching the other side of the city and piercing the night sky. Maria Khan muffled her cries with one hand at the sight of the mangled car. She grabbed her mother with the other.

Collapsing into a heap next to Zan was Akbar Khan. He ran his fingers through his son's hair, wiping the blood from his forehead – 'Ya Allah! Ya Allah! YA ALLAH!' – on his knees, drenched in rain, his supplications getting louder and louder, as though exorcising the devil. The old man's calls to his Lord were the last thing Elyas heard before the ambulance sirens closed in and drowned out everything else. They arrived from all sides, white against the darkness.

Events unfolded in front of Elyas like a grainy, silent film. Around Jia everything seemed to be in slow motion: a paramedic cajoling her to let go of her broken brother, his words lost in the cold, damp air, her eyes dim. Jia was in another place, another world, one where she could rock Zan back and forth, back and forth, to this place. Streams of whispered words came from her mouth as tears dripped from her face to his. Only Akbar Khan was close enough to hear what she was saying, and it was her madness that forced him to resume control. He raised his head and straightened his back.

His eldest son was gone, a boy who had come to life through him and become a man under his watch, become so much more than he could ever have hoped. Akbar Khan had started to believe in Zan's plans for the family business. It had been a long time since he had allowed himself to dream, but handing over his empire had begun to seem like a reality. He should have known better; he had developed ideas above his station, and he had forgotten he was not the master of final judgement, although he had dealt it out enough times over the course of his life. He had brought destruction to those he believed deserving, and to others who had simply become collateral damage in the battleground of business. Today that destruction had been visited upon him.

He leaned in and whispered something to his daughter and she immediately loosened her grip. The paramedics moved in swiftly, lifting Zan's broken body on to the cold stretcher and into the ambulance. In the distance, Elyas watched his wife. Behind her swarmed paramedics, policemen, and other faces, some but not all familiar. But she saw none of it. Her head down and her palms upwards, she looked as if she was praying. She wasn't, though; she was staring at the blood.

Only Akbar Khan saw Elyas standing alone in the distance. He had lost his son and he would not give up his daughter. He put his arm around her, and like the old-fashioned wooden toy, the kind that stands and collapses, collapses and stands, she clutched her father. She could not watch them take her brother away. Through the sea of people, Akbar Khan led his family – what remained of it – home. The doors of the ambulance slammed shut as they left, and the gates to the house swung closed after them. Elyas knew then that his marriage to Jia Khan was over.

CHAPTER 18

Sanam Khan knocked on the bedroom door and waited. The house was dark, the only light coming from the living room, where she'd left the men waiting.

She blamed herself for their presence. She chided herself for not having given more alms to the poor; she should have offered more of herself, of her time and her money, and now it was too late: the evil eye had them and there was nothing to do but pray. She spoke her daughter's name into the darkness. She was glad she was here.

Jia sat up. Her mother's voice was soft, but Jia was a light sleeper. She had been since Zan's arrest, her senses always on alert. She climbed out of bed and opened the door. 'Your father's brother is here,' Sanam Khan said. 'I don't understand what he's saying.'

'Where is Baba?' said Jia.

'Come, wash your face quickly, they're waiting.' Her mother was always practical at times of difficulty, and Jia had come to see the value in her ways. Tasbeeh in hand, the old woman waited, counting prayer bead to prayer bead, as Jia made her way to the bathroom.

She washed the tired out of her eyes before looking at her reflection. Cleansed of the day's make-up, she ran her hands over her cheeks and neck. Her face was free of lines and yet to wrinkle – the benefits of brown skin – but tiny age spots had begun appearing on her cheeks. Her eyes were worn, her skin not as taut as it once was – she was definitely older, and a lot wiser. She checked her phone for messages, hoping for something from Benyamin, but there was nothing. She wondered if he was home yet, and made a mental note to spend some time with him away from here. She wanted to make things right between them and knew that her mother's shadow wouldn't allow the frank conversation they needed to have.

Her mother was waiting for her outside the bathroom, clutching Jia's shawl. She wrapped the soft material around her daughter's shoulders and brought it up to her head, covering the loose hair the way she used to do when Jia was a teenager. The duplicitous world of men expected women to be draped in honour. 'This looks like the kind of thing Akbar Khan would choose,' she said, her voice faltering at the name of her husband.

'He sent it to me,' said Jia. 'I never understood why he gave us gifts on Father's Day.'

'Your father, always a gentle soul,' her mother replied, her voice quieter than usual. 'Few people know that about him. But, then, he lived every day for his children…' Her voice trailed off and Jia noticed her hands were shaking. She put her arms around her mother as Sanam Khan had done to her so many times throughout her childhood. She found herself swelling with tenderness and sadness in equal measure.

'It's OK, Mama, I'm here now,' she whispered. She helped her mother down the stairs, Sanam Khan leaning heavily on her daughter. Jia reached for the bannister; the wedding flowers that were wrapped around it crumpled under her touch.

Sanam Khan took each step carefully, holding her daughter tight, afraid of what letting go would mean. Akbar Khan had left the house abruptly after the party ended. In his youth, he would have taken the stairs two by two to tell her he was leaving, but his knees weren't what they used to be and so he had called up to her, saying he'd be back soon. But he wasn't, and instead Bazigh Khan was here, his face solemn, his eyes pitch black. This house had seen some dark days and her God had demanded His dues. Something told her that there was worse still to come.

***

Standing by the fireplace, watching the embers rise and fall, Jia listened to Bazigh Khan, his words chilling her to the bone. She pulled her chador tight around her shoulders and up across the nape of her neck to warm herself. 'Tell me again, from the beginning, Lala,' she said.

But Bazigh Khan wasn't prepared to repeat the story so soon. 'The words almost took my life the first time they left my lips,' he whispered. He had been standing since he arrived at the house. His legs were getting heavy but he dared not sit for fear of not rising again.

'Baba, sit down,' said Idris to his father.

'How can I sit in the warmth while Akbar Khan lies on a cold slab?' he said. He took a deep breath, letting the alien feelings that ran through him settle. He knew that other people, normal people, called them guilt and fear. But he had not been like everyone else for such a long time. He was Bazigh Khan, defender of the Khan: his job was to stand between death and his brother and snatch him back from the heavenly farishtay when they came, but he had failed. He had left his brother's side and his duties early, and the angel of death had taken Akbar Khan.

He'd only gone because Akbar had pressed him. 'The Khan should be guarded day and night. It is one of the unwritten rules of the family,' he had reminded his brother. But shortly after, when Akbar Khan received the call about Benyamin, he'd ignored protocol and chosen to travel alone, telling his guards to meet him at the place where they'd heard Benyamin was being held.

When he didn't arrive, the guards went looking for him. It didn't take them long: a black Bentley with private plates is hard to miss on a winding country road. Less than two hours after saying good-night to his brother, Bazigh Khan got a call telling him the Khan was dead.

'It was not like him to take such a risk,' said Bazigh Khan, shaking his head.

The moon had been full and fat that night, casting its light like little drops of honey on the leaves that filled out the lush hills and valleys. The guards had found the car parked in the layby of a nearby beauty spot, Akbar Khan beside it, still wearing the black shervani Maria had picked out for him for the wedding reception. A grey blanket had been draped over him, as if to stop him feeling the chill. The men had moved the blanket to find his face pressed deep into the soft brown mud, five bullets in the back of his head. He had been shot at close range. The black brocade hid the bloodstains well, and from a distance he looked like an old man who, feeling tired, had taken a nap next to his car after a picnic. The men who found him had fallen to their knees and wept like children at their father's grave. They had lost their protector, and who now would answer to God on their behalf?

Idris stood by his father's side, one hand on his shoulder. He caught sight of his reflection in the mirror – his clothes crumpled, the red lines of sleep still evident in his eyes. This night had aged him. Standing by the window, his cousin Jia, however, looked fresher than her middle years. Her hair covered, her face washed clean, she seemed to have shed some of her burdens.

He remembered his Quran teacher telling him that believers are mirrors for each other, silently reflecting back their truth. Unwittingly, Jia Khan's mirror cast light on the weaknesses of others. The strong among them took note; the weak, no doubt, blamed her for their own inadequacies. It was something he had observed at the wedding, but he realised now that she had always had this presence about her. She was clever and unflinching, and he saw in her a hierarchy of destructive potential and his place within it. Maybe it had seemed more pronounced tonight because she no longer cared about anything in this world – Zan's death had seen to that – or maybe it was just the way she was made, only he hadn't recognised it before.

Whatever it was, Idris knew that if he could see it, then so could everyone else. There was no honour among thieves; the pack needed someone they feared to keep them in line. Idris wondered if Jia Khan could accept who she was before it was too late, and in so doing save the family before its demands destroyed her.

The call for Fajr interrupted his thoughts. It was followed by silence, and each person playing their part. Sitting in an armchair by the window, Sanam Khan wiped her tears with her shawl. She was heartbroken at her husband's death. The thought that she might be mourning her child as well as her husband skirted her mind, and she resolved only to mourn when Benyamin returned home.

'We must proceed carefully or face financial ruin,' Bazigh Khan warned. He was not a slow-hardened man; it was the heavy hammer of a single experience that had shaped him, and his words were often blunt. In other families, this was not the time to mention business and money, but they were not like other families, and Jia understood his reasons well. Her uncle was readying himself for war. But the warning sufficed; the rest of that discussion could wait. Today, he would speak of his brother.

'Akbar Khan was a great man, a good man, one who knew that to steal was more honourable than to spread one's hands before another,' he said. 'He chose to face the wrath of God rather than bow to a master. And on this day, my sister, as he stands before his Lord, no curtain between them and no earthly body, I pray for great mercy on him, as he showed mercy to so many of us.'

It was customary to talk of the dead in this way, to scoop out memories and feast on them for three days, no more, no less. It was how the mourners healed. The coming days would be full of this.

'We must make preparations for the Janaza and for his afterlife. I have given orders for five hundred poor families to be given flour and meat and provisions across the provinces of our people. I hope you feel it is enough. We can do more if you so wish.'

Sanam Khan nodded without really listening. She was unable to focus on the afterlife of her husband while her son's earthly life was in the balance.

'There will be time to mourn my father, Lala,' Jia said softly but firmly. 'Right now our concern must be for Benyamin. We don't know how much time we have. Please tell us again everything you know.'

It was beginning to get light by the time Bazigh Khan finished recounting the night's events. Unbeknown to him, his brother had sent men to bring news of Benyamin after he failed to show up for the rukhsati.

'He received a call soon after the wedding,' Bazigh Khan said. 'I must have just left. The men had found out that Benyamin was being held by a group called the Brotherhood in the old textile mills.'

The factories had once been the financial backbone of the city, a flourishing industry that had attracted workers from India and Pakistan, feeding their families and changing the course of their lives. Then everything changed. The workers stayed but the work travelled to the countries they had once called home. The mills remained dormant for decades until regeneration projects opened them up again. The Khan had business interests in these buildings and some of his foot soldiers owned apartments there. It wouldn't have taken long for the information about Benyamin to reach him.

Bazigh Kahn groaned again. 'I wish I had known what was going on. I would have stopped him going. I could have handled the situation myself.'

'He would not have listened to you. You know what Baba was like.'

'You must not think ill of your father, Jia, he was a brave man,' said Bazigh Khan. 'We will defend your honour, and when Ben jaan is home and our Khan is buried, we will have vengeance – we will invoke badal. As his eldest child, you are the only one capable of doing what must be done. The law of Pukhtunwali demands it.'

'This life of ours has already swallowed one of my children – must it take more?' said Sanam Khan. She was tired and unable to hold it together any longer. The tears came and she wept.

Jia wiped her mother's eyes. 'We will find a way to fix this,' she said.

'If they were going to kill him, they would have done so by now,' said Idris, kneeling beside his Sanam Khan. 'Instead they have moved him – we've checked the old mills. He's not there. They must be hoping to buy some time. Don't worry, we will bring Ben home. Now, why don't you go and see if the chai is ready?' He understood that his aunt needed a task, and feeding her family would give her a sense of purpose. She nodded, kissing his forehead as she left the room.

When she'd gone, Jia took her seat. 'What do we know about this Brotherhood?' she asked Idris.

'Not much,' he replied. 'Andrzej Nowak is the head of the group – he's fairly new in town.'

'I've met him,' said Jia, with a grimace. 'I defended his cousin on a drugs charge last year.'

'They are from across Eastern Europe, but the kids here assume they're all Polish, hence the name "Brotherhood". They've been here for a few years, making in-roads in a couple of other cities. Some of the kids whose parents came here when our fathers did have joined them. But some of our boys have married their women and so we keep track of things. They've not really caused any major trouble until now. Your father asked me to look into their dealings last month. He said they were angling for control, trying to take apart the Jirga and pick its proceeds. He knew they were planning something but I never thought they would be brave enough to kill him, and this soon.'

Jia listened intently to her cousin. Idris was the Khan's lawyer and chief adviser. He knew everything there was to know about the family business. If the old ways had continued he would have been her husband, and it was widely known that Akbar Khan had hoped his daughter would choose her eldest cousin as a spouse. The arrival of Elyas had ended the hope of a familial union, but while the open secret could have caused bad blood between other families, Jia and Idris were different to most people. He held her in high regard and she recognised in him sound judgement. She knew that the death of Akbar Khan would leave a gaping wound in the Pukhtun brotherhood; it required the kind of 'handling' that only a Pukhtun man with a steady hand and a steel mind could do. She was glad he was here. 'You should speak to the Jirga, Idris. This is not my world, but you understand it,' she said.

Trusted, respected and obsessed with detail, her cousin was an important linchpin in the Khan empire. But he knew he was no leader. 'No,' Idris said. 'It's not my place. I have laid the groundwork and I'll do whatever you need, but the succession must continue with you.'

He had spoken briefly to key members of the Jirga on his way over to the house, to break the news and to reassure them. 'The families are setting up a meeting for later today. They are demanding justice,' he said. 'Akbar Khan worked hard to unite them through marriage and business alliances, but I'm afraid the ties of kinship may not be enough. If you do not assert your right today and in front of the collective Jirga, they will see it as weakness and there will be war.'

The death of Akbar Khan would have far-reaching consequences if not handled correctly. It was Jia's actions that would now determine the future of the city and those who lived there. Idris prayed to God that she understood the gravity of what she was about to undertake.

CHAPTER 19

'Good or bad, he's closer than your jugular vein,' said John, raising his eyebrows at his old friend.

Elyas laughed. 'Since when does an atheist quote the Quran?' he said.

'Round these parts it's what they'd say about your father-in-law,' said John. He was one of the few people Elyas trusted. He told the truth and he told it cold. It came with the territory. John and Elyas had known each other for over two decades and despite distance their friendship had remained strong.

When the *Recorder*'s editor had announced he was taking a sabbatical for six months, Elyas jumped at the chance to work beside his old friend. Taking over the chief's office was not just another job for him. It meant more than warm news-sheet and black ink. This was the Khan's local paper. If anyone knew what was really going on with Jia's family, it was the reporters who worked here. And Elyas needed familiarity.

'It won't happen,' the school careers adviser had said when he'd mentioned his plans to become a journalist. 'Media is not for people like you.' For a while Elyas believed him. But, thankfully, university changed that, giving him back the confidence to follow his dreams. After graduating, he'd gone to work at his local paper. The first day on the job, he'd understood his careers adviser's warning: Elyas's was the only brown face in the newsroom.

The distance from the cub reporter's desk to the chief's corner office, inch by inch, was a measure of how far he had come. He looked out at the team of weekend staff through the glass wall that separated them, as they sifted through the details of the day's breaking story – the death of Akbar Khan. He'd been left reeling when Jia had phoned him with the news. So when John got in touch to see how he was, he offered to come into the office to help piece the story together, even though he wasn't officially supposed to start until Monday. It would take his mind off the personal fallout from this news. Ahad's grandfather was dead before they'd even been introduced.

The newsroom hadn't changed much in the years since Elyas had left. Newspapers were still strewn across the floor, desks and printers, some of them yellowing, their edges beginning to curl. Subs still shouted at fresh-faced journalists, and endless cups still filled the kitchen sink. The smell of the fridge left Elyas wondering if anyone had cleaned it since he'd left. Reporters still hunched over desks, stared at their screens, bashed keyboards and snapped pens, as news editors with papers to fill remained as antsy as ever, if not more so. The arrival of the internet age had made life for print journalists precarious.

John, who'd never left, was now their crime reporter. His reasons for staying were mainly family-related. His wife was the social affairs correspondent and their three children were settled in local schools. He'd thought of moving, especially with the industry dying, but had never quite found the right post. John was an old-fashioned hack: TV and radio were not for him, and the jump to internet... Well, that was too risky with a family. 'I've got a comfortable seat on a sinking ship,' he'd told Elyas. 'Let's see if a lifeboat turns up, eh?' And so he'd stayed. Easy to get along with, he looked like a newspaperman out of one of the 1920s detective novels he read and wrote for a hobby.

First day back on the job and Elyas found himself knee-deep in photographs and clippings as he and John looked through the background on Akbar Khan. Not all content had been digitised. Elyas knew most of Akbar Khan's history by heart and the cuttings did little more than refresh his memory. Heartbreak and Google were stalking companions, and while there wasn't much about Jia online, there was plenty about her father.

The men stopped as one of the reporters came in carrying newspapers fresh off the press. The reporter piled them on Elyas's desk and left. 'Why are we going through these old stories and not getting someone else to do it?' John asked.

'This is personal to me.'

John nodded. He knew exactly how personal it was. Tentatively, he broached the subject. 'Did Jia say anything else?' he asked.

Elyas shook his head. 'Just that the funeral will be on Monday. And that I should bring Ahad.'

'What? She wants you to bring Ahad?'

'Yes.'

John shook his head. 'Are you sure that's wise? I mean, her dad told her that he was dead. Is his funeral the best place for a reunion?'

Elyas shrugged. 'I don't know. Ahad wants to go. He's getting a train up here this afternoon. None of this is easy.'

'What I never understood was how she believed that he was dead. Surely she needed to bury her child, name him, find some closure, something? But she just carried on. And then Khan left him with you. What the fuck was that all about?'

'It wasn't like that,' said Elyas.

'It was exactly like that. There's something else going on here, mate.'

Elyas already knew meeting at the funeral wasn't a good idea, either for his son or the boy's mother, but nothing about his relationship with Jia had ever been straightforward. He wondered if that was what had kept him addicted to her for so long. He was no different to a junkie, hungry for the next fix, willing to blur the lines of right and wrong to get it. Unwilling to confront his shame, he brushed the thought aside. Age had never stopped a grown man making a bad choice. Work was best. News was salvation. Work was where he made his best decisions. 'So, what else do we know about the Jirga?' he asked, picking up a copy of the day's paper and handing it to John. Akbar Khan's face was splashed across the front page, the headline 'Gangland Assassination' above it.

John shook his head. 'Things are bad,' he said. 'They're worse than when we first started. Everything has gone – the big companies have left, unemployment is high, and hardly anyone who goes away to university comes back. The city has been drained of hope. My contacts tell me the police have been after Akbar Khan for years. They know about the Jirga, about the drug runs, the money laundering, the prostitution, the tax fraud – you name it, they know it. But the CPS just can't seem to make it stick. People whisper and gossip but when it comes to giving evidence, no one comes forward, stories don't corroborate and reports go missing.'

'People are that afraid?' said Elyas.

'They're not afraid of him, they respect him.'

Elyas was surprised by his answer. Things had become so bad that criminals were now among the highly respected in society? He was so steeped in privilege that he hadn't seen it coming.

John watched his old friend grappling with what he was learning. He had always admired Elyas's drive. It was the kind of drive that required commitment, the kind that got you kicked in the teeth. Repeatedly. But that had never stopped Elyas. It had been evident the first time they met. They were at college and Elyas had just narrowly escaped a beating from a group of rival university students over a long since forgotten political discussion. John had dragged Elyas to the pub to escape. Once there, Elyas had ceremoniously suggested they write down their plans for the next ten years. John had thought it a bit weird but agreed. 'The back of a stained beer mat is probably the best place for my plans,' he'd told his new friend. Over the years, Elyas had crossed off every single one of his goals, and hung the mat in his study. John hadn't. He now used his as a coaster on his desk 'as a reminder that plans are for losers', he told Elyas.

John was genuinely pleased for his friend and glad that success had not changed him. To Elyas, achievements were just road markers that allowed him to feel worthy. John knew this – and where his old friend's demons lived. Elyas's career trajectory had been inversely proportional to his personal life. John, on the other hand, had a job he liked and lived with the woman he loved, who loved him back. The equations of life were balanced.

'Do you think Jia knows the full extent of her father's criminal activities?' John asked.

'I don't know,' Elyas said. 'They were close. But by the time she and I split up there was a lot of bad blood. I think it was more from her than from him.' Jia would talk to Elyas about her father's business from time to time, but only in general terms. She had never been comfortable on the subject.

They continued looking through the archives, separating out anything they thought useful.

'This is from the night Bazigh Khan's wife died,' said John, handing Elyas a cutting. It was a photograph, black and white, of a young man being pressed against a wall by two policemen, his hands behind his back, his face turned to the camera, expressionless, emptied of feeling. It showed his children looking on, their faces bereft, one clutching a soft rabbit, Sanam Khan kneeling beside them, her dupatta wrapped around her head tight, her figure blurred as if she was moving when the camera clicked. Her husband was standing next to her, his eyes locked upon his brother. Elyas wanted to take the picture to Jia and ask her about it, but he knew it would be pointless.

'Here's what we've got so far about last night…' John said, picking up his battered old notebook and squinting as he tried to make sense of his shorthand. 'What does that word say?' He pointed to one of the squiggles on the page. 'Oh yeah, I remember now. A big drugs shipment was supposed to come in last night. The biggest that the city has seen in a long time...'

'Where did you hear that? Not from official police channels, surely?' said Elyas. He was impressed at John's work.

'I have my sources,' John replied. 'You're not the only award-winning reporter here, you know.'

'Seriously?'

'It's all over the community website,' said John. 'A guy called Andrzej Nowak was out celebrating with a group of his men last night. I'm told he's been under police surveillance for a while. They're not sure what he's doing here but they know it's not to do charity work for Islamic Relief. Your man Ben Khan was also seen at this gathering with some girl, probably his girlfriend...'

John knew Elyas thought of Benyamin Khan as a little brother. What he had to say next was difficult. 'Apparently Ben was trying to steal Nowak's drugs consignment. Maybe he was trying to impress his father, maybe he was just doing it for a lark, who knows. The drugs were in the guy's car, so he stole the car.' He spoke slowly, choosing his words carefully, his eyes on Elyas, watching for a sign of when to stop. 'The word is that the Brotherhood have Benyamin Khan. Andrzej Nowak is not known for his...mild-mannered ways. And if they do have him, and he's alive...from what I hear, he'll be praying that he wasn't.'

CHAPTER 20

'Yes, John, I'll be careful,' Elyas said as he left the car park. Just a day into management and he hadn't been able to hack it, watching reporters leave the newsroom to find stories as he sat behind a desk and read reports and looked at budgets. He couldn't do it. He'd collected his keys and left.

John was better at that stuff and should have got the job in the first place. 'Look, I'll call you as soon as I know anything,' Elyas said, not letting John speak in case he told him to stop being stupid and head back. Which would have been a reasonable demand. Elyas ended the call and dropped the phone on the passenger seat.

He couldn't stop thinking about Benyamin.

Elyas had heard enough about the Brotherhood now to know what they were capable of. A cold chill ran down his spine at the thought of them. He straightened his shoulders, leaning back in the seat; he needed to stay focused if he was to be of any help to Jia.

It had been years since he'd driven through the city. It was a set of memories to him, memories filled at first with sunny days, walking through town eating bags of salty chips from the shop on the corner of Moonbridge Road, and later with dark and rain-soaked days, collar pulled up and battling through the wind to catch the bus home. He couldn't say exactly when the warm and bright had turned to cold and gloomy, but it was then that he had made the decision to leave. Today, as he drove through the same old streets with the same grey skies overhead, past the broken windows and peeling

128

paintwork of the stone buildings, few signs of the city's better days remained.

His time here had been mixed, but Elyas still loved this city. To him, she was a grand old lady who'd enjoyed her time in the sun, but had burned too brightly and faded all too fast. During her glory days in the late nineteenth and early twentieth century, her beauty and potential drew traders from far and wide. With the merchants came lucrative deals and soon mills of honey-coloured stone began to spring up against the green landscape. Thousands of workers followed, crossing continents in the hope that some of her success would rub off on them. She became the wool capital of the world, and the district of Hanover was the jewel in her crown, home to her courtiers, who built huge houses for their families.

But then the textile industry moved overseas, where production was cheaper, and the mills that had once been filled with looms, humming love songs to her bounty, stood empty. As her charms faded, so did her suitors. The merchants fled when the money dried up, taking their families with them, leaving behind only high ceilings, covings and mouldings. Neighbourhoods dropped out of favour, prices fell. Immigrants and factory workers moved into the opulent Victorian houses. The multiple floors, numerous bedrooms and large living spaces made them perfect for the extended family system of the city's South Asian communities.

It was to one of the old mills that Benyamin had been taken, rumour had it. Driving to it through the city meant taking a refresher course in clutch control, and as the car engine revved at the traffic lights on top of another steep hill, Elyas realised he had missed driving through this quiet beauty.

He arrived at the mill to find it cordoned off, two policemen patrolling the perimeter. He parked up and jumped out, taking the road in his wide stride as he walked towards them. 'What's going on, officer, if you don't mind my asking?' he said.

'There was a nasty incident 'ere last night,' the policeman replied, his accent white working class, but his tone warmer than expected. 'From press, I s'pose,' he added, watching as Elyas pulled a notebook from his pocket.

'Mind if I look around?' said Elyas.

'Knock yourself out, mate. Not past the cordon, obviously. The press officer is on her way if you're looking for information – if you are, you know, press, like. Because if you were…I'd tell ya to ask in that shop over there.' He pointed at a minimart across the road. Elyas thanked him and headed over to it.

Inside, an old man at the counter was chatting with an equally antiquated fellow behind it. Deep in conversation, they were oblivious to the arrival of new customers. Elyas looked around at the shelves. They were half empty except for crisps and chocolate, bread, booze and dust. A musty smell permeated the air, almost as if emanating from the old men, dense and pungent. Elyas lurked behind the shelves, eavesdropping on their chatter. He picked up a faded bar of chocolate. They were talking in heavy dialect, one he'd heard before but wasn't fluent in. The shopkeeper noticed him loitering. He used the words 'lamba', 'gora'… They were talking about him as though he was white.

'Just this, please,' Elyas said, coming forward and handing over his money. The old man fumbled in the cash register before giving change. Elyas thanked him. 'Do you know why the police are here, Uncle?'

The shopkeeper shook his head vigorously, his eyes shut tight. 'I no know what happened,' he said in a thick accent. Elyas nodded and thanked him again, this time in Urdu.

'You speak Urdu? Where you from? You Pakistani? You no look Pakistani,' he said.

'Yes, I am. Well, my grandfather was. He's Pathan,' Elyas replied.

The shopkeeper's face lit up. 'OK! You wait. Wait, OK?' he said, picking up his phone. The man dialled a number and spoke to someone on the other end, then held out the phone. 'Here, speak to my son, he will tell you everything,' he said.

Elyas took the battered old Nokia and put it to his ear. The warmth of one's own kith and kin, and their need to pass on what they knew, never failed to inspire him. 'Hello?' he said.

'Bloody drug dealers, in't it!' said a heavy voice on the other end. 'They moved in couple o' weeks back. Rented some storage units. Said they were selling mineral water. Tried to give me some.'

'What did you say?'

'I said no thanks! Best steer well clear of them Eastern Europeans. Two weeks after they moved in and they're driving round in flashy cars. I knew it were dodgy. I mean, who sells water and makes enough for a Lambo? Then water board came out, sayin' summat about a water leak. Sayin' we usin' too much of it. Think they moved premises after that, kept the units for storing their cars.'

The shopkeeper's son spoke fast, making it difficult for Elyas to keep up. As he listened, he gauged the man was as dodgy as they came in this city, but everyone deserved to be heard. Elyas had a knack for getting people to open up. He could get them to reveal things in private conversations, with cameras pointed at them and down phone lines. You just had to care enough to listen.

Malala Food Stores was the kind of establishment that shouted money laundering: bare shelves, tins past their sell-by date, pins and needles in little packets, and plastic toys that looked straight out of the eighties, all signs that this was some kind of front. Experience told Elyas that the shopkeeper's son was no stranger to the police. That's why he wasn't at the premises today, and why his fumbling old man was working the cash register.

'You know Akbar Khan?' the young man asked. 'I work for 'im. I told 'im what these scum were doin'. Said we need to clean 'em out!'

'And Ben Khan? Do you know what happened to him?' Elyas asked. No reply. He waited. A less experienced man would have interjected but Elyas understood how to draw answers out of people by leaving a silence hanging. The void seemed unending but Elyas was patient, and then, 'Hello? You still there?'

'Yeah, I'm still here,' came the voice. More silence. And then, it happened. When he finally started talking, his words were drained of their bravado and street kid arrogance. He spoke for quite a while, his voice low, so that Elyas had to press his ear to the phone, listening hard, swallowing every word. When the son hung up, he handed the mobile phone back to the shopkeeper.

'Are you OK?' the old man asked in Urdu. 'You look even paler than when you came in.'

Elyas smiled weakly and thanked the old man for his help and his concern. Once safely in his car, he scrolled through his phone for Jia's number. He held the phone tightly in the palm of his hand, staring at it, his heart ready to jump out of his mouth. He had to pass on what he knew. But it had pained him to hear it himself – how would he tell her?

The young man on the phone had been quite sure about what had been done to Benyamin last night. 'I couldn't get hold of Idris so I called Phats – he does security for the Khans – told 'im where Ben Khan was,' he'd said. 'But I couldn't bring myself to tell 'im all of it. Tauba! I ain't slept all night since I heard his screams, bro!'

'What happened?'

'They took him to the parking lot by the storage units. I saw them with my own eyes. That Brotherhood, if you do 'em wrong, they want you to suffer as a warning t'rest of us...' He took a long breath. His voice trembled. 'He's a good kid, our Ben. Looks out for my dad. What they did to him was not human, man... I heard his screams... They just wouldn't stop... They just kept revvin' up those cars, man. Revvin' 'em up and parking those fuckers on him. Reckon they only stopped cos they heard the Khan had got wind of what was goin' on. They were gone before anyone showed up.'

CHAPTER 21

Jia emerged from the house to find Michael waiting for her at the bottom of the stone steps. He was empty-handed, his phone tucked away in his jacket pocket. He'd been admiring the valleys from this vantage point. The air was clean and crisp, filled with the smell of freshly cut grass. Jia looked at the grounds of her father's house, the pathway weeded clean, the neat edges of the lawn. The wedding had left none of its mark thanks to the Khan's men. The family never left business unfinished.

She had spent the rest of the morning handling the details of death. The post-mortem had been expedited, thanks to Bazigh Khan. He had pulled strings and ensured that the process would be completed quickly; even in death, Akbar Khan came first. The coroner's office was not as easily persuaded. Its bureaucracy was as a heavy ship, difficult to change direction once its course was set, so the inquest date was in a few weeks. Men and women who deal with death on a daily basis do not fear much, and so bribery was out of the question. That said, the coroner was a fair man and had agreed to issue an interim death certificate so that the burial could take place within the three days recommended under Islamic law. It wasn't an unusual request in this city.

Michael held the door of the Range Rover open, ready for Jia to take her seat. The Bentley was in the police compound, being examined for evidence. They were on their way to meet her father's men. The car's music system began playing old Rafi songs as the engine turned. Michael moved to turn them off but she stopped him, hoping her father's favourite tunes would ease her discomfort. The old memories kept on coming.

Row upon row of small terraced houses came into sight, then the roads widened to open green fields. The landscape brought a mix of melancholy and nostalgia. With its dry-stone walls and winding roads, its green and grey and brown countryside, its cold, crisp air, this would always be home to Jia. And though the hills and valleys merged with ease, she knew that people who lived here stood apart.

It was an apartness that had begun when men like her father had crossed sea and land to come here in search of a better life. Her father. The thought of him brought a sudden, sharp shot of sadness, but she had no time to indulge the emotion and she knocked it back.

She thought of the tangas and taxis and ships and planes carrying their passengers from rural parts of sixties Pakistan. They had settled slowly, some marrying here and others 'back home', and their families had grown. Their sons and daughters, the next generation, were born and raised in the city, and schooled in places that would later be described as 'enclaves'. They'd worried they'd lose their heritage, their language, their way. But that hadn't happened.

Instead, the next generation of children had become something else, something caught between the land of their heritage and the place of their birth. Something that would find more acceptance in the village of their forefathers than in the green fields of the county where they were born. Cocky and confident, the boys held on to tribal divisions, speaking of them with pride in their own form of patois. Using the same mash-up of English and Punjabi, Pashto or Mirpuri, and dressed in the vibrant pinks and parrot greens belonging to the bright shine of the Indian sub-continent, the girls were caught in an even bigger crossfire. The East gave them grace, the West gave them freedom. And of course they wanted both. They were proud to call themselves Pakistani, wearing the cricket shirts and flying the flag of the crescent moon on Eid, but their mindset belonged to the land where they were born.

Their patriotism was lost on Jia. She wondered why they boasted about a nation that was built on blood, sweat and rape, run by power-hungry, money-grabbing misogynists. What did it offer them? Life would be simpler without the troublesome burden of her bloodline, without the battle for identity that drove young people to places like Syria to fight a war that was never theirs to begin with, for a people that would slaughter them, given half the chance. How easy it would be to change her name to something more European and lose herself in the majority society. But she was a Pukhtun and to the Khans that meant more than patriotism. It meant heritage and responsibility. It meant loyalty and love of nation. It meant changing the world for the better.

She had believed she was chosen. Her father had told her as much. Repeatedly. Tell someone something enough times and they believe it. But somewhere along the road to being the favourite child, their paths had diverged. And now, travelling to meet her father's men, she had to summon all the old ways and values and sacredness of that choosing. She wondered what she was doing in this rundown, forsaken city, a place whose children, according to the media, had run into the arms of extremists overseas. Even the men and women who ran agencies of intelligence, who possessed 'in-depth information', couldn't tell them why these children were strapping bombs to their bodies. But Jia knew why. She knew what it was to run, and a part of her could sense the desperation that had pushed people so far into the wrong, just to find understanding and identity.

It was a long way from what Akbar Khan had wanted for his children. He had wanted them to do well, and in order to do that he understood that they had to integrate with the country into which they had been born. He had impressed this upon them and encouraged them. Both he and her mother were keen for them to leave the family business behind and start anew on unsullied lines and cleaner foundations.

The push and pull of old and new flooded back in through the windows as the car entered the city, threading its way through streets lined with sand-coloured buildings, ice-cream parlours, shisha bars and boarded-up pubs.

She leaned back into the warm leather of the seats, reminding herself that she had always been a good daughter. She had tried to live life the way her family had wanted, even though it had meant breaking away from them, and to some extent she had succeeded. But things had changed so suddenly, and now it seemed the life that had opened up to her was closing back in.

CHAPTER 22

A guard sat reading an Urdu paper in a small outbuilding by the iron gates. The emblem of the Jirga was set in the centre of the gates, its red and gold roses both warning and welcoming visitors. The guard glanced up and then quickly rose to attention as he recognised the approaching vehicle's licence plates. The heavy black gates swung open slowly and the Range Rover slipped through and on to a private road. They drove for almost a mile before reaching the end of the winding driveway, where ten neatly parked black Bentleys signalled that the members of Akbar Khan's Jury were here and waiting. A white Rolls-Royce, the only one of its kind in the line-up, was being buffed by a chauffeur in a neatly pressed Nehru jacket. Keeping up with the Khans was an expensive part of business, but the accoutrements of privilege were necessary if people were to believe they were living in times of plenty, and that their loyalty would be repaid.

Jia glanced at her watch; they had made good time. Idris had been in touch with the arrangements. 'The Jirga had to start strictly controlling locations and timings after the attempt on Akbar Khan's life in '95,' he'd said. Jia remembered those days vividly, her father in hospital, men in and out of the house checking security and ignoring everyone around them. A dark cloud had descended on the family business. Tensions had been high then, much as they were now, but this time her father wasn't here to navigate them.

The riots of that year had left their mark on the Khans and taught them an invaluable lesson: organised crime cannot operate without the rule of law. So they had drawn up a clear set of rules on which the family business now ran. These rules ran alongside the ancient tribal laws, and were enforced and adhered to.

There was a clear protocol for meetings. Decisions were finalised last minute to minimise leaks. Representatives from each family met an hour before the scheduled arrival time to draw straws, with the man with the longest straw making the venue arrangements. It was a great honour, but the work required was hard and they had to move fast. After all, they were Pukhtun and hospitality was as great a concern as security.

Today, Mubarak Khan and his establishment had been tasked with the honour. A master baker, he was among the closest and most trusted of Akbar Khan's allies. The meeting was being held at his bread-making business on the outskirts of the city, in a pink building that nestled among the landscape like a gentle rose.

He was standing by the entrance when Jia arrived, his portly body reminding her of a wholemeal dough ball waiting to be dusted and flattened and rolled into a chapatti. Mubarak Khan was bound by a deep loyalty. His empire was built on the foundations of the Khan brotherhood that some called 'biraderi', but as with all great patri-archal cultures, his family business was in fact started by a woman for her one great love, her son.

Despite his success, Mubarak Khan had not forgotten his debt, or his place in the Khan brotherhood. His feet were planted firmly on the ground and ready to follow the Khan into battle. After all, it was his money that had enabled the uneducated but ambitious baker to start the venture; it was his guiding hand that had helped it prove, and his insistence on 'taking care' of competitors that had allowed it to rise and become golden. Mubarak's mother had baked the code of the 'Old Country' into everything she made, and that included her son. It was mixed in with the red clay of his ovens, the salt that seasoned his flour and the blood that ran through his veins. And so Akbar Khan's daughter was now Mubarak's daughter; her wishes were his command and her honour was now his duty. He greeted her warmly, kissing her forehead, tears in his eyes.

Jia hadn't visited the bakery since she was a child. She reached out to touch the walls, letting her fingers move across the once-peeling paint, and saw that they had been restored with care.

Mubarak Khan led her through the building, the fragrance of hot naan and cinnamon swirling through the air as they walked the length of the corridor. He pushed open a door at the end and together they entered a shiny stainless-steel kitchen where men wearing black cotton aprons and matching linen hats were mixing and kneading and baking. Light dustings of flour covered their faces and everything around them. Jia watched as three men took pieces of dough and plied them into balls, rolling each one out into a circle before placing it on a kind of cooking cushion. A fourth man picked up the cushion and reached into the burning tandoor, pressing the uncooked naan against the hot clay wall to make it stick. She thought of her father's words the last time she had been here. 'Respect these men,' he had said. 'Every day they put their hands into the depths of hellfire to bring you food.' Watching the men work, Jia wondered how deep into those hellfires Akbar Khan now found himself.

Beyond the kitchen and hidden in the heart of the bakery was a large, windowless conference room. A select few knew of its existence, and if its whitewashed walls could talk, they would have destroyed many a powerful man. The room was a place of shura, of consultation, and this was the way of the Jirga. Akbar Khan had long held that debate and discussion gave people a sense of control over their destiny, and prevented rebellion, and he had encouraged it in his tribesmen. Consultation was the closest they came to democracy.

Today, the room was empty of most of its furniture, the twelve leather armchairs that were usually there having been replaced by white cotton sheets spread across a polished parquet floor. The Jirga sat cross-legged, their heads covered with soft prayer hats and bowed in solemnity. Some of them prayed silently, some a little louder, others discussed personal matters quietly between themselves.

Their Khan had gone on to the next world, leaving them in a place between life and death; their affairs were unfinished, their questions unanswered. They needed a leader who could bring them together. Like fatherless children they waited for someone to show them the way. They waited for the child of their Khan, as was tradition, but a woman had not led their people in centuries and few had faith in her abilities.

'Of course, nowadays these youngsters want to put us aside and think for themselves, as though we are stupid and know nothing of the world!' Sher Khan said to one of his fellow Jirga members. While his sons had been in prison, they had developed opinions that did not sit right with him. He wanted to hand over his responsibilities as a Jirga member, but he had little faith in their ability to step into his shoes. He had been relying on the Khan's power and wisdom to bring them into line. With Akbar Khan gone he was forced to seek counsel elsewhere. 'What are we to do?' he said. 'I am afraid our ways will die if something is not done. Akbar Khan promised to help but now he has passed to the next life, may Allah be pleased with him, and I do not know where we will turn for answers.'

The man beside him nodded in understanding; the demise of their homeland and scant hope of pure-blood Pukhtun grandchildren in this new land concerned them greatly. A way would have to be found to navigate issues of marriage and still maintain family loyalties. But for now it would have to wait. The Khan was gone and rumours of a rebellion were surfacing. The limbo in which they found themselves could quickly turn to purgatory if plans were not put in place to restore faith.

Fitting then, that it was the aroma of burning coals that greeted Jia when she walked into the room. In one corner a chef carved a slow-roasted baby calf with a sharp knife. Jia's stomach turned at the sight of the flesh falling to the platter below. The chef's table was plump with meat of all kinds; chappal kebabs and chunks of lamb sat amid mountains of rice with slim strands of carrots, sultanas and raisins, and, of course, fresh naan.

Mubarak Khan handed her a piled-high plate. There was nothing on it she could eat, but meat was the staple of her people. 'You have fulfilled the law well,' she said to him. 'I'll take this with me and share it with my mother. She hasn't eaten since the wedding.'

Mubarak Khan nodded. 'Your father always said that it was our laws that set men apart from beasts,' he said. 'The old laws give our lives meaning.' Jia nodded. She knew the laws of Pukhtunwali well. They were deeply ingrained in her people. Melmastia and nanawatai were laws that demanded unconditional generosity and gave Pukhtuns their reputation as the most hospitable people in the world. It was the law of badal that gave them their other reputation, for invoking vengeance. She knew that history's ledger was filled with the body count of those who had attempted to avoid its fulfilment, and that the path of the Pathan flowed red with the blood of feuds. But she hoped that time had brought change and that a more enlightened group of men sat before her today.

Having worked hard to disentangle herself from her father's empire, she was conflicted about agreeing to meet with them. She had raised this with Idris, but he had offered no alternative. Power lay in the Jirga, and she needed their support. In the end, Benyamin's safety was paramount, so she had resolved to put her pride aside. The drive over had given her time to peel away some of her concerns and develop a kind of strategy.

She would ask her father's allies for zmeka, the law that demands a Pukhtun defend his property. She would remind them that as a daughter of their tribe and the child of their Khan, the code by which they lived obligated them to defend her and her honour. She hoped they would respond to her call. She had lost one brother; she would not lose another.

The men rose as she entered, and waited for her to take her place. Her head still covered and bowed, solemn and aware that every eye was on her, she walked across to where Bazigh Khan was waiting. Her hand in his, he led her to her place at the front of the room. The men sat down again. The atmosphere was heavy with the work Bazigh Khan had done to pacify them; the residue of reined-in arrogance and the scent of testosterone still lingered. The room felt thick with resentment, their hostility thinly veiled. Like a pack of hungry wolves, they waited. She knew that these men could sense fear and twist it to their will. In that moment, she was glad of her father's tutelage and his raising her not to fear men.

'Jia jaan, you are the daughter of our Khan,' Bazigh Khan said. 'We would like to offer you our condolences. "*Inna lillaahi wa inna ilayhi raaji'oon.*" If you are in agreement, we would like to start with the Fatihah to pray for maghfirat for Akbar Khan.' Jia nodded, joining the men as they placed their hands before their faces, shielding their eyes from the world to recite seven of the most powerful verses of the Quran, calling upon their God. Jia hoped He was listening.

With the word 'ameen', Bazigh Khan signalled the end of the prayer, the men's voices chiming with his. Then, drawing from the Quran again, he said: 'And give good tidings to the patient, who, when disaster strikes them, say, "Indeed we belong to Allah, and indeed to Him we will return."'

Jia wondered what her father would have to say about the situation in which she now found herself. She had considered his dispensation of justice to be ugly and misguided, feeding only his ego and having no place in the betterment of society. She had argued endlessly with him over this man's value and that man's virtue, but nothing had ever been resolved. And today, these dangerous men, these men whose reign she had long wished to see end, stood before her awaiting her guidance and instruction. She reminded herself of Benyamin and steeled herself for the onslaught.

Jaanan Khan spoke first; he was the eldest of the men. His tone was cold, his manner frosty, yet he began with kind words to her: 'I would like to offer my condolences to you. Your father was a true Pathan and a king among our people. We will miss him and pray you find peace.' A wry smile spread across his face, and he bared his teeth. 'You are many things, Jia Khan, but you are not our Khan; you are a woman,' he said.

'I am here to listen to my father's people,' she responded. Silence fell across the room, followed by a sound from deep within Jaanan Khan's belly. He was laughing at her. He turned to his comrades, smirking, and they joined him. Their half-suppressed scorn awoke an old hatred in Jia, one that she had not felt in some time. Anchoring herself with a reminder of who Jaanan Khan was, she refused to take the bait. His ways were the old ways, his sensibilities the old sensibilities. His green eyes had greyed watching time and people change, but his archaic interpretation of honour and loyalty had not, and he believed that women should know their place. Jia knew hers, and it was not at the feet of these men.

She raised her hand to silence them the way she had seen her father do many times. She was on course to become a judge under British law, so she knew how to control a room. Maybe that is why they stopped laughing. On the other hand, this was not that world, and this was a world in which her worth remained unproven.

She waited, allowing the silence in the room to grow until it became unbearable and Jaanan Khan exploded. 'She will lead us into destruction! Look at her, so frightened that she dare not even speak.' His anger infected his comrades and their voices rose like a rabble.

Bazigh Khan tried to silence them again but Jaanan would have none of it. The two men's voices became louder and louder, with others at the table trying to out-shout each other. Harsh words were exchanged in English and Pashto, accusations flung and age-old wounds torn open. Jia listened, their words watering the anger within her, and she blamed her father. Was this his badal for her? To let her walk in his shoes? The rage that had taken root when she'd heard what had happened to Benyamin wrapped around her sinews like ivy. She straightened up, her head being pulled by an invisible string that hung from the rafters.

She looked at the old men who had built the family empire alongside her father, the men who owned the city and intimidated its inhabitants. She watched them spit and seethe and goad each other, unable to control their tongues and their tempers, and a calm came over her. She was better than this, she was smarter than them, and she had nothing to prove.

Her voice even, her tone gentle, she looked at Jaanan Khan. 'You benefit from the business of women. If women stopped buying from and selling to men, then where would you be?' she said. The room fell to a hush. 'We have not buried my father yet, and I have still to weep my share of tears, Lala.' She moved forward and placed her hand on the old man's arm, knowing that calling him uncle had softened him a little. 'I was your Khan's favourite child and this is how you repay him. Does his death and a woman's pain and honour mean so little to you?'

He had expected her to light the fuse, not pour sand on his vitriol. A look of shame flashed across his face and in that moment Jia knew she had him.

She glanced around the room at the other men. She had watched them grow old, from fathers to grandfathers, and she understood that they were withering away and clinging to their views in the hope of remaining relevant.

'Do not be offended, Daughter,' said Bazigh Khan. 'We want in no way to dishonour your father's memory or to take from you this time of grief. It is justice we seek. These are our ways, and so it has been for centuries.'

'These ways of which you speak have killed my father and endangered my brother's life,' said Jia.

One of the men, a little younger than the others, nodded at her words, leaning forward as he spoke, his Pashto not as clear as the others: 'If we do not impress upon the perpetrators the error of their ways, how will they learn? Jia jaan, it is as a mercy to them that we must act.'

Afzal Khan was the first member of the Jirga to have been born in England. Seated at the far end of the room, he had inherited the family business only a year ago, after his father passed away. His factory was crucial to the Khan's economy and was one of the major links in the drug import chain. His blood ran hot, but his loyalty to the Khan was unmatched.

'Your father was a respected man, a great man,' he went on. 'He kept the peace in our streets for decades. But the young men have been getting restless for some time. The Brotherhood is feeding them lies and we need to show them the truth of justice. You can decide which law you follow, that of your British courts and your education, or that of your ancestors, and if you choose to leave us, that too is your right. Know that any one of us is willing to step up and take the responsibility of your father's place. Indeed, I would name myself if my uncles here would accept?' Afzal Khan's forthright words impressed and shocked the gathering in equal measure, and sent murmurs running through the room.

Bazigh Khan raised his hand to calm the men. 'That will not be necessary,' he said. 'We must allow the daughter of our Khan to hear what each of us has to say. That is our way and has been since time began.' So, one by one, they came forward and put their case.

Jia listened, paying close attention to every word. They put their plight before her, heaped praise upon her father and demanded justice for his death. And as she listened, she realised they would never accept her as their equal, so she resolved to play a different game.

'You have done me a great honour by inviting me here,' she said. 'I know that you have done so out of love for our laws and for my father. Jaanan Khan is right, I am only a woman and I know little of the world of men. Women know only the pain of leaving their family behind to help a man build his name and his family; the pain of being heavy with child, a child that will carry a man's name; the pain of giving birth; of love, of suckling your male child for two whole years, pouring every ounce of life into him only for him to turn around and tell you he knows better than you. The West would have us believe that women are equal to men, but you and I know we are not. Women can only live as equals if men permit it, if men support us, step aside to allow us to progress, if they help us stand and place our feet on the ladder of success. My father was one such man and he was proud that his Jirga was full of such men. And so, because I know you to be men of honour and forward-thinking, and because you know my weaknesses, I am asking you to stand by me as your daughter and sister. I am your honour. We are Pukhtun. Help me to make things right, help me to deliver what you need. Give me time and I will bring you badal and my brother, your *son*.' She paused, emphasising the word, reminding them that they were family. 'But you must trust me and assist me in this process. I cannot do it without you.'

As she spoke she saw each man's face soften, his head bow, some in shame, others in understanding, and she knew she had won. They had expected her to defend her position the way a man would; they had been ready for a fight but not for her surrender.

One by one they came and offered their allegiance. Placing their hands on her head, the way a father does to his child, each man gave his blessing. Women were strange creatures, difficult to gauge, impulsive and emotional. But some, the ones who were pure, like their mothers, could see into men's soul and beyond the naked, shivering wreck that housed them. They found themselves wanting to protect her and, in so doing, win her favour. They were afraid both for her and of her.

The meeting was over. One by one, Bazigh Khan showed each man out until only Jia Khan remained. 'That was smart,' he told her.

She smiled at him gently, putting her hand on his. 'Now, Uncle,' she said, 'sit by me and tell me everything my father knew about the Jirga and its weaknesses.'

CHAPTER 23

She knocked on the door and waited. No answer. She rapped harder, her knuckles bearing the brunt. The sound of footsteps and the turning of a key followed. She could see he'd been sleeping. His hair was ruffled but he was dressed. She understood this was why he'd taken so long to open the door: he'd been searching for his clothes.

He stood aside to let her in.

'Coffee?' he asked. She nodded.

She watched him moving around the kitchen looking for clean cups, trying to find milk, all the things one does when someone drops by unannounced in the middle of the night. She noticed his body was still taut and lean and it made her glad she'd driven over.

'I couldn't sleep,' she said, taking the cup. 'I keep thinking about Ben and what state he must be in...' She paused, waiting for him to speak, but he didn't. He just kept looking at her, wondering why she was here now, after all these years, and in the middle of the night. She was worried about her brother, which was understandable, but her concern for him while still no mention of her own son angered him. He wanted to ask her why, but he was afraid that she would leave, and he had waited so long for her to come to him this way.

She shifted uneasily from one foot to the other, not ready to tell him her real reasons for visiting, instead talking about other things. 'I've been meeting with my father's old cronies,' she said. 'Remember them?' He nodded, now as interested in her words as her lips. He blocked out his questions, wanting her to keep talking. He also wanted her to stop. She noticed the light behind his eyes, the one that would come alive when he was wrestling a knotty problem or when he was pursuing her. She wanted to see it burn and so she began telling him about her meeting with the Jirga, the things they had said, the way it had made her feel. As she spoke, bits of Jia Khan, criminal barrister, began to fall away until she was just Jia. The words spilled out of her, and she let them. She knew he would clean up the mess; he was the only one who could. He always had been, hadn't he?

He listened quietly and when he finally spoke it was only to say, 'Perhaps warm milk would've been better, then?' She laughed. Maybe at his joke, maybe at herself for being there, maybe because if she didn't she'd cry. She didn't really know which it was.

'Yes, perhaps,' she said, then added, 'I want to stay...'

He was about to say something about their son being in the house and the inappropriateness of the situation when she kissed him. He pulled away, unsure of what was happening. She leaned in closer, her warm breath caressing his neck. 'I want to fuck your brains out,' she whispered. He decided he would leave the emotional fallout until tomorrow.

She bit him, she gnawed at his lips, she sucked the kisses out of his mouth. Her hands held him fast and tight, and he let her. They moved to the bed, falling into it as they had when they were young, but this time it was more about forgetting than making memories. His mind kept wandering and he kept dragging it back. What would he tell their son in the morning? That was the difference between youth and age. Youth was always in a hurry, while age was eager to slow everything down, to think things through before acting.

His scent entered her bloodstream and hit her hard and fast, sharpening her senses, cutting the cord of self-restraint and destroying all logical reasons not to do this. She wanted to press him into her; she wanted to make herself whole again, the way she used to be.

The old Jia, the innocent Jia, the one without blood on her hands, the one who was fearless. Her hands moved lower, unbuttoning his clothes, pulling him closer, making him hard, taking him into her. She wanted to lose herself in his smell and make him bend to her will, to control him, own him, make him feel things that only she knew how. And he, in shock from the moment she'd arrived, allowed himself to give in to her will.

Afterwards he lay on the bed, spent, exhausted, still reeling from the shock of it all. 'Did you find what you needed?' he said, as she came back to the room from the bathroom.

'Yes, thanks,' she said. She was wearing his shirt, and in the faded light she looked exactly the way she had done when they'd first made love. She began to take it off and he wondered if he had the energy to do it all again. But she put on her own clothes.

'You're leaving?' he asked.

'I can't stay,' she said. 'It's not a good idea for Ahad to see me here.' Her directness, the mention of their son, took him by surprise again. It was the first time he had heard her say his name.

'But this just feels sort of wrong somehow, your leaving, I mean.'

'It was just sex.'

She was right. But these words, from those lips, were unexpected.

'How have you changed this much?' he whispered, intrigued and a little afraid. Because she had changed more than he could ever have imagined. He watched her dress and tie back her hair in that way she used to when they were together. He'd never really stopped loving her. She collected her things and she left, kissing him as she did so, telling him to bring Ahad to the funeral. And in that moment, watching her walk away alone, in the dead of night, the same way she had come, he understood just how broken she was and that he was never going to get over her.

CHAPTER 24

The cups rattled on the tray as the old man set it down with trembling hands, removing the items one by one and placing them in front of Nowak and his guest. Some of the coffee spilled from the pot and he grabbed a cloth, mopping up frantically. 'So sorry. So very sorry.' His throat was dry, his words afraid to leave his mouth.

Nowak smiled at him. 'Don't worry, old man,' he said, baring his teeth, then his smile vanished. 'Now, get out.' His clipped accent added to the directness of his words. The owner of the restaurant backed away quickly, relieved to be able to do so. He knew men who had lost their limbs for less.

Sitting across from him, Jia waited patiently. 'Would you like this with your coffee or later?' she asked, pointing to a box by her feet. The words 'World's Finest Sweethouse' were embossed on it, a claim as confident as the gold it was written in.

'Later. We can deal with these things in good time. I don't like to do business without getting to know my associates first. Let us get acquainted,' he said, and smiled wide, every tooth visible. 'Last time we met, you weren't very forthcoming, as I recall. Funny, isn't it? You were working for me then, and a fine job you did.' He paused. 'My cousin, whose name you helped to clear, he was there on Friday when your brother tried to steal from me. In fact, he's the one who's been looking after him.'

Something in the way he said the words made a shiver run down Jia's spine, though she did her best to hide it.

Nowak sat forward, his long, tapered fingers clasped into a steeple, and Jia was transported back to the café where he'd approached her a year ago. He was wearing the same cologne. It was gentle, inoffensive, expensive. 'You know, in my country, women usually pour the coffee,' he said, leaning in as if about to share a secret and then changing his mind. 'I like the ways of the English. They claim to make no distinction between men and women. But you and I know they do.' He paused, waiting for her to agree, continuing when she didn't. 'I like my coffee strong, like my loyalties. How do you take yours?' he asked, lifting the pot.

'I am your guest, I will take whatever you offer,' she said. The room was hot, the air musty, like the red velvet curtains that were draped across the windows, blocking out sunlight and any sign of a breeze. Nowak's talk left Jia impatient, but she knew men like him must be indulged and so she thanked him, putting the cup to her lips gently. The coffee tasted even worse than it smelt but she drank it as if he'd handed her nectar.

They were at the county's longest established and only authentic Polish restaurant. The owner was a trusted friend of the Nowak family and his daughter was married to a young Pathan from Mardan. The restaurateur worried about his grandchildren, their health, their well-being, their future, and so in a world of lines and sides he had negotiated himself a neutral place.

Idris had been at the Khan residence early to brief Jia about Andrzej Nowak. He'd flicked through the notes he'd prepared for Akbar Khan, his iPad balanced carefully on the breakfast table. His uncle had relied heavily on Idris for such matters. 'Andrzej Nowak, handsome, young, erudite.'

Jia had raised an eyebrow at the description. 'Is this a date or business?' she'd said.

'He's the son of a wealthy doctor who came to England in the sixties,' Idris went on. 'Dr Nowak married the daughter of a shop-keeper, the owner of a local delicatessen. Andrzej was their middle child. He was sent to boarding school in the south of England, and then his parents decided to move back to Poland. He was a brilliant student, studied history and modern languages at Cambridge, and then he disappeared. We don't know anything about him between then and his arrival in Yorkshire, including why he is here. He certainly doesn't need the money.'

'I guess we'll find out what he wants this afternoon,' Jia said, closing her book. She had been making notes; it helped her focus, and looking down at the page meant her thoughts remained her own.

She had been finishing up with Idris when her mother arrived, the perpetual murmur of protection prayers coming from her lips. She blew them over her daughter, her hands passing from her head to her tocs. Jia bristled a little. Her mother chose prayer over action every time and it irritated her, but she knew better than to brush her away; besides, they needed whatever higher power there was on their side. Before leaving, Maria had given her a twig, the kind they used to collect as children when they pretended to build bonfires. 'It's from the apple tree,' she said. 'Baba was going to have it cut down. Its roots are damaging the house.'

Sitting before Andrzej Nowak now, Jia picked up that twig and placed it on the small leather notebook. The talk so far had been inconsequential and Nowak was yet to mention her father, or the business at hand. 'I am surprised they sent a woman to such an important meeting,' he said.

'Do you consider women to be less capable than men?' she asked.

'Me? No, I do not. But your men do,' he said.

Jia pulled the notebook towards her and opened it. She traced her finger down the seam, pushing the pages flat. 'I think... Mr Nowak, that there has been a misunderstanding...'

'In that case, please do clarify, Ms Khan.'

'My brother is young and headstrong,' she began. 'He doesn't always understand our ways —'

Nowak held up his hand to stop her.

'You sadden me, Ms Khan. Your brother was caught trying to steal from me,' he said. 'I would not call that a misunderstanding, would you?' He had gauged that Akbar Khan's daughter was sharp and astute, but most of all she was patient. She knew when to listen. He liked that, and he hoped she would prove worthy of his time. He was tired of the common criminal. They were boring, too easy to manipulate, easily triggered, with little self-control.

Life was a game to Andrzej Nowak – he liked attention, he liked winning – but a game was only fun when one's adversary was worthy. Charm flashed across his face, and he sighed deeply. 'I had hoped for a smarter response from the daughter of the mighty Khan. Perhaps you've been sent to negotiate with me on more…intimate terms?' His eyes fixed on her. She could feel them boring holes into her.

He began removing his tie, sliding it from his collar, and then folding it once, twice, three times. He placed it on the wooden table close to where Jia was sitting. Then he unhooked the brown leather belt he was wearing and pulled at the strap, each of his movements slow and deliberate. Jia glanced around the room: there was one exit and Nowak was sitting between her and the door.

'What do you say, Ms Khan?' he said, leaning in towards her, the stale smell of coffee on his breath making her sick. Alone with a man who was feared by many, she could see where his power lay. Andrzej Nowak was a man of no honour, the kind of man who brought a grenade to a knife fight. He cared for nothing but the win. And even that mattered little. She realised that she was his opposite.

Her words came calmly, slowly, decisively. 'I say that the misunderstanding, Mr Nowak, is your calling me here, and holding my brother hostage in order to negotiate a deal. I understand your grievance, but my father's business associates are not so sympathetic. They think you killed him.'

A cold smile spread across Nowak's face. 'Your father's colleagues must be upset,' he said, relishing the moment.

'As you already know, I am not involved in the business of my family. I won't disrespect you and pretend that they have not asked me to take over from my father. They have. But I have declined. I want my brother, that is all. After that, the city is yours.'

Nowak leaned back. 'That is a shame. I like you, Ms Khan. You're an intelligent woman and I can tell that you have an inquisitive mind. I was hoping we could spend some time getting to know each other but I see now that you are not inclined that way. Truthfully, I'm disappointed to hear that you're prepared to hand the great Khan empire over so readily.'

'Really? Why?' Jia said.

'Because, Ms Khan – and I feel you of all people should be able to understand my predicament – I'm bored. This life of privilege that you and I have lived, it's dull. I envy ordinary folk, and their daily need to wake up and go into the world and make something of themselves. No one ever wanted anything of me. It's hard watching the ants go about their business. You understand that, I can tell. I start thinking I've met an equal, I plan, I wait, and then they disappoint me. It's always the way. I need distraction.'

His face broke into another smile and Jia noticed that one of his teeth was cracked and yellowing, his face lined like the contours on a map. How had she not seen it before? She recognised exactly what he was; she had come face to face with his kind in court countless times. She leaned back in her chair, grateful for the cashmere cardigan she had picked up before she left: his words had chilled her to the bone.

'My brother, Mr Nowak,' she said. 'That is all I am here to talk about.'

'Just like a woman, thinking always of her family. Come, then, I will take you to him. He is in our guest quarters,' he said, rising. 'This way.' He pointed to the back of the restaurant.

Jia got up and signalled to Michael, who was standing out the front by the car. He entered and they followed Nowak across the dining area to the back door, which opened on to a cobbled alleyway.

Nowak led them along the alleyway and on towards a dark archway, where two of his men were waiting. He stopped by a discreet wooden door recessed into the wall of the arch and turned the cast iron handle. It creaked opened slowly to reveal steps going down.

'Ladies first,' said Nowak and waited for Jia.

She looked into the stairwell, cold air and the smell of iron and petrol wafting up from it. It occurred to her that this could be a trap. She turned to Michael, who understood immediately. Without hesitation, he descended the clanging metal staircase. There was a thud as his boots hit the ground below – and then silence. It felt like an age before he called up, 'OK.' She followed him down.

They found themselves in an underground car park, the only light coming from the stairwell behind them and a ramp at one end of the long basement.

Nowak gave a shout and somewhere in the darkness an engine began to roar. The noise was followed by the bright beam of headlights flooding the room, and Jia raised her hand against the glare. Through squinting eyes she made out five heavy black Range Rovers, and sitting on the ground in front of them, the outline of her brother. He was holding his hand in front of his face to shield his eyes from the light. She heard Michael's gasp before she could see for herself, but as her eyes came into focus and she stepped closer to her baby brother, all feeling left her limbs.

Marks from tyre treads were embedded into the right side of his face. His black hair, usually straight and gelled back, was caked in congealed black blood. Lacerations ran across his cheeks, and his eyes – his beautiful brown, soulful eyes – were swollen to the size of small plums.

Nowak laughed, soaking up Jia's shock and horror. His entire body twitched with anticipation of her anguish. But she didn't flinch.

She just stood there silently, loyal to the tendrils of cold hatred that were spreading deeper within her. Insidious, slow and powerful, they wrapped themselves around her legs and feet, driving deep into the ground, rooting her and strengthening her will to kill him. It was an intoxicating sensation; she had felt it fleetingly once before. This time it was stronger, purer, more sustained. There was no denying her destiny. There was nothing left to fear. It was everyone else who should be afraid.

She glanced down at her right hand and noted its paleness. She flexed and clenched it into a fist to bring the blood flow back. She spoke the words, 'Michael, bring the car,' her voice steady and distant. Michael hurried away up the ramp.

From the corner of her eye she could see Nowak's face fixed in its cruelty, and she knew he was waiting for an outpouring of rage. In his position she would have done the same. She turned to face him, taking him in, piece by piece. 'Thank you for your hospitality,' she said. 'You have been most gracious.' There was no trace of irony, just simple words strung together, and with them she robbed Nowak of his victory.

She saw his eyes flash and narrow, and the vein in his neck throbbed until almost blue. This momentary lack of composure was enough to prove to Jia that she'd rattled him. 'Let us conclude our business now, Mr Nowak, as agreed,' she said, holding up the box of mithai she had brought with her.

Her coolness snapped Nowak back. 'As agreed,' he repeated. 'Fly back to your nest. Make sure the others understand that this is our territory – and we will not steal your young.'

'That is not my business. I am taking my brother and leaving. Here is what you asked for.' She handed him the box. He took it and placed it on the bonnet of one of the cars, then pulled a pocket knife from inside his jacket and flicked it open with well-practised ease. He slid the blade along the seal, before passing the box to his associates, who began carefully lifting out the wads of purple notes it held.

'You understand I need to check the amount?' he said.

She nodded. Silently, the men counted. Jia waited, watching the money pile up on the bonnet. The air, heavy with the smell of engine oil and metal, made it difficult to breathe, and she felt her head becoming opaque. The men continued to count. From the corner of her eye Jia could see her brother. The blood pounded in her ears and a metallic taste filled her mouth. She just needed to hold on a little longer.

She was grateful when the screeching of tyres on the ramp broke the silence, signalling Michael's return. But the sound sent Benyamin crumpling to the floor, whimpering, his arms covering his head as he lay there in a heap. It took all the self-control she had not to rush forward and gather him up in her arms. But she knew she could not show Nowak any sign of weakness, and this made the rage in her rise further. She called it forth from deep inside her soul and held on to it, feeding off it, one eye on her brother and the other on the men slowly counting the money.

When the men gave Nowak the nod, Jia went over to Benyamin and pulled his arm around her. With Michael's help, she led him to their car and lowered him into the back seat, closing the door firmly after him. With her brother safe, she took a deep breath and glanced down at the apple twig in her hand.

'You've got this,' Maria had told her on the doorstep of Pukhtun House.

'I know.'

'Remember that gruesome book of Pukhtun tales we smuggled in from the One World Bookshop?'

Jia had cast her mind back and remembered a yellow hardback book with strange pictures. Maria went on to remind her what they'd read in it, of wartime executions, prisoners pegged out, their jaws forced wide open as wronged women urinated in their mouths repeatedly until death overcame them. And of the women who carried out castrations, beheadings and 'death by a thousand cuts'.

Maria's words were matter-of-fact, as though relaying an oft-used recipe passed down through generations.

'They would slice the man open,' she'd reminded Jia, 'and then push grass and thorns into his wounds. And they were no kinder to their own men, punishing a cheating husband by forcing thick and thorned twigs down his penis. Why do you think our father never strayed? Sometimes they would just tear a man's tongue out by the roots after gang-raping him. I'm not trying to say we are barbarians; the British were no better. They flayed and filleted our people. But war for us is an honourable pursuit. We nurture it within us, and each generation proves its worth through it. And, of course, our wars are ruthless. No mercy is shown and none is expected. We don't take prisoners. If this man Nowak was to be captured by the Jirga, he could expect not only to be killed, but to be carved up and quartered before having his cock cut off and stuffed in his mouth for good measure.'

Jia didn't know if it was Maria Khan's stories or her support that had strengthened her. But she'd left for the meeting filled with a confidence that made her care little about proving her worth to Andrzej Nowak.

Now, though, with her brother safely in the back of the car, Jia couldn't resist, the way a cat can't resist a mouse. Drawing herself up, she turned and looked at Nowak, her eyes as cold and steeled as his, and she said to him, 'Have you heard of execution by golden shower?' He flinched, and she pounced. 'It was carried out by Pathan women on prisoners of war. I hadn't thought about it until this morning when my people reminded me. But there's no need for you to worry. These are civilised times, and as you mentioned earlier, in today's world our women are controlled by men – and by that token I have no power and can do nothing other than take my brother and leave. If, however, by some chance I did have power and the might of my people behind me, you should know that you have shown my brother more mercy than I would show you. There is also the matter of my father's death.'

Nowak was suddenly unsure of his course of action. Something in Jia's voice unnerved him. 'I didn't have anything to do with your father's death,' he began, but he stopped himself. He knew she wasn't interested in his denial.

Nowak was a man who had seen conflict of many kinds; he had sought it out and studied it and buried himself in it to the point where he had become practically fearless. But even he knew there were men and women in the world against whom you could never win. And there was something in Jia's voice that day that reminded him of that. He had heard it before in men with no will to live, in kamikazes and jihadis.

CHAPTER 25

Her face unflinching, Jia buckled her seatbelt. 'Let's go,' she said to Michael. He drove out of the dark basement and turned into the street, the soft hum of the car's heating system tempering the silence. It was only when they reached the edge of the city that Jia exhaled. She leaned across the back seat and gently wiped her brother's brow. She tasted iron on her lips when she kissed his forehead. He whimpered, his eyes closed, and she took him in her arms, pressing him into her, trying to absorb his pain, as she had done when they were children. 'I've got you,' she said. A myriad of thoughts ran through her head; she pushed them down. Leaning forward she put her hand on Michael's shoulder. 'Drive for a few streets and then stop the car somewhere quiet,' she told him.

He did as she asked. Turning into a small backstreet, he stopped outside the Ali Baba Fabric Shop. The metal shutters were coming down, evening was falling and the owner, Wasim, was closing up for the day. He turned to see who had pulled up as Jia got out of the car. She looked left and right. The street was empty except for Wasim and a group of boys playing football at the end of the cul-de-sac. Wasim rushed forward to greet her, just as she threw up all over his shoes. 'Water, I need water,' she said, wiping her mouth.

The fabric merchant looked from Jia to his shoes and then back to Jia. She opened the door to where Benyamin was doubled over and Wasim's eyes widened, a slow realisation crossing his face. He ran to his car and began fumbling around in the boot, returning with a plastic bottle and a bag of dates. He placed them in Jia's hands. 'This is all I have. It's Aab-ae-Zamzam,' he said. 'My parents have just come back from Umrah.'

Jia took a long swig from the bottle then wiped her mouth with the back of her hand. She felt better but didn't know whether it was the holy water or just the action of throwing up that had eased the knot in her stomach. What she did know was that she would not find loyalty like this anywhere but here. 'I won't forget your help, Wasim,' she said.

'No worries. It's only water! You could've got that at Tesco,' he replied. Then his face turned solemn. 'We are here for the daughter of Akbar Khan in any way you may need.' That he knew who she was, didn't surprise her: she had been recognised as the daughter of Akbar Khan in this city her entire life. That someone like him held her father, a criminal kingpin, in such high esteem always took her aback. But this was a city of contradictions; nothing was black and white and no one's loyalties were straightforward.

She handed the water and dates to Michael. 'Here... I'll take over the driving now. With your medical training you'll be able to take better care of Ben than I can. Do what you can until we get home. I'll call Malik when we get there,' she said, taking the keys from his hand. He did as she asked. Once in the back of the car he put the water bottle to Benyamin's lips, and the boy gulped fast, almost choking. Pouring some of the holy water on to his scarf, Michael began wiping his wounds.

As she drove through the streets of Hanover Green, Jia caught sight of her brother in the rear-view mirror. He winced in pain and she couldn't help but blame her father for it. 'Day in, day out, my father dealt with these people, wallowed in their crap. What the fuck was he thinking?' she said bitterly. 'And what the fuck am I doing cleaning up his shit?'

In the time that Michael had been with the Khan, he had seen him for what he was. He couldn't stay silent. 'You think your father was a demon, and there are plenty of folk ready to agree with you, but what do they know about struggling and climbing out of the gutter? Akbar Khan kept the devil from the door for a lot of us. Without sinners, there aren't saints. If you want to help good people, you have to learn to be bad. Because that's what it takes in this world.'

Her eyes on the road, her hands on the steering wheel, Jia held her tongue until they got to Pukhtun House. Sanam Khan was already at the door, waiting anxiously. She moved aside as Michael carried Benyamin in, then hurried after them with Arabic words, Maria close behind with water and bandages. Placing the patient on the sofa, Michael carefully began cleaning his wounds. The cuts were deep, the bruises thick. He was worried about internal bleeds and concerned he didn't know enough to prevent further complications. 'We need to get him to a hospital,' he said.

'Jia...' Benyamin reached out for his sister. She took his hand in hers, kneeling beside him.

'No hospitals,' she said. 'They'll ask too many questions and we can't be dealing with the police right now. Do what you can for him and let me figure something out. Benny, I'm just going to get changed and I'll be right back, OK? Mama is here with you, and Maria will get you whatever you need.'

She transferred his hand gently to their mother's. Jia would spend the night by his side, watching over Benyamin as he slept, ready to fetch painkillers and water every time he stirred, but for now she had things to attend to. She left the room, closing the door behind her. Her head was spinning. She looked at her phone: another missed call from Elyas. He'd left a voicemail. She deleted it without listening. She couldn't hear his voice right now; she wouldn't be able to think straight. She'd call him later.

She scrolled through her contacts for Malik's number. Her cousin was a qualified doctor. 'I need you to come over, now,' she told him. 'He's in a bad way. He needs to be in hospital but I can't take that risk.'

She hung up the phone and turned around to find Bazigh Khan standing at the door, his face awash with concern. Even killers and criminals worried about their kin. 'He is hurt badly?' he asked.

Jia nodded. 'Malik is coming.' She leaned against the wall, exhausted. 'Is it always this hard, Lala?' She looked small, but he knew better than to underestimate her.

'Yes,' he said, taking her in a fatherly bear hug. 'It is. You must eat, and then we must get on with business. The chief of police is here. He pulled up outside just as I was coming in the door. He says he has been calling since the day your father died. I have asked him to wait in the study.'

Jia looked surprised. 'He's come to see me? Do you know what he wants?'

'Maybe he wants to offer his condolences. I always thought these Angrez sent cards, but maybe our ways are rubbing off on them, eh?'

'Maybe,' Jia said, 'but I doubt it. And I'm sure you know more than you are letting on.'

The way the policeman sat in the chair, unapologetic, with his arm sprawled over one side, irked Jia. His voice, nasal and patronising, did not help matters. 'Ms Khan…I have a dead white bouncer, severely injured white revellers and an eighteen-year-old girl, also white, who may never walk again thanks to these two thugs. You must know something.'

The last words were spat out; he could see that her mind was elsewhere. Reeling from her meeting with Nowak and the damage he and his men had inflicted on her brother, the thoughts running through her head were not pleasant. The problems of one chief of police didn't figure high on her agenda. But she tried to feign interest, her eyes on his lips as he repeatedly uttered the word 'white', his mouth stretching so wide it almost split his cheeks. His face was flushed as though he'd been drinking and Jia wondered if the job was a little too much for him. His annoyance at the situation was apparent. He wasn't used to having to chase people to get back to him and she had inconvenienced him by making it necessary to seek her out in person.

'Eyewitnesses describe these thugs as anywhere between five foot eight and six foot, with brown hair and – wait for it – Asian. They took it into their hands to exact mindless revenge in my city, a city that is already at boiling point, and being watched by outsiders, right-wing groups ready to rip it open again and drag its intestines out on to the streets to chants of racial hatred!'

'I understand, but what can I do? We're preparing for a funeral here,' Jia said. She was tired of listening to the sound of his voice.

'I know, Ms Khan, and I am sorry for your loss.' Briscoe's voice suddenly became practised, as if reading from a script. 'We are doing all we can to find out who was responsible. But we could do with your help in return...'

'Are there any leads on my father's death?' Jia said, substituting his request with her own.

'Not yet. We're working our way through the information. But as you know, your father had many enemies...' His eyebrows furrowed as he spoke, and his eyes disappeared further into his face.

Jia bristled at his words. 'I'm sure, Chief Constable, that in your line of work you also have many enemies. If you met an untimely death, would you expect to be treated with less respect?'

The policeman looked disappointed. 'I am not here to mark territory, Ms Khan. I don't think you understand the severity of the situation. Look, I love this town, but she is not like other cities. This is not a melting pot, it's a pressure cooker. And unless you help me we will have a riot on our hands of unprecedented proportions!'

'And how should I do that?' Jia asked.

Briscoe sat back in his chair. Her lack of emotion vexed him. He was no stranger to bending the law, knowing that there were times when ethics had to be put aside for the greater good, but this privileged brown woman was beneath him, and asking for her help was akin to walking on ground-up glass. But he had little choice in the matter: the order had come from above. The police and crime commissioner himself had called him to a private meeting.

'By calling in your father's…associates,' he said. 'The Jury, the Jirga. And by telling them to control the streets. They have done it before. They have been doing it for years. Why can't they do it now?'

Up until that moment, Jia had assumed that the Establishment regarded the Jirga as a myth; that it was known about and actually worked in conjunction with Yorkshire's police forces took her by surprise. She hadn't realised how far her father's network had spread. She decided it would be unwise to let Briscoe know this. 'Allow people to underestimate you,' Akbar Khan had advised her. 'Sabar and salaat. Sabar and salaat – see how "patience" is mentioned before "prayer"?'

'My father is dead,' she said to the police chief. 'And here you are, asking my family to do the job you are paid for? We are an ordinary family, sir. I'm not sure what influence you think we have –'

'Ordinary, my arse!' he snapped. 'Just because I can't do anything about the Jirga doesn't mean I'm blind to its existence!' His anger was obvious now, but he hadn't risen to his position without the necessary skills, and he quickly pulled his temper back. 'Look,' he began, 'I know you're a good woman. You're a smart, sensible, successful woman…'

'Patronising me won't help any,' she said.

'I'm sorry,' he said quickly. 'This thing is out of control, though. And there are enough brown kids in jail from the last time the situation boiled over. They're only just picking up the pieces of their lives.' He paused, thinking he was fighting a losing battle, and slumped back in his seat. 'My son-in-law, he's one of you. I have no issue with your people. Hell, my grandkids aren't two shades from you!'

His words had little effect on her. 'Mr Briscoe…Chief Constable, I'm afraid I have another meeting to attend, so if you'll excuse me.' She stood up to show him to the door. He sighed, almost relieved that it was over. He could tell his daughter that he had done his best.

Bazigh Khan escorted Briscoe out. As he opened the front door, the police chief turned to him. 'We've known each other a long time, you and I,' he said. 'Your brother's death… It's obviously very early on in our investigations, but our forensics experts have pointed to the possibility that Akbar Khan knew his killer. I know that's not rare in your business. But the way he was found, and the lack of bruising or signs of physical restraint, suggest he had no warning of the threat, and that could be because he trusted whoever killed him.'

The butcher didn't flinch. He put his hand on the policeman's shoulder. 'Come, let me walk you to your car,' he said.

But as Briscoe went to get in car, Bazigh Khan stepped forward, holding the door firmly shut. 'I'd like you to keep that information between the two of us. Do you understand?' he said, fixing the police chief with his gaze. Briscoe nodded. 'I need you to say the words,' said Bazigh Khan. 'The way you did when I helped out your son.'

The mention of Timothy and a long-forgotten deal with the Khan family left Briscoe cold. 'Mr Khan, I promise to do what I can for as long as I can,' he stammered. 'But I can't guarantee anything. It will come out sooner or later.' Bazigh Khan nodded and stepped back, allowing him to open the car door.

CHAPTER 26

Jia pressed the small key into the large iron padlock. It jarred slightly and then clinked open. She unhooked it and put it to one side before lifting the lid of the wooden trunk. Everything inside was still neatly wrapped and labelled, just as she'd left it. She picked up the package marked 'Ahad' and unwrapped the tissue, pulling out a small blue blanket. It was brighter than she remembered, a midnight blue with pale stars all across it. It had been a gift from her father to Ahad on the day he was born. She couldn't help but bring it to her cheek, the scent and softness of it evoking long-forgotten feelings. She hadn't been in the attic of her dead father's house for years, and the sight and smell of it brought on a wave of emotion that hit her hard and fast, bringing with it memories she'd rather not recall. Immense and intense feelings towards her son overwhelmed her and the tears came. Slow at first and then faster, they streamed down her face, over her cheeks, her lips, and she let them fall to the ground. For the first time since his birth, she mourned the little boy she had lost. She wept for the childhood years she had missed, and the teenage angst she was part of. This outpouring of grief was precisely what she'd been desperate to avoid all those years ago when she'd attempted the unspeakable.

She heard footsteps coming up the stairs and quickly wiped her face as her mother entered the room.

'My child,' she said. 'What are you doing here?'

'Nothing, Mama,' replied Jia, turning away. 'I was just looking for something. I'll be down in a moment.'

Sanam Khan took her daughter by the shoulders and turned her towards herself. 'You can't hide your pain from me,' she said.

Jia smiled wearily. 'I'm tired of fighting,' she said. 'I don't sleep any more, not since I left this house. They make you weak…children, don't they?'

'Is that why you did what you did?' said Sanam Khan. Jia flinched. The question had taken fifteen years to reach Sanam Khan's lips. 'You were wrong then and you are wrong now, my child.' She paused. 'You gave me reasons to be strong. Reasons to fight for a better life, to fight my fears, to fight your father.' She smiled at the memories of her husband, Akbar Khan, gentle at the birth of his daughters, proud at the birth of his sons, watching with concern the day Jia learnt to walk, quietly bereft at Zan's funeral. Then the smile left her. 'It is fear of our children suffering that makes us weak, but the desire to protect them that makes us strong.'

'I don't know how to be his mother,' said Jia.

Sanam Khan brushed the words away as if they were flecks of dust on her shirt. 'Of course you do. You are my daughter. I know what you are capable of.'

'But this pain inside me,' Jia said. 'I am ashamed.'

Sanam Khan took her daughter by the shoulders again. 'You should be ashamed, but only because you are stronger than this. Listen to me. Tears are considered a sign of weakness in the world of men but they are not. They are the water that feeds our soul and keeps our roots strong.' She wiped her daughter's eyes with her chador. 'This fear and these tears,' she said, 'will keep you human, keep you close to Allah, His people and His mercy. Shed them, wipe them and begin again. But remember this: show them to no one but your mother, because no one will understand, and people will try and use them against you. "*Inna lillaahi wa inna ilayhi raaji'oon*,"' she said, and with that declaration of submission to the will of the Lord, she closed the matter, taking her daughter by the hand and leading her out of the room of memories and regret.

At the bottom of the stairs, though, she stopped. 'Trust your blood, Jia. Tell him the truth,' she said. 'And make peace with your husband. You will need him.' And with that, she left to prepare to bury her husband.

CHAPTER 27

A low, respectful hum surrounded Pukhtun House. The sky was cloudless, the day cold and crisp. The third day of mourning had begun. Yesterday's trickle had turned into a torrent as people began to pour in to pay their respects. The news had travelled fast and the Pukhtun tabar had descended swiftly to help with the practicalities of an Islamic funeral.

The tabar was extended family – the tribe. It was allied and divided into groups called 'zai' along lines of blood, cooperation, business and conflict. The complicated nature of these lines meant members often belonged to more than one zai. But the only man who belonged to all was their Khan: he was the one man for whom they dissolved old feuds and put aside bad blood and stood united. The death of the Khan required that they come together to mourn him. It was tradition, and it was in tradition that their power lay.

Bazigh Khan's sons were in charge of overseeing the funeral. The younger members of the tabar had arrived at the first sign of light, and were going about their business like worker bees.

Dressed in white, Idris Khan moved from room to room, organising the house and household. Furniture had been removed and the floors were cleaned, ready to be covered in white cotton sheets. Wasim, the fabric merchant, was responsible for them. His mother and wife cried silent tears as they embraced the Khan's widow, handing her the neatly pressed sheets they had spent all night hemming. Sanam Khan took them with gratitude before ushering them into the room where women were sitting in remembrance of their God and His servant.

She was reading verses of the Quran and wiping her tears from its pages, when Benyamin came to collect her. They were to see Akbar Khan for the last time.

Across the city, the Jirga were arriving at the morgue to participate in the most important ritual in a Muslim's life: that of his burial. Formally dressed, some in shalwar kameez and others in Western suits, each man's head was covered by a small white cap or Afghan topi, of the kind worn during prayer.

They shook hands and embraced, their emotions deep and bubbling over, the elders wiping away tears of regret and fear, as much as of sorrow. The ghusl, the ritual bathing of the body, was a reminder of the transient nature of life. Intimate and poignant, only the trusted were asked to take part. It was, therefore, a great honour and a reinforcement of each man's place in the family to be here.

The smell of camphor and disinfectant filled the air. Akbar Khan's cold corpse lay on a steel table in the centre of the white wet room, ready to be cleansed and then placed in the ground. The imam waited by the door. He knew the Pukhtun tabar was an emotional tribe and he warned them that the soul of Akbar Khan was still present. 'It will remain connected to the earth for forty days. So, please, keep your anguish under control.'

The men nodded respectfully. Though young, the imam had proved himself to be worthy. By day he was a lawyer, working at the world's largest legal firm and navigating the laws of the land. By night he helped believers understand and follow the laws of Allah. The two sides of his life stood him in good stead with all generations of the family. He was an honourable man.

When Sanam Khan arrived, she stood at her husband's side, one hand on Benyamin's shoulder, the other on the back of the chair that had been brought for him to sit on. As the wife of the deceased, she was the only woman allowed to participate in the final rites.

A shroud lay loosely over Akbar Khan's body. He would never pray again; his spiritual accounts were complete and ready to be submitted. But his men could ask on his behalf, and they called upon their Maker to forgive their old friend and leader. Seeing him lying there, empty of his soul, brought a strange calm upon them, and as the solemnity of the ritual came to a close their eyes dried with the drying of his body. Camphor was sprinkled on three large pieces of white cotton, once, twice, thrice. The men stepped back and professed their faith: '*La illah illallah, Muhammadur rasool Allah.*' As the cloth was brought forward and the kafan wrapped around the man who had terrified generations, he looked like any other corpse about to be lowered into a grave.

By noon the steady stream of visitors to the house had become a river. What had begun as hundreds grew to thousands. The streets around the family home and the mosque filled with parked and queuing cars.

The women wiped their tears with their chadors as they prayed, their heads covered and bowed. Young and old sat side by side, some veiled, others not, safe in the knowledge that the house of Khan held no judgement in matters of faith.

Jia stood by the front door, greeting the visitors as they arrived, Maria leaning on her, her hennaed hands clutching her chador as she tried to muffle her cries.

The Jirga had left the morgue and would be arriving shortly. Afraid that the sight of the casket would overwhelm her, Jia asked her sister to see to the mourners inside.

Sher Khan was the first of Akbar Khan's business associates to arrive. Two tall men stood either side of him. They had been working closely with Idris all morning. 'Jia Khan, our prayers are with you,' he said, and then, introducing the two men, 'My sons, Razi and Raza. My daughters and wife have been here since Fajr.'

'Yes, Khan Baba. My family is grateful to your family,' Jia said. It had been a long time since she'd been thankful for the support of her own people.

Sher Khan and his sons took their place with the mourners, waiting where the casket was to be brought. They were followed by an elderly man slowly navigating the stone steps of the house. When the man stumbled, a young woman with him reached out a hand to assist, but he knocked it back. Seeing Jia in the doorway seemed to give him the momentum he needed. His pace quickened and he eagerly placed his palm on her head upon greeting her, speaking in a dialect of Pashto she could not understand. Taking his hand in hers, she tried to thank him in a mix of English and the dialect of her family. The old man replied, tears in his eyes, and Jia looked to the young woman beside him for an explanation.

'He is saying he owes a great debt to your family,' said the young woman. 'We are from your grandfather's village in Afghanistan. Your father's people, they helped us when we were in troubled times. We were one of many families who were captured by warlords. Your father helped us escape and brought us here. He looked after us. There were twenty families that he saved, good families, educated families, who had lost everything. But thanks to him we have rebuilt our lives. Thanks to your father, may God rest his soul, I am now able to support us, and my cousins, too, are educated professionals.'

In all the years that Jia had spent at her father's house, he had remained tight-lipped about those he helped. The stories of the families, and the work that he had done to give them a life, were secrets he had taken to his grave.

The young woman's words left Jia reconsidering her own experience of her father – of the small ways in which he had showered her friends with kindness, of the gifts he had bought them, knowing what each of them liked and disliked, winking at her as he handed them out – and she melted a little.

'I work at the Akbar Khan refugee centre on weekends,' the young woman said. 'I would love you to visit and see how we plan to continue your father's work.'

Jia smiled at the old man, still holding his hands in hers.

'We will never forget this debt. Our lives are your lives,' he said, this time in a language she understood. He stopped, and kissed the palms of her hands, his display of gratitude embarrassing her. She would need to learn to handle such things better if she was to stay.

By afternoon the city had come to a standstill. Mourners lined the streets around Pukhtun House and police officers were out in force.

The coffin was placed in the living room, ready for each visitor to pay their respects. When it was time for the Janaza prayer, the men lined up facing the casket, the imam beside it. He placed his iPad on the pulpit, open at the final draft of his sermon.

'When God commanded the angels to bow before Adam, Satan in his arrogance refused, and with that refusal he declared war upon mankind. Our souls are both the prize and the battleground. The complexities of life, the choices we make daily, are part of this fight. As warriors, we are grateful that only God knows the intention of man, and that only He will judge us.' He paused and looked at the faces of the mourners, knowing that he could never gauge their hearts.

He cleared his throat and spoke again. 'Many will ask what this city finds to honour in this man. Many will turn away, because to them he is not a man but a monster, and an enemy of the law. They will say that he brought evil and hate to our daily struggle. But we will answer them: did you ever talk to Akbar Khan? For if you did, you would know why we must honour him. Akbar Khan restored our self-respect and gave us dignity. This was his meaning to his people. And in honouring him, we honour the best in ourselves. Come, let us stand for prayer.'

Some shaken, some silenced, the men took their places, each one facing the direction of the qiblah, the imam leading them, Akbar

Khan before him. The rows of men had been painstakingly counted: odd numbers were considered pleasing to Allah and blessed for the deceased. The women stood behind the menfolk, their chadors pulled over their bosoms. They shuffled closer together.

A hush fell across the building and its grounds at the first takbir: *'Allahu Akbar!'* The Janaza prayer had begun. The congregants spilled out into the garden, across the lawn and into the streets surrounding the house, standing shoulder to shoulder. At the fourth cry of the takbir they turned their faces right and then left, re-entering the world of material things. It was time to bury the dead.

'Stay with me, child, I need you here,' Sanam Khan said to Maria, holding her back from the funeral car as Jia took her seat. She knew she could not stop Jia accompanying her father's body to the cemetery, and so she pressed her lips tight on that matter, but she did not want both her daughters breaking tradition and the rules that Muslims had followed for centuries. 'Let the men bear this burden,' she said. 'They do what they want their whole lives. They must face the consequences of their actions alone.' Jia was still within earshot, and couldn't help but wonder if the words were directed at her.

The funeral procession made its way slowly through the streets that Akbar Khan had been the talk of for so many years. Her father's men walked the distance from the house to the cemetery, as a mark of respect, the casket on their shoulders. Jia was in the first car behind them. The drive felt longer than any she had ever taken and her heart was a storm of emotions. As she tried to brush aside her thoughts and consider what her father would have done in her place, the heavens opened. Akbar Khan had loved the rain, often standing by the window, watching it soak the ground, listening to its rhythm. Jia wondered if this was a sign. Rain was a mercy but also a punishment. Armies of angels descended to take the souls of the good, but who would be coming for the Khan?

As the car turned into the cemetery, Jia spotted the elderly man she had met at the house among the crowd. The pull of his Khan had been too strong. Row upon row of black umbrellas, suits and shalwars spilled through the cemetery gate and ended at the plot where Akbar Khan was to be buried.

The cars stopped by the waiting Jirga. Their Khan would have to face his Lord alone but they would go as far as possible on the journey with him.

Michael helped Jia out of the car. She was the only woman in attendance. Muslim men buried their dead, because women were considered too emotional to witness the event. Coming from a race that was hot-headed, whose men were known for holding grudges, and being rash in their actions, the irony of this was not lost on Jia.

Still not strong enough to walk far unassisted, Benyamin was helped to his place by Bazigh Khan. He stood beside his sister as their cousins carried the coffin to its final resting place. Jia reached out to take his hand. Akbar Khan had been the shoulder that others looked to lean upon; today he was on the shoulders of others, and even his son could not help him.

The siblings watched silently as the coffin was lowered into the ground, each outwardly controlled, each aware that they would be leaving their father alone in that pit. Neither had feared for him until this moment. They hadn't yet found an opportunity to speak properly about the events that had brought them to this point. Standing in a sea of men, still aching from his injuries, Benyamin felt awkward holding his sister's hand, leaning on a woman for help. He let go of her, and she barely seemed to notice.

One by one, the members of the Jirga stepped forward, deepening Jia's sense of loss with each handful of soil cast into the grave. Distanced from the hearts and hearths of Pukhtuns for years, the warmth of their love was evident to her now. It enveloped her. Unable to weep, she stared at the ground, and emotions she had long since buried began to rise. The umbrellas did little to stop the rain, and her white kurta and shawl soaked through, clinging to her body. Cold and shivering, she was acutely aware of her every move; every inch of her felt pain, from her skin through to her bone. Mourners filed past, paying their respects, their feet splashing mud from the water-soaked ground, leaving dark stains across her shawl and kameez and her soul, stains that would never be cleansed.

CHAPTER 28

The men stepped back and raised their hands in prayer one last time. The sounds of crying and muffled Arabic seemed to get louder before the imam finally called out: 'Ameen!'

Jia passed her hands over her face and opened her eyes. The rain made it difficult to see clearly but she knew she was being watched. The boy's features were familiar, and as he began walking towards her she knew the time for reckoning was here.

'Ahad, my name is Ahad,' he said, holding out his broad, olive-skinned hand.

'I know,' she whispered as she took it in hers. The last time she had held it, it had fitted snugly in her own palm; now it was large enough to envelope hers.

'Why didn't you come and see me?' the boy asked. They had moved away from the graveside and were standing under a tree, waiting for Elyas. He had left them alone under the pretence of bringing the car closer. The burial was done and the mourners were returning to Pukhtun House.

It was Jia who had asked Elyas to bring Ahad to the funeral and now she wondered why she'd done it. The timing was not perfect, but then when would it ever be? At least the rain had stopped now.

'I thought you were dead,' she said. Her voice was empty, her glance anywhere but on her son, as though an anvil had fallen inside her, pushing all feeling deep into the ground.

She felt Ahad's eyes examining her, hoping, no doubt, for some shred of understanding, remorse, something, anything. He must have wondered why she wouldn't look at him. She couldn't; he reminded her too much of her brother. His eyes, the shape of his brow, his expressions: it was a face that conjured up Zan Khan. Ahad had inherited none of his father except his name and his need to ask questions.

'How could you not know I was alive?' he said. 'How does that even happen?'

'I just didn't,' she said. The truth was that simple and that complicated. She wanted to hold him, to soak in his smell, the way one does with a baby, but he was no longer a baby. He was almost a man, with the beginnings of facial hair, and deep-set eyes filled with troubling questions.

Ahad fell silent. He had waited so long for this moment, and here she was, his mother, as cold as the body she had buried. 'How does that even happen?' he said again, more to himself than to her.

He hadn't known his mother was missing from his life until he was four years old. It was only when he noticed his friends' mums collecting them from school that he realised he should have had a mother too. Wide-eyed and ice-cream-covered, he'd asked his father, 'Where's my mummy?' Elyas's answer was to pack up their things and move closer to his parents, hoping that his own mother's presence would make things easier. But the questions kept on coming and became more and more persistent. Elyas muddled through fatherhood, telling Ahad fantastical stories of his mother, in which she was a princess held captive by pirates or by a witch's spell, but one day they would rescue her and bring her home.

The magic soon wore thin, partly because the lies began to grate on Elyas himself, and in the end he had to promise to explain Jia's absence when the time was right. The letter from Akbar Khan had been that time. Elyas had told Ahad a little of the night Akbar Khan had arrived at his doorstep with a tiny bundle wrapped in a pale blue blanket. But not everything. So much of it was still a mystery to Elyas himself.

Akbar Khan had handed his grandson over to him. 'Name him Ahad,' he had said. 'And do not let my family, especially my daughter, know he is alive. He is of your bloodline, and by bringing him to you I am absolved of responsibility.'

Akbar Khan's face was lined; he had lost much sleep over his decision, but Elyas found it hard to have any sympathy for him. He was, after all, responsible for the demise of his marriage and the loss of so much more.

With Zan's death, something inside Jia had died too. Without word or warning, she cut off all contact with Elyas. He had called her every day, written her lengthy emails, sent her letters and texts, but she had not replied. Left without explanations and only assumptions as to what he had done to deserve such treatment, Elyas arrived at Pukhtun House but was turned away by security. He waited at the gates until darkness fell. No one came to ask after him, not even Sanam Khan, who had always been kind to him. The police were called and he'd spent the night in a cell, accused of harassment. Nothing had come of it except an official letter requesting the dissolution of the marriage. Elyas had ignored it, putting it to one side, thinking that she would reconsider. And then one day his father-in-law had arrived with a child he said was his.

Still standing in the hallway, dressed in his pyjamas, Elyas had been bewildered by what was unfolding. He looked down at the swollen but tiny baby, sucking hard on its tiny fist. He'd read somewhere that newborns resembled their fathers to give them a greater chance of surviving. It was evolution's way of confirming paternity. And sure enough, when the baby looked back at him, his warm brown eyes wide and accepting, Elyas saw his own features reflected back. He stared up at Akbar Khan for guidance, but the crime lord and kingpin, looking almost comical clutching a feeding bottle, with a baby bag swung over his shoulder and a burp cloth in his other hand, was in a hurry. The surreal situation in which he found himself meant questions were left unasked and unanswered.

Now, so many years later, waiting in a cemetery, having buried the man who created this situation, Jia was having to answer questions about her part in what played out that night. She thought back to the day her father had told her that Ahad was still alive.

He'd arrived one summer's evening last year, almost unannounced. It was late on a Friday. The last appointment. Her PA had brought him to her office, grinning, thinking she'd pulled off a raise-worthy stunt. Jia had thanked her firmly and asked her to close the door behind her.

'It's not her fault,' he'd said. 'I told her it was a surprise family reunion. You don't come to me, and I was here on business anyway, so I asked her to list the appointment under a pseudonym.'

Jia moved to take his cane, gesturing for him to sit, his smell reawakening her childhood. He looked older, his brows slightly unruly and greyer than she remembered. In another life she would have leaned over and tidied them up, then given him a kiss on his head. His lion-headed walking stick, which had always been about style and not assistance, was now necessary. 'It's about your son,' he'd said.

She'd sat back in her chair. 'I don't have a son.'

'Jia jaan.' His voice was gentle, reminding her of all the times throughout her girlhood when she'd played him for toys and books and money and he'd let her. She felt herself filling up with the sadness that she'd long tried to suppress.

The years had passed quickly but the days were often endless. Seeing families picnicking in Hyde Park, friends' holiday snaps on Facebook and tourists wandering around London together, was beginning to leave her hungry for connection with her own. It would be good to find a way forward. She had resolved to tell him that, to lay her cards on the table. She was ready to make amends, but fate had other plans.

'He is alive,' said Akbar Khan. 'He is with Elyas. I took him there.' He paused and looked at his daughter, waiting for a reaction. None came. 'You weren't well. And I thought it would be best for you and for the family.' He watched as she began rifling through papers. He'd anticipated annoyance, anger, a visceral reaction, but none came. Instead, she picked up the file she'd been searching for and walked across the room with it. Opening the door, she stepped into the walkway where her PA was working. Akbar Khan watched, knowing this to be the height of disrespect in his world, but equally aware that her anger was justified. He was afraid it was too late, that her pride would convince her to make the wrong decision. They had both lost sons, but hers, he could return. That's why he was here.

He heard her now, a little louder than before. 'Could you bring some tea?' she said to the PA. 'From across the road. That place that does chai, and something to go with it, please.' She returned to her office and closed the door.

'Forgive me,' she said to her father. 'I forgot my manners.'

The path between the said and unsaid had fallen away that day, leaving Jia unable to find her way back to her father. For her, it was the final disappointment. She would not allow it to happen again.

'Didn't you care about me at all?' Ahad said, breaking into Jia's thoughts.

'I did care. I still do,' she said.

'You don't seem to care,' Ahad said, his frustration at her coldness growing.

'I'm sorry you feel that way. I'm not devoid of feeling. Emotions run deep in my family, in many ways deeper than in others. We have learnt to control our emotions to stop them controlling us.'

Experience had taught Jia hard and long-lasting lessons, and she'd survived by cleaning the slate of whys and regrets and the left-behinds of life. But now they were reappearing, one by one, and demanding to be heard. 'You're taking my choice not to feel as a reflection of my not caring, when in fact the truth is precisely the opposite. Do you understand?' she said.

He did understand; he understood better than most. She looked across at the mourners. 'We're not like them,' she said. 'My father used to say that every herd has a master. I never really knew what he meant until now.' Jia had stopped explaining herself years ago, but something about him encouraged her to keep talking. 'I wasn't always like this. There's a story about Hazrat Ali that my father used to tell us often when we were children. During the height of one of the battles Muslims fought for their freedom, the caliph found himself standing above an enemy soldier, ready to take his life. But the man spat in his face, and so he let him go. You know why he did that?'

Ahad shook his head.

'He said that the anger that had risen up in him had clouded his judgement, and if he had killed the man he wouldn't have known whether it was for revenge or for the universal rights of mankind. It takes great strength to control one's emotions. Killing someone else is easy; killing your own ego, that's hard.'

From a distance, Elyas sat in his car and watched the two of them talking.

He still didn't know what had happened all those years ago to make her leave, and why she had decided to sever all ties with her son, or indeed if she had thought him dead for some of that time. In the days and weeks that followed Ahad's arrival, Elyas had tried to contact her again, but to no avail. Not knowing the background to the situation, and understanding Akbar Khan's manner that night to be a warning, he didn't discuss Ahad in his letters. Not that it would have mattered if he had: they were all returned unopened and his calls were unanswered.

Years later, when Ahad was older and had begun asking questions, Elyas considered contacting Jia again, but he decided against it.

Something told him it wouldn't be in the boy's best interest. Things had changed since then. Ahad had changed.

Elyas had hoped to introduce his son to his mother in better circumstances, but choice was something that life rarely offered him. He watched them walk towards him. Jia covered in the residue of the day, Ahad subdued, they wore each other's faces. He wondered now if he'd done the right thing by bringing Ahad, and what was to come of it.

CHAPTER 29

It was relatively quiet when Jia arrived at Pukhtun House. Most of the mourners had left. Those who were still there were having dinner in the marquee. It would probably remain this way until the next morning, close family trickling in and out until Fajr prayer, when the floodgates would open once again and prayer books, hats and the soft hum of Arabic verse would return.

Sanam Khan's warm embrace when Jia came in was just what she needed after the wet cemetery.

'How's Benyamin?' asked Jia.

'He went out to see some friends, although I don't know what kind of friends don't come to the funeral.'

Jia wondered when she would find time to sit down for a chat with her little brother. The chaos of circumstances, the responsibilities upon her, and Benyamin being triggered by almost everything she said, made even simple conversations difficult. She worried about him.

'You must be hungry. Let me get you something to eat,' Sanam Khan said, ushering her towards the kitchen.

'Wait, Mama, I have some guests with me.'

Sanam Khan squinted past her daughter, her eyes falling on Elyas, standing in the doorway. His hair was grey, unlike the first time he'd crossed the threshold of Pukhtun House, and by his side stood a teenage boy.

'Who is that with Elyas?' she asked. Then she stopped, a quiet realisation spreading through her. 'Ya Allah, forgive us,' she murmured, clasping her hand over her mouth, as if trying to push the words back in. She squeezed her daughter's hand and whispered, 'He looks like Zan.' Unready to meet her grandson, overcome by affection but overwhelmed by the things she knew and had seen, she moved at speed, reaching the kitchen door as he stepped into the house. It was trite, but true, that she loved him more than her own children; it was that way with grandchildren. It was why she had sent him away with Akbar Khan: she wanted him safe. She would live with the shame of that secret her entire life.

'Where's the bathroom?' Ahad asked.

Jia gestured to a room across the hall. 'We'll be in the study. It's the second door on the right,' she said.

Elyas followed Jia through the hallway, past the odd mourner and into the study. The smell of furniture polish and oranges flooded his mind with memories of the night Zan had died. This was the room he'd argued with Akbar Khan in. The oxblood chair in the corner looked a little more worn, its leather now softer and more inviting. It crossed his mind how different things could have been if he'd held his tongue, if he had left it to Jia to fight his corner. They could have raised Ahad together, Zan may still have been alive, and maybe Jia would still be the woman he'd married. The silence felt heavy. Elyas didn't know if it was the circumstances of today or the past that weighted them down, but he knew if he didn't ask now, he never would.

'What happened to us, Jia?' he said.

She looked up at him through her tired eyes and he wanted to hold her, to support her, the way he always had, smooth life over and make everything better.

'I don't know,' she said. 'I am sorry.'

He wasn't ready for the apology, but he didn't want to fight either. Time was a precious commodity, one he didn't want to squander on bitter words and accusations; but still, answers were needed. And so he measured himself.

'You didn't answer my calls, or reply to the letters I sent. I thought you blamed me for Zan.' He was afraid of what she might say but he also had to know. He tightened the lid on his need, knowing it to be futile. None of it would bring back what he really wanted, the life he had wanted with her.

'Maybe I did,' she said. The air in her lungs felt musty; it was time to speak. 'I needed time to process everything. But by the time I was ready, too much of it had passed, and for that I will always be sorry.'

'I waited for you. We waited for you...to hear from you.'

'I know. Believe me, I know what I have lost.' As if on cue, the door opened and Ahad came in. He looked oddly small, and Elyas was overcome with the desire to scoop him up and take him home, to avoid the questions and conflicts that were to come, to halt the heartbreak on this path. But they were here now, and there was no turning back.

Jia watched her son walk around his grandfather's study, stopping at a collection of photographs. He picked up a faded picture of Akbar Khan, their resemblance undeniable. The answer to so many questions had been buried today, alongside him.

While it was true that some of what he had learnt about his mother's family was difficult to accept, he respected his father's decision to tell him. Better to know your grandfather is a criminal than hear it in whispers on the day of his funeral from news crews and reporters.

Ahad's paternal family were nothing like the people he had seen at the funeral today. The pomp and circumstance of the mourning, the array of expensive cars, the over-groomed women: it was all very different to the world of his buttoned-down grandparents.

He was thinking about all this and more when he felt Jia's eyes on him. 'My grandfather says your people are cruel. He said that when they fled Afghanistan, they slaughtered their wives and children.'

Jia had readied herself for difficult questions from her son, but this was not one of them. She considered her words carefully. 'I am a proud Pukhtun, and you and I have the same blood – are you cruel?'

'Is it true?' he asked.

'Bravery requires difficult decisions. To do good for the many, one must sometimes do questionable things to the few. If your grandfather knew the Pukhtun ways he would understand why the women and their children were killed. Every action has a reason, a measured reason. If you wait long enough, time reveals it. The men believed that their womenfolk would slow them down, allowing the enemy to catch up, and death at their hands was a kinder end than what that enemy would have done to them. Life demands harsh payments and difficult decisions. Those who don't understand that, don't understand life,' she said. The conversation was intense but Jia considered it best to be honest with her son.

She was acutely aware that, despite giving birth to him, she had not had the opportunity to be his mother. She knew that the foundation parenthood is built on, the endless drudgery that proves and causes love to swell and grow, was missing between them. Their absence of history left her feeling stilted.

Ahad reflected on her words. Had his mother just lectured him? He had waited years to meet her. The way his father had described her, she was warm and gentle; but Jia did not seem to have been awaiting him with open arms. He looked across at his father, hoping to find some anchor, and Elyas responded, nodding, nudging him on to say what he had come to say.

But Ahad was frustrated by the situation, by it not being the way he wanted it to be. Years of anger, confusion and unanswered questions bubbled under his skin and stopped him from speaking.

It was Jia who finally broke the silence. 'I hear you've been in trouble with the police,' she said. 'What did you do?'

'Why does everyone think it's my fault?' he said, his anger finding an outlet. 'The bastards were picking on me for no reason!'

She looked into his eyes, eyes she'd last seen on her eldest brother the day he'd died. 'Well, we'll have to do something about that,' she said, leaning forward and touching his arm.

'You can't say things like that to him,' said Elyas.

'Like what?'

'He's a teenager and you were offering to solve his problems the way your father would have done.'

'I was just talking.'

'He's a kid. He believes everything.'

'He's nearly legally old enough to leave home or get married. I think you're being a bit overprotective.'

Elyas realised Jia hadn't been around children since she was one herself, and as a result she was ill-equipped to speak to anyone who wasn't an adult. He had expected too much of her. But her words forced him to recognise that, though he disagreed with her method, she might be right about some things. He *was* overprotective. He had told himself it was because he was doing the work of two parents, but maybe his approach had been wrong, and maybe, despite his best efforts, he had let his son down.

Although the conversation between mother and son was strange, their interaction awkward, Jia knew that there was no other way it could have played out. She knew that the strained circumstances and her reluctant honesty made it difficult for Ahad to like her, but she hoped that her trust in him and her obvious loyalty to her bloodline would go some way to calm the waters.

Her mother asked her about it later that evening, once Elyas and Ahad had left. 'A woman is incomplete without her child,' she told Jia.

'Will I ever forgive myself?' Jia replied. She thought about the things she couldn't talk openly about with her mother, the darkness that had once consumed her, and that was again knocking at the door – things they both knew but could never quite bring themselves to admit. She pushed the thoughts aside and shook her head.

'It is what mothers do, feel guilty,' said Sanam Khan.

***

On the other side of the city, Benyamin waited in his car, hiding behind its tinted windows, the night drawing in around him. The funeral had been even harder than he had anticipated. The morphine Malik had prescribed was wearing off and he knocked back a couple more tablets, followed by a glug of water. Thanks to Malik's contacts, he'd been seen last night by medics at the private hospital nearby, and received the best 'off the books' medical treatment possible. The scans had shown he'd been lucky: there was no internal damage to his organs. His face was still swollen, and his body badly bruised, but by some trick of fate, he hadn't broken any bones. He couldn't stand for long periods of time, but he'd managed the drive OK – he was glad his Beamer was an automatic.

This had always been his favourite time, sitting in the warmth of his car, encased in the velvet night. That feeling of comfort had been marred now, but he still preferred it to being at home, especially with so many people around, so much fussing and high emotion. Here he could watch the world go by from the shadows, like a film, the orange street lamps spotlighting the actors: working girls, junkies, pimps and punters. It was a place for the lonely, for the strung out, the desperate. It felt like escape.

CHAPTER 30

Two months later Nowak made his next move. 'Why would he target that building?' said Idris. 'It doesn't make sense.' Jia, Idris and Nadeem were sitting in a shisha bar across from where the bomb had exploded. The large plasma screen on the wall opposite was tuned to News 24, showing the rubble that was once a refugee centre. Plumes of smoke poured out of the old warehouse, as young and old ran out on to the street.

Jia had been nearby when it happened. The explosion had shattered glass, pulled roofs off buildings and taken walls apart brick by brick. It had cracked the road wide open. Jia and her cousins had spent hours fielding the injured. Exhausted and broken, they had retired to Pasha's shisha bar.

The images on the news kept coming. 'I know her,' said Jia, pointing at the screen. The woman from Akbar Khan's funeral, the one who had accompanied her elderly father, was standing behind the reporter. The side of her face looked raw; she was hysterical, paramedics patiently helping her into an ambulance. The chaos was a message from Nowak, a sign that there was no line he would not cross. He wanted the city and he would take it as a corpse if he had to. He'd sent Jia a text just before it happened, like an attention-seeking child, she thought, her blood boiling; he wanted everyone to look at him, talk about him, be afraid of him.

'If it wasn't for the proceeds of crime, this city would have nothing,' Idris went on angrily. 'No one cares what happens in this place. And no one's going to care about these people who come here, the refugees, people who have escaped war and persecution! So why target them?'

'I care,' said Jia. 'We care. And his fight is with us. I've seen men like him before. They don't care about anything. They don't love anything. He's targeted the most vulnerable people he can to get to us. Because he knows we do care.'

For too long, Jia had hidden herself away in her ivory tower. She had closed her eyes to the silent injustices of society, to the ease with which her white counterparts, from their own towers, passed judgement on enclaves and ghettos, a symptom of their arrogance and luck. For too long she had lived apart in a society of indifference. Now Nowak was dragging her out.

'Is Ben joining us?' asked Nadeem.

'I think he's at home,' Jia said.

'I hear he's got a new lady friend,' said Nadeem. The TV volume ramped up out of the blue and they turned to find someone had flicked to a music channel. Nadeem's words were lost in the mix.

'Any news of Malik?' said Jia.

'He's at the hospital. Says he'll join us when he can,' said Idris.

It felt good to be with the strong foundations of family. Pasha's chalky walls were built on community, and recalled those found in the generational and palatial homes of Lahore's old quarters. The smoking ban had brought Prohibition-style speakeasies to the city, where the poison on sale was not booze but tobacco. Remixed Arab-English tunes, bubbling hookahs and chatter filled the place. Pretty hijabistas sucked on hubbly-bubbly tubes as plumes of smoke rose up and permeated the air with a variety of shisha fragrances.

The cousins fell into conversation in the way that only those who live closely and share blood can, picking up strands of the past and intricately weaving them with the here and now. Jia began to remember what it felt like to be surrounded by people she'd grown up with, people who shared her values and understood her ways without explanation. The conversation was simple, easy, comfortable. The waiter handed her a glass of juice and she took a long, slow drink. She leaned in to the sugar hit and the warmth of her family, and spoke about the issues confronting them, about Nowak, the Jirga's request and the police.

As the family lawyer, Idris had known the day would come when they would need to discuss the family business openly; he had just had to bide his time. 'We've lived long enough to know that British law does not offer people who look like us justice. As members of the judiciary, we choose to live by it and implement it, but no one is going to give us our rights. Like Zan said, we have to take them.'

Jia listened, the mention of her brother tightening the knot in her heart. Before Zan had been arrested he had discussed bringing their fathers to justice, showing them the error of their ways, and then using their money and influence to improve the lives of others. They were going to call themselves the Verdict, and they were going to bring down their fathers, whom he described as 'backward and bent on destroying the fabric of society'.

Sitting here all these years later among the rubble of life, Jia saw his words for what they had been: childish idealism.

'Before I came here,' Jia said, 'I wanted to end this life of our fathers. Now...I'm not so sure.'

Malik appeared behind her. He pulled off his coat and placed it on the back of a chair. He looked exhausted. Jia handed him her juice. He took it gratefully.

'Are there still injured people coming in?' said Nadeem.

'No, we finished up a while ago, but I had another kid come in with stomach pains,' he said. 'Like Jimmy Khan's little girl last year, frightened to death she was... We found a kilo of heroin in her stomach. A kilo! The Brotherhood had her swallow seventy-nine condoms full of heroin before putting her on a flight to Manchester. If even one had burst she would have died.' He finished the juice. 'Sorry, did you want that?'

Jia shook her head and ordered another drink.

'Nothing like that ever happened under the Jirga,' Malik added. The family had enforced a strict code of honour – no child was to be harmed, the elderly were to be respected and women were allowed to choose their destiny. Decades had passed since anyone had dared cross the line. Nowak's new wave of criminals was changing all that.

Nadeem shook his head in disgust. 'Whatever the Jirga did, we knew our children were safe,' he said. 'But these new guys, they have no code, no honour. And the police can't handle them…or won't. They couldn't deal with the organised crime of our disorganised fathers, never mind these people. They're younger, more ruthless and better organised.'

'The Jirga is getting old,' said Idris. 'The last ten years have seen them losing business and getting sentimental about the old ways. They reject change, change that could benefit them and the city. They've weakened and that's what's allowed Nowak to get his foot in the door.' He paused, turning to Jia. 'Your father said he was ready to retire, wanted you to take over. I always said you were too straight, but he disagreed; he said you'd like the new projects.'

'What projects?'

Idris opened a leather notebook. 'I wanted to distance the way we do business from the family,' he said. 'Modernise it and make it more lucrative. A lot of the younger kids are tech-savvy. There's a girl called Haines, Chilli Chacha's granddaughter – she's brilliant. Tech city would snap her up but her family won't allow her to leave home until she gets married, and she's brighter than all the boys they've tried to set her up with. She's got an idea for a website… This is the age of eBay and Shopify, and yet the Jirga is still running things like a cash-and-carry corner shop!'

'What stopped you implementing any of this?' asked Jia.

'You did. I wanted you to be here, to take over. I knew you had it in you, I just didn't know if you'd follow through,' he said, watching her face closely, waiting for a reaction, a flicker of resistance. But nothing came. He was right, she had always been her father's daughter, but it was the cumulative effect of life that had brought her to this place. She could no longer sit back and ignore the equal expectations society put upon people from unequal circumstances. Seeing the blood of her people run in the city had awakened something in her. She was the Khan. She always had been. It had just been a matter of time.

'Show me,' said Jia, pointing at Idris's book. 'Show me what you think we should do.'

He handed it over and she began leafing through the pages.

'You're talking tech but staying old school?' said Malik, nodding at the pencil and notebook.

'It's easier to shred than an iPad,' Idris answered. 'And it's just reminders. Most of it is up here,' he said, tapping his head. Idris had an eidetic memory; he remembered everything. 'The old men are tired. It's time to step up and take charge, Jia. Once we are settled we can convince them to retire and bring our people out of the dark ages.'

Jia listened to Idris, his words genuine, grounded in loyalty and sound judgement. She trusted him more than she trusted anyone else. Her mother, the old man at the funeral and now Idris – they were all asking her for the same thing.

'Nowak will be planning to take out more members of the Jirga. He won't stop with Akbar Khan,' said Idris. 'He wants to throw the city into chaos before taking over the operations and then tearing them apart.'

Jia watched her cousins. They had grown up here. Their father, and hers, had worked hard to make it their own. The blood of Bazigh Khan's family had been spilled on the streets. Her brothers had offered up their innocence and their lives at the altar of Pukhtunwali. Now Nowak had decided to play with the lives of the city's children and women, as if they were worthless. Somewhere along the way, Akbar Khan had become the voice in her head: *These are not the ways of honourable men. Make them pay.*

The surge of rage she had felt when she'd collected Benyamin began to flow again, bringing images flashing through her mind: Ben's tyre-marked body, young children with heroin pouches in their intestines and Nowak's smug face. It didn't consume her, it didn't overwhelm, it renewed her. It coursed through her veins, spreading to her extremities, making her feel powerful. She formed a fist with her right hand, before letting her fingers fall loose. 'Sabar and salaat,' her father had said. Patience and prayer. The time for both was done.

'We will make them pay,' she whispered, her voice ice cold. 'I am going to do this,' she said. 'And you're going to help me. There will be no more corner-shop crime. There will be a new Jirga, and it will be run the way I say.'

Benyamin had been a few streets away when the explosion happened, Sakina in his car once again. She'd unbuttoned her burqa, and the scent of her perfume filled the car. He was pleased. She'd liked his gift. 'The usual?' she said. He nodded. His face was red but the tension in his head was beginning to subside.

'It's OK,' she said. 'Just try and relax.'

He leaned back in his seat and closed his eyes. The deliciousness of drifting into sleep swept over him as her hand moved down his arm. And that's when the blast happened, reverberating through the car and all around. Sakina gasped. 'What the hell was that?' But suddenly, Benyamin couldn't breathe. His airways constricted, the oxygen trapped and unable to pass into his lungs. His chest felt tight, his stomach heavy. He reached up to his throat; he was frightened and fighting to breathe.

Sakina rooted around in the glove compartment and pulled something out. She reached over. 'Breathe into this,' she said, giving him a brown paper bag. He put his face to the bag and began to take deep breaths. As the panic attack subsided, he leaned back in his seat and checked his phone. There was a message. 'It's an explosion on Durban Street,' he said. 'Jia is there. She's fine.'

'You don't have to help,' said Sakina. 'They don't know you're nearby.'

Shame flooded through Benyamin. 'I'm sorry,' he said, 'for being like this.'

He was grateful for her presence, but conflicted. He'd never needed anyone before, and now, when he did, it was a prostitute. They'd been doing this for weeks. Him coming here, just to sleep. Her watching over him, soothing him.

His family thought he was collecting the milk money. Jia had suggested it might be good for him to keep a hand in the business as he recovered. But what did Jia know? She wasn't the one having the nightmares. She wasn't waking up in a cold sweat, or being triggered into panic mode by the flash of car headlights.

He'd caught sight of Sakina on the milk round and had recognised her, the way souls recognise each other. He'd watched as car after car came to take her away.

He found it hard to be around family now. He felt embarrassed, afraid, conflicted, all things he thought men weren't supposed to feel. He needed to talk to someone and not feel ashamed. 'Being around you calms me,' he'd said to Sakina. 'I know that sounds stupid.'

'There's a hadith that says, "Souls are like conscripted soldiers,"' she'd replied. 'Some of us were together before we were born, and recognise each other when we meet in this life.' Benyamin didn't know about that, but he knew he needed to talk to someone about what happened to him.

'I can't go to a shrink. This isn't *The Sopranos*,' he'd said. The two of them had laughed at that. He hadn't laughed in a long time. She was clever and funny, and she knew how dark life was. Mina hadn't understood. She'd wanted things to revert back to how they used to be almost instantly, but he couldn't do that. She'd been lucky, managing to escape in the chaos that followed him getting caught that night. He hadn't been so lucky, and Nowak had changed him.

'Funny, the culture we come from. It's fine for you to pay for sex, but tell someone you're struggling emotionally and they lose all respect for you.' Sakina could say things like that and he wouldn't mind. When Jia said words like that they would trigger something in him that made him want to distance himself from her. But he still hoped she would take over Akbar Khan's duties. She was the only one who could.

CHAPTER 31

The day after the explosion, Jia and Idris set to work. They began by strengthening their network. Their first port of call was an old school friend who ran a business close by. Jia wanted to explore options for the Jirga and its various operations.

Through an internal glass window in the reception area, she watched workers draping deep-red chiffon scarves across high ropes that stretched from one side of a room to the other. The lobby was empty, except for a young man in a grey suit, who sat on a sofa behind them. Clipboard in hand, he was filling in some paperwork. Idris checked his watch and then looked across at Jia. They were waiting for the owner of the business; he was running late.

Bespectacled and dressed in a laboratory coat, he arrived a few minutes later and greeted them warmly before leading them down a narrow corridor. 'Apologies for my tardiness,' he said. He opened a door and led them on to the factory floor. It looked like an illegal version of Willy Wonka's factory. To the right of them, vats of red liquid bubbled away like hot blood. Factory workers dressed in boiler suits and hairnets dropped dry fabric into the large pots and stirred them with broom-handle-like wooden sticks. Liquid from several of the vats was being siphoned off, and evaporated through a complicated system of glass pipes to leave behind a solid substance.

'All these scarves are to be sold in Mumbai Mart,' the owner said. 'They're all pure silk. Take a look.' He handed Jia the scarf with the flourish of a souk trader.

She passed the fabric through her hands; it felt like an ordinary dupatta.

'Thank you for showing us around, Safaid Posh.'

'No problem, and please, no one calls me that any more. Everyone translates it to "White Coat". It's a bit naff but it's easier,' he said, and then quickly moved on. 'The scarves are soaked in a solution of the product at our factories by the border of Afghanistan, dried and then imported here as ordinary scarves. This plant is where we reconstitute the product.'

'The product?' asked Idris.

'Monkey water,' White Coat said. Idris looked at him expectantly, waiting for him to explain. For the son of a dealer, his drug terminology was limited. 'You know, liquid heroin. We sell it by the syringe or in a dropper bottle. Costs a bit more to us but our contact at the needle exchange helps us keep prices low, and I figured the cleaner we keep our users, the bigger our market.'

Although both had known about this side of the city's industry for years, they had not seen the operation first-hand until now. They were impressed and told White Coat as much. 'That means so much to me,' he said. 'Please, come into my office. I've ordered tea.'

They agreed to his hospitality and took a seat in the sparsely decorated but highly organised office. Filing cabinets lined one side of the room. Planning charts, delivery dates and detailed drawings of operations lay across the desk.

'Do you worry about keeping so many records?' asked Idris.

'No. Everything is encoded. Besides, this is just delivery dates for our halal operation. A large percentage of our business is just ordinary fabric retail,' said White Coat. A young woman in a white headscarf came in carrying a tray with a cafetière and glass cups. She placed the tray on the desk in front of White Coat. He began pouring kava into small cups. 'Remember Nighat? The girl you set me up with at school?' he said to Idris.

Idris laughed aloud. 'The one with the handlebar moustache who always smelt of stale curry?' The young woman left the room quickly.

'Er, yes. That was her. We got married last year,' said White Coat. He blushed profusely.

An overweight child, his mother hadn't helped matters by dressing him in short trousers and knitted tank tops, and giving him his lunch in a margarine tub. So, what could the bigger kids do but bully him? Thankfully, the beatings ended when Jia Khan befriended him. Every school kid knew not to mess with the Khan's children or their friends. Or even friends of their friends. She'd helped him up and handed him his glasses after a particularly nasty encounter, smiling as she told him that his spectacle prescription was similar to hers. That was the day he fell in love for the first time.

White Coat spoke without pausing for breath, as if in a perpetual state of excitement. Today, more so than ever, he was nervous and desperate to impress. 'It was all my idea, this plant. I came up with it when I was studying for my chemistry degree at Manchester. Where did you go to uni?' he asked, and then without waiting for an answer continued, 'You see, I was speaking to Dad about the family business and I told him out and out: smuggling, not something I can do. Dad was disappointed. We didn't talk for a bit. Then…I came up with my plan!' White coat's eyes glistened as he talked. Here was a man who loved his job.

'The plan being this place?' asked Idris.

The scientist nodded.

'We hear Nowak contacted you,' said Jia. The colour drained from White Coat's face.

'I'm a businessman,' he said. 'I'm in business to make money.' Jia smiled at him and nodded, allaying his fears.

'What did he want from you?' Idris asked.

'Their shipment's already in the system – nothing to do with us. But they were looking for friends to help maintain their supply, clean their money, that kind of thing.'

Jia listened, leaving Idris to ask the questions. 'What did you tell them?' he said.

'I don't like to turn business away, but I don't like their methods. It's dirty. Bad for long-term business. I see myself as a sort of social worker, providing a service of care if you will. Some people need help surviving and if I don't do it someone else will. But the Brotherhood, they're dishing out the drug to children, women, no idea of hygiene. Sooner or later these diseases will filter back to our people... So I told them I'm too busy at the moment to take on new work.'

'Do you know anything about their operations?'

White Coat looked uncomfortable. He possessed information and had not passed it on. If Akbar Khan had been alive this would have gone badly for him; even though he didn't work for the Jirga, his family, business associates, people he worshipped with, did, and that was how the Khan's power worked. It was why it was difficult to escape it. He turned to Jia. Hanging out with her had been the best part of school. Not only was she the smartest girl he had ever met, she also always had time to hear about his schemes, ideas others usually thought were crazy. He had tried to stay in touch with her, but after her brother's death she had stopped responding to his emails.

'I wanted to work with your father but he didn't always understand our operation, see?' he said. 'But if you're stepping in...I mean, taking over, I'd like to help. I know the Polskie's shipments are sold on in bulk, cheap and fast. I gather they've been talking to Hajji Taj, you know, the travel agent? I reckon they're gonna send the money through his place.'

Jia leaned over and took White Coat's hand. 'Thank you, Abdul,' she said. 'That information means a great deal to me. Keep your ear to the ground and let us us know if you hear anything more? We will be in touch with you very soon.'

White Coat's brown cheeks reddened further.

CHAPTER 32

'It makes sense,' said Idris as they left the factory. 'We'll need a strong team, and he's got the experience, and we can trust him. My advice would be to ask him to head up the drugs. Quality control, alternative ways of distribution and bringing the product over.'

The sun was getting low. The light was turning the stone buildings the colour of chamcham, and it made Jia think of the Sweet Centre, where her father used to take them on Sunday mornings for halva and puri. There would be rows and rows of sweetmeats, squares of barfi, round and fat gulab jamun steeped in syrup, and soft milky rasmalai. It seemed like only yesterday. Memories of Akbar Khan had been coming thick and fast over the last two months as she figured out her place and her plan.

She pulled the black collar of her coat up high. The bitter wind bit hard.

'And while we're talking, I have some more advice for you,' said Idris. 'Buy some warmer clothes now that you're sticking around. You look like you're fucking freezing in that southerner get-up!' Jia laughed at his outburst and he joined her. Idris so rarely said anything unmeasured it eased the tension. Things were about to get harder, and without a sense of humour they'd lose themselves to the darkness they were stepping into. Idris had her back and she had his. Jia was glad he was here, especially now that they were going to war.

'You would have made your mother proud, you know,' she told him, when they stopped laughing.

'Let's go home,' he said.

They crossed the road to their car, where a group of young men were deep in laughter and conversation.

The man in the grey suit, who had been waiting in reception earlier, was with them. He asked for a light. 'You should quit,' Idris said, handing over his silver Zippo. 'And so should I. But not today. Today we smoke.'

'I know, you're right,' said the man in the suit. 'But there's not much else to do round here. Unless you want to deal drugs.' He lit his cigarette and took a long drag, then handed the lighter back to Idris, who lit his own. Jia took a step back from the smoke.

'What kind of work are you looking for?' Idris asked.

'Anything. Most of us are trained developers,' the man replied, nodding towards his friends. 'UX, apps, software, you name it and one of us can do it. But there's no jobs around here and some of us have got family – we've tried applying everywhere. It's all a bit shit. I probably shouldn't complain. I'm sure something will come up.'

The men weren't much older than Zan was when he died. They weren't much older than Ahad. They were eager, intelligent, street-wise and smart, but living in a city that was dying had placed them on the bottom rung of life. Even those who'd moved away found themselves judged when they told people where they had grown up and gone to school. No matter where they went, others stepped on their knuckles to rise to the top. So in the end they came home. They were somebody's brothers and somebody's sons, but the rest of the world didn't see it that way. Jia did. She understood. She understood that they lived in a restricted world, and that it was the world, not their abilities, which held them back.

The smell of Jia's own son as he had been lowered into her arms still lived in her memory, as did the overwhelming need to protect him, and with that, of course, the overwhelming fear that she would somehow fail to. 'He will teach you what love is in its purest form,' her mother had said. Jia had held on to him tightly, tormented by the fear that she would lose him the way she had lost Zan, that he would disappoint her the way her father had disappointed her, petrified at the thought that love like this was fleeting. She was convinced that love was no longer something she did well.

So when they told her he'd died, she'd been oddly relieved. The doctors had blamed MRSA. She knew it to be a lie – that wasn't how he had died, or how she *thought* he'd died – but she had stayed silent, worried they might blame her. Then, of course, years later her father told her Ahad had survived and that he had taken him, as he had taken all that was good in her life.

She wondered what kind of man Ahad was becoming. Was he kind, like Elyas, able to forgive? Was he whole, intact, or had the world damaged him the way it had her? She felt a pang of regret, wishing she'd held on to the letters Elyas had sent. She wished she'd opened them, had a taste of her son's life, experienced his childhood. But she hadn't. She'd sent them back, one by one. She'd blamed Elyas for Zan's death as much as her father, and she had wanted him to suffer as much as she did. But meeting Ahad now, seeing how much he reminded her of her brother, she wished she hadn't. He would have helped fill the void Zan had left. What kind of a mother was she? How cold? How disinterested must she have seemed to him?

He was waiting for answers but she didn't have any to give, not yet. As she stood under the street lights with these young men, contemplating her takeover of Akbar Khan's world, she realised her father had done the right thing. Elyas was a better parent than she could ever have been.

Idris, on the other hand, was like her. Broken, unflinching and unforgiving. His past had stolen away the privilege of forgetting; that was for other people. He believed in little, but he believed in Jia Khan, and he made her want to be the mother the city needed.

'It is time for change,' she told Idris as they drove back to Pukhtun House. 'We have to help our own people. Pakistani families only help those who toe the line. If you want to do something different, there's no one to help. The little girl from Bradford, the boy from Luton, or the teenager in Ilford – who steps up for them when they need a job, or an internship, or money to finish their education? No one. And no one will, except us.'

And she told him her plan, and he listened, nodding at her every word. Things were about to change.

CHAPTER 33

The plan was simple, and was operational in just four weeks. They took the brightest and the best, the youngsters who couldn't get ahead because of their skin tone or the way they spoke, or because they just didn't know how to get to the place they wanted. The rude boys, the dropouts and the misunderstoods. The artistic, the creative, the risk-takers and shortcut-makers. The broken men and women the extremist mullahs wanted to lure away with false promises, twisted surahs and skewed images of pop culture, only to abuse them and turn them into instruments of mass destruction.

And they built their empire, a brave new world, alongside the old, a world that stood on the foundations of the past but was slicker and digitised. Jia's rules were clear. 'They have to be here because they want to be,' she said. 'Not because they have to. That's the only way they'll stay loyal. If they're with us under duress they will succumb to a better offer or be seduced into disloyalty. We can't take that risk.'

They did what they set out to do. They trained them, gave them a place to go, a place where they were understood, valued and their skills known. They were given a salary, their taxes were paid, and under the table they were handed a cut from the job. Students enrolled in the educational arm and the press loved it: they were 'helping the disenfranchised'.

'Who in their right mind would name a drug-dealing business after an illegal substance?' Malik asked.

'We would. And we have,' said Idris. The name was his idea: the Opium Den. 'They may know what we're doing, they may eventually gain some understanding of it, but they will never prove anything. We're smarter than they are, and so are our people. They like to underestimate us, so let them.'

Jia always knew the venture would succeed but the speed at which it did surprised even her. Then there was the sideline business…

Jia had instructed Idris and her team to take the old mills that stood off Canal Road and redevelop them. Situated across from the shopping precinct and the hotel known for its hourly knocking-shop rates, it wasn't the sort of place you'd expect a successful tech company to build its headquarters. But it worked and it thrived. She put Benyamin in charge of the day-to-day running of the organisation's buildings. It meant he had a significant role but very little to do with the illegal operations. She needed him to stay safe and out of harm's way. At least for now.

After decades of being reminded that they belonged to an underachieving and unemployed community, the people of this city had stopped trying to climb out of the black hole in which they found themselves. Those who did were pulled back in by the weight of others wanting to hide from their misery. But when 'The Company' (as those who worked for the Opium Den referred to it) told them they deserved better and gave them better, they grafted. Jia made sure her employees got everything they needed. The Khan's philosophy of trust and loyalty became the cornerstones of the Opium Den.

There were two sides to the business, legitimate and illegal. The illegal arm disrupted the country's drugs market. There were few rules other than: 'Get it done, do it right and don't tell anyone.' The young developers devoured the work. They were hungry for opportunity and starved of validation. The Company gave them a place to belong and a sense of achievement. Their cultural background was an asset, not a problem to be managed or a box to be ticked.

Their time spent late-night web-surfing for pot and porn was paying off; they had developed an extensive knowledge of the darknet. It allowed them to build a modern drugs marketplace that gave buyers anonymised access to any illegal substance they wanted. It was an eBay-like set-up, and payment was taken using Bitcoin and other virtual currencies through a system similar to Paypal.

Drugs and consensual sex was what they sold. Akbar Khan's death had turned Jia's monochrome life various shades of grey. She cast aside her belief in the rule of law, leaving the balance of sin and virtue to God. He could sift and sort and allot after she died. But while she lived she knew that the good she did outweighed the bad. Children were fed, women slept soundly and men had self-esteem, and that was all that life came down to in the end. If heroin, meth-amphetamine, cocaine and marijuana helped rich men sleep and poor men exist through another day, then who was she to stop it? Then there was the simple question of economics. Someone was going to supply, so why not them?

There were, however, lines that Jia and her men were not willing to cross. Clients demanding weapons were told 'no', clients demanding paedophilia were told 'sure' – and then their virtual lives were hacked into tiny pieces, evidence handed over to the authorities, and their actual lives destroyed.

The Company's reputation for secure and high-performance delivery soon turned it into a world-class organisation. In the begin-ning, clients brought their legal business with them to mask their illegal purchases, but when the firm began delivering slicker products than its competition, and solving unsolvable tech problems, it found itself with new and lucrative accounts that were only interested in its software development skills. They built niche apps, taking a chance on ideas that mainstream venture capitalists would pass on. From social media to salah, their cultural knowledge gave them insight into the markets of India, Pakistan and Bangladesh, countries whose tech users were hungry for relevant content. Living in extended family systems gave these users deep pockets and made them early adopters of technology. Then there was the billion-dollar Muslim market. Jia's company understood their needs instinctively.

New business was always carefully scrutinised before being taken on. Users were given unique invite codes to websites only after vetting procedures had been carried out. As the clean money stream flowed in, it laundered the black money that flowed alongside it.

Clients that were trying to break into emerging markets across South Asia found themselves in a multilingual, highly skilled hub, working with men and women with chameleon-like abilities to switch cultures. Eventually, what had started as a front organisation soon became a lucrative business.

It was only six months before employees were being headhunted by multinationals, start-ups and Silicon Valley's biggest exports. Jia was clever. Because dirty money secretly holds hands with clean, she encouraged the men and women to take up the offers, knowing that they were planting the seeds of a powerful network. The Company celebrated their success. The plan to expand the network and make it global in the next ten years was right on track. No one asked questions. The police stayed away; the streets were being cleaned. The unemployment figures were going down. No one knew what was really going on. They were running the country's biggest drugs delivery operation all from the centre of this city.

Jia had agreed with Idris that the best place to hide something was in plain sight. 'The best cons are the biggest ones,' she told her cousins. 'The ones that everyone can see but can't prove. People won't believe we have the guts to be so brazen. They'll see it and ignore it. And the ones that won't, we buy them. Buy enough people and they'll drown out the voice of dissent.' By the end of the year they were cleaning money for international syndicates and some of the world's biggest crime families.

But she also never lost sight of the endgame. 'If someone wants to get clean, let them, help them. We're not in this forever. We're in this to help our people get clean and get out. That is how empires are built.'

They built their new empire tall and high and with walls of steel to guard it. Its reach spread from the small-time client to the highest echelons of society, and they worked hard to get there.

· Its success helped relieve the pressure that had been coming from the Jirga to exact badal on Nowak for what he did to Benyamin and for her father's murder. Jia had not forgotten what was owed, it was just that her priorities were elsewhere. Reshaping the family business was a matter of urgency – it had been left far too long. Revenge, however, was a dish best served cold.

CHAPTER 34

As soon as Jia stepped through the door of her London apartment, calm descended and the responsibilities of her new-found life slipped away. It had been her sanctuary for a long time. More than a year had passed since she made Pukhtun House her permanent residence. She had few regrets about it, but as she walked through the hallway and into her bedroom, she realised she missed the freedom of this life.

She'd kept the apartment as a bolt-hole but hadn't been able to visit often. Work stole all her time, but this week Maria had forced her to leave. 'It's half-term, I can come with you,' she'd said. 'We'll spend a few days together, try the Darjeeling Express Biryani Supper Club and take in a show.'

'Although maybe not on the same day,' said Jia. 'I can't imagine anything worse than turning up to a West End show smelling of salan.' It wasn't the offence taken by others that worried her. The lingering aroma of curry on clothes and fingertips, no matter how expensive the hand soap, made her anxious. You only had to have had someone hiss 'Smelly Paki!' at you once for it to leave its brand on you forever.

Maria and Jia had taken the train to King's Cross, enjoying Northern Rail's hospitality of English breakfast tea and moreish shortbread. Jia felt the tension leave her shoulders as she lay her burden down in the presence of her sister. They had an unspoken agreement never to discuss the family business, but everything else was on the table. Relationships, the state of the city's schools, Elyas, Ahad and their mother were all topics they covered in the two hours ten minutes they were on the train.

'Mama seems even quieter than usual,' said Jia, as the dining-car attendant refilled her teacup and walked away. They were in first class, the carriage busier than Jia had expected. She wasn't bound to travelling during school holidays, and it crossed her mind that she never had been.

'It's her age,' said Maria.

'She leaves the room when I walk in.'

'You know what she's like.'

'You're right. It's like I'm an extension of her, as if she can say and do whatever she likes to me without consequence. She was never like that with Zan.'

'Zan was golden,' said Maria. 'The way Mama talks about him, as if he was some saint.'

'She adored him, but I don't think she likes me.' This was the first time it occurred to Jia that it was possible for her mother to love her and not like her. Perhaps Sanam Khan could sense what Jia had become, or knew what she had done, but it was more likely to be something else, something simpler.

'You have lived a completely different life to her. She stayed home and looked after Baba, raised us. She sacrificed everything for her husband, and gave no thought to how people should treat her. You and I, we draw clear lines about how we expect to be treated. She just doesn't understand that.'

Jia knew her little sister was right: their mother didn't understand them and never would. Much of their love was lost in translation. Maybe it was always this way with the children of immigrants, separated by the gap that grew between culture and generation. Her mother had never laughed with them the way she laughed with those from her home country, and although Jia spoke the languages of her mother's land, they sometimes felt heavy on her tongue.

Once in London, Maria had dropped her bags at the apartment and headed to New Bond Street with her sister's credit card. Jia liked nice things but had little interest in shopping; Maria knew what suited her, and what she liked. It was the perfect arrangement. They would head out to dinner later, but for now Jia placed her case down and sat on the edge of the bed, taking off her shoes. Her feet ached a little from being on her feet. She used public transport when in London. Here she could be just another face in the crowd.

The smell of the apartment took her back to another time, the scent of wood polish and floor cleaner and lilies reminding her of the career she had worked for here and how close she had been to achieving her goal of becoming a judge. She now realised it had been an empty existence, that family was what was needed to feel whole. Losing Zan and Ahad had left her raw, as if the very skin had been taken from her. It meant everything was painful; even innocuous comments about birthdays and anniversaries were like shards sometimes, a painful reminder of what she didn't have. In order to survive she had armoured up and carried on, numbing herself to the pain. But Akbar Khan's death had changed all that, forcing her to face up to her responsibilities and to the island that she had become.

Now, she was responsible for the happiness and livelihood of scores of families. And she found herself looking for ways to sew up the rift her father had created between her and her son, and make sense of her relationship with Elyas.

She picked up the letters her assistant had opened and organised ready for her return. Invitations to official luncheons, the Law Society Excellence Awards, a former colleague's wedding – all reminders of a life once lived. A life distant from the one she was living now.

She thought of all the letters Elyas had written her. The ones she had sent back, unopened. The ones he had kept and handed to her as she left for London this morning. She'd been afraid to open them on the train, afraid of her reaction to what was in them, to the opening of the floodgates she had locked and barred.

Alone in her apartment, she took them out and read them one by one.

CHAPTER 35

'I'm outside,' said Jia. She'd been knocking on the front door for a while with no answer.

'I was in the bathroom.' Elyas pulled on a jumper and went to open the door. 'It's the middle of the day. What are you doing here?' he said, letting her in. He found an old tissue in the pocket of his pyjamas and wiped his nose. She was holding a box, and a bag from the pharmacy.

'I've brought you soup and painkillers.'

'I don't drink canned soup.'

'I made it. Is that so hard to believe?'

'When do you have time to make soup?'

'When did you get so mean?'

'I'm sorry,' he said, shaking his head. 'I'm not well and my accountant needs some papers for my tax return. I'm just a little stressed.'

She kissed him on the cheek, accepting his apology. She slipped off her shoes by the door and hung up her mac, before walking to the kitchen with the provisions she'd brought. 'I've got some time before my meeting. Why don't you finish your work, and I'll heat this up for you?' she said.

He was going to protest, but changed his mind. It was rare for him to be looked after by someone else, and so he accepted the help graciously, taking a seat at the kitchen table. He watched her move around the room, taking out bowls and glasses and warming up food, like this was normal. 'So, this is how it feels,' he said. 'I could get used to this.'

She put the bowl down in front of him, along with a napkin and spoon. The fragrance of chicken broth, cooked with onion and garlic, cloves, peppercorns and whole coriander wafted towards him. She waited expectantly as he put the spoon to his mouth. His face conveyed the right response: it was delicious. 'Don't get used to it,' she said, and then laughed.

Little by little Jia began to seep into Elyas and Ahad's life more and more. Elyas had extended his stay after the previous editor of the paper decided he didn't want to return from his six-month sabbatical. He was eighteen months into the job now and didn't know whether to take up the permanent post they had offered him – a lot depended on what happened with Jia. Things had remained steady and secretive and he'd been too busy to ask questions up until now.

'So, are we going to talk about what's been going on or just pretend that nothing is?' Elyas said one day, waving at Ahad on the pitch. They were at a rugby match. Ahad was on his college team.

'Where do you want to start?' she asked.

The way he felt about her made him uncomfortable. He had built his house on a fault line and was expecting to avoid an earthquake. People always said that there were two sides to every argument but he knew that wasn't true. There were always three: your side, their side and the truth. In this case the truth was a distant hope and Jia's side had never been told. They discussed everything around them except her leaving him. And they never talked about her stolen visits to his house in the night.

'You would never have said that ten years ago,' he said.

'Things change.'

'That they do,' he agreed. 'You and I being whatever we are… and me sending Ahad to this poncy school with all these middle-class white boys in blazers and hats. What has happened to us?'

'You always said I was the champagne socialist.'

'It's true. But you were right. About everything. Public school does give you a great network. Amazing what having a child does to one's perspective,' Elyas said. 'But you always did see things more clearly than I did. I always envied that about you.'

'You mean I had vision and you were wearing bifocals?' she said.

Elyas laughed. 'Like Butch and Sundance? And we both know how that ended.' She smiled, and for a moment they were an ordinary couple.

'This is not the Wild West,' she said. 'And going out in a blaze of gunfire is not on the cards for us.'

'I used to feel as though I was playing snap while all the white kids played poker. I fought hard to get where I am. Up against rich boys who played tennis in the afternoons and went to country clubs on weekends. Guys whose fathers made calls to get them wherever they wanted to be.'

'And now our son is one of those entitled types,' Jia said, raising an eyebrow.

'Isn't that our whole problem? We want things and then when we get them we don't feel we deserve them? I don't want Ahad to struggle just because of my principles. The older I get, the more I understand that values and ideals get lost along the path; you lose a few and damage some of the others. We're all compromising in some way or other. People talk about underachievement and a lack of brown kids at the top – well, you can't be what you can't see. People recruit in their own image, or pick someone they know. That's how the ladder is climbed. At least your company seems to be giving young people a network.'

'My father believed in the network,' Jia said. 'He ran his life on it and sent us to the best schools to build it. But networks have their own class system, and when your father is the kind of law lord who'll have your kneecaps shot off, and NOT the kind that adjudicates British law, it's not that straightforward. That's what I want these guys to have, a future without shame of where they came from, you know?' It was easy to be around Elyas; that was why she was with him. He accepted her for who she was, without judgement. But there were things about her that he didn't know, and things she didn't believe he would take well. So she gave him what she could, and kept what she couldn't locked away.

'Sometimes I wonder what would have happened if my parents had stayed in Pakistan,' he said.

'I know where I'd be: sporting a Hermès Birkin as I was being driven around by my chauffeur,' said Jia.

'You do that now,' Elyas said. She realised she missed her youth and the lightness he had brought to it, that time when she couldn't tell where she ended and he began. And now she only met him in the darkness of a bedroom or here in the park. The two parts of their relationship were divided; something inside her wanted to find a way to bridge them. But what was that bridge? The mundane daily tasks of shopping lists, lunch and laundry-basket arguments? She had an army of men ready to go to war at her command, on land and online, but she couldn't navigate a relationship outside that world.

She looked up and a tall good-looking man waved at her from across the grass. He was waiting by the play area with an old-fashioned pram. His wife, a handsome woman, was keeping an eye on their five-year-old son. The little boy was confidently climbing the steps to the slide. The man looked familiar.

'I know that guy. Who is he?' Elyas asked.

'That is Marcus Massey. He's an investment banker,' she said.

'Why do I know his face?' Elyas said.

'Maybe you covered the story? Marcus was accused of assaulting – sexually assaulting – a trainee risk analyst. She dropped the charges. Story was, Massey's father put the screws on her father's business contacts and paid her off too.'

'I suppose the police couldn't do anything about it?'

Jia shook her head. 'I knew her. She used to work with me. Power makes men unfit for normal life.'

Elyas saw that something in her had hardened and it frightened him. But he couldn't say whether he was afraid *for* her or *of* her. 'Jia, what's going on?' he said. 'I'm worried about you.'

'Nothing,' she replied. 'Let's get a coffee, the weather is changing.' Elyas felt the warmth of her against him as she took his arm and led him towards the café. It was the first time she'd touched him in public.

She waited at a table while he bought the drinks. 'So, are we going to talk about what happened between us?' he asked, tearing open a sugar sachet and pouring it into her cup.

'No,' she said matter-of-factly.

'Why not?' he asked.

She sipped her tea slowly. 'There's nothing to say. It was all such a long time ago,' and she turned away from him, caught between wanting to talk and not talk; and then she saw Ahad walking towards them, which settled the matter.

It began to rain and Elyas went to get the car, leaving Ahad waiting with Jia. The silence was uncomfortable. She took her phone from her pocket and began flicking through emails, more out of habit than obligation. This was how it had been for months, her not speaking, him pretending it was OK. But today would be different. Ahad had decided it so. 'Why did you hate your father?' he asked.

Jia looked up from her phone. 'What makes you think I hated him?'

'Because I hated you too.'

She put her phone down. That she was important enough in his life to be hated, that his feelings towards her despite her absence were so strong, surprised her.

'I get it now, though,' he said.

'Get what?' She looked straight at him, into his face and the eyes that had once belonged to her brother.

'That you had your reasons,' he said. 'I'm not like everyone else. But I am like you, and you're like your dad. Other people don't see the world like we do. We're different.'

'That's a lot of introspection,' said Jia.

Ahad shrugged. For a sixteen-year-old he was articulate in a way that most teenagers were not. Jia could see that private schooling had paid for itself.

'I know you blame everyone for your brother's death, including my dad. The thing is, he's still hung up on you.'

He stopped, seeing her reaction. His words had removed her mask and behind it stood a woman who did not know she was loved. He took something from his back pocket and handed it to her. She found herself holding a single photo-booth picture. Black and white, curled at the corner, it was of her and Elyas pulling faces at the lens. There was a date on the back, the year slightly smudged, the words 'Leeds Festival' still readable. Looking at it reminded her that she had once been full of life and love and trust. But she only understood that now that she wasn't.

'I found it when we were packing. He keeps it with his passport, won't travel without it.' Ahad took the photograph back from Jia. 'You think that because he wants you and ignores all the chaos that goes with you, he's weak. That being cold and distant somehow makes you strong. But you need him to keep feeling something. Anything. Look, I know you've been sleeping with him. I know you come to our place late at night. I keep finding your fucking stuff. And I don't care, OK? Just don't hurt my dad. He deserves better than that.'

For the first time since his birth, Jia saw her son clearly for who he was. He had changed since she'd met him at her father's funeral. He was poised on the steps of manhood. The family business and the fallout from Akbar Khan's death had consumed her. She had compartmentalised the things she dealt with in depth and the things she dealt with superficially. She had been skating the surface of her relationship with Ahad but he had taken a pickaxe to the pond and doused her in icy water. She could see him now, clear as day, and sharply focused. He was the best of the Khans, and the worst, and despite all her efforts, she loved him.

The old feelings took her by surprise, and she pushed them down. The fear that had arrived with his birth was alive and well. And this time there was no stopping it.

CHAPTER 36

Idris left Jia at Barbican and walked down Silk Street, past the offices of the Magic Circle law firm where he'd started out. He was on his way to a friend's law offices. The day had been productive, but being patronised by rich men who liked to shoot their mouths off exhausted him. He knew that the most powerful people spoke the least.

The legal side of the family business had been growing steadily, and Jia had decided it was time to consolidate the bedrock on which it was built – the drugs. Sales of illicit substances gave them more than a steady income stream; it also gave them a network that penetrated the highest echelons of society. It was essential to their long-term plans.

Edward Mason was an old friend from university, and he ran one of the world's most successful boutique law firms. He and Idris had shared an apartment until Idris left to join Akbar Khan's business. Edward went on to take over his father's prestigious law firm. His client portfolio read like a who's who of the *Sunday Times* Rich List, and while Idris's did too, it was for very different reasons.

Their meeting was scheduled for the end of the day. As Idris walked through the quiet, suited-and-booted snobbery of St Paul's he was glad he no longer worked in this area. There was a lot to be said for being around people who looked like him.

He arrived at the office on time and took a seat in the lobby, remembering how intimidated he had felt the first time he'd been here.

Idris knew he was a brilliant lawyer. He had an eye for fine details and loopholes that had saved clients millions and made them as much if not more. Working in London had been enjoyable at first; the bright lights and luxury had seduced him. But then time had taught him the truth: that success did not always come from hard work – it came from who you drank with, fucked, and your family name – and that power and money came to those who had wielded it since birth or were willing to sell the meat of their morals for it. It was they who controlled the political landscape, business and high society, and they who decided your fate.

And so he found himself falling out of love with the British justice system; it didn't bring him the salvation he needed. He saw how easily the law was manipulated to control people, people who were like him in race and religion, the ones without connection and network. He listened as so-called educated types spoke of their attitudes, beginning sentences with phrases such as 'I'm not racist but' and ending them with 'not you, of course, you're different'.

He found himself floundering, unable to make sense of the path he'd chosen. He began staying home instead of partying with clients, which was bad for business. He dabbled in religion online, meeting like-minded types who claimed to be purer, more virtuous, than the corporate West; but when he dug a little deeper he found their ideologies twisted. He retreated further into himself.

In the end, it was the law of his family, of his ancestors, of Pukhtunwali, that saved him. It made better sense to him than the rules of crown and country, and it needed defending. He turned his back on the London career, and went home.

So when the large clock that hung behind the reception desk of his friend's firm told him he'd been kept waiting for almost forty-five minutes, he was not surprised. It was a sign that he had been downgraded on the ladder of business courtesy.

When he finally arrived, Edward was apologetic but only super-ficially so. He looked dishevelled despite the sharp suit and shirt.

'Idris,' he said. 'Sorry I kept you waiting so long. Billable hours! Some days I wonder why I go home. Come on, let's go get a drink. I could use one after the day I've had. And the little something extra, if you've brought it?'

Edward's car was waiting outside. Fifteen minutes later they pulled up outside a nondescript black door. A young brunette greeted them with a warm smile reserved only for the clients of London's most exclusive private members' club.

Inside, the conversation flowed, as did the drinks, and Edward was on his fourth when they began to talk business. Idris was still nursing his first. He'd tried drinking when he was young but it hadn't been worth the guilt. It wasn't that he was looking to appease Allah; it was that every time he put a step wrong he felt his dead mother's disapproving eyes on him, and that was enough to stop any man drinking, let alone a Pukhtun. Still, a social drink was an integral part of the lawyerly life, and clients and colleagues were wary of networking sober. Saying no to a drink meant dragging up that great wall of difference, the wall that separated 'them' from 'us' and led to the sort of questions about religious ideology that every Asian Muslim kid dreaded. The only respectable answer to 'Why aren't you drinking? Is it against your religion?' was 'I'm an alcoholic'. But no one wants to do business with a man who overshares. And a man who overshares and can't handle his liquor might as well declare himself bankrupt. So Idris would order one drink and keep it in his hand all evening.

'I've been dealing with suppliers since Jesus was in nappies. You expect me to believe that you can seriously supply all the needs of our one hundred and forty thousand employees every week? What are you operating? Some kind of Deliveroo for drugs?'

Idris took a black folder from his briefcase and handed it to Edward. He flicked through the file, stopping at the first page. It detailed the names, addresses and personal details of every one of his employees, from the cleaning lady to the senior partners, and there were pictures. Pictures of powder being cut and snorted, sexual liaisons, of partners doing things they shouldn't. Edward unbuttoned his collar. 'How did you get this?' he said.

'It's part of the service,' said Idris. 'We run a tech company. Data is our business.'

'If I didn't know you to be a man of integrity I'd think you were about to blackmail me.' Edward laughed nervously. 'You know my crowd, my colleagues, my clients – they aren't your average street-corner junkies. They're connoisseurs. While I trust you, I need to make sure you understand?'

'I do,' said Idris. 'You're in safe hands. I wouldn't be here if you weren't.'

Jia arrived. Edward greeted her warmly. He knew her well from the old days. She took a seat opposite the two men.

'Why hasn't this been done already?' asked Edward.

'Because people always try and complicate matters,' said Idris. 'We have spent months developing systems with untraceable layers to launder money through eBay, Gumtree and other second-hand selling sites. We have created algorithms for money-transfer sites that allow black money to piggyback on white and be secreted into offshore accounts. And the most beautiful part of it is that we can give you receipts and invoices for legal products.'

'If you're so sure it works then explain it to me so that I can understand. None of this algorithm bullshit,' Edward said.

Jia remained silent on the details, as she had with the Jirga. She hadn't felt either the need to let them know her plans, or the desire to gain their support. She would tell them what she needed to when she was ready. She knew, in any case, that men responded better to each other; the patriarchy was the domain of all men, regardless of race and religion.

'The internet is too big for search engines to index every single website on it,' Idris said. 'That means some get left behind and these are the ones that make up the deep web. The only way to find those sites is if you know their web address. Follow me so far?' Edward nodded. 'The dark web, or darknet as it is also known, is not only not indexed, but the user needs to have something special to be able to access it, like an authentication code. To add an extra layer of security, we use it with Tor – "the onion network". It's a software program that you load on to your computer, like a browser. It hides your IP address and it hides the route your information takes by bouncing it through a network of up to five thousand servers around the world. Think of it as a huge network of hidden servers that keep your online identity and your location invisible. It means websites can't track the physical location of your IP address or find out what you've been looking at online…and neither can law enforcement or government agencies.'

'The *onion* network?'

'Like the layers of an onion, the websites you're visiting are hidden behind layers of anonymity.'

'Do I need to wipe my history or anything afterwards?'

'It's always a good idea. We'll install a cleaner on your machine that will do this and clear your cache automatically.'

'And you are sure she's up to running this?' Edward said to Idris, looking at Jia. 'She's always been a little too softly spoken. She needs to be more forthright if she's going to succeed at business. You know you need to make money, right?' he said, addressing Jia now, and she knew she had been right to let Idris handle the negotiations. Edward was the kind of man who thought he was 'woke' but who said what he liked. His privilege and place in society made him believe he was infallible, but he was clever enough to know that in this day and age he needed at least to appear to show women respect. It was the kind of attitude that Jia despised. But she thought long and hard before she responded.

'Edward, I don't need to prove my credentials to you, because I know and you know that you've already done your due diligence on me and my company. Don't ask me how I know, just trust that I do and think for a moment what that says about me and the information I have on you.' She pulled a blue file from her bag and placed it on the table. 'Idris showed you what we know about your employees. I hoped I wouldn't need to show you this.' She slid the folder across the table towards Edward. 'Now, you can choose to do business with us or you can go elsewhere, but don't underestimate me because I'm not a white man.'

Edward's mask dropped. His face was now cold and devoid of all emotion. Stripped of his power he seemed to disappear a little, and Jia couldn't help but enjoy the moment. He slid the blue folder back towards her.

'We need something in seven days,' he said. 'We have an important client coming into town and need to show him a good time. I was looking for something a little different, if you get my meaning?'

Jia nodded and leaned over, putting her hand on his arm and smiling. He didn't know whether it was fear or relief that washed over him, but he felt compelled to comply.

'So, let me see if I understand correctly: after the first delivery, we can buy online through the website by placing an order for…I don't know, stationery or something, and depending on what I pick you'll know what my order is?'

'Yes. The code is pretty simple. You'll pick it up in no time,' said Idris.

'Forgive me, but this all sounds crazy. You're openly selling this stuff online? You're either brave or stupid.'

'Bravery has nothing to do with it,' said Jia. 'I trust our system. Our IT experts make sure all transactions are obscure. If the authorities wanted to track down our users, they would have nowhere to look. The only money good here is crypto-currency. It's the online equivalent of a brown bag of cash.'

'And how will you explain all your crypto-currency?' said Edward.

'Our income comes purely from Bitcoin mining,' said Jia.

'So what about delivery?' said Edward. 'How does that work?'

'There are a number of ways,' Idris replied. 'One way is through the breakfast or lunch order system. Every morning you get your PA to place an order at this number.' He handed Edward a business card. 'These are the contact details for your friendly neighbourhood narcotics shop. They also do a mean mozzarella panini and the best all-day halal breakfast in town.'

Edward laughed. 'That's what I like about you pick'n'mix Muslims: priorities, you've got them straight. Your business may be strictly haram but your food can't ever be!'

'We will have told them to expect your call,' Idris continued. 'Place your order and at 10.00A.M. and 1.00P.M. sharp the delivery boy will drop it off. Along with your sandwich. The only thing you have to do is wait, and make sure he delivers the breakfast box directly to your office. Lunch deal works well if you're looking for a hit a day.'

Edward nodded. 'What if I need deliveries throughout the day? For various people, you understand,' he said.

'Then I suggest you go with the Caretaker package. You put one of our guys on your office payroll as a janitor. We handle all the details, vetting, references, employment history, and make sure he has a clean record. He maintains the building, keeps the boys topped up through the day and cleans up – it all works beautifully. Of course, this works for your day-to-day needs. Any parties you want us to cater for, they'll need our events management services.'

They were unsure what convinced Edward in the end. Maybe it was their sales pitch, maybe he liked their product, or maybe he was afraid of what they had on him. Whatever it was, they knew that this big fish was enough to bring in the ocean.

CHAPTER 37

It was the smell of urine soaking through his father's trousers that the shopkeeper's son would never forget. That and the screams coming from within the shop as it burned to the ground.

The knife had been pressed into the sinews of the old man's neck, his eyes wide: he'd looked like a little child, afraid and helpless. His son had moved towards him, instinctively, but one look from Nowak stopped him dead in his tracks. He stepped back, impotent, angry and afraid in equal measure. They had refused to pay the protection money. Their allegiance had always been with the Khan, but he was dead, and now Nowak and his men were demanding blood.

'Malala Food Store,' said Nowak, reading the sign above the cigarette display stand. 'After the Nobel laureate girl?' Silence. The shopkeeper's son only had eyes for his father, and the urine that had pooled by his leg. He felt sick to his stomach. This was his fault. He should have asked Idris for help. He should have called earlier.

'If you'd paid my men your father would not be embarrassed in this way. But now we have to make an example of you.' Nowak grinned, brandishing the knife the way a conductor leads an orchestra and then placing it back on the old man's throat. His men hulked closed by. One of them kicked a box of laundry powder off the shelf. It fell with a thud, breaking open and spilling its contents across the floor. Another took a bottle of detergent and poured it over the powder, mixing it in with his boot, like children in a sandpit.

'What are you doing?' said Nowak. 'We're here to send a message.' The men smirked at each other. 'Fetch the cans,' he said. He wasn't used to getting his hands dirty but today was about more than this shop. It was about getting a reaction out of Jia Khan and the Jirga. He felt ignored, as if they didn't consider him worthy of their time. Like a petulant child, Nowak thrived on chaos and the attention it brought him.

His men returned with red canisters full to the brim with fuel. They unscrewed the caps and began pouring petrol all over the shelves, holding the cans high and slopping the oil around. The thick smell permeated the air. The shopkeeper's son could feel the stench in his throat. He tried to formulate a plan. There was a baseball bat by the till if he could only get to it, but he was by the door. He had been about to lock up when the men had forced their way in.

'Here, give me one of those,' said Nowak, taking one of the canisters and tracing a circle of petrol around the old man. 'Who can help you now?' he sneered.

The old man opened his eyes wide and looked at Nowak, the fear now gone. He was short, a few inches over five foot. He tilted his head up. 'Allah,' he said. 'Allah can save me,' and he spat at Nowak's feet.

Nowak picked up another can of petrol and doused the shopkeeper's son in fuel. One of his henchmen held the door open and pushed him towards it. Desperate not to leave his father, he grabbed hold of the doorway to try and stay.

'Get me my money,' said Nowak. 'And tell Jia Khan what you have seen. Tell her this is her fault. That if she does not give me the city, more of this will happen. Go!'

The young man fell out of the shop, scrambling for the nearest cashpoint, searching his pockets for his keys and his cards. They were empty. He had nothing but his phone. He dialled Idris. 'They've got my dad! They're going to kill him! I need money! Now!'

But by the time Idris arrived, the building was ablaze, the young man on his knees outside, his head in his hands. Idris dragged him back to a safe distance.

He was delirious, his eyes red, his body soaked through with sweat and petrol. 'They set the place alight as soon as I called you,' he said. 'They covered me in petrol so I couldn't help him! They were never going to wait! They have no mercy! He was an old man! Just a frail old man.' He cried out in agony, his spirit broken, his mind on the verge. 'There was no one to help us!' he said. 'No one.'

News of the incident spread quickly across the region. Rumours mixed with facts, turning the story into a myth that would be spoken of for years to come. By the time the fire was put out and the building safe enough for the old man's body to be brought out, there was nothing left. Dental records confirmed who he was.

The streets were filled with silence that night, as the city mourned the death of an innocent shopkeeper, a victim in a turf war that had little to do with him. His only crime: standing up to Nowak. The air was crisp, the orange glow from the street lights bathed the lanes, and the smell of coal and shisha wafted over the cobbles. Despite the great evil that had been done, the landscape remained unchanged. But something unseen had changed. A tipping point had been reached, a critical mass, and things would never be the same again.

CHAPTER 38

'They are upping their game,' Jia told her men. 'They are trying to take apart the grassroots of our operation and this cannot be tolerated.'

The attack on the shop had come hot on the heels of a blaze at a Khan storehouse. It was the third time the Brotherhood had done this. They had been building inroads slowly, taking advantage of the fact that Jia and her men were putting all their energies into restructuring the business.

The Company was bringing in more money than ever before and empty bellies were being filled. There was work for those who wanted it and education for the rest. From cleaners to coders, designers to project managers, sales associates to call-centre personnel, The Company offered jobs from entry level to professional. And if you didn't have the skills but showed the promise, the business would take you under its wing and train you up while paying your wage and rent. They hired in their own image. Instead of seeking outside investment, they pumped money into the area and kept it circulating.

The city was starting to flourish in ways it hadn't done in years. The future looked hopeful, with one serious exception.

Jia had let the Nowak problem fester for too long. The Brotherhood was trying to push the streets towards chaos again. While The Company had brought money and opportunities to people, the world outside it hadn't changed. The white structures that maintained control still existed. The city was still an enclave, and Nowak and his men knew how to take advantage of the tensions this caused. They had slowly been pouring oil on the fire that was lit the night of the drive-by club shooting. Nowak understood animal rage, how to draw it out, how to feed it. The most primal of all human urges, he planned to use it to tear the city apart.

Over the past six months, Jia had received several calls from community leaders asking for her help. The police were losing control of the city and had no way to bring things back into line. Maybe if they had brought Akbar Khan's killer to justice, things would have been different, but they had failed to find anything to link Nowak to the murder. Jia had listened to Mark Briscoe, still cautious about his intentions and undecided about her desire to work with him.

But when Idris had brought news of shopkeepers being targeted by Brotherhood gang members and being 'invited' to pay protection money, she knew the time for caution was over. The line had been crossed. The realisation of where that line was, had surprised her. She'd leaned back in her father's chair as Idris paced up and down, turning the thought over in her head, wondering if circumstances had changed her, or simply revealed what she had always been. 'Protection racketeering is what got my mother killed,' her cousin said. He was angrier than Jia had ever seen him. His eyes were stone cold, his voice resolute. 'We have to stop him. Nowak is salting our wounds. My father may be silent but we will never recover from what happened to our family. We will never flourish.'

Jia knew that Idris wasn't alone in his anger. Tensions were rising among her people. The wives of the men who had been hurt in the latest attacks were calling Pukhtun House to speak to her. Having a woman at the helm of the Khan family gave them the courage to make direct requests. The sisterhood was growing.

So Jia had gathered her most trusted men together. As well as her cousins, Bazigh Khan was there, the only one of her father's colleagues to be invited, being trusted by both Jia and the Jirga. And despite his not being family, Michael's presence had also been requested. Benyamin watched quietly from a corner of the room. Since his injuries had healed, he'd been pushing for more operational involvement and he had earned his place. They stood in Akbar Khan's study awaiting her direction.

'We must make a final decision today about how we want to resolve this,' she told them, 'and follow it through. Now is the time to exact badal.'

The Jirga had displayed uncharacteristic patience in their wait for badal. The returns from The Company had filled their gaping mouths and satisfied their greed; but it also meant they had allowed their old patch to fall to the side in favour of the bigger money. While they had been eating at the table, the dogs had taken their tossed-aside bones and turned them into a feast. Revenge had been placed in the cooler long enough; it was time to serve it up. The attacks on their territory reignited their demand and they had sent a message telling Jia that her time was running out. She must act.

Jia had spent much time contemplating her options before calling this meeting. Men had been sent to gather information about Nowak's plans. Foot soldiers had brought back intelligence that pointed to a massive haul by the gang, one so lucrative that it would allow the Brotherhood to solidify their hold on the city. Nowak was planning on selling his stash and was counting on Jia Khan's ignorance to get away with it.

'We know when Nowak and his men are meeting the buyers,' Idris said. 'We've fixed it so that the buyer is one of our men. He's from the Newcastle zai. We know the guys will be driving a black Beamer and we know where they intend to make the drop. The money and goods will be exchanged at the same time, at a service station thirty miles from here. We have arranged for police to be thin on the ground.'

'Michael, who is in charge of our cars?' Jia said. The medical student had become one of the most trusted members of the group.

'That would be Fat Bob,' said Michael. Jia raised an eyebrow. 'That's his name,' he added. 'I can't do anything about it!'

'OK. Tell him, this Fat Bob, what we need and tell him to sort it tonight. We need two cars, and we need them to be clean,' she said.

Bazigh Khan listened, watching the young woman carefully lay out her plans, and he thought of his brother. Akbar Khan had known his daughter would take his place, and it had come to pass just as he had predicted, the demise of the Khan and the rise of his daughter. 'Your father kept a car especially for a job like this,' he said. 'It's in the garage, untraceable.' Headstrong and proud, he could see that Jia was smarter than her father had been. But she also knew when to ask for advice, and he was pleased with the respect she accorded him. Jia thanked her uncle for the information and arrangements were made for the car to be brought out of storage.

'How is buying their shipment going to help us any? Whether we buy it or someone else gets it, they still get what they want,' asked Nadeem.

Jia didn't answer but turned to Bazigh Khan. 'I would like you to convey to the Jirga that we are handling the situation,' she told him. 'Thank you for coming over this late. You must be tired. Why don't you rest a little while we finish?'

Bazigh Khan nodded. He understood the request was a respectful way of asking him to retire, and he had been prepared for this. She was slowly disentangling him from the knotty business and allowing him to hand over his responsibilities to his sons. The loss of power would have made a lesser man angry, but Bazigh Khan knew the ways of his family; he knew they would still call upon him for counsel, just without the pressure of practical matters, and he was also glad this meant he'd be able to spend time with his granddaughter. He left the room.

'I understand your desire to bring the family business out of the dark ages,' said Nadeem. 'And I'm with you on that, but I don't understand how buying Nowak's stash constitutes badal or solves our problem. They're still going to be here, they're still going to be demanding protection money from our people. They'll just have our money and be stronger because of it.'

'What are we missing, Jia?' Malik said. 'There's obviously more to the plan than this. Otherwise we wouldn't be here. So what is it?'

'We do the switch,' she said. 'We give Nowak the cash. We send the shipment out, as I've explained to our own dealers.' Her eyes were stone cold, her voice steady. 'Then,' she said, looking at her brother and pausing, 'we kill them.'

There was a silence. Nadeem looked uncomfortable. 'I know Idris is with you but I need time,' he said. 'You're talking about us physically killing someone. Don't get me wrong, Nowak needs to die. But taking a gun and pulling the trigger at point blank range? I don't know if I could do that. The drugs, the rest of it, that's easy, but this…the practicalities of it… I need time to get my head around it.'

'Of course,' she said. 'Think it over. Make sure you can live with your actions. Because once we do this there's no going back.'

CHAPTER 39

The last time Jia Khan slipped into his house in the dead of night, Elyas had told her it was over. 'I can't do this any more,' he'd said.

'Well then, stop taking my calls,' she'd replied, a little too quickly. And he knew that would never happen. She would call, and his heart would race and his greed for her rise up, and he would have no choice but to answer and unlock the door and take her into his bed. His desire for her was gnawing at his senses, inhibiting pathways of reason and logic. She was calamitous but he was in love with her. When she said 'stop taking my calls', the thought that she might no longer come to him threatened to become real, and he knew that the need was as much his as hers.

But he had Ahad to consider. Watching her every move as he spoke, making sure she wasn't spooked, he'd told her that, in that case, they must spend time out of the cover of darkness, doing the things that normal families do. She agreed, and so it was that Elyas and Ahad arrived at the domed turrets and Corinthian pillars of the Alhambra, where Jia had arranged for them to go to a concert.

The lobby was a sea of sherwanis and tuxedos, and over-processed brown women teetering on heels with backcombed bleached-blonde hair. Elyas noted that his son looked out of place in his faded T-shirt, ripped jeans and blazer, but Ahad didn't seem bothered by it. Elyas gave him one of the tickets. 'Thanks for doing this,' he said. 'I know it's not been easy.' His phone buzzed. He looked at it. 'It's Jia, she's running late. Come on, let's find our seats,' he said, and led Ahad through the bustle to their places.

The auditorium was slowly starting to fill up. Elyas and Ahad squeezed past a couple in their row and dropped into their seats.

'Dad, you need to tell her how you feel. You can't keep pretending you're OK.'

'Who says I'm pretending?'

'If she's going to stay over, she needs to start staying over properly and not leaving before dawn like some teenager. This has been going on for a stupid amount of time. Did you really think I hadn't noticed?'

Elyas laughed, nervousness covering his embarrassment. 'OK, you're right and I'm sorry. We've talked about it. We're working through it. She's just…you know. Your mother, she's been through a lot. She's just scared.'

'Dad, you must be the only person on the planet who would describe that woman as scared.' The hum of musicians filtering on to the stage and tuning their instruments interrupted their conversation. The sound of sitar and tabla mingled with the hum of the audience speaking to each other in Mirpuri, Urdu, Gujarati, Hindi, Hinko and English. They quietened down as an old Punjabi folk singer seated himself centre stage, his waistcoat matching the velvet bolsters he reclined on. To his right stood a beautiful young woman. Her jeans clung to her curves, oversized headphones covering her thick black hair. She moved slowly to the melody of the songs, adding her voice to them, softening their sharpness with modern tones. They were nearly an hour into the show when Jia arrived. The couple in the neighbouring seats stood up to let her pass, and she whispered an apology to them in Pashto, which the man acknowledged with a nod.

'Where were you?' whispered Elyas. 'You've missed most of it.'

'Meeting the police,' said Jia, her eyes on the stage. He wanted to ask what the police wanted with her, but he knew she wouldn't tell him, and even if she did she'd swear him to secrecy, and that would be excruciating for the journalist in him.

As soon as the interval arrived, Elyas made his way to the men's room to give Ahad and Jia some space. He was washing his hands when someone tapped him on the shoulder. He turned round to find an old friend from school grinning at him.

'Elyas!' he said. 'How long has it been? I keep seeing you on those documentaries, man! You have done well!'

'Thanks! How are you? Still playing footie?'

'Only on Sunday mornings now, I'm afraid. I'm in the police force. Keeps me busy. What brings you to this neck of the woods?'

'I'm taking some time out of TV to work at the local paper. You must hear some things in your line of work?'

'I used to. I'm working as a community liaison officer these days, visiting mosques, speaking with the imams.'

'How's that? I guessed with things getting better on the job front, tensions might have eased.'

'They did for a while. But sometimes it feels like one step forward, ten steps back in this city. Remember the guys who shot the bouncer? I can't remember the date, but it was over a year ago now. The ones who went on the run and were finally caught? Well, their case is due in court next week, and it's stoked up old feelings. There's talk going around that the men were mistreated, bullied into confessions – that it may not even have been them pulling the trigger.'

'Really? The evidence is overwhelming, though. Right down to eyewitnesses.'

'I know that. But the kids would rather believe in conspiracy theories than what the police are saying, because the police haven't historically been their friends. I mean, even you and I will have experienced that.'

They walked slowly back to the lobby, Elyas listening attentively, his concern growing.

'With Akbar Khan gone, there's been a power vacuum,' his friend went on. 'Some of the younger members of the community, they're vying for positions. It's complicated. The city has become a powder keg. It feels as if nothing can stop it from blowing.'

Before they parted, Elyas suggested they exchange numbers. 'Give me a call if you want to talk on the record?' His friend nodded, and they said their goodbyes. Then Elyas headed to the bar, where he found Ahad ordering drinks. 'Where's Jia?' he asked.

'She's back in the auditorium, being the ice queen,' Ahad replied.

'It's not that bad, is it?'

'Let's not do this again,' said Ahad. 'Don't make her spend time with me. She hates me.'

'She doesn't hate you.'

'She won't even look at me half the time and the rest of the time she speaks to me as if I'm on work experience.' Elyas could see the hurt in his son's face. He reached out but the boy turned away. 'I have to go pee. I'll see you in there,' he said, heading towards the toilets.

Elyas made his way back to the auditorium with the drinks, his head spinning. He was worried about Ahad. He was ready to confront Jia. But she wasn't in her seat when he got there. He looked around and saw her standing near one of the fire exits, deep in conversation with a man Elyas recognised as the one who'd been sitting next to her. His complexion was pale, his eyes deep blue, making him stand out in the sea of brown faces. Elyas watched them for a moment; the man looked as though he was leaving – he was putting the package he was carrying into his pocket and pulling his coat on – so Elyas decided to head over.

'He read it?' he heard Jia ask as he approached. She took something from the man and placed it in her bag. Elyas was surprised they were speaking in Pashto not English, but he reminded himself there were Caucasian-looking Pathans.

'He did,' came the man's reply.

'Thank you. For taking it to him,' said Jia.

His gaze lowered, the man placed his right hand across his chest and bowed his head before leaving.

Jia turned around to find Elyas behind her.

'Who was that?' he said.

'Someone who knew my father,' Jia said. 'He wanted to introduce himself.'

'Wasn't he sitting next to us? The man you apologised to in Pashto when you arrived?'

'Yes, I think so.'

'How did you know he was Pathan? I couldn't help assuming he was white.'

'I don't know, Elyas, maybe I don't make assumptions like you.'

'It was just a question.' Her dismissiveness was beginning to grate.

'Shall we go back to our seats?' she said. Her voice was distant and detached, and it riled Elyas further. He had kept his emotions in check for the sake of his son, but he couldn't do it any more.

'What's going on with you?' he burst out.

'Excuse me?'

'Ahad. He's really trying, and you're not. Why are you being cold with him?' His voice was loud, his face agitated. A few people turned in their seats to see what was happening, but he didn't care. 'He's upset. Our son is upset. You don't seem to give a damn. What kind of a woman are you?'

'I don't know what you're talking about,' she said, stepping out of the stream of concert-goers making their way back to their seats.

Her empty words angered him further. 'I'm talking about the fact that you left me!' he said. 'I'm talking about the fact that you walked out on me and you never even thought to give me an explanation! I've been raising him alone. Yes, it made me stronger, and I'm probably a better man for it, but I don't want to feel like this any more. And Ahad has no choice but to crave your love, yet you dangle it in front of him and then don't make any effort!'

'Are you done?' she said.

'No!' he said. 'I'm pissed off!' He inhaled and shook his head. 'I'm done.'

'Go back to London, Elyas. You're a nice guy, but this isn't the place for nice guys.'

'Listen to me, Jia. He's a good kid. But he's not had it easy and that's led to him making some bad choices. I'm worried that once he crosses the line he won't be able to find his way back.'

Standing behind them, Ahad heard every word, and he knew that the line had already been crossed.

They sat awkwardly through the second half of the show. Elyas was glad the couple next to them had gone. He wasn't in the mood to make polite conversation. When it was over, the three of them left the theatre in silence. Orange street lights studded the night sky, and there was a steady backdrop hum of traffic, punctuated only by the distant sound of the odd siren. They set off down the road to the curry house where he had parked his car. Jia was about to cross the street, her foot stepping out on to the tarmac, when she heard a screeching of tyres and felt her chest being crushed as a strong arm hit her full on, pushing her to the ground. She landed heavily, her handbag spilling its contents across the road, and there followed what sounded like a volley of fireworks, so loud that her eardrums felt as if they would burst. Time seemed to slow down and then speed up as people ran towards her and then past her to help someone else. Jia looked across to see a man on the ground, his body heavy and lifeless. Something was seeping into her clothes and on to her hands. She brought her fingers up to her face to see what it was, and was hit by the unmistakeable smell of iron. It was blood. Where was Elyas? She looked around frantically, her head cloudy, her eyes trying to focus on the body. From the angle at which he lay, she couldn't tell who it was. Then she heard Elyas's voice, followed by Ahad's, and relief flooded over her.

The ringing in her ears had subsided by the time Elyas reluctantly left her on the doorstep of Pukhtun House. Everything that had happened since the shooting – the rush to get to safety, dropping

Ahad off, the journey home – had gone by in a blur. As soon as Elyas had handed back the things he'd picked up off the road, she thanked him and said goodnight, stuffing them back into her handbag. She didn't want him to stay. When she got in the house, she rummaged for her phone. Everything was covered in fine powder – her compact must have smashed when it fell to the ground. She brushed off the phone and dialled.

'What happened? Was it Nowak?' she said when Idris picked up.

'No, not as far as we know. We can't be sure yet who the target was, or if there even was one. The streets are turning rogue without a Khan. They're trying to fill the void he left, fighting among themselves.'

'And the man? The one who was shot?'

'He's dead. Shot by one of the men on the motorbike. He was just some guy who had stopped to buy milk on his way home from work. Wife, kids, steady job.'

Jia ended the call with the feeling that Idris blamed her, that on some level this was her fault. That the entire city was on the verge of self-destruction because she hadn't acted sooner to stop it. And she knew he was right. She'd shunned the old ways of doing business in her pursuit of a shake-up, but if she wanted to keep control, she was going to have to do some of the things she hated her father for.

CHAPTER 40

He pulled the collar of his jacket up around his neck and blew into his hands to warm them. The holding cell was cold. He didn't know how long he'd been there and he didn't know long it would take for his father to realise he was missing. The police had picked him up at the Cuedos snooker club in Burlington. He'd gone there after the shooting to blow off some steam. After dropping him at home and saying goodnight, his dad had driven off with Jia. Ahad knew he would be more concerned about her than him tonight.

He'd been in a place he shouldn't be in, doing things he knew he shouldn't do. The officers had been heavy-handed and he'd mouthed off, tried to resist arrest, and had ended up paying the price. He traced his finger over his eyelid, afraid, hoping he would be able to see once the swelling went down. He wondered how he was going to explain this to his father. His bravado was gone; waiting alone in a police cell took him to dark places. He had never been caught before. He thought of Jia and wondered what he would have felt if she had actually died today. He thought of his dad, and the disappointed look that would flash across his face. When were the police going to call him?

Ahad had always been a clever child, even labelled 'gifted' by the child psychologist who had seen him at the age of six on the school's recommendation. That was when things had changed. He'd begun being disruptive in class, throwing ink on his school bible and using indelible pens to write complicated equations on walls when his teacher's back was turned. The teachers had been more excited by the possibility of his ability than worried. They'd worked hard with him and he realised 'gifted' didn't mean anything without work. He lacked focus; he didn't really know what he wanted other than to learn the things that interested him. He didn't need therapy to know that his 'no fucks given' hardwiring for everything other than his father was his mother's fault. It was all her fault.

His father was the best among bad men. After spending years trying to reach up to the pedestal on which he'd placed Elyas, Ahad had come to the conclusion that it was pointless. Besides, his father did have his flaws, he'd discovered, chief among them his inability to resolve conflict. And so, sitting in that freezing cold cell in a police station, waiting for what was to come, he blamed his mother and his father too.

He heard the cold sound of metal turning in the lock and the heavy door swung slowly open, screeching along the stone floor. A policeman stood on the other side, his smile wide, like a clown in a uniform. 'Well, sir,' he said, 'it's time for you to leave our premises.'

Ahad stood up as the officer stepped forward, expecting something terrible.

'Would you like a Hobnob?' the policeman asked, offering him the packet he held in his hand. Ahad looked visibly confused, unsure of what he was being asked. 'You know, in case you're peckish?' the policeman said.

Ahad looked at the biscuits and the years dropped from his shoulders. 'I'm OK, but thank you,' he said.

'No worries, I just thought you might be hungry,' said the officer. He led Ahad out of the cell and down a corridor. 'You should've said you were Jia Khan's son. If I'd have known... We didn't treat you too shabbily, did we?' Ahad didn't answer.

Jia was in the reception area signing some paperwork.

'Shall we go?' she said.

'Where's my dad?' he asked.

'He doesn't know about this. Probably thinks you're tucked up in bed. You want me to tell him?'

'Not really,' Ahad replied.

'He'll know something happened when he sees you, though. I'm going to send him a message, to let him know you're with me,' she said.

'I'll handle it,' he protested. She ignored him, typing a quick text and hitting send before Ahad could stop her. 'How'd you know I was here?'

Jia picked up her bag. 'Does it matter?'

He didn't answer. Jia noticed his eyes were red and he'd been crying. 'Are you OK?' she asked. Her words angered him. He hadn't wanted her to see him like this; he didn't want her to know how much he cared, how much he resented the power she held over him. They walked out in silence, Ahad a few steps ahead.

'I'll find my own way home, thanks,' he said. The police station was in an isolated spot, high on a hill overlooking the city and beyond. The street lamps extended rivers of artificial light across the county. The air was biting and fog was beginning to descend into the valley. Stuffing his hands into his pockets, Ahad looked around for a street sign, a bus stop, anything to help him get home without having to call his father. But there was nothing.

Jia watched him, and understood that he was trying to figure out his next move and save face. 'Here.' She held out his keys and mobile phone. He took them from her and turned away again. 'Let's go,' she said, as if she'd picked him up from his mate's house not the police station, and as though this was any other day.

He pushed his fists into his pockets, the cotton threads digging into his knuckles, hoping that the pain would cut through his anger at her lack of understanding, but it didn't work. 'Fuck you,' he said. 'Fuck you and your uppity white calm ways.'

The abruptness of his words surprised her. She had expected to face his anger at some point but not today. Not when she was finally stepping up to take responsibility for him.

He had looked so small and so innocent when the officer had led him out of the cell; he'd reminded her of herself in the days before things changed. She wanted to tell him this and more but she was proud and she wouldn't allow anyone to speak to her in that manner, not even her own son. 'When you hurl abuse at me, we have two problems,' she said. 'First, you're trying to hurt me and I've not given you permission to do that. And second, hurting me now may hurt you in the future. Do you understand?'

'Thanks, Oprah, not quite the "aha moment" I was looking for but thanks. You're going to lecture me now? Because if you are you're sixteen fucking years too late.' He felt the blood rushing to his head, pounding harder, drowning out all external noise. He would never speak to his father like this, but he needed her to understand what she'd done. He wanted to bait her and hurt her the way she had hurt him. It was time to do this.

Words continued to fire out of him like nails, hitting her hard. 'Where the fuck have you been?' he said. 'You're picking me up from a police station. The first time you're picking me up *ever*, not from school, not from football, but from a police station! Does that not affect you at all? Where were you when all the other kids' mothers were making them packed lunches and crappy Halloween costumes? Or when I lost my first tooth, spoke at my first assembly, learnt to kick a football? Where were you all those nights I was too scared to sleep in case Dad died and they put him in the ground? Where were you, Jia Khan?'

Jia watched him shouting at her, the vein on his forehead pulsing the way her father's and brother's had, when the blood was still flowing through them. Ahad's words didn't hurt her in the way he hoped; the pain she had inflicted on herself was far worse than anything he could say. But her heart did break for him. It cracked inside her chest, the pain spreading into her limbs. This was what she had been running from.

She wanted to go to him but she didn't know how. She hadn't held him since he was a few days old. And he kept shouting without pause, the angry tears running down his face as he pleaded with her for answers. 'What kind of woman shuts her husband and kid out of her life? And he, Dad, brings me here to see you, and you have no explanation! Nothing! You talk to me about shitty family crap and history and Khans and Pathans! What about me? How about we talk about me for a fucking second? Remember me, the kid you gave birth to? You fucking waltz around like the queen of fucking everything and you couldn't even call your own son? Because you know what I think? You're a liar. It was all bullshit. I think you knew I was alive. Because if you really thought I was dead, why didn't you call my dad to talk to him about it? To share your grief? Or is that it? You didn't feel anything? Your old man may have been a crim but at least he was honest about it! You, you're just a lying cunt of a bitch.'

The word snapped her back to the here and now. She remembered all the things she had done and all the things she was about to do for family, and the emotion in her drained away. 'Yes. I am,' she said. 'And that makes you a son of a bitch.'

He stopped, shock spreading across his face. He had expected her to argue, not accept his accusations. He had wanted to hate her so much but she hadn't let him. He had wanted her to say so much more but she wasn't prepared to. And now he was exhausted and he didn't have any fight left in him to make her see what she had done.

'Get in the car, kid,' she said, her tone cool. 'Just get in the car and I'll drive you home. You were caught trying to deal class A drugs, remember that? I'm the one who's pulled strings and got the charges dropped, so unless you want to spend the next few years in a juvenile detention centre, I suggest you get in the car.' She pointed towards an Aston Martin DB9.

He looked over at it, and found it hard not to be impressed. It was a beautiful car.

'You want to try it out?' she said.

'What? Really?'

'Yes, just wipe your nose before you get in. I don't want your tears and snot all over the interior.'

He did as he was told, all his anger gone in an instant. How had she done that without giving him any answers? He walked to the driver's side and tried the door.

'Other side,' she said. 'One arrest in twenty-four hours is enough. There's plenty of private road at Pukhtun House. You can try her out there.'

Ahad stared out of the window for most of the journey; his head hurt from the events and the sound of his own voice.

'Elyas told me you were a good kid,' Jia said.

'I am a good kid.'

'I think the police would disagree.'

'What about you?'

She smiled at him, and for the first time in a long time it felt like genuine emotion. 'No. I don't think you're bad. You're my son after all.' She had never spoken those words before and something inside him warmed. 'Sometimes, the best people we know do the worst things just to keep the good people safe. Like my father. And maybe like your mother.'

They reached the gates to the house, swapping seats once safely inside. Ahad clicked the belt buckle into place and put his hands on the wheel, wrapping his fingers around it. He started the engine, pushed his foot on the clutch to move the gearstick but lifted it off too fast: the machine jolted forward and stalled. He tried again and again with the same result. Jia waited patiently, her face stoic, letting him try and fail and try again. She hadn't been there when he'd learnt to walk, but she was here as he learnt to drive and she planned to stay.

'It's harder than it looks,' he whispered. In the space of a few hours, Ahad had been arrested, and then rescued by the woman who had abandoned him, the woman he hated; he'd let her rile him and had spewed venom at her. He had wanted so desperately for her to be impressed and instead he felt like a fool. 'I am clearly a loser of gargantuan proportions,' he said. 'You can't even bear to look at me. Can you? Do you still dislike me that much?'

She didn't answer. Her mind was back at the police station, running through the things he'd said. The police chief had called to give her a heads-up. 'I hope now we can be friends, Ms Khan?' he'd said on the phone. Ahad had been caught up in a routine raid, a small fish in a big net. 'If my tiddler was mixed up in this kind of thing I'd want a friend looking out for him. Probably just needs his mother to set him straight. Most of these young men do. But then, you know him better than I.'

But she didn't know Ahad. And sitting next to him, trying to make sense of things, she realised that in protecting herself she had inadvertently damaged her son. Something she had never intended. She reached into her handbag and pulled out her lipstick. There were certain things that simply shouldn't be said without lipstick, and times where its application gave a woman the space to gather her thoughts.

'You know…when they handed you to me you were so tiny, so helpless,' she said. 'I didn't want to let you go, and I kept you on me, on my chest, all night… Before, when I was pregnant, they told me there was something wrong with you, and I went to have a termination. But I couldn't do it. By the time I found out I was pregnant, you were kicking…and I was afraid.'

'You were scared? But nothing scares you.'

'You don't think I'm human?' she said. He doubted her ability to feel, and she knew many thought the same, and while she didn't care what others thought, she did care about him. He was her son, and though buried, her love for him ran deep. And so she cut open her chest and took out her heart for him to see. The words felt trite and saccharine on her tongue but they were the truth, and she knew that the bitter taste left by their sweetness said more about her than her choice of them. 'Life is about losing,' she said, 'losing time, the people we love, our innocence, our ideals. That is all I know of life. So yes, I was afraid, I was afraid of the pain that comes with love. And so…when they told me you'd died, I was relieved. Relieved because I loved you so much that it hurt me. It's not something I expected until I felt you within me, growing slowly, listening gently to the things I heard.

'Ahad,' she said, and for the first time he heard the weight of a mother's feeling in that address. 'Great love is not the thing of romance novels. It comes from blood. It comes from opening a vein for family, from seeing your face in each other, in your child, your brother, your father. Seeing yourself look back at you through someone else's eyes, knowing that you would sacrifice yourself, piece by piece, for them, until there was nothing left of you.'

Ahad was afraid to look at her in case it broke the spell. 'You were so perfect, so alert,' she said. 'But you were unable to protect yourself. How I felt about you, it was such an overwhelming thing I couldn't look at you. The way I loved you was all-consuming!' she said. 'If I had returned to your father…been reunited with you… stayed with you…it would have destroyed me and you. You made me afraid. For the first time in my life I was afraid of everything. You were my weakness.' She looked at him. 'But I will make you my strength. If you will let me.'

Hot, salty tears washing away years of anger, loss and loathing flowed down his face as he broke down. And as they flowed she reached over and put her arms around him. He couldn't tell how long they sat there, or how long he wept, but the velvet night deepened and then abated around them, and the azaan was calling believers to prayer when they finally walked through the door to Pukhtun House. Jia covered her head and showed Ahad the way to the ablution room. 'Do you pray?' she asked. He nodded. 'Good.'

Ten minutes later, ritually cleansed, heads bowed and arms folded, they stood side by side on the prayer mat, a very different mother and son from the pair who had met the evening before. When they were done, she whispered the words of the Ayat-ul-Kursi and blew them across his face. Her mother had done the same for her every night when she was a child, telling her the verse of the Quran would protect her.

'What is that for?'

'The world is full of sharps and shards. I can't save you from them – I have come to terms with that now – so I place you in the protection of Him in whose hands and control my life rests. He is all people like you and I have,' she said. 'He is all we have.'

CHAPTER 41

'Some men are here to search the house.' Maria's voice came through Jia's dream, waking her up. She dreamt of the events that led to Zan's death so often that it took a few moments for her to realise this time it was real. It was starting to get light outside. Maria was standing by the bedroom door in her pyjamas, much older than the last time she'd said these words. She should have been tucked up in bed beside her husband, but had stayed over to comfort Sanam Khan, who was still having trouble sleeping alone and suffered bouts of insomnia. The coincidence that led to this moment of déjà vu was not lost on Jia.

She picked up her mobile phone to look at the time, noting a couple of missed calls on the log. She'd have to check them later. She hurried downstairs and looked at the video screen. There were five of them, all dressed in black, waiting by the gates to the house. 'We are here to search your premises,' said the lead officer, speaking into the intercom. It took a moment for Jia to recognise her. She cast her mind back: it was the officer whose reputation she had sullied in court a few years back, the one she had accused of having an affair with the wife of one of Nowak's men. She was glad that Maria had been smart enough to leave her out in the cold.

'Do you have a warrant to search the premises, Officer Swan?' asked Jia.

'We don't need one,' she replied. Her face was still, but her eyes flashed with anger. Jia could see that that day in court had changed her, and she had been nursing this grudge for quite some time, waiting for the day she would show Jia Khan who was boss. But this wasn't that day.

'I'm afraid I can't let you in.'

'You are legally obliged to allow us entry,' said the officer.

'You don't have a warrant.'

'Under the Police and Criminal Evidence Act of 1984, we are allowed to enter and search the premises after the arrest of someone linked to the property. We have made such an arrest.'

'No one who lives here has been arrested.'

'Benyamin Khan was arrested at 1.00A.M. this morning.'

Jia flinched. She had spoken without having all the facts. Her mind flipped back to the missed calls: it must have been from her contact at the station.

'For what?'

The woman pressed her lips together into a thin smile. 'Kerb-crawling,' she said.

Jia turned to her sister with a questioning look. She shrugged.

'I heard him come in about an hour ago. Someone must have bailed him out,' said Maria.

'Idris,' Jia said, under her breath.

'How long can we leave them out there?'

'Go and get Ben. Bring him down.'

As Maria hurried up the stairs, Jia picked up her phone and flicked through her contacts for Mark Briscoe. He answered after the third ring; his voice sounded groggy. 'What time is it?' he said.

'Mark, five of your officers are outside my house,' she said.

'Let me get back to you.' He hung up. His instant response pleased her and she logged it in her mental ledger. Over the last couple of months her relationship with the police chief had gone from cold to cordial, and was warming towards friendship. While not entirely throwing caution to the wind, she had accepted the fact that it was in both their interests to cooperate given the deteriorating situation in the city. Jia's connections gave her access to red carpets, VIP passes to shows, and private boxes at Premier League matches, which she was happy to pass on to her friends and colleagues, especially those who had earned her favour.

She looked up to see Maria coming down the stairs, Ben a few steps behind. He stopped halfway, just as he had the last time the police had come to search their home. His face had healed, his cheekbones returned, and despite having had little sleep, he looked refreshed. Jia loved her brother, but she wished he would make better choices.

'What's going on?' he said, wiping the sleep from his eyes.

'The police are here to search the house.' She wanted to add, *because of you*, but her phone rang. It was Mark.

Maria and Benyamin waited as Jia took the call. She didn't speak at first, just listened, and then eventually said, 'I understand. You don't need to apologise.' She turned to her brother and sister as she spoke, and smiled. 'Yes, Mark, I'll see you tomorrow morning.'

'What do we do?' asked Benyamin when she'd hung up.

'Nothing.'

'But Maria said they want to search the house. We can't just let them in.'

'Where were you tonight?' Jia said, ignoring him. 'What were you doing that made them think you were kerb-crawling?' The intercom buzzed loudly before he could answer, and Jia pushed the button to let the visitors in. She looked at Benyamin. 'This is your mess,' she said. 'You should get this.'

A look of uncertainty passed over Benyamin's face. He walked to the door slowly, turned the handle and stepped outside to find Officer Swan pulling up alone in her unmarked car. There was no sign of her colleagues. She climbed out and walked to the front steps, her face burning up as she approached. Benyamin, confused at first, regained his composure, remembering who he was.

'Officer Swan,' said Jia, stepping forward. 'I believe you have something to say to my brother.'

The policewoman stuttered and stammered her way through an apology. Something about crossed wires, Chief Constable Briscoe, and being more careful next time. Jia watched, her eyes on Benyamin; he seemed rooted to the spot with relief. She hoped that this would go some way to making him whole again. Even though it was Nowak who had inflicted the most recent wounds, Jia knew the trauma ran deeper than that. It had started years earlier with Zan's brushes with the law. Benyamin had been a child then, but those who had raised him had been coloured by the incident.

Her father had used bribery and corruption to keep the police in his pocket, and now Jia had sweetened the deal with favours and buttoned them in for good.

CHAPTER 42

An elderly man in a tired suit carefully spooned biryani into his mouth, his eyes on the curry house, watching customers order, eat, pay and leave. Despite the late hour the restaurant was filled with families young and old. Children played in between the tables as parents and grandparents folded pieces of naan into morsels and dipped them in sauce for them. Across the other side of the restaurant, Elyas was dining with John.

They'd been eating at Café de Khan for as long as John could remember. The place was a cultural institution, having been around since the sixties. One of the first Pakistani eateries in the country, through the years its clientele had gone from homesick immigrants looking for a taste of home, to Hindi film stars and white middle-class food connoisseurs. Now with branches across the country, its newer establishments were slick, with modern interiors. But the original restaurant maintained its old-fashioned school-canteen feel. Prices were low and service was fast, and alcohol was strictly prohibited, but that didn't stop the crowds.

'Will you put that thing down, for God's sake!' said John to Elyas. He'd been on his phone since they arrived.

'What? I'm working! That's why I am who I am and you are not,' said Elyas.

'You're on that bloody social media site again, aren't you? What's it called? Tip-off?' John found new media irritating, probably because it had sounded the death knell for newspapers.

'One of these days it's going to help us find a big story before the police sirens get there,' said Elyas.

'I'll stick to police media lines and tip-offs from real people, thanks,' John replied.

Elyas looked up. 'Did you know that South Asians are more likely to take up new technology than their white counterparts? And did you know that the brown pound is stronger than the equivalent white pound?'

'And did YOU know you're buying me dinner with that strong brown pound?' said John. 'Speaking of money. Did you get anywhere with the "havala" story?'

'The money-laundering one?' Elyas had been looking into the money transfer method after a tip-off from the police. 'Yeah, a little bit. I know that travel agents are involved, and that there's no paper trail. It's pretty complicated and I'm not sure anyone really understands it and that's what makes it such a great way for criminals to hide and move money. Why do you ask?'

'Just something I've been looking into recently,' answered John. 'There are lots of hand car-wash places opening up across the city. I'm wondering if they're dodgy.'

'Probably,' said Elyas.

The waiter brought their order and placed it on the table. They began eating even before he'd left, Elyas tearing large chunks off the chapatti and dipping it in the karahi. 'Who needs plates?' he said.

It had been a long day. The city had been boiling over with news and they hadn't had time to eat. When John finally looked up from his plate he saw they were being watched. 'Why do they let that old homeless man hang around? He's always stalking the staff, judging the customers.'

'Maybe because he owns the place?' said Elyas, smiling.

John looked at the elderly man he'd thought was homeless. His suit was oversized and his grey hair dishevelled, but Elyas was right: he was in charge. He called one of the waiters over and pointed to a table that needed cleaning. The waiter bowed repeatedly, fear written across his face, before rushing to clear away the dishes beside him. 'I'd like to have people be that scared of me when I'm old. And have them do my bidding,' John said.

'What, on eBay, you mean?'

'Funny,' said John. 'Any leads on anything on that thing then?'

'Plenty. I'm using this site called Yik Yak. People use it to post stuff about specific places,' Elyas said. 'Remember that shooting last year, the one outside the club? Well, there's a lot of differing accounts about who was responsible.'

John raised an eyebrow. 'It's a bit late for that, isn't it? Trial's already begun.'

They were deep in conversation when Jia walked in. She spoke with the owner; Idris was with her and Michael waited by the door. The old man said something to the waiter before leading his guests to an office in the back of the restaurant.

'Did you know she was going to be here?' John asked Elyas. Elyas shook his head. 'I'd give anything to know what business a high-flying legal eagle and a slick city boy are discussing in the back of a curry-house kitchen with that homeless man,' said John. 'Do you think she's getting mixed up in their business?'

'I don't know… Anyway, how are things going with your new novel?' Elyas replied, changing the subject. His relationship with Jia was now public knowledge. She was spending more time with Ahad, which was good, but something was wrong. The Jia he had fallen in love with and the one he knew now were very different. It was as if the sun and the moon divided her personality. During the day she was devoid of all emotion, her behaviour alien to him.

As John settled the bill, Elyas hoped she was not about to pay a price too high for her heritage.

Waiting at the back of the restaurant, Jia knew exactly what price life was about to extract from her and she was ready to make the payment. The old man spoke slowly, with the confidence of someone who knew his worth. 'I know you have come to me because I am childless and so have no part in the power struggle that is happening. I know what you are planning, Jia Khan,' he said, leaning forward as he spoke, looking her straight in the eye. 'We all do. We are old men, Jia jaan. We have lived. And we have learnt from that life.'

'My father spoke highly of you,' she said.

The old man smiled. 'You must know by now that to run this city is not easy. You must command the respect of the masses and the minorities. Sometimes it is the smaller groups that hold the power. Don't underestimate anyone. At your age your father had the respect of his people.'

Jia considered his words carefully before answering. 'You are right, respect must be earned. And I will do all I can,' she said.

Samad Khan was part of the landscape. The only member of the Jirga without a family, his wife – another Jia – to whom he had been betrothed from birth, had been the only person he ever loved. He was a short, dark-skinned Pathan, she pale and attractive, as intelligent as she was fierce. He would show her off and bask in her beauty, both of them laughing privately at the comments they received about their contrasting skin tones. They had wanted for nothing in life. Except for good health. Doctors had advised them that childbirth would prove disastrous. But his wife was stubborn and ignored the warnings. The baby didn't survive, and neither did she. After she died, Samad buried himself in work, emerging only when called by the Jirga.

Without a family to distract him, his business flourished. His curries were served by royal warrant and found on supermarket shelves and kitchen cupboards across the country. He knew power, how to wield it and take it, but it meant nothing to him.

His curry house was next door to the travel agency Nowak was using as his money-laundering headquarters. That was why Jia was here. She and her men needed access to put their plan into action. Samad was no threat to their operation, but without him and his blessing there was no plan.

'There is nothing you can do,' Samad Khan said. 'The paving of the path to respect began many years ago. Only with time will you know if it reaches your front door. And besides, you are a woman, what will you do in the world of men?'

'It is because I am a woman that you should trust my judgement,' Jia replied.

Samad Khan was intrigued. She was his wife's namesake and reminded him of her. 'Explain,' he said.

'Under Islamic law a man must divorce his wife in the presence of a qazi three times before they are no longer bound,' Jia said. 'After the first two talaq they can still reconcile. Men are easily angered, slaves to their passion and makers of rash judgements, as you and I know. A woman, she must only say once that she wants it and it is done. We women are more tolerant, we measure and weigh up before we make our decisions. This is God's ruling, not mine. But there are few who understand it. There is little choice here, Khan Baba. Nowak must go. He destroyed some of your storage centres, he has sent informants to the police saying that you hire illegal workers. It was only by my providing you with a tip-off that the raid came to nothing. On this you agree?' she said.

Samad Khan nodded. 'Those boys save every penny I give them to send home to their parents,' he said. 'They sleep ten in a room some of them, work all evening and late at night to help their families, marrying off their sisters, educating their brothers. They are not here to enjoy living off the benefits of the state. Nowak and his men, it is a sin what they are doing.' Speaking about the kitchen staff had unnerved Samad Khan. With no sons of his own he thought of these boys as his children, paying for their airfare, finding legal representation to iron out citizenship problems, helping them when they were sick. He was shaking now as he spoke.

Seeing this, Jia softened her tone. 'Yes, Baba, you are right,' she said. 'That is why you have my promise that by cooperating with us in dealing with our mutual problem, no harm will come to you or your staff. Just make sure your insurance is in order and I will do the rest. When this is over we will sit down and discuss how to assist you further. My legal team and expertise will be at your disposal. You have my word.'

The old man smiled. He had spent more than sixty years of his life toiling, and most of that without his wife. He was ready to retire. He had just been waiting for someone to hand things over to.

'My wife would have liked you,' he told Jia.

'And I would have liked her, I'm sure,' Jia said. 'You have my word…as the daughter of Pukhtunwali, I will help your people.'

The old man stood up. 'Please excuse me, it is time for my Isha namaaz,' he said. Then he placed his hand on Jia's head and brought it forward, kissing her forehead. She smiled and thanked him for his hospitality. Before leaving, she turned to the old man. 'Pray for me, Khan Baba,' she said. 'It seems the time for sacrifice is here. And we must all pay. You with your place of business, and I with my soul.'

CHAPTER 43

Nadeem awoke to the sound of his daughter crying. The little girl was standing by his door, clutching the shawl her mother had embroidered before she was born, her hair as red as her grandfather's. That was where the similarity to Bazigh Khan ended.

'Sweetie, what is it?' Nadeem asked.

The little girl rubbed her eyes and swallowed hard. 'Baba...Baba, there's a monster in my room. Can I stay here? With you?' Nadeem pulled the bed covers back and his daughter raced to climb in. She snuggled up to him, her tiny five-year-old feet ice cold. Nadeem rubbed them gently. 'Haala jaan, did you really see a monster?' he asked.

'No. But...Sarah at school told me that Uncle Akbar was a bad man and a monster and now that he is dead he will come and get me.' Haala stopped. She was embarrassed. 'She said that's why the girls won't come to my birthday party. Is it true, Baba? Is Uncle Akbar a monster?' The little girl looked up expectantly at her father.

Nadeem kissed the top of his daughter's head. 'No, my love. It's not true.'

'I'm glad,' she said. 'I liked him.' She paused for a moment and then spoke again tentatively. 'Baba,' she said. 'Is Mama a monster too?' Nadeem hugged the little girl tight and told her to sleep – she had school in the morning. But Haala had more questions. 'Baba, what is a Parkie? Sarah Mathews said I was a Parkie. I told her we weren't Parkies, we were Pukhtuns. That's right, isn't it, Baba?'

'Yes, darling. That's right. Now close your eyes,' he said. Nadeem looked down at the little girl, who was already starting to drift off in his arms. She was the most beautiful thing in his life. She had her grandmother's eyes, eyes that he hadn't seen since his mother died that day in the fire. Growing up without her had been hard. Nadeem had been his mother's favourite child. He felt her loss infinitely, even now. He'd buried himself in work; taking on other personas brought relief, at least for the time he was on stage. But Haala's birth had meant having to leave that life.

Nadeem's girlfriend, the little girl's mother, had left early on and he had raised Haala alone. Looking back, he didn't blame her. They had met at work and had fallen fast for each other. Their relationship had been passionate and addictive, drinking each other in and living life to the full. It was a fairground ride on love heroin. But a baby brought change, one that she could not handle. The passionate debates that at one time had ended in sex now became arguments that led to her throwing whatever came to hand. So she had left. But if she'd found the relationship difficult, she found separation from her daughter even harder. Unable to make peace with either option, her addictive person-ality had led her down dark corridors from which she could not escape.

Unable to sleep, his daughter's words ran through his head. She was so much like him it made him afraid. He remembered how the cruel words of school children stung hard. And with no mother to run home to for comfort, the stings swelled and multiplied, until eventually you were numb. You had to be to survive. This was the future his daughter faced. He had hoped for better, but all these years on and little had changed in the world for Haala and for other brown children like her. The thoughts gnawed at his wounds. As he brushed the hair from his daughter's forehead he knew he wanted to protect her innocence. He did not want her to become like him or like Jia Khan. He wanted words like 'Paki' and 'terrorist', and the negative connotations of her heritage, to be wiped clean from her life path. She was worth slaying monsters for.

He gently moved his arm from behind her neck letting her head rest on the pillow. Covering her with the duvet, he carefully walked across the room so as not to wake her, and into the kitchen. He opened the fridge and took out a bottle of milk, gulping it back to ease the heartburn he'd been experiencing for the last few days. He placed the plastic bottle on the worktop and picked up his phone, flicking through for Jia Khan's number before deciding it was too late to call. He wrote a text and then hit send. '*I'm all in*,' it said.

Seema pushed the pram along the cobbled street. She didn't understand why her friends wanted to meet in this part of town. Head down, she quickened her pace as she approached a group of young teenagers. They began to jeer and joke among themselves. One of them spat on the ground before her. The group's ringleader stepped out behind her and shouted, 'Oi! you wan' some o' this?' He pointed at his crotch and gestured obscenely.

Seema stopped in her tracks. She turned around, and looked at the boy and his group of friends. They were still laughing. She smiled back at them. 'Do you want some of this?' she said.

The ringleader looked confused and then angry. 'That's wha' I said an' that. You bein' funny, hain?' he said.

Seema nodded at him, still smiling. The teenager began walking towards her, his friends close behind, but she stood her ground. Her baby began to cry. As the gang drew closer, she reached under the blanket that was spread across the pram hood. She pulled out a pistol and pointed it at the youngsters. 'Now. Tell me. Do you want some of this?' she said.

The ringleader took a step back, walking into his friends.

'No? Thought not,' said Seema. Then she turned and carried on striding towards her friend's house. Behind her she could hear the teenagers.

'Woah!' said one of them. 'Was that thing for real?'

A young girl ran past Seema and up to the dazed group. 'What was she sayin'a you?' she asked.

'Nowt,' said the ringleader.

'Good. Yasser Khan's wife that is. You shoun't say owt to her unless you want the Verdict to cut off yer balls.'

'Who the 'ell's the Verdict?' asked another kid.

'Han't you 'eard? Ma brother an' his mates all been talkin' 'bout it. They say it's time for new blood. A revolution's comin'! The Jirga's time is over. Ma brothers, they say they gonna be respectin' whatever comes.'

CHAPTER 44

'We can't have organised crime in a disorganised city. We need law and order restored,' Jia told the men.

Sher Khan's eldest son, Razi, listened carefully to her words. He had been tasked with arranging this meeting, inviting handpicked and trusted sons of the Jirga. The men had come eagerly and sat side by side, eating roti and rice with large cuts of mixed grill, as Jia told them of her plan.

She had met with each man personally in advance of this gathering. Idris had done the background checks and collated the information. They had found their cousins ready to speak and amenable to a meeting. The atmosphere was relaxed and informal. The clatter of plates, the sound of freshly cooked karahis being spooned and drinks being downed filled the air. The fragrance of coriander and ginger, tempered with simple spices, made them feel at home. A decade had changed the family dynamic; ideals had been shed, dreams smashed and reality had set in. The men were tired of living under the iron rule of their fathers at work, and then going home to negotiate the arguments of their wives and mothers in the extended family system.

But they had been raised to be respectful, and needed guidance on how to extricate themselves. The emotional blackmail used to keep them in place had started to wear thin. The threats of dishonour and shame upon family were becoming old. This last year, under Jia's watchful eye, had brought new hope.

She knew that getting the old men of her father's Jury to retire would be easier if it was their children who asked them to step down. The old men had run the city for too long. Their decisions had started to weaken along with their limbs. Rebellion under the guise of retirement was what she offered her cousins. It meant their fathers would retain their dignity. Further, as each Jirga member was replaced by his own son, he could act as mentor and counsel. But the cousins still needed a little convincing.

The dinner was being held on the first floor of one of the old mills owned by the property-rich Khan family. Land was important to the Pukhtuns and when the city's old businesses had started to close the family bought up the premises. Unable to get mortgages at the start, they had used the old ways of 'committee'. Large families meant that deposits were accumulated quickly and without the need for interest. The system worked by each person giving a fixed monthly amount over a set period of time. Each month all the money was collected and given to one of the committee members. Weddings were paid for, businesses backed, deposits collected and, more recently, university fees covered in this way.

Some of the buildings had been converted into apartments and kept by men for their mistresses, or second and third wives, and sometimes for gay lovers.

Much of Akbar Khan's property had been bought in his children's names. This mill belonged to Jia. In its heyday it had been filled with textile workers and wool merchants. Now, some of it still housed those ghosts and memories of the past, but the rest, Akbar Khan had rented out to an antiques dealer. It was a sentimental move on his part, one of his few indulgences. There wasn't much call for antiques in this place and the dealer was unable to meet the rent requirements. But Akbar knew of his daughter's love of antiquities and curiosities and had hoped that when she came to learn of it she would see it as a sign of his affection. And coming into the building today, she had.

As she had made her way up to the first floor, she'd wondered what her father would make of her now.

The mill was a vast expanse of space. Row upon row of grey industrial columns ran down the length of the building and parallel to each other, fixed into the ceiling and floor with heavy metal bolts. The twelve men had been standing around an industrial kitchen when Jia had entered the room, their voices low, punctuated by the occasional laugh. They watched as a portly chef stood behind a huge hotplate, getting ready to cook, an array of tomatoes, red onions and green chillies to one side of him, a butchery of entrails to the other.

Jia Khan was hungry. She had been waiting patiently and could wait no more. She asked the chef how much longer it would be, and he handed her the cleavers, gesturing for her to take over. He was a jovial man, respectful, but also one who liked to tease his cousin.

'Can you even cook?' Malik had asked. Jia didn't answer. She took the cleavers and nudged the chef aside. She folded back her sleeves and stepped up to the hotplate. She could see it was blackened from years of serving kat-a-kat and parathas and masala fish; she could tell the spices and butter had seeped into it and seasoned it through and through. She poured oil on to the plate and waited for it to smoke. She reached over and took the raw meat, adding it to the plate and watching it sizzle, measuring spices, adding tomatoes and fresh chillies. She used the cleavers to cut through the hearts, lungs, liver and brain, chopping them until they were tiny, and cutting them further until they resembled minced meat. The days of quinoa and oat milk felt a lifetime away.

'You know how to cook,' said the men. And they tucked in, the food giving them heart for the discussion at hand.

'So you want us to fight for you, and to turn on our fathers,' Razi said. 'Why should we trust you?'

Jia spoke slowly, her words measured. 'Trust is not something one can convince another to have; it is earned. The fact that you are here shows that I have earned it already. I will ask you to make hard choices; these are hard times, but then you already know that too.'

Jia had asked Idris to tell the men of the plan to kill Nowak. Their coming to her with questions reassured her that they held her in high esteem, and she knew that once won, their loyalty would be unwavering.

She listened intently. 'I spent a lot of time inside because of this kind of thing,' said Razi.

She nodded. 'The system let you down. I will not.'

Razi picked up one of the deep serving dishes from the centre of the table. It was filled with large chunks of mutton, cooked with potatoes and fat and seasoned with salt and lemon juice. He passed the dum pukht to Jia, who took it graciously. She filled her plate and ate heartily, the taste of mutton reminding her of the dinner parties her mother would throw when she was a child, how they would all sit around a dastarkhan on the floor together, eating nothing but boti and tikka and occasionally rice, and the elders would ask her to bring toothpicks to fetch out the bits of meat that had caught between their teeth.

Razi had been little when Jia had left for university. She used to carry him off to the garden on her hip whenever Sher Khan and his wife visited. She could tell from his face that what he was about to say was difficult. His words came slow and separated.

'My brother and me, we trusted our parents,' he said. 'They trusted the British justice system but they locked us up for throwing one stone. One stone! Almost identical case in Ravenscliffe a week earlier and the kid got a non-custodial sentence. You know why? Because he was white. The system is stacked against us. It's a game, a big fucking game of dress-up and fancy barristers getting fat on it.' His eyes were full of anger, the rest of his face contorted as he spoke. 'You know how old I was? Nineteen. I was nineteen. He was eighteen just a week before it all kicked off. They fuckin' locked us up for time. We stopped trusting.'

'The Jirga let you down,' Jia said. 'My father let you down. He was a good man but he lacked knowledge of the British way of doing things, systems that we have worked in and have access to and now control. We've become more powerful in the last year than our fathers did in twenty. We understand the white mind and we can manipulate it.'

Razi shook his head, not at her words, but at his own pain. He pointed at his brother, Raza, who hadn't looked up from his plate since they sat down. He was eating in silence, a spoon in one hand, the other resting on a battered notebook that lay next to his plate.

'He was a good kid,' said Razi. 'He was just walking the wrong way home from college that day. Art college, he was at – I fought Mum and Dad to let him go, and for what? Here, pass me that,' he said to Raza.

Raza reluctantly handed over the book.

'Look, look what he does. Draws these all day.' Razi handed the notebook to Jia. She opened it, carefully turning each page as if looking at a priceless artefact. Page upon page of grotesque images confronted her, bearing witness to the effects of the so-called British justice system on boys with brown skin and Arabic names. She stopped at a self-portrait. It was a sketch of a head cut open and a hand pouring guns and pills into it. Closing the book and putting it down in front of her, she leaned back in her chair. The boy had had talent once but the system had damaged him. Less melanin in his skin, and art teachers and lecturers would have given character statements and told tales of future promise at the Crown Court on his behalf. He would have walked away with a bruised ego and a lesson learnt. The verdicts in the case of the white rioters in Ravenscliffe that Raza spoke of had been lenient, something that was widely known in legal circles. Jia had studied them at the time and then put them aside. The thought that she could have helped was acerbic; it grieved her.

'We want to help,' Razi said, 'but we want to make sure everything is done respectfully, you understand?'

'I understand your concerns. It is time to take responsibility, but we will do it without offending your fathers. Some of us tried to leave this life behind, but the outside world wasn't as simple as we hoped. Our elders paved a path for us, we can take it further. Maybe one day one among us will be the parent of a government minister or even the prime minister. But until that day comes we are Pukhtuns, we live by our own law and we should die by it. It is time we brought the family business into the new era. But I need your help to do it.'

'All we ask is this one job to clean up the place,' said Idris. 'Then, if you want, we'll train you, we'll give you jobs, we'll pay your tax and your national insurance contributions, everything. The tech centre will give you a step up and a place in society. You have already seen what we are doing. Your children won't have to lie about what you do. You will live like honourable men but without the boot of white privilege on your necks.'

Razi turned to Jia. 'White society did not give us justice. If we do this with you, you will give us justice?' he asked.

'I don't know about justice, but I will give you back your dignity,' she said. 'If you want it. The only thing that separates us from the rest of the country is opportunity. The politicians, the wealthy, the people with power – they are not going to give us what we want. We will have to seize it for ourselves.'

She could feel the energy in the room, the dead dreams of men coming alive as she spoke. Sitting so low in the well, surrounded by the skeletons of those who had tried to escape, the men had no idea how to climb out. But she had thrown them a rope and they were going to hold on to it with both hands.

CHAPTER 45

'I won't let you do this!' the woman screamed at the boy, grabbing him by his hood. His feet dragged across the asphalt as she pulled him into the white van that was waiting close by. The door slid shut hard behind her, and she slapped her son for the first time in her life. 'Beta! They want to kill you! They want to kill you, my flesh and blood! I carried you for nine months inside me, I nursed you for two whole years. Why? Because I love you, and no one will weep for you except me! Do you understand, you little shit?'

The boy pushed his mother aside, trying to clamber over her and out of the van. 'Mum! Let me out, you crazy woman! What the fuck!'

An old lady, strengthened and fattened by desi ghee, pushed him back into his seat. '*Tu bai ja,*' she said, telling him to sit in the way only Punjabi grandmothers can, before adding '*ulloo da patha!*' for good measure.

He'd been called worse than a 'son of an owl' before, but the insult, like the push, came with a force that shocked him. He sat back down, rage and embarrassment burning up his cheeks. 'This in't our homeland, Mum! We gotta show them what's what. You should just take me home to Pakistan!'

His mother banged the palm of her hand on her forehead and then raised it up to heaven. '*Ya khuda!* How is my son this stupid? Pakistan is not your homeland! This is your home. Your homeland is where I am! You listen to me, you! You lived in me before you lived anywhere else! I am your mother and your homeland! And I was born right here on Morley Street. You think I'm going to let you ruin your life for this? You are going home with me. And all your other friends are going to do the same!' She turned to the boy's grandmother. 'If it wasn't for Jia Khan, who knows what would have happened,' she said, shaking her head. At the sound of Jia's name, the colour drained from the boy's face.

The message had come through the grapevine: the women were to gather at the Pakistani Community Centre on White Abbey Road. They waited, eager to hear why Akbar Khan's daughter had called them, voices of dissent rife among them. Rumours about her had been perpetrated and perpetuated in these circles for years. Was that why she had called them together? Despite misgivings, they came to listen, some out of loyalty, some out of curiosity, but mostly they came for the gup shup, chai and chaat.

Jia stood before them, dressed in a chador much like their own. Her words were strong but her manner mild and what she said made sense. She told them rumours had reached her about men travelling from other cities to cause trouble, as they had once before. That time the community had done nothing. But this time they were being called to arms.

'You must keep your boys safe,' Jia said. 'The menfolk will not do it. You and I know that while they talk a lot, it is us women who actually do the work.' She would give them practical help, she said. And she offered them vehicles to do the task, and her voice gave them the courage and permission to do what needed to be done. And most of all she promised to stand by them in a way that no one had done before.

'We experience the sort of pain that would kill a man in order to give birth and carry on his family name. I am a mother. I know your fears. If our sons get caught up in this, the police will not give us justice. We have already lost some of our children to this violence. My cousins Razi and Raza have just returned from paying a heavy price. We can't allow others to do the same.'

And so when the violence started, they were ready and waiting to take their sons home. It was a Friday afternoon when things began to simmer; Jumma prayers had just finished and people were returning to their places of business. It was contained at first, having started within a mile radius of where the two bouncers had been shot, but by midnight it had spread out past Valley Parade and into Burlington and Hanover, and on the other side from Bowling towards Leeds.

It was 2.00P.M. when Elyas stepped out of the cafe and into the growing demonstration. In the time he'd had lunch, police in riot gear had moved into the centre of the city and were gathered around the edges of Centenary Square. Protesters with placards filled the place. '*Education + Opportunity = Integration*,' read one; '*Laundry is the only thing that should be separated by colour*,' said another, and '*Why should we integrate with those who denigrate?*' A line of mounted officers hemmed them in, watching from the perimeter, their eyes hawk-like, waiting for trouble to kick off.

Elyas's phone buzzed in his pocket. He pulled it out and hit the green symbol. 'Yeah. I'm right in the middle of it!' he said. 'I can't see much…' He turned to find a mob moving towards the steps of City Hall, their faces contorted in anger. The police circle began to tighten. Elyas broke into a run. 'I'm on my way back.'

On the other side of the city centre, Nowak and two of his henchmen were getting ready to hide their money. They walked into the travel agency that had been helping them launder and transfer their ill-gotten gains, each one of them carrying a black holdall. Previous monies had been small amounts, but this was the big one. Dressed in suits, they looked like three business reps about to sell generic paracetamol to a chemist. The owner of the establishment, Hajji Taj Mohammed Akram, ushered them in quickly before reaching up to the top of the turquoise door and turning the key in the heavy mortise lock. He repeated the procedure three times along the length of the door. No one could get in and no one could get out. He led the men into his back office and turned to face them. Each silently placed his holdall on the desk, unzipping it to reveal wad upon wad of neatly rolled banknotes. The travel agent looked up and grinned at Nowak.

Jia waited patiently outside the back door of Café de Khan. The restaurant was housed in a terraced row. The backyards were open, without fences or walls between, and customers often parked across the invisible boundaries.

It was some time before it opened, but it gave her the opportunity to put her car keys in her purse and look through the bag just long enough for the CCTV camera on the corner of the building to get a clear shot, and allow her entry. The game was officially in play.

On the worn stone steps of the Inner City Gym, in a dingy doorway, Razi Khan waited with his brother. Their eyes on the road, they watched as the ranks of men surrounding the English Defence League began to swell and turn nasty. A scuffle broke out between a skinhead and an Asian boy with a Scouse accent. Tempers flared and language became more and more colourful; others stepped forward and fell into the fight. Fists flew and heads were cracked; bottles of Newcastle Brown were smashed before being held out as assault weapons. Some cuts and bruises later, a group of policeman stepped in, pulling the men apart.

Back in the newsroom, Elyas and John tried to figure out what was happening. 'What have we got?' said Elyas. 'I don't understand how this happened without warning. And in the middle of winter!' He was staring over John's shoulder at his screen. The building buzzed with ringing phones and staff arriving, dropping their bags and switching on their computers; the quiet hum of a weekend newsroom had turned to a roar.

'We've got several snappers and a couple of reporters on the scene,' said John. 'Guys in here are making calls and I'm on your social-networking sites.' He was staring at the screen, scrolling down the list of tweets, Facebook messages, Instagram and Snapchat posts.

Elyas glanced around the room. Almost every journalist on the payroll was there. 'Who called these guys in?' he asked.

'No one. They're hungry for a story. Like you. Only younger,' John said.

'Thanks! You got anything?' asked Elyas.

'Nothing yet. But look at this guy. I don't even know what he's saying here,' John said, pointing to a message full of acronyms.

One of the junior reporters shouted over to the Elyas, 'Police have advised people to shut up shop and go home!'

John turned to him. 'Something is not right here, Ely,' he said. 'It's like this EDL march just happened, without any visible planning. Since when did these people get so bloody spontaneous? And so organised at such short notice?'

'You're right,' said Elyas. 'I've just walked through a crowd of young Asian guys, and not one of them sounded like he was from this city. Newcastle, Liverpool and London, yes, but not here. Something is definitely not right.'

'Do you think Jia knows anyone who can shed light?' asked John.

'I just spoke to her. She's having dinner with her cousin at Café de Khan. Didn't seem to know any of this was happening.'

In the middle of town, Basharat Bashir began pulling down the shutters to his halal meat shop. Across the road, James Davis was doing the same for his butcher's shop. 'Didn't expect this so soon. Did you hear owt?' James said, his voice carrying across the road.

'No,' said Basharat. 'I would have told you straight away if I had. Will you be OK getting home? You can come and stay at ours till it's over if not.'

James lived on the other side of the city. To get home he would have to drive through Hanover. The last time the police had asked local businesses to shut up shop, his drive home had been blocked by rioters. He had no idea what was going to happen today. 'We can't go to yours – it's right near where all the trouble was last time. Come with me, I know where we can go. I'll call Julie and let her know. You give Shagufta a ring and tell her you're with me.'

The two men finished closing up and got into James's car. Basharat's son Bilal had dropped him at work that morning before heading in to buy last-minute things for the new baby. Basharat prayed Bilal had got home before the trouble kicked off.

Jia entered the private room at the back of the restaurant. It had seen off the last of its lunchtime customers and was closing due to the streets protests; the staff were starting to leave. Sitting cross-legged on thick red carpets, as Pukhtuns had done for generations, Idris, Nadeem and Malik were waiting with the owner, Samad Khan. The men stood up as she entered. Idris stepped forward and pulled the runner from what looked like a small coffee table. Underneath was a large black trunk with a heavy padlock. He took a key from his pocket and unlocked it. Nadeem pulled up the lid and let it rest on the floor. The men stepped back as Idris reached into the trunk.

He took out a pair of brown leather gloves and a mask for each of them.

Nadeem looked at him. 'What the fuck is this?' he said, holding up the rubber face he'd been given.

'It was all they had at the pound shop,' said Malik. 'I thought it was kind of funny and appropriate, considering they're homeboys.'

'What's the problem?' asked Jia.

'I'll tell you what the problem is,' replied Nadeem, pulling on the mask. 'It's bloody One Direction, that's what! The masks are all of Zayn Malik!'

'Actually, this one is Dynamo,' said Malik, handing the rubber face to Jia.

She took it. 'Thanks. Now stop messing around,' she said as she pulled the gloves over her slim fingers and took a semi-automatic pistol from her bag. 'Looks like that summer we spent hunting in Pakistan is finally going to pay off.'

Malik picked up his weapon tentatively. 'I can't say I'm looking forward to this,' he said.

Nadeem laughed nervously. 'Really? Because the rest of us are so thrilled to be here, right?'

'You can back out now,' Jia told Malik gently. Then she turned to Nadeem, her voice harder this time. 'And so can you,' she added. 'There's no room for nerves on this. We will understand. None of us are looking forward to putting a bullet between a man's eyes. I need to know you're in this for the long haul. Once we step through that door there's no going back.' She waited for their answer.

Nadeem nodded. Malik straightened up. 'I'm coming,' he said. 'There's no way I wouldn't. We're family and loyalty is all we have.'

Each man took his weapon from the arsenal in the trunk. Samad Khan watched from the sidelines, stepping forward only when the guns were dealt out. He took out a cloth bag.

'I have a gift for you,' he said. He gave them each a cloth cap. They recognised it as the kind worn in the North-West Frontier Province and across Pakistan and Afghanistan. 'These pakol were given to me by my wife,' he said. 'Each time she visited her family she brought one back…to remind me where we come from, she said. She had planned to give them to our children, but as you know we were never blessed that way. But I think she would have wanted me to pass them on to you. She believed it important to remember our history. The leaves from an oak tree fade, fall and are replaced, but the roots remain. No one sees what detritus the roots feed on, all they remember is the beauty of the branches and the colour of the leaves. This is a symbol of those roots. Guard its honour well,' he said. 'Jia Khan, you must take the red one. It has been waiting for you for quite some time.'

Jia thanked him for the hat. It resembled a small woollen bag with a round base. Rolling up the sides, she placed it on her head as she had seen her father do many times throughout his life. The brown of her eyes deepened. They were better suited to the cover of a magazine, the kind found on the bedside tables of aspirational Pakistanis, than the back of a curry house in a rundown northern city.

Samad Khan knelt on the floor and lifted the Bokhara rug on which the men had been sitting before Jia arrived. He folded it once, twice, and from the middle to the side, affording it the respect a worshipper gives his prayer mat. Beneath it, hidden away, was a door. He took a small key from his pocket and placed it in the lock. It clicked open with ease and lifted like a lid to reveal a set of stairs. 'There is no light down there, but your eyes will soon adjust,' he told them.

Jia moved forward to step down into the darkness, but Samad Khan stopped her. 'We must pray first,' he said. 'As with everything in life, it is our way.' And with that he raised his hands, uttering the Bismillah loud enough for them to know he had begun calling on his Lord. They followed, some not knowing if this was the time to pray, and others saying the protection prayers they had learnt in childhood, until they heard his 'ameen'. They were ready.

Back in the travel agency, Mohammed Akram counted the money carefully, each pile neatly laid out on the table, and growing steadily. Nowak stood back and watched. He could see Akram's greed growing, and he liked it. It was the travel agent who had approached him to offer his services. He had been removed from the Khan's inner circle and all because of a small matter. His ego had not recovered, and his izzat was blemished. He swore blind he had thought the girl was older, but the Khan had ignored his pleas. Mohammed Akram was bitter, and angry enough to agree to finance Nowak's operation and help clean the cash using his transfer contacts. But all of that was an excuse; the truth was, his business was dying, killed by the internet. Even the older generation were getting their kids to buy Umrah and Hajj packages for them online.

The travel agent had long known the havala method would be the perfect way to move black money, and now he would prove it. With no paper trail, and no actual movement of goods, there was no way for the police to prove anything. He had tried to explain the system to Nowak when they had met the year before. 'We use my havaladar in Rawalpindi. He is a trustworthy man. He inherited the broker job from his family, and they've been doing this for generations. You give me the money to be transferred to his country. I contact him by phone and ask him to pass on an equivalent sum of money to your man in Pakistan. Your man can then transfer it to the Isle of Man. We move thousands of pounds in a matter of minutes, with no questions asked and no record of any kind. Between us – the brokers in Rawalpindi and myself – we balance our books through a reverse transaction…when someone on his side wants to send money here. But, and this is the clever part, because the system is based on our long-standing relationship and trust among the havaladar, there is no need to balance accounts at the end of the day, or even at the end of each month. We don't keep records for long and it's all perfectly legal.'

'What does that mean to me?' Nowak had asked.

'It means that the transactions are difficult to track,' Akram had said. 'It means we balance our books on both sides and no one ever really knows what money is where or how it got there. It means your money gets to your tax haven safely.'

Nowak was sold. It sounded complicated and risky, but he'd liked that.

As Akram counted the cash and calculated his share, he was thinking all the while about 'the great Akbar Khan' and what a shame it was that he hadn't lived to witness his rise and Jia Khan's failed attempts to take the city. He had once craved the Khan's respect – what a fool he had been. He looked at Nowak. The man was ambitious but impatient. He was here for the game and the money but not for the people. It would be a shame to see him take over Yorkshire operations, but not that much of a shame. Akram carried on counting. A loud noise made him glance up at the CCTV screen across the room.

He watched as Nowak sprang into action, moving quickly towards the doorway to see what was happening outside. The sounds of the riot hit before the CCTV images registered what was going on. Loud and angry, it was hulking closer.

Nowak came back shouting at his men in his mother tongue. 'Let's go! Now! Put the cash back in the bags! Move, move, MOVE!' They dropped the bags on the floor and began sweeping the cash into them. Nowak looked afraid, almost as if he knew what was to come.

Razi Khan watched the violence unfold as he stood outside the travel agency, his brother beside him. They waited in silence, their holdall bags in their hands, as Asian men swarmed up the street. Row upon row of faces advanced, hidden under scarves or cloaked with hoods, filling the usually quiet street with the roar of angry men. Police vehicles were parked bumper to bumper across the road, closing it and signalling where the stand-off would be. The officers remained ready behind sheets of riot gear.

As the roar grew louder Raza flinched, but Razi Khan put his hand on his brother's shoulder to calm him. They had come too far to lose their nerve. The crowd surged ahead of them and stopped, unable to move past the police and unwilling to move back. Pushing the men aside like a Spartan on a battlefield, Razi Khan moved to the middle of the crowd. He looked around at the men and waited. He placed his gym bag on the ground next to him, then dropped to his knees as if tying his shoelaces. Once there, he unzipped the bag and pulled it wide open. On the other side of the road, his brother had done exactly the same. Their eyes met and they calmly walked away, moving seamlessly back through the crowd.

Idris tried to push open the trapdoor, but it felt jammed, as if something heavy was on it. He turned to look at Jia. 'It's a rug. Push harder and it will budge,' she said. Idris did as she asked, using his shoulder to force the door up – she was right. When he managed to wedge it up, he could see the rug hanging over its edge. He pushed it aside and climbed out into the light. He squinted through his mask, his eyes reacclimatising, before reaching down and helping Jia up. Nadeem and Malik followed. Jia put her finger to her lips and they listened. To the backdrop of the angry crowd in the street outside, came Nowak's voice from an office across the room; he was shouting in a language they didn't understand. The door was slightly ajar and they could see the men packing the cash into bags, an urgency in their movements.

A delicious rush of coldness flowed through Jia as she reached for the door. Her mind was clear, calm and focused. The events that had led her to this point aligned and everything made sense. The sound of the riot rose, punctuated by the crack of fireworks, and she gestured to her men: it was time. They moved stealthily into the room. *Bang, bang, bang!* went the fireworks, coming closer and closer together. The Brotherhood didn't have time to react. Idris was the first to pull the trigger, the dull thud of the bullet leaving the pistol through the silencer masked by the noise outside. He hit the target square in the back of his head, the man collapsing into a heap, his blood seeping through his blond hair and on to the oak floor.

Akram cowered in a corner of the room. 'Please, I have small children!' he begged Malik, who was towering over him. 'I ask you for mercy.' Malik froze, the reality of what he was about to do taking hold of him. He stepped back. Seeing him flinch, Jia moved her gun swiftly from Nowak's head to Akram's. The sound of a crack followed and his face crumpled like a concertina. Jia's senses were heightened, the air around her cooler; it was like nothing she had felt before. She soaked it in.

Nadeem's mark lay dead, his blood running along the grain of the floorboards and dripping through the cracks.

Nowak was the only man left standing. He faced his attackers, his hands in the air, blood spattered across his shirt and in his hair. He looked afraid, until Jia removed her mask, and then he smiled. For a man staring death in the face, he seemed very relaxed. 'It's you! How lovely to see you here. For a moment I thought I was about to die. But now I know it's you, well…that changes things. After all, I already broke one Khan,' he said.

Idris stepped forward, his arm outstretched, but Jia stopped him. 'Let him finish,' she said.

'Yes, listen to the little Pakistani woman. You know this is a game for men, don't you? But then again your brother, he couldn't take it either. He begged me to stop. He cried like a child. Like a little boy. Benyamin Khan, son of the great Khan, begged *me* to let him die. See? Look, you're angry, your judgement is clouded. Women think with their hearts and not their heads and that is why you'll never be any good at this. You know, for me it was only business. It was never personal,' he said. He waited for her to respond.

Something crashed outside the building and Jia flinched, only for a second, but it was enough for Nowak to make his move. He lunged forward, grabbing for the gun, his hands around hers, shoving her towards Nadeem and Idris. He roared with rage, hammering Jia's jaw with his head, all the while holding on to the gun. She could feel the trigger cutting into her as he forced her finger on to it. *BANG!* The recoil propelled them both backwards, hard. Jia clutched for the corner of the desk to steady herself, as Nowak slipped on the blood that had poured out of his men and pooled on the floor. She looked up to see Idris slumped on the ground, Nadeem crouching beside him, Malik standing silent at the back of the room, his back against the wall. The gun was still in her hand.

Time slowed. The air cooled. She looked at Nowak staggering up from the floor. In the coming years, her cousins would recognise the look in her eyes and remember this as the first time they'd witnessed it.

'Mr Nowak, everything is personal,' she said, and she pulled the trigger. The bullet erupted square between his eyes and he fell backwards, his body hitting the wall behind him before thudding to the floor.

Bilal looked around for his friend Majid. He'd been getting in his car to go home that morning when his mother had called to complain about his wife again. He was tired of the constant arguing, the accusations and the emotional blackmail. He'd shouted at the old woman. She'd cried. He'd hung up the phone and called Majid to see if he was free for lunch. The crowd of Asian protestors was already heaving by the time Bilal reached the curry house. Someone knocked into him; he ignored it and carried on, trying to spot Majid in the sea of faces. The crowd continued to jostle him and Bilal's agitation rose. 'Get the fuck away from me!' he'd said to the guy behind him. Hatred spewed out of him. Hatred for this street, for this city, for the people – this continuous shit that destroyed any hope of a future. Someone pushed him again. 'Fucking watch it, mate!'

All around him men began to rage. Bottles and bricks, and whatever came to hand, were flung at the police wall. Their collective fury seeped into Bilal. A boy in a hoodie with a scarf wrapped around his mouth shoved him from behind. He fell forward, almost tripping over a bag that someone had left in the middle of the street. The stench of petrol rose up. As he steadied himself he noticed that the bag contained glass bottles and some kind of oil. He watched as five men gathered around a car and began to rock it back and forth before turning it over. Behind him a group of young boys cheered and raised their hands in victory. His anger rose and he considered picking up one of the bottles in the bag. But the police began to move forward in formation in an attempt to herd the men down the street. Bilal backed away.

He spotted Jimmy Khan; the men had been neighbours for years, exchanging pleasantries on the way to work and at Friday prayers. He was standing by the bag, a bottle in one hand, his phone in the other. Bilal watched as Jimmy looked at his phone and then flung the bottle into the window of the travel agency across the road. The glass shattered and as mob mentality kicked in, a volley of other bottles were hurled into the building, creating explosion after explosion. The shop was alight, flames licking up the front to the roof, as though trying to escape into the night sky.

Jia stood motionless, looking down at Nowak, her phone in her hand. She was jolted back by the sound of smashing glass coming from the next room. Nadeem helped Idris to his feet. The bullet had only grazed his arm. The temperature began to rise quickly. It was time to move.

'Take the money,' said Jia.

Her cousins grabbed the bags of cash, throwing in the last few wads lying on the floor, and began making their way back to the basement from which they'd come.

Jia stood by the trapdoor and waited until her men were safely underground, flames rising rapidly all around her. From the back of the room, she watched the travel agency burn, the fire devouring everything in its path. She turned off her phone and threw it on the flames before she left. It exploded behind her.

Back in the restaurant, Jia's cousins pulled off their masks and threw them into the trunk with their gloves and guns. Once Jia had emerged from the basement, Nadeem and Malik closed the trapdoor and pushed the box back into place. They looked at each other, sweat pouring from their faces. The heat was intense, even here. 'Well –' said Idris. His words were cut short by the sound of an explosion nearby.

'What was that?' said Nadeem. 'It sounded close. I think we should get out of here.'

But when they entered the dining area they were greeted by thick black smoke coming from the direction of the kitchen. They headed down the corridor towards it, but when they tried to enter they were beaten back by flames. The fire from next door had spread at an alarming speed.

'Doesn't look like we're going to be able to get out the back way,' said Nadeem.

'Or the front,' Idris added, staring hopelessly at a wall of flame blazing across the shopfront.

Malik looked at the others. 'I don't think we thought this through properly,' he said.

Back in the newsroom, Elyas and his reporters watched the drama unfold online. The news helicopter showed plumes of smoke pouring out of the travel agency, the surrounding streets swarming with rioters, like locusts, beyond control and demolishing everything in sight as the police looked on, helpless. All they could do was wait for the violence to subside.

A local TV reporter was interviewing self-styled community leaders, local MPs, councillors and one university expert, who grabbed the microphone: 'I have a question,' he said. 'How long do people endure you riding roughshod over their lives before they no longer have any respect for yours? Violence has an interesting way of changing definition. When it's used against us, you call it justice. When we utilise it, you call us criminals. There is no such thing as reverse racism. There is only a response to racism. This is not racist violence, this is violence born from rage of oppression, and it will happen again and again until you stop seeing us as the problem and you as the solution.'

'Elyas,' said John, looking up from his screen. 'Jia... Apparently she's trapped next door to the travel agency.'

'What? How? Surely the restaurant was evacuated after the police warning?'

'I don't know, mate. I'm really sorry. It's all over the net,' said John. 'She's developed quite a following over the last few days, become a bit of a local hero. The online chatter is using the hashtag #TheVerdict to describe her and her cousins. Sounds like people on the ground there have been waiting for her to come out, but there's been no sign.'

Elyas was already on the phone, dialling her number, but the call failed. He tried again as he started pulling on his coat.

'Where are you going?' John asked.

'I have to get out there, I can't stay here,' said Elyas.

'Elyas, mate, you don't want to get mixed up in this. She runs her father's operations, you must have known that?' But the door had slammed before he had finished speaking.

Somewhere deep inside, Elyas had always known the truth about Jia, what she had become, what her business really was and the danger that put her in, but he hadn't wanted to admit it to himself. He didn't stop running until he reached Morley Street. Pounding the pavement, out of breath, his heart racing, he clawed his way through the crowd towards the blaze, only to be pulled back by a policeman. 'Sir, you can't go any further.'

'But my wife is in that building!' said Elyas, his voice frantic. He couldn't lose her, he had come too far. 'I have to get in there!' he shouted, his hands shoving the policeman aside. Two other officers stepped in to restrain him but he continued to struggle, knowing that the orange and yellow flames licking the sides of the building were taking Jia further and further away from him. 'Look, you don't understand. I have to get in there! Please, let me go, I have to help her!' On his knees now, head in his hands, he watched helplessly as flames rose upwards, shattering windows and devouring the upper floors of the shop and restaurant.

The policeman he'd struggled to get free from looked at him. 'If she's in there, the only one who can help her now is Allah, mate,' he said.

The police, the shattered glass, the sirens, the concern for Jia, all brought back memories of Zan's death and Elyas felt nothing but despair. He had let her down again. If only he had been less proud, if only he had told her how he really felt, and if only he had accepted what she offered as enough, then maybe, just maybe, she would still be here. His head hurt and his throat burned from the petrol fumes. He needed to talk to Ahad, to prepare him. He looked back up at the building where his wife was trapped. There was nothing he could do.

The men were destroying their own city – it had given them more than the place they considered their motherland ever had, and whether they knew it or not, they belonged here. Tomorrow they would awake to the damage they had inflicted and wonder what colour of jinn had possessed them to bring down the apocalyptic fire of hashr on this place. And what would follow would be another day of judgement, one that would see them locked up for decades if history was to repeat itself, one brought about by the legal system that his wife had spent her life defending, but never would again.

On the other side of the city, Benyamin was meeting Sakina, waiting for word that everything had gone according to plan, oblivious to the disaster that was unfolding. He was furious that Jia had refused to let him go along. She had made up some bullshit about needing someone she could trust on the outside in case something went wrong, but he knew she was being overprotective again. She didn't trust him to keep his nerve. She didn't get that he wasn't the kid brother she'd abandoned so many years ago.

'Can I say something?' said Sakina. Benyamin nodded. 'This is never going to end for you.'

Smart, unafraid to do what needed to be done, she reminded him of his sister. He respected her, maybe even cared about her a little. He had no idea what this thing between them was, or what it would become, but in among the chaos that was life, she steadied him.

'Why?' he said.

'Because you're fighting with people who don't exist any more.'

'What do you mean?'

'Who are you angry with? Your sister, right? But Jia as she is now, or the Jia who left you behind? Because she's here now, and she has been for some time. When it matters, she is here.'

Dressed in his favourite leather jacket, Benyamin looked the picture of health. His hair jet black and styled to perfection, his cheekbones chiselled, he could have been an Instagram influencer. Hours of physio and days spent at the athletics track meant he had regained his strength fast. The only physical trace of his ordeal with Nowak was a single scar which cut his left eyebrow in two. The scar ran deeper than anyone knew, down into the recesses of his mind where it had begun to fester. The truth was, he had been carrying all this anger around with him even before Nowak, and he was tired. It was time to put this burden down, to pour out the contents of his head in front of Jia, but he didn't know how. He was hoping Sakina could offer advice.

'You want to fight with the sister who left you all that time ago, because maybe if she had stayed you wouldn't have gone looking for Nowak, and things would be different now.' But she hadn't stayed, and then she'd returned and stepped up, and somehow that had made him angrier, because he couldn't hate her. He loved her, and he wanted her acceptance. 'This is the great tragedy of your life? That you can't make peace with someone who doesn't exist any more, because she changed and got better, all without you getting the chance to tell her how you really felt?' Up until now, Sakina had been respectful to Benyamin Khan, careful of his position as the son of Akbar Khan, brother to Jia Khan. But now he was just wasting her time.

She could still smell the sweat of her clients on her even after she finished scrubbing her skin in the shower at night. When she looked at herself in the mirror, her face gaunt, her skin having lost its shine, all she could think of were the beer guts and flabby bodies that pressed against her as she made her living, the way they heaved and sighed their way to ejaculation, the smell of booze and fags and body odour lingering long after they had left. No one washed for sex workers. Maybe if they did, they wouldn't need their services. This was her life and she accepted it, not gratefully, and not forever, but for now. She would make plans once her brother had finished university. For now, her life wasn't about happiness, it was about circumstances. But Benyamin, his circumstances weren't the problem. He was. Sitting in the warm leather interior of his prestige vehicle, spending more on a bottle of perfume than a punter paid her to suck him off in the back of a beaten-up Toyota Corolla. His bills paid, his belly full, and here he was afraid to talk to his sister about unimportant things.

'You're entitled,' she said. 'You're angry because your big sister rescued you. Because the way she looks at you, the things she says, makes you feel like less of a man. Well, guess what, that is all on you. Real men handle shit. So a woman came to rescue you, so what? No one ever came for me.' She wanted to add, *Get over it, just fucking get over yourself*, but a knock on the tinted window interrupted her. They both turned and looked through the passenger-side window. It was Khalid the pimp.

Benyamin climbed out of the car. He didn't care what Khalid thought if he saw Sakina in the car, but he didn't want him talking over her. Khalid looked distressed, like he was in a hurry to get somewhere. 'Bro, it's your sister,' he said. 'She's in trouble. Down Morley Street.' Benyamin went to get back in his car but Khalid stopped him. 'You can't take your wheels there, man, it's chocca. You won't make it.'

Benyamin turned and ran. He ran like he'd never run before, his mind emptied of everything except getting to Jia. If she died, his family would not survive the loss. She was their Khan; he knew that now. He smelt the fire before he spotted the smoke, plumes of it rising and spreading across the city, thanks to the strong north wind. The pungent smell of burning plastic, wood and petrol was almost intolerable as he approached Morley Street, but he pushed his way through the crowds.

He spotted Elyas, saw him sink to the ground in front of the blazing buildings, unable to get up, and he knew that Jia must be in there. As he approached, their eyes met, their faces speaking a thousand words, their mouths empty. There was a stillness in that moment, a sickness in the pit of their stomachs. They had lost so much already – how would they survive this? Benyamin reached down and helped Elyas stand, their heads made of stone, their legs of jelly. Elyas tried to speak, but what was there to say?

Around them the men raged. 'Pray,' shouted a voice from the crowd. It cut through the testosterone like a hot knife, and a hush fell across the street. It was instantaneous. The men raised their hands to their faces. Then someone shouted 'Takbir!' and Elyas turned to see the sea of men ebb like the tide before rising on the crest of '*Allahu Akbar!*'

The call for the Omnipotent rang out again and again, getting louder each time as the crowd's response became ever more fervent.

'God is the greatest!' they shouted, each man putting aside his ego and professing his smallness in the universe of God and all His prophets. There were men who swore blind that in that moment they witnessed armies of angels descending from heaven. Some put it down to the euphoria, others the weed, but when Elyas and Benyamin looked around, there was no denying the power that was reverberating around them. It was huge, like the pull of a giant magnet. Then, something happened. The crowd that had gone from rampage to religious experience began to part in the middle, chanting all the while.

'We've done what we can. It's time to go,' Jia said, pulling the damp material away from her mouth to speak.

'I guess we're leaving the money,' said Nadeem, as he hurriedly wrung out a cloth and wrapped it around his face.

'We're leaving the money,' she said.

They'd done all they could. They'd started by searching for fire extinguishers. Malik had spotted one near the toilets and had run to fetch it. 'What now?' he'd said, picking it up, ready to shoot. 'One of these is not going to be enough to get us through there.' They looked towards the screen of fire spreading towards them from the front of the restaurant.

Jia scoured the room for something else that could help, her eyes landing on a pile of tablecloths. She'd moved swiftly, throwing them to her cousins. 'Quick, take these to the toilets and soak them in cold water.'

The sinks were small, so they'd used the toilet bowls too, Malik and Nadeem soaking the cloths, Idris and Jia running back and forth to the dining room with them. Jia wrapped the first one carefully around her face, then ran down the short corridor to the kitchen and placed another at the foot of the doors in attempt to reduce the steady stream of smoke. The paint on the outside was bubbling and she knew it wouldn't be long before the doors gave way.

Then she joined Idris, throwing more of the wet tablecloths over the smaller fires bursting up from the sparks of flame burning at the restaurant windows and door. They sizzled as they landed, quenching the flames beneath them and forming a white pathway.

When they ran out of tablecloths, they pulled more from the tables. Eventually Idris had signalled to Jia that it was time to go. Some of the flames had been doused but they'd soon be back and the smoke was getting thicker and more toxic, the temperature unbearable. If they didn't hurry, all their efforts would be undone. That was when they'd run back to the toilets to get the others.

Now they stood at the door, as ready as they'd ever be to face the flames.

'OK?' she said. Nadeem and Malik nodded. 'Stay close to the ground and follow us.'

She pulled the cloth back up over her mouth and nodded at Idris, who opened the door. Then they moved at speed, crouching low and holding on to the back of each other's shirt as they traversed the dining room, Idris at the front, spraying the extinguisher. The kitchen door was ablaze now and smoke poured down the corridor unimpeded, stinging their eyes and making it impossible to see. They felt for the pathway of damp, steaming tablecloths, following it towards what they hoped was the front door.

Idris stopped suddenly. Everything was pitch black, the heat coming at them from all sides, the smoke heavy. The wet coverings on their face meant it was impossible to speak. Sensing something was wrong, Jia pushed past him swiftly to discover the way was blocked by the burning door, buckled and blistering in the intense heat. Without flinching, she stood up, placed her hand on the searing metal push plate, and heaved it with all her might. The door shifted, and she fell forward into the light.

One by one the rioters moved aside, slowly at first and then faster and faster, until the mass split, separating like the sea for Moses. Elyas squinted through the heat, his eyes transfixed, waiting, willing the restaurant door to open, and when it did he felt his heart in his throat. Through the smoke she emerged, her forehead smeared grey, her eyes focused, a cloth around her nose and mouth, calls of '*Allahu Akbar!*' still reverberating around her. The carcasses of cars burned on either side as she stepped across a river of shattered glass and debris, Idris, Malik and Nadeem stumbling in a line behind her, coughing and spluttering as they came. Paramedics hurried forward with silver blankets to wrap around their shoulders, but Jia walked past them towards Elyas and and collapsed into his arms. Elyas held her tight, and she let him, the fight having left her body. She reached out to her brother standing beside them, grateful for his presence. He held her hand and nodded, then went to check on his cousins. The paramedics moved in to help, checking Jia's pulse, wrapping her blistered hand, administering oxygen, asking questions. Elyas heard nothing, saw nothing, except Jia Khan.

CHAPTER 46

'I'm pregnant,' she told the doctor in A&E, then turning to Elyas, added, 'ten weeks.'

Elyas was speechless. The doctor seemed unconcerned. 'We'll do a scan just to make sure everything is as it should be, but you seem fine,' he said. 'It sounds as if your quick thinking kept your exposure to smoke to a minimum. Wrapping those wet tablecloths over your face and mouth was a brilliant idea.' He turned to Elyas. 'Keep an eye on her. If she has any shortness of breath or chest pain when you get home, you'll need to bring her back in.' He left the two of them in the examination room.

'When were you going to tell me?' Elyas said.

'I don't know,' she said. 'I was waiting for the right moment. I haven't had time to process it myself…but it's going to be OK.' She was going to say more but a nurse came in.

'Ms Khan, the police are here for you. I've told them that you'll be a while,' she said.

The doctor discharged Jia after the scan. She was ready to answer police questions, but the arrival of Mark Briscoe put her on edge. 'I know you've had a long day,' he said, 'but, if you don't mind, I'd like you to accompany me to the station. There are a few things that need clearing up.'

Though they were on friendly terms these days, Jia still didn't fully trust the chief of police. But she agreed to go. The adrenaline rush had worn off, leaving her exhausted, and she wanted to get this over with fast. Elyas walked her to the police car, acutely aware that sirens and ambulances had been involved the last time Jia had been carrying his child, and that he'd lost her then. 'I'll call you when I'm done,' she told him.

'I'll be waiting,' he said, as he watched the car drive away.

It was late evening when she finally rang Elyas from the police station. She knew he'd be waiting by the phone, but that wasn't why she'd called him. She wanted to tie up loose ends, return life to a kind of simplicity. The gates of Pukhtun House were swarming with news reporters when they arrived, so Elyas suggested they go to his place. She agreed.

They climbed the stairs of the building in silence, both too tired to speak. And when he brought her a cup of tea he found her asleep on the sofa. So he covered her in a blanket and sat down alongside her, watching her breathe, afraid to touch her in case he broke the spell.

She awoke to find him snoring, the TV tuned to some late-night shopping programme. His eyes closed, his face emptied of worry, he looked younger, almost like the boy she had married, and she was compelled to lean in. He smelt like stale cigarettes and the aftershave she had bought him for his birthday the first year they were together. She kissed his cheek. He tasted like her youth and the years she could never revisit. She kissed his lips in the hope that time would roll back, that she would open her eyes and find herself innocent again, just shy of three decades of life, that his kisses would somehow cleanse her soul and set her free. Maybe it was the years of separation and the secrecy accompanying the rekindling of their relationship that brought a sense of newness to each time she was with him. Whatever it was, she knew it had to be fleeting; she was surprised by its having lasted this long.

He reciprocated, tasting her lips as if they were ripe fruit, opening his mouth wider and wider, extending the promise of passion he'd made her years earlier.

The rhythms of their love-making were slower than they had been in their youth. But in his bedroom, behind closed doors, his arm around her waist, their legs intertwined, his kisses deep and heavy, she received him as hungrily as she had done the first time.

'The thing about sex in your forties is that you take the time to fold your clothes neatly before you begin, because you know from experience that you're going to need them when you're done,' he'd joked afterwards, as he handed her an oversized T-shirt. She'd laughed at his commentary.

Later, she sat on the edge of the bed, her back to him, thinking of what to say. 'You wouldn't want any more than this if you really knew me,' she said. The darkness hid her face, but the curve of her shoulders, her back, her lips and the slant of her neck were all clearly outlined by the slivers of moonlight that slipped in through the curtains.

Elyas watched her from the bed, his back against the pillows, knowing that one wrong word could make her bolt. Her fears had pushed her to the edge of the bed; had he put too much pressure on her in his desire to have her back, not just for Ahad's sake, but for himself? But he owed it to them both to be honest. So he took his time, thinking, weighing up phrases against each other before finally settling upon his response: 'There is nothing you could tell me that would make me leave. I want this baby and I want you.'

His naive confidence saddened her, but she wanted to believe him. She wanted to believe that he would still love her if he knew about Ahad, about what she had attempted to do to him in the hospital on the night he was born. She wanted to believe that he would still feel the same if he knew what had happened the night her father was killed, and Benyamin was taken. But she knew that openness, trust and honesty were for other people. People with simpler lives, who carried smaller burdens. Her choices had taken her down a path that few would accept and fewer still understand. A path that had her believe spousal love was the domain of the weak and that familial love was the higher calling. It was the warrior path, the path of self-sacrifice, trodden by few – the qurban, the Pukhtun.

'I can't give you anything. And there are things about my life that would make it very difficult for you to stand by what you say. You don't know what you're asking for,' she said.

Her words vexed him. 'I do, Jia. You think I don't know that you're running your father's business now? What kind of journalist would it make me if I was the only man in town not to know what sort of criminal network your father headed up?' he said. Then his tone softened. 'But I love you. Not some vague idea of you. But you. You with the half-finished cups of tea with the tea bag still left in them. I miss the smell of your hair, and finding all my razor blades blunt because you've used them, and the weirdly organised crockery cupboard. I want us to be a family. I know what life is about, Jia, I'm not under any illusion. You're a complete hard-arse, and I'm OK with that.'

'That's not it,' she said.

'What else is there? Tell me something that would keep me away, then. Life isn't black and white, I get it, and you're trying to clean up your father's mess and I want to stand by you while you do that. You're a good person, Jia.'

His words weighed her down. They were so far from what she was that they left her lonely. The human capacity to lie to oneself, to pretend that the obvious was not so, no longer surprised her, but that Elyas was willing to deny evident truths in order to be with her did.

But then she thought of the pregnancy… Maybe it was enough, or he was enough, or maybe enough was enough, and rationality returned. The Khan needed a spouse, some semblance of normality. A woman without a husband in this city was a target for talk, and that was something she didn't need. She remained silent for a time, and when she spoke her response was measured. 'If we were to be together you would not be able to ask questions about my work. There are things I wouldn't be able to talk to you about. Things I will never be able to tell you,' she said. Elyas nodded. 'It was only recently that I realised how much my father really loved me. He was a good man, a great man, and I misunderstood him. He lived by his own rules and ancient laws, and for a long time I thought that was wrong. I believed in the British justice system. I believed that hard work and honesty was the answer. I know now that although many claim to live that life, few in fact do.

'Maybe in a few decades our people will have become equals in this country. But it's unlikely. British courts speak of honour but they set up secret courts to judge us. They hold our sons without charge for years, they put our husbands in planes and send them to the US for crimes they say have been committed on British soil, all the while hiding the menfolk of Elizabeth and Mary and Katherine behind their skirts. In the West, justice and mercy is reserved for the light-skinned, the Christian-named.'

'That is what you believe?' Elyas said.

Jia's eyes were dark like coal. 'This much I know: if your name is Mohammed or Ali or Usman, you are a rapist or a terrorist, you're a danger to society. You are guilty unless you can prove innocence,' she said. 'But those with power will find respect wherever they go. They are a law unto themselves. They belong to every country and to none. My father knew this and he was right.'

'I respect your views,' he said. He moved forward and took her hand. 'I know you, Jia Khan,' he said. 'I know that whatever you do is for others. And I know that we are better together. Let me help you.'

Jia considered his words and knew that it was time to tell him the truth. Her eyes locked on to his. 'There is a bitterness inside me. It comes over me slowly,' she said. 'And it makes me want to wipe the happiness right off their privileged faces. I watch people struggle, good people, kind people, struggling through life with bills and poor health and clever children born on the wrong side of the tracks. I pray to God to help us. I recite the Durood over and over, asking Him to help the people of Muhammad, but I cannot tell you who I am praying for any more. Who are these people? Are they the ones who stand in the mosque, who are wealthy enough to give alms to the poor? What about the women who sell their bodies to feed their babies? The men who get high to hide from the shame of their past mistakes? The sinners who pray in the cover of darkness and feed the poor their own blood and soul? All of us having to make sacrifices, over and over again. And sometimes the one you'd take a bullet for is the one holding the gun.'

Her eyes flashed. She let go of his hand and stood up.

'I'm sick of patronising eyes and pursed lips,' she said, turning to face him. 'Our blood is the same colour as the pale but that doesn't matter because our skin is brown and our Prophet is a man not a god. Nowak could acquire that last mantle of privilege and respect-ability that you and I will never have, that our son can never have, because he was a white Christian man. That is why I killed him. Not because of business – fuck business. Business does not keep you warm at night; business does not bring back the dead. It does not bring you a respect that goes beyond cold, hard cash. No, this was not business, this was personal. He came here thinking he could take what was ours. His privilege brought him here; his arrogance got him killed.

'I've seen who I am and it's something I'm going to have to live with for the rest of my life. But I don't see why anyone else should.'

She looked away now, waiting for his response, thinking he would be shocked, that he would stand in judgement. But he didn't. Instead, he got up and kissed her. And she knew that he hadn't heard a word she had said.

CHAPTER 47

'We have identified the three other men as members of a crime family from Eastern Europe, known as the Brotherhood,' the chief of police said. 'We understand they hired men from outside the city to create tensions and bring disorder to this great city so that they might take advantage of the disruption to conduct illegal drug activities.'

He was speaking at a press conference outside the steps of City Hall. He looked tired as he spoke. The last seven days had been difficult and he was looking forward to going home to his wife tonight. Tomorrow they would take the dogs and head to the moors, without having to worry about what was to come. Jia had made sure of that, and he was relieved. The clean-up operation would begin on Monday. Right now, the press must be dealt with. He wasn't sure how they would react, but was hoping the questions would be few. He spoke clearly and firmly as he had been trained to do.

'It is proving to be a difficult investigation,' he said, 'since most of the evidence was destroyed in the fire. But we believe the owner of the travel agency was their money launderer and the shooting was the result of an altercation between him and the Brotherhood.'

A week had passed since the day of the riots and Ahad and Elyas no longer felt like guests at Pukhtun House. Jia had also been asked to give a press statement outside the gates of the family home. Father and son watched the events on television from inside. Idris was with them.

The news moved away from the press conference and a mugshot of a man flashed up on the television screen. 'Dad, wasn't he sitting next to us at that concert we went to with Jia?' said Ahad.

'Yes, he was,' said Elyas, remembering how he'd seen Jia talking to him in the interval, before they'd had that argument. He turned the television volume up.

'Police announced today that they have arrested a man in relation to the killing of local businessman Akbar Khan. Waleed Karzai is due in the magistrates' court tomorrow charged with his murder,' the news presenter said. 'Karzai denies the charges.'

'Why would he kill Akbar Khan?' said Elyas.

'He wouldn't kill anyone,' said Idris, 'unless someone paid him to. He's a finisher.'

'A what?' said Elyas.

'He's the man you call when you need to close the books on someone important. My father told me once that this guy was the best. Said that if anyone wanted to end the Jirga, he's the man they would have to call. That's probably why they got him on Akbar Khan's security detail – he'd have had to have sworn an oath of allegiance to the Khans. Makes you wonder what could have persuaded him to renege on his oath.'

'Money? Like you said?' said Ahad.

'Yes, but Pukhtuns don't act out of greed alone. Karzai's bloodline is sworn to protect ours – his allegiance is not to the individual but to the bloodline and its succession. He would need to be persuaded that breaking that oath was in the service of the bloodline and for its own preservation. But even then he would be honour bound to inform his Khan – which means, if Karzai had been asked to make an attempt on your grandfather's life, Akbar Khan would have known about it, he would have told us, and we'd have stopped it. So I'm not sure what's happened here, unless Karzai went rogue. Or the police have simply got the wrong man.'

'What if the person who wanted him dead was someone he cared about? Then the choice would be between saving his own skin or theirs,' said Ahad.

Idris's face was dark, his eyes cold. 'Just like your mother,' he said. 'Always looking for a loophole.'

Elyas sat down slowly; the fog in his head began to clear. Something was waiting for him in the corners of his mind. He thought about Jia, her words, how she had talked with Karzai in the concert hall that night. Something had bothered him about it – perhaps it was simply her caginess. Whatever it was, he'd put it to the back of his mind in the chaos of the shooting afterwards. He closed his eyes and replayed the memory, and recalled how Jia had taken something from Karzai and put it in her handbag. Had it been an exchange? Was the brown packet he'd seen Karzai putting away one that *she* had passed *him*? Money? But it made no sense. Why would she pay him? Unless she had found her loophole? '*It was only recently that I realised how much my father really loved* me... *Sometimes the one you'd take a bullet for is the one holding the gun.*' Her words came back to him. Had she always planned to take over her father's empire?

Elyas suddenly remembered something else from that night at the concert. He made his way quickly to the bedroom and opened the walk-in wardrobe that was now his. He hadn't unpacked properly yet. He unzipped his suitcase and began searching frantically. He found the jacket he'd been wearing that night and emptied the contents of its pockets. Nothing. Then he remembered the internal pocket. He reached in and his fingers touched the edges of an envelope. He'd forgotten to give it to Jia when he was handing back the things that had spilled from her handbag during the shooting.

He opened it, taking out a piece of folded paper. He recognised Jia's handwriting.

Baba,

You were my hero. I had no way of knowing what life had in store for us, but I knew that as long as you were with me, everything would turn out well.

I was naive.

When Zan died I broke. You watched over me for months as I grieved. Then the baby came and went and I broke again. The grief was bubbling up inside me, leaving me bitter. So I left. Life was hard without you. But it would have been harder with you.

And then you called and told me about my son. That he was alive. You'd kept him from me. Because you had thought it best.

I had been in a haze after Zan's death. I had been unwell. I had trusted you to protect me, but you failed. Instead you took advantage of the situation.

Your actions took from me the people I loved, the people I could have loved the most.

I didn't get to see him grow. I didn't get to be there for his first day at school. I never got to hold his hand in mine when he was afraid, or sad, or when he was lonely. And now you tell me he is alive, and expect no repercussions. You raised me like a son but treat me like a daughter.

I love you, Baba. But you took away my choice. You took away my freedom. You took my life. And I cannot allow that to happen again.

Your daughter,

Jia Khan

Elyas pressed his hand against his chest. The air felt thin, leaving him unable to breathe. He scanned the letter again, hoping he'd misunderstood. He folded it up and put it in his jacket pocket. His head began to hurt, and he rubbed his temple with his thumb, trying to figure out what to do. He ran through the conversation they'd had in his bedroom a week ago. He hadn't got it then, but he did now. He finally understood who Jia was. She was Akbar Khan's daughter and she had had him killed – and possibly betrayed the man she hired to the police. She had planned her father's death, paid for his execution, and then carried on as if none of it was her doing. That's what she had been trying to tell him, but he was too blinded by love to listen. Jia Khan was a stone-cold killer, and she was carrying his child.

He walked into the living room and stood by the fireplace. He took a log from the pile and put it on the fire.

'Are you OK, Dad?' said Ahad.

'I'm fine,' he said, turning round. Behind him the cream corners of the letter curled under the log, disintegrating into the flames.

CHAPTER 48

Jia stepped back into the house. Satisfied with her words, the reporters were moving away from the gates of Pukhtun House. Inside, the Jirga were gathered.

Sanam Khan waited in the hall, in her hands her husband's favourite chador. She unfolded it and wrapped it around Jia's shoulders. She could not stop her daughter entering the world of men, but she would make sure she kept her honour. The familiar smell of Akbar Khan's aftershave mixed with the scent of stale tobacco enveloped Jia, triggering memories of childhood and her father. She pulled the shawl tight around her and walked towards the study.

The men had been called to Pukhtun House to discuss important matters. They had been told about the events of last week and they knew that badal had been exacted. With each man stood his son and representative. Jia Khan walked over to the desk and invited the men to sit. Idris poured her a glass of water and placed it by her right hand. She waited until each man was seated before beginning.

'I have called you here for the last time as members of the Jirga,' she said, her voice full of authority, her words absolute. 'As of tomorrow my father's Jury will be retired and a new Jirga sworn in. They are your sons, and they have shown themselves worthy. They were prepared to put their lives on the line for the good of our people. I hope you will show them respect.'

These were clever men, they were smart men; they had left their homes and travelled to a foreign land and they had succeeded in

their hopes of providing security for their children. Jia knew that
they were aware of her plans to place them in retirement. She would
not disrespect them by assuming otherwise.

'I assure you that we will continue to follow the ways of the Jirga
and in doing so seek your consultation in major decisions,' she said.
'Shura is the way of the Quran, it has always been the way of the
Khans, and I will honour that. You have worked hard for us. Now
it is time for you to rest and for us to work for you. People of honour
stand by their word,' she said.

The men nodded in agreement. The daughter of Akbar Khan had
proved herself worthy. She had exacted badal and she had brought
their sons together under one banner. They were pleased. The one
or two dissident voices among them had been quietened, if not by
the actions of Jia Khan, then by fellow members of the Jirga. Unity
made them strong. It had been this way for centuries. A divided Jirga
could lead to bloodshed and decades of unrest in business and
matrimonial matters. Many of the men had daughters and they had
secretly been worried about their futures. But the new Khan had
allayed those fears. After all, she was a woman and had an understanding of these things.

Jia spoke again. 'Rest assured that I am responsible for those who
call me their Khan. And I will honour that responsibility until my
death.'

It was time. Each man turned and placed his hand on the shoulder
of the one in front and took the centuries-old oath. The sound of
their voices rippled through the house as their emotions overcame
them. Promising to honour the laws of Pukhtunwali and keep the
covenant of secrecy, they were now bound to each other and their
Khan by more than blood. Jia pulled her chador over her head and
tight round her shoulders. One by one, the men came forward, each
one placing his hand on her head, offering words of prayer and
praise. She was their sister, their mother, their honour. What was
said within the confines of the Khan's study could not be repeated

outside those four walls. And what was confided to the Khan by a Jirga member was sacred and secret.

The men embraced each other heartily as though meeting for the first time in a long time. Watched over by Jia, they were safe once again under their appointed leader. It was a day most blessed.

As they turned to leave she raised her hand. 'Before you go, I would tell you one more thing.' She picked up the glass and drank from it deeply. The men waited to hear what else their matriarch had to say.

'Know that I would not hesitate to kill anyone who attempted to hurt our family and bring an end to our peace,' she said, her voice cold and her hand steady. 'Even if that meant someone from this room.'

Idris and Bazigh Khan were the last to leave. It had been a long day and they had not yet spoken about the day's events or those that had preceded it. As Idris was driving his father home, Bazigh Khan pulled a crumpled piece of paper from his waistcoat pocket.

'*She will prove herself a worthy Khan,*' he read out. 'Your uncle gave me this the night he died. It was as if he knew it was coming.'

'Baba jaan, I wish to respectfully ask a question,' said Idris.

'Go ahead,' his father said.

'How is that you have such faith her? Pukhtuns have traditionally subjugated their women, and yet here I see your unquestioning loyalty to one. What am I missing?'

'She is our mother now. Our people have always held their mothers in high esteem. Paradise is said to be found at their feet,' his father replied. 'And...Jia Khan has more Pukhtun in her bloodlines than most of these menfolk. She will do what she must to keep the family honour. Do not underestimate her. I have seen what she is capable of with my own eyes...' Bazigh Khan stopped.

Wanting to hear more but understanding the subject required delicacy, Idris stayed quiet, hoping his father would trust him enough to tell him exactly what he had seen. They travelled in silence for some time. Then the old man spoke again.

'Son, I know that you have wanted to make her your wife since you were young. I know that even living with Mary, you consider Jia Khan the other half of your soul. But know that you were saved when she married Elyas.'

Idris pressed his father. 'Baba jaan? What did you see?' he said.

'I saw your uncle's anguish. Sanam Khan and I were the only ones that did,' he said. 'It was pitch black the night he came to me with the child. It was his grandson, Jia and Elyas's son, Ahad. I had never seen Akbar Khan that way. He was a hard man but not heartless, and what he had seen had shaken him. He handed me the child and asked me what we should do. I had no idea. I had raised you but with the help of Sanam Khan.'

Idris was stunned. 'Akbar Khan wanted you to kill his grandson?' he said.

'No! My brother wanted me to help him save him! I had seen her try once but had thought it the madness of post-partum women. I had spoken to her and called her mother to keep watch and feed the child. But Akbar Khan, he told me he had caught her a second time, the child on her lap, and the pillow over the baby's face...'

'Who, Baba jaan?' said Idris.

'The child's mother. Jia Khan.' Bazigh Khan stopped. 'She told me it was the Pukhtun way. That in times of war such things were necessary. That she had far to travel, that the child would bind her and be used by her father against her.'

Idris pressed his foot on the brake hard. His car screeched to a halt inches away from a crash. Engrossed in his father's words, he hadn't noticed the lights change or the car in front stop. His understanding of the situation had always been that Jia hadn't wanted the baby, and had sent him to live with his father. That the truth was much darker made his blood run cold.

'You are worried, my son,' said his father. 'I would be too. She bided her time for fifteen long years. The night of his death Akbar Khan gave me a letter with instructions not to read it until the following day. In it, he told me to forgive Jia Khan and to stand by her. He knew she was coming for him, and he was in submission to the will of the Almighty. She has long planned the demise of the Jirga. Surprising, then, that she has bound it tighter and herself in it. Surprising but fortuitous. It is a cold woman indeed who would not spare her own offspring. And this cold woman will make a great Khan for our people.'

EPILOGUE

Jia sat on the bed, the baby in her arms, wrapped in the pretty pale green blanket that Maria had crocheted. Maria was due next month. Her legs swollen, her blood pressure high, she was on bedrest. She'd taken up the craft to stay busy.

Jia looked at the newborn, who had been safe inside her until a few hours ago. Closed eyelids, perfect pink lips, tiny fingers wrapped around hers, now out in the cold, mean world. Skin to skin, she pressed the baby against her breast. She protected those she loved, but one's own children were a different matter. They didn't listen, they pushed boundaries, they scattered tacks under their parents' Achilles heels. Last time, the burden of parenthood had outweighed the love. She wondered how it would be this time. She closed her eyes and leaned back in the bed. She was exhausted.

Her labour had been long and intense. Everything had been fine and then the baby had gone into distress. A rush of po-faced medical staff into the room had alerted Jia and Elyas to the gravity of the situation. She'd been taken to surgery. Shortly after, the cry of a newborn signalled everything was going to be fine.

Elyas had been by her side the whole time. He'd looked tired and she'd sent him home a few hours ago. The baby had gone down, but sleep wouldn't come to her. Her mind was exhausted, discombobulated, and her body broken. She made a note to speak to the doctor in the morning.

She looked up to see her brother at the door to her hospital room. He was holding a teddy of the kind only people without children would buy, and in his other hand was a flat brown box. She felt a rush of love and calm descend.

'From Tarantino's.' He held up the box. 'I'll see that baby and raise you cold pizza,' he said. 'Breakfast of champions.' He took the baby in his arms and placed it gently in the cot.

'You OK?' he said. She nodded, overcome by his presence and by all the things they had been through together. This was family. Here was someone who knew her beneath the armour, before the world took hold of her.

They sat in comfortable silence, Jia eating slice after slice. 'Elyas doesn't have a clue about food,' she said.

'What can you expect from a man who has oat milk in his chai?' he replied, and she laughed. They hadn't laughed together in years. He looked relaxed, fresh-faced and golden. He seemed easy in a way that she hadn't seen since her return to the city. She felt herself relax and sleep came. When she awoke he was still there, sitting beside her, watching her, his face covered in brotherly love.

'You snore just like Dad,' he said, teasing her. 'Must be the nose...' He paused. 'You know, for years I wished you'd died instead of Zan.'

'I know,' she said. 'Me too.'

'That baby looks like me.'

'Yes,' she replied. 'You were a beautiful baby. So much hair, and huge eyes.'

'I feel sorry for this little one...' He looked down into the cot, at the baby wrapped tight in blankets, unaware of the world unfolding around it. 'And I worry about you.'

His soul chose that moment to crack wide open and everything inside him poured out on to the hospital floor. Maybe it was because he finally felt strong again, maybe it was because Jia appeared weak, or maybe this was just how love for family was, messy and uncon-ditional, made of ties that even knives could never sever.

'I'm the one who stayed,' he said. 'I'm the one who looked after Pops, and took him places. I'm the one who held Mama when she cried, night after night. I'm the one who Maria leaned on.' His face looked distant, and Jia wanted to take all his pain away and into herself and numb it with the morphine drip that was attached to her. 'Do you know, she still sometimes calls me Zan? Maria and I are just shadows. Do you know how it feels never to be good enough?' He looked tiny in that moment. He began to cry, his head in his hands, the sound of a man breaking in two echoing around the disinfected room.

Jia leaned over and put her arms around him, and he rested his head on her shoulder. They stayed that way for a long time, the tears rolling down his face and on to her neck, and her hands wiping them away.

'I'm sorry I wasn't here,' she said. 'But I am now and I'm not going anywhere again.'

ACKNOWLEDGEMENTS

Here is my Jirga, the people without whom this book would not be what it is.

Thank you to Nikesh Shukla, if it wasn't for your kindness, support and practical help this book would not be a reality. So many people offer help, but few go the distance. You're a bona fide superhero and I'm honoured to know you.

To my agent Abi, I waited my whole life to hear someone say 'I got this' and to know that they really did. Thank you for fielding emails, handling calls and navigating deals. If I ever go into battle, I'd like you with me.

To Arzu and Helen, thank you for your invaluable advice, brilliant insight, and attention to detail during the editing process. You shone a light on all the dark places I was hiding from and forced me to raise my game, but you did it with kindness.

To my editor Jenny Parrott, for the 'dancing' emails, the 'yes' and the pep talk. I love your enthusiasm!

To my sisters, Khola and Javaria, who read early drafts and kept telling me I should keep writing, and to Fozia who always brings the funny.

To Sabena, for always being on the other side of the phone and reminding me I'm not mad. I'm so glad I got on that flight.

To Mary, I could not have got through these last few years without you. Life feels easier when you're around, I miss you.

To my husband, Adnan, for believing in me, even when I quit, thank you for rescuing me from myself.